SWORD & SORCERY
FROSTFIRE

SWORD & SORCERY
FROSTFIRE

ETHAN AVERY

Stories By Storytellers

Copyright © 2022 by Ethan Avery

Edited by Seldon Writing Group

Cover art by Sarah Hassan

Map by JonahPaul Butterfield

Chapter art by Danielė Buivydaitė

Library of Congress Control Number: 2022901720

Publisher's Cataloging-in-Publication Data

Names: Avery, Ethan, author.
Title: Sword and sorcery : frostfire / Ethan Avery.
Description: First edition. | Cincinnati, OH : Stories By Storytellers, 2022. | Series: Sword and sorcery ; book 1. | Audience: Ages 13-18. | Audience: Grades 8-12. | Summary: The lives of a penniless young swordsman and a wealthy apprentice mage intertwine due to a mysterious, magical mirror.
Identifiers: LCCN: 2022901720 | ISBN: 9798985622829 (hardcover) | ISBN: 9798985622805 (ebook)
Subjects: LCSH: Magic—Juvenile fiction. | Social classes—Fiction. | CYAC: Magic—Fiction. | Coming of age—Fiction. | Fantasy. | LCGFT: Novels. | Fantasy fiction.
Classification: LCC PZ7.1.A93 Swo 2022 | DDC 813.6 [Fic]—dc23

ISBN 979-8-9856228-2-9 (Hardcover)

ISBN 979-8-9856228-0-5 (eBook)

First Edition

This book was typeset in Adobe Devanagari

Stories By Storytellers

www.storiesbyethan.com

For Lamont Kristian Turner,
a far better writer than I
and an even better friend

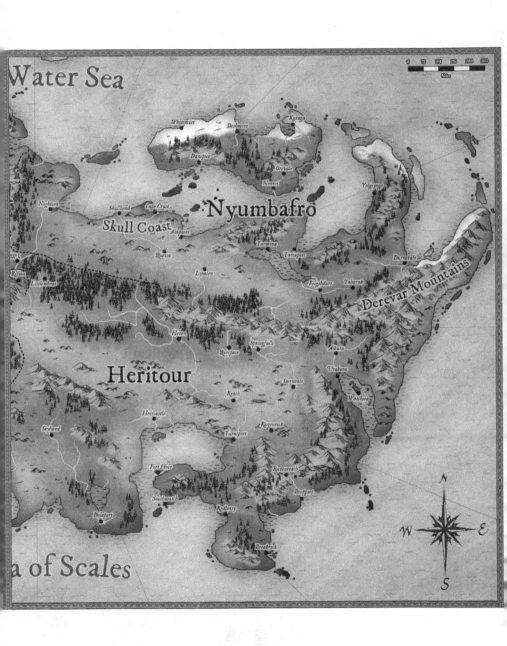

Water Sea

Whitemist · Deshmire · Karaga

Danspice

Otevale

Newest

Nyumbafro

Nightsea · Skullbrad · Cape Crust · Yelgrago

Skull Coast · Alspant

Quessa

Tarmiaa

Lynaion · Taristport · Durravale

Kifton · Frightdarr · Talsarak · Derevar Mountains

Littlewreat

Horen

Springfalls · Atkara

Heritour · Quespass

Urakara

Reach · Sterrwale · Watchra

Heircastle

Skyland · Turnport · Ravenrock

Fort Heir · Ravenreach · Dropport

Southwatch

Delaport · Redberry

Breakrock

a of Scales

N
W · E
S

PART
I

Reflections are false
perspectives are true until…
they gaze at mirrors

~ Chapter 1 ~
A Most Mysterious Mist

LOSING WASN'T AN OPTION. EREVAN WAITED TOO LONG for this moment. The sword of his opponent warned him not to rise under the cloudless midday sky, but Erevan's boots twisted the soft grass beneath them anyway.

Ignore the pain, keep fighting, Erevan thought, leaping from the ground and brushing dirt off his sleeve. He hoisted his blade and charged three swift paces along the field. One good swing was all he needed to bring down the man before him. His father.

Missed.

"You're not even close," his father said, dodging Erevan's slash in an effortless sidestep. His feet moved far faster than an ordinary man his age. Then again, he wasn't an ordinary man. He was Sir

Lee, the finest swordsman in the entire country of New Lanasall. Maybe the finest swordsman in the whole western world and Erevan wanted... no needed, to beat him.

"I'm not giving up!" Erevan yelled and let out a flurry of swings at his father, only to watch each one be parried and tossed aside.

"Think. Don't just act. Plan your second move before you go for the first," his father lectured, waving a hand in the air. Erevan swung again, this time with all his strength.

Sir Lee spun around him and cut at the back of Erevan's neck. Or. He would've, if they'd been using *real* swords in a *real* battle. Thankfully for Erevan, the swords they wielded were made of wood, fashioned into blades from the branches of a nearby dying oak tree. Their real swords were still sheathed on their belts.

"You fail," his father said with a disapproving grunt before tossing his wooden sword down and adjusting the sheath of the blackened blade on his waist belt. Then the man walked to the oak tree and sat down by their things, two adventuring packs and a hat made of straw. They rested against a gnarled trunk that smelled of wild, scurry-happy critters.

"How long before I can try again?" Erevan asked, readying his stance in the grassy farmland fields and practicing his swordsmanship against an opponent he could actually beat. *The air.*

His green make-shift hooded half cape swishing as he did so, while little drafts of wind slipped in the patched-up holes of his tattered, dirt-ridden clothes.

"Hmm, give me a moment to think," Sir Lee said, blocking the sun from his eyes until he put on his wide hat. A gift from Erevan's mother, the hat was thin but tall and weathered, like Sir Lee himself. The man went nowhere without it.

"The last time you said that, it was five months before I got another chance," Erevan noted.

"And apparently that wasn't enough time." His father gave another grunt. Then he closed his eyes and laid back against the tree trunk.

"I am trying," Erevan said, still slicing the wind attempting to perfect his form.

"But you aren't learning," his father said, sighing.

Erevan stopped and looked at him. "I thought I was getting better."

"You are."

"Then why can't I beat you?" he asked, studying his father's face for a clue, but it was as stoic as an ancient tortoise. The thin, greying strands of hair on his head signified wisdom and experience, a far contrast from Erevan's full head of black, twisted locks with golden tips. They both carried scars on their faces. Years of close calls with death as a mercenary were visible on Sir Lee's square face. Erevan, however, received most of his from a life growing up on the streets of Bogudos. A large cut across his left eyebrow sat as the crowning trophy on his round head.

"You're not improving at the right things. You've gotten faster, your footwork is good, and your instincts are impeccable for someone your age."

"But?" Erevan pressed, knowing what was coming next.

"But, you're too reckless," his father said, shaking his head. "A man must think before he acts." One of his father's many, *a man must* quotes, most of which he'd told Erevan a hundred times before.

"You always say that."

"It's always true."

"You told me to be aggressive so I could punish my opponent's mistakes."

"I also told you to be patient to avoid making mistakes of your own," his father said, sighing. "And yet even with those big pointy ears of yours, you only managed to hear half of what I told you."

"You always say that too." Erevan frowned. He felt the tips of his slightly pointed ears, proof of his half-elven ancestry. He looked at his father's ears. Rounded, like any other human. Only able to hear half as far and clear as Erevan could. Ears were one of the two easy ways to tell humans and elves apart. The other clue was their eyes. Like his skin, Erevan's eyes were brown with a little amber, but their color was more vibrant than a human's and they saw twice as far.

Unfortunately, it was like that for all his senses. The stench of cow droppings was impossible to miss coming on the breeze from a nearby farm. Their next destination.

The local townguard captain wanted to meet with them, and supposedly, there was someone of mild importance in his care.

"You'd think some elven wisdom would've passed down to you. Or that you'd inherit some patience at least," his father said, shaking his head.

"So, if I learn to be more patient, can I try again today?" Erevan asked, holding his breath for the answer. He knew he could beat his father... *probably*.

"Trying again today would be the opposite of patience," Sir Lee said, chuckling. He stood, and his heavy armor clattered. Then he nodded off to the west, where a red and white barn stood half a mile away surrounded by fields of wheat. "Let's get this over with. It's a long road back home." He slung his pack over his shoulders and walked toward the barn.

The assortment of items within the pack jingled as he did so, coin, torches, a compass; the man carried everything in that bag. Then he lobbed the other pack to Erevan which contained their rations and carried the welcoming scent of bread. Erevan tossed the bag over his back as well and followed his father.

"This job wasn't too bad, you know. I can see why you chose this life," Erevan said.

"Escorting a traveling merchant wagon along the safer roads of the country is not my typical mercenary work, and that's the only reason I let your mother talk me into allowing you to come. Things might've went fine this time, but it didn't involve bandits, goblins, or any of the deadly creatures in the wilderness of this country."

"I'm not afraid of them, I'm a better swordsman than every townguard in Bogudos, you said it yourself."

"Being a mercenary is about a lot more than your skill with a blade."

"Then why are you making me beat you in a duel before you let me join you as a mercenary?" Erevan asked. And when his father didn't answer, Erevan continued, "I'll listen to whatever you say while we're on a job, I promise."

Sir Lee grunted. "That would be a first."

"If it's two of us working, we could take on bigger missions and earn more coin," Erevan pointed out. He needed gold, and lots of it to fix his mistake from two years ago. But that wouldn't convince his father. "Besides, we both know someone who could use the extra coin for the school she wants to build," Erevan said, and his father's face went flatter and drier than an old prune.

"Don't bring your mother into this. She'd have my neck if I got you killed."

"Well, I could use the extra coin to—"

"Egg the townguard barracks?" Sir Lee asked, cutting him off and clearly trying to shift the conversation away from what Erevan was going to say.

"That was a long time ago. I'm mature now," Erevan assured.

"Is that so? I seem to recall them chasing you through the city rather recently," his father said with another of his grunts.

"You're just getting old. The last time that happened was when I was fifteen."

"You turned sixteen last month," his father said. Erevan grinned.

"Like I said, a long time ago," Erevan repeated, holding back a chuckle. "And I was only being chased because they thought I was selling magic dust. Like I'd ever do that after what happened two years ago."

"Running from them doesn't make you look very innocent."

"You're the one who told me to be wary of the townguards."

"I also told you to follow their orders," his father said.

"You give a lot of conflicting advice." Erevan frowned.

"It makes perfect sense, son, you're simply too young to understand. That's why you aren't ready to be a mercenary," his father told him. "Now, let's see what the good captain wants," he said with what might've been a hint of sarcasm in his ever-calm voice.

They were a little ways from the front of the barn, but Erevan could still see the three people that stood there. One was the townguard captain of the area. They'd met only once and already weren't on good terms. He'd been the one to inspect the merchant wagon Erevan and Sir Lee escorted to the capital city, and the captain had made more than one rude remark about the city of Bogudos and all its inhabitants.

The captain's glossy, leaf-colored badge shone on the chest of his leather armor as he tapped a finger on his sword's pommel, waiting for an excuse to unsheathe it. He stood there; his nose turned up as though having to walk on his own two feet was beneath him.

Lurking nearby was a stranger with a black hood pulled so far over their head that their face couldn't be seen, even under the noonday sun. Their hood extended into a long dark cloak that covered them down to their fine leather boots.

Before them both was an old lady with creaky old bones, white hair, and dirty farm clothes. She held firm to a shovel too heavy for her to lift as she cowered in the presence of the captain and his dark-hooded companion. Erevan perked his ears up and listened as he walked.

"Whether or not you can spare it is not the issue. Taxes are owed," the captain said. The old lady's head drooped. She gave a quick glance behind her. A couple cows sat indifferently in their stables, unaware of their owner's predicament. Next to them, behind a barrel, was a small child hugging a stitched toy and eavesdropping on the conversation.

"We can hardly afford to eat," the old lady said. "Trade with the home country has slowed so much since the war—"

"I don't need a history lesson. I was there," the captain said, raising a hand to cut the old lady off. "You must understand these are challenging times for all of us."

"Are they challenging times for you?" the old lady asked, pointing a finger at him. "You and your men come and take from us, and for what? Where's our coin going? That's what I'd like to know?" The hooded person shifted at the old lady's words but didn't speak.

"Consider it an investment for a brighter tomorrow," the captain said, revealing an unpleased smile.

"Those aren't your words. That's what they told you to say," the old lady said, scowling.

"If you'd like more information, there are weekly meetings not ten miles west from here in the capital to discuss—"

"I can't up and leave my farm to go stroll down there, I have mouths to feed," she said, stopping him. "Are my grandchildren supposed to tend to the farm themselves?"

The captain rolled his eyes. "Where are their parents?"

"Dead," she said with a glare. "I had to hire a field hand just to keep the place running. He's a hard worker, but I can barely afford to pay him." She pointed a finger out into the wheat fields where a black-bearded dwarven man who stood maybe four and a half feet tall fumbled a bushel into a sack.

"I am, of course, willing to overlook your offenses due to the circumstances. If you can offer me something off official records. Otherwise, you'll need to come with me."

"I have nothing except the clothes on our backs. If you're here to arrest an old widow for non-payment, then do what you must. But please, make sure my grandchildren aren't left here to fend for themselves."

"No promises," the captain said, grinning slightly.

"Leave her alone!" Erevan yelled, hurrying their way. The captain turned to Erevan and his grin widened.

"Ah, the boy from the city of swamprats," the captain said, tightening the grip on his sword.

"And yet none of them are as filthy as you," Erevan snapped back.

"That's enough, son," Sir Lee said from behind him. The captain's face shuddered at the sight of Sir Lee, and he promptly released the grip of his sword, but he continued to tower menacingly over the old lady.

Erevan looked back at his father. "I won't sit around and watch them treat her like this."

"We won't," Sir Lee said.

"Evlynna bless you two," the old lady said. Sir Lee forced a smile in return. Sir Lee was many things, but unlike his wife, he was not a believer in Evlynna. Erevan had yet to fully make up his mind on the matter.

Crack. Breaking bone. A scream pierced the air. Erevan snapped his head to it. An eerie growing cloud of fog swelled, already the size of the barn. Inside of the swirling mist were a faint pair of eyes as it enveloped the spot the dwarven man had been in the wheat fields. And the mist was expanding.

Erevan's feet were already moving. "He needs help!" he shouted. Without another thought, he rushed to the screams which grew more desperate with every step. And to *the fog*. Losing sight of everything, even himself.

Chapter 2

A Most Magical Mirror

LOSING WAS NOT AN OPTION. NOT THIS TIME, NOT again. Aireyal concentrated as best she could, eyes closed. But her best had never been good enough. The last time she tried, everything went… no. That was not the way to think right now.

Aireyal let out a deep breath, opened her eyes and threw ruby red dust at the candle burning on the table before her. "Igno," she said, wishing the magical word would work.

The candle's flame flickered a hair, but it might have been because of the wind. She glanced over to the open window in her mother's wide rounded study as the gentlest of breezes made its way in past the bookshelves and sighed. All she had to do was make the fire spark, dance, or anything that showed she could control it. It was the only simple step of the overly complicated sparks test she'd have to pass. Unfortunately, the candle before Aireyal burned calmly, *taunting* her.

"You're almost there, I can feel it," her mother said, holding a cup of mirthroot tea and cheering Aireyal on with an overly enthusiastic smile. Lies. There was no *almost* with magic. You either did or didn't, even Aireyal knew that, and she was the worst apprentice mage in the entire school. Though, *mage* suggested she had actually done magic.

Aireyal ran her hand past the awful freckles on her face and down through her long brown hair. Not too long of course, that might attract attention. Instead, she kept it cut just the right length to fade into the background when other people were around. No elegant curls, no pin-ups, no dyes. It was best to keep it plain and dull, like all her clothes. Silky fabric but patternless with bland creamy colors, unlike the school uniform she'd have to wear soon. At least all the other girls would be stuck in the same purple long-sleeved blouses and ruffle skirts too.

"Try not to lose concentration next time," her mother said. Her own rich, silky attire swishing as she moved toward the table, though hers was sunny yellow. She peered at the clutter of red fey dust. A mess to clean up, but that was for the future. For now, it scented the disheveled study room's air with a swirling blend of sweet cherries and spicy cinnamon.

"It's hard not to," Aireyal said, slouching. She grabbed another handful of dust from the pouch in her hand. Aireyal's eyes betrayed her, glancing at the plaque hanging above the table. *Grandmage June Ando* shined in fancy golden letters. Her mother's name. Being *magicless* was one thing. But still being magicless as the sixteen-year-old child of a Grandmage, one of the most important people in the Senate of Mages, was unheard of.

"Something the matter?" her mother asked, trying to hide the concern on her face with a sip of tea.

"Just thinking," Aireyal said, gripping tight to the dust in her hand.

"Take however long you need," her mother said in her softest, sweetest voice, like a swan floating on water. "I know you'll get it this time."

Another lie. Aireyal knew her mother wasn't foolish enough to think she'd succeed. Then again, Aireyal got herself in this predicament because of her own lie. A lie that she could never admit to *anyone*.

It would be fine if her entire future didn't depend on going to this school... but it did. Other schools taught magic, but since Darr-Kamo had been built, it was the only school the Senate of Mages had accepted candidates from. And Senate-Mages got to settle magical concerns in Lanasall's cities by making laws.

The country of Lanasall was more prosperous than ever... for some. But that fortune came at the cost of rising taxes on everyday workers, mostly thanks to the laws enacted by Lanasall's other governing body, The Parliament of the People. And partially thanks to Parliament following the lead of their new sister country New Lanasall's laws.

The irony of the situation was endless. Parliament was supposed to work in the people's interest on non-magical concerns. But in the smaller towns of the country, the working class toiled and even injured themselves at jobs they despised so they could make enough to survive. All while the Members of Parliament and wealthy citizens in big cities like here in Longaiya lounged in luxury, doing little to no work at all. *Citizens like you,* Aireyal's inner voice said, and she looked down at her splendid, silk clothes.

But the guilt of her inherited affluence pushed her on. She could change things as a Senate-Mage in one city, and from that example, others would surely follow. But to become a Senate-Mage, she had to make it through Darr-Kamo. And to make it through Darr-Kamo, she had to be able to do magic. Something everyone else who had ever attended the school proved they could do in their entrance exams. *Everyone but you,* her inner voice reminded her.

"What if I'm not good enough?" Aireyal asked. The failures of her past refused to permit her to look her mother in the eyes, so she scanned the tall bookshelves that lined the walls instead. They were overstuffed with novels, textbooks, and maps. More books piled high below with barely enough space to see the hard stone floor under them.

"You'll get it next time, lollidrop, I'm sure of it," her mother said as though Aireyal were still the same small girl that once needed help reading the long words in giant tomes.

"No, I mean, what if I'm not good enough for this school?" Aireyal asked, picking up a book from the top of a stack, hoping it would distract her from the impending dread in her nerves. *The Law of Dragonslaying* by Sir Bard.

Pass, she thought, placing it back.

"Aireyal Ando. What have I told you about believing in yourself?" her mother lectured, laying her tea down and placing her hands on her hips.

Aireyal looked at the floor, hoping her mother wouldn't make her recite the—

"I want to hear you say it," her mother said before Aireyal could finish the thought.

Sigh.

"I can do anything if I put in the time to study it," Aireyal said, repeating the phrase that had been burned into her memory for as long as she could remember.

"And have you studied to prepare for school this year?"

"I've been studying my entire life," Aireyal said, thinking of the countless books she'd read. *The History of Lanasall and its Great Split, Every Volume of The Core of Magic, The Rivalry of Heritour and Nyumbafro...*

"Then you will be ready, because she who trains to learn..." her mother started, waiting for Aireyal to speak.

"Trains to lead," Aireyal finished. It was a quote from Ilizabeth Kamo herself, co-founder of Darr-Kamo. She'd said it in a speech the day she died. No. The day she was *killed.* Aireyal had read the address at least a dozen times... *today.*

She was Aireyal's biggest inspiration, even more so than her mother. At least being like Ilizabeth Kamo was possible. She was a normal magicless human that hadn't gone to Darr-Kamo. But that was *only* because she founded the greatest school in the western world, where *the best and brightest go,* or so people said. It was certainly the place the wonderfully wealthy went; even here in her mother's messy room, the prestigious golden-leaf designs painted on the walls proved that.

Aireyal turned her attention back to the candle. Her mother was right; she had studied magic inside and out, down to the smallest details. All she had to do was believe *in her studies.* And *in her training.* And *in herself.*

She faltered. That was the hard part. She wasn't an elf; it was normal for humans to be magicless. Only one in ten humans could do magic at all. But this was Darr-Kamo. Everyone here could do magic. *Except you,* that pesky inner voice noted. Aireyal took a deep breath.

You can do it. Stop your doubting, she told herself, fighting the voice. Aireyal pulled another handful of red dust from the bag and threw it at the candle. "Igno," she said. It seemed like it sputtered… maybe? Then again, it was probably only the wind. She stared at it and tilted her head to the side as though it would help her discern more.

"Hmm," her mother exhaled. There was a dejected tone in it that Aireyal knew her mother didn't mean to have, but it was there all the same. And that is what sank Aireyal's heart. Being a failure was one thing. Failing the person that believed in you most was another.

"I'm so sorry," Aireyal murmured and dropped her head. "I don't belong here. I should've gone to—"

"You *are* in the right place, Aireyal, you'll see. This school will become your home before you know it, just like it did for me when I was an apprentice." Her mother walked over and placed a caring hand on her shoulder.

"No one here is like me," Aireyal said, picking up another book to flip through.

"It's a school, Aireyal. I'm sure you'll find someone who loves books as much as you do," her mother said, smiling. "The librarian is a good friend of mine after all."

"You know that's not what I meant," Aireyal said, frowning.

"Don't doubt yourself so much." Her mother pulled her in for a small hug. "Stop thinking so much, just act."

"Sorry," she said, taking in a deep breath. The cherry-cinnamon fragrance of the room burned into her lungs. A sweet-scented reminder of how pathetic she was. *No. Stop that. You can do it.*

Aireyal huffed out a breath. A determined one. *You know what to do.* Magic was simple. She thought back to her readings,

'*Controlling the elements of nature requires red fey dust. This dust may affect nature in an amount up to but not more than its own size. In other words, to control an entire glass of water, one needs at least an entire glass of dust.' -Antoni Darr, co-founder of Darr-Kamo, page 13 of 'The Core of Magic, Volume I: Evoking the Elements'.*

Now was the time to make her magic as reliable as her memory. Perhaps her mother was right. Instead of thinking, she needed to act. Or try to at least. *No.* She *could* do it.

With a handful of dust, Aireyal took one final deep breath, then tossed it forward onto the candle. "Igno," she said, and this time... nothing happened. *Again.*

Aireyal's eyes betrayed her once more and peeked at her mother, whose lips were pressed together in veiled disappointment. Aireyal's heart shattered.

Knock. Knock. Her mother's head spun toward the door. "Why don't we take a little break," she said to Aireyal, trying to fake a smile, then visibly giving up on it and going to open the door.

Behind it was a boy with light blond hair curled to perfection. His face was pale like he'd sat out in the cold autumn air for too long, though that didn't stop him from being the most handsome boy Aireyal had ever seen. He stood tall in his purple school uniform which might have been baggy on some but fit his form perfectly. And the sophisticated jerkin was embroidered on its front with the leafy designs of Lanasall's flag.

Best of all though, the boy was an elf. He had soft, but somehow sharp facial features like elves tended to, unlike the broader, more rugged features of humans. And Aireyal loved the vivid color of elves' irises. She found them so much more interesting than mundane human eyes like her own. She stared into the twinkling, ocean blue eyes of the boy before her. That is, until those beautiful eyes flitted over to her.

Pump, pump. Her heart raced, so she dashed over the stone floor to a corner of the room, barely in sight. Aireyal pretended to be interested in the contents of her mother's mahogany table. It was a mess, like the rest of the room. Even the chair behind it was loaded with papers and books. How her mother managed to find anything in here was a mystery. Then again, this was her private study, not her main office that influential people were always in and out of. Which is surely why she had such a curious collection of things atop it. Aireyal risked another glance back at the handsome boy and his eyes met hers again. *Pump, pump.*

Aireyal snapped her head back down to the table and picked up her schedule for the first half of the school year.

1ˢᵗ Hour – First Year Apprentice's Breakfast – The Banquet Hall

2ⁿᵈ – 5ᵗʰ Hour – Morning Leisure

6ᵗʰ Hour – History of the Western World, Docent Tolk – Phoenix House

7ᵗʰ Hour – Introduction to Magic, Grandmage Ando & Docent Stewart – Darr Hall

8ᵗʰ Hour – Afternoon Tea – The Banquet Hall

9ᵗʰ Hour – Tarot Reading, Seer Levi – Sybill Observatory

10ᵗʰ Hour – Sylvan for Beginners, Docent Eldmer – Adatin Tower

11ᵗʰ Hour – The Economy of Magical Goods, Docent Mountaincoat – Palo Pavilion

12ᵗʰ Hour – Supper – The Banquet Hall

Aireyal's eyes dropped from her schedule and skimmed over the rest of her mother's table. Pouches of dust, strange colored paper, an ash black egg that was a little smaller than a goose's. *A black egg?*

Something flickered in her eye, and she flinched, but it was only a hand mirror, maybe nine inches wide, laid flat against the desk. Its golden-rimmed edges suggested it was expensive. But it was frosted along its glass which... didn't reflect the room at all.

Instead, the mirror showed what appeared to be a field of wheat shrouded by something too foggy to make out. And for the slightest of moments, a pair of eyes appeared behind the fog. Aireyal reached down to pick up the mirror and wipe the frost from its face.

Sssss. The mirror's handle was sizzling hot to the touch. Aireyal jumped, startled and her knee slammed into the table, shaking it. The commotion sent the egg rolling until it fell right onto... no, *into* the mirror, as though the mirror's glass was a hole.

All of it would've been fascinating if Aireyal wasn't in so much pain. She was unsure whether to attend to her bruised knee or burning hand. *Wait. Burning?!*

Aireyal screamed as flames scorched her fingers. Agony, like her flesh was being cooked alive. It coursed through her hand into her body. The faint sound of her mother shouting something filled her ears as Aireyal's knee buckled, sending her tumbling forward. The last thing she heard was an ominous thud and a gut-wrenching shatter.

~ *Chapter 3* ~

The Court's Courier

ANOTHER SHATTER ECHOED AS EREVAN RAN ahead in the fog. As did cries of pain, which became clearer with each step. He couldn't see in the thick mist, but at least he could hear where he was g—

Erevan tripped over a stout silhouette that managed to come in view right as he crashed into it.

"Didn't see you there, sorry," Erevan said, standing up and offering a hand to the dwarven field hand, who lay atop a thick bag of wheat, groaning. He didn't notice Erevan at all. Instead, the dwarf stood up and stumbled about like he'd left a tavern several drinks too late. He lasted five seconds on his feet before falling back down. His hands caressed a crisscrossed bloody gash on the side of his head.

"I heard you screaming. What happened?" Erevan asked, staring at the gash.

"Erevan!" Sir Lee's voice called from behind him.

"I'm here! The dwarf's with me, he needs help!" Erevan shouted back, then he looked again at the sturdy little fellow before him. "What happened to you?" Erevan asked again, but he got no response. "Don't worry, I'll get you out of here," he said, this time reaching to help the dwarven man up. But the moment Erevan touched his shoulder, the dwarf flinched.

"THE MIST IS HERE! IT'S A SIGN! WE'RE ALL DOOMED!" the dwarf yelled as he swayed around with blood dripping from him onto the wheat.

"Erevan!" Sir Lee called again, this time closer. His father's heavy armor jingled, and soon enough, his figure emerged through the fog at Erevan's side. Moments later, the captain's hooded companion showed up as well, though they stayed further away as a mere silhouette covered by mist. The captain, however, was nowhere to be seen.

"He refused to set foot inside the fog," Sir Lee said as Erevan peered around for the captain. "A wise choice I'd say. Fog doesn't appear out of nowhere. Whatever caused this could be dangero—"

Sir Lee stopped mid-sentence as a muffled groan came from below them. Erevan looked down at the dwarf, who now laid with his face planted in the blood-soaked ground. "Friend of stone, what did this to you?" Sir Lee asked, but there was no response. And so, he took both hands to help the dwarf up. The moment he touched him, the dwarf screamed again.

"FEAR THE WHITE MIST! IT HIDES THE SPECTRES WITHIN!"

Spectres. Dwarven merchants passing through Bogudos spoke of them. Their stories, however, were unconvincing at worst and improbable at best.

Sir Lee scoffed. "This nonsense again." But this was different. The dwarves Erevan had met in the past were at least... *sane.*

"Do you think he lost his mind to some enchantment from the mist?" Erevan asked.

"Perhaps. Either way, we should get out of here as soon as we can," his father said grimly.

"What about the dwarf? We can't just leave him," Erevan said, looking down in pity as the dwarf rubbed the bleeding gash across his head once more.

"He's already lost too much blood, he's as good as dead."

"But—"

Crack. Another shatter. This time, from behind them. Erevan turned, but mist clouded his vision. The sound rang in the distance for several moments before fading away. He looked to his father, but the man was completely unaware, still watching the dwarf. The captain's hooded companion, though, had also tilted their head toward the sound. Then, without so much as a warning, they dashed off in the shatter's direction. "I'm coming too," Erevan said, starting after them. Sir Lee yelled something as Erevan ran into the billowing clouds of fog, but his ears were focused on something else.

Metal against metal. Getting closer by the second until... a cry in anguish. The kind made moments before death. "Igra morta asi asu," a voice said as Erevan approached. A lady's... no, a girl's.

Soothing though not soft, and particularly rebellious in nature, like a current rushing the wrong way.

Erevan arrived to see the captain on the ground unmoving, a series of crisscross slashes across his chest just like the dwarf. The captain, however, wasn't breathing. He was dead. His hooded companion stood above him silently.

"What happened? Did you see anything?" Erevan asked. The only response he received was a shake of the head. *What's killing them?*

Suddenly, the mist around them faded as quickly and eerily as it appeared, leaving them in the sunny wheat fields of the farm.

"Erevan!" Sir Lee called. Erevan turned, his hand on the hilt of his sword, expecting trouble. But his father was perfectly fine unlike the captain or dwarven field hand. Another scan of the area led Erevan's eyes to the old farmer lady. Dead, with crisscross slashes across her chest. He looked inside the barn to see if the farmer's grandchild survived and found a stitched bear torn apart. Next to it was a tiny corpse.

Who or whatever did this had no conscience or morals, Erevan thought. He tried to ignore the sick churning in his stomach as his father's footsteps approached. There was no time to mourn. He needed to stay alert in case the mist and whatever was inside it came back. Dropping your guard near the freshly dead was a good way to join them. People had learned that lesson firsthand on the unforgiving streets of Bogudos before his eyes.

"Stop running off. That's how you get killed," his father said as he approached.

"I was following them," Erevan said, pointing at the captain's hooded companion. Sir Lee grabbed the hilt of his sword, studying the figure, but there wasn't much to see. All Erevan could tell for sure was that he was maybe half a foot taller than the person, every other detail was lost in the long black cloak that covered their body down to their boots.

"Who are you?" Sir Lee demanded.

With a cautious, black-gloved hand, they pulled their hood off, revealing a girl. She had big chocolate brown eyes that matched her flawless skin. Eyes more vibrant than Erevan's, so colorful in fact, that he knew she was an elf, even with her ears hidden in her thick, coily, black hair. "I'm a courier from the court of Nyumbafro. Sir Lee Eston, I've been searching for you," she said with a stunning smile.

"Nyumbafro?" Sir Lee repeated, scratching his beard which had grown scruffy out on the road. The courier's claim made sense though. She fit the description of the country full of brown-skinned elves. "You're quite a ways from home."

"I could say the same of you. Bogudos is what, three weeks travel from here?"

"Less than that by sea, if the weather's favorable."

Which it definitely isn't, Erevan noted in his head, thinking of the mist that had just surrounded them. But that's not what concerned him at the moment. "Why were you looking for my father?" Erevan asked. The courier glanced at him, then at his father, then back to him, squinting. He was certain he knew why too. Erevan didn't resemble Sir Lee because Sir Lee wasn't his birth father.

Not that he wanted to talk about that with some stranger and his expression must've shown as much because the courier's full lips parted to say something, then she decided against it. Instead, she chose to pull a rolled-up parchment note from her cloak and hand it to his father who opened it. Erevan read behind him, pausing every so often to check the area in case the mist returned.

Sir Lee,

The courier carrying this letter is in need of an escort back to Nyumbafro and I believe there is no candidate more ideal than you considering you're currently traveling back to Bogudos. It is of dire importance to the entire country of New Lanasall that she and the item in her possession make it to their destination. So much so that you'll be paid one thousand gold pieces for the completion of this mission.

For a brighter tomorrow

One thousand gold pieces. Most people in New Lanasall only made one or two silver pieces from a day's worth of work. One gold piece was worth ten silvers. That meant one thousand gold pieces was worth... well, a lot of days of work. It was also more than enough to fix Erevan's mistake from two years ago.

His friend Isaiah had spent the last two years in jail for something he didn't do, and unless someone came up with a five hundred gold fee on Isaiah's behalf, he'd spend the rest of his life there. *He wouldn't be there if it wasn't for me.* Erevan clenched a fist. He owed it to Isaiah to save him, no matter the cost.

"This letter isn't signed by anyone," Sir Lee noted.

"It's from your Magistrate. She wanted to keep this assignment off official records," the courier said, taking the letter back from him and rolling it up neatly. "Rest assured, you will be paid upon my safe return to Nyumbafro."

If the Magistrate, leader of the entire country of New Lanasall sent such a letter, then this courier must've carried something beyond valuable. Erevan looked her up and down but there was nothing to see except the dark cloak she shrouded herself with. Whatever she had was small enough to carry on her person.

The offer sounded good, really good, but things that sounded really good, typically weren't. That was another lesson the streets of Bogudos taught all who grew up on them. Sausages, shoes, swords, didn't matter; if the deal seemed in your favor, there was a downside, *always.*

"What aren't you telling us?" Erevan asked.

"I'm not sure what you mean," the courier said with an all-too innocent shrug of her shoulders.

"It's a bit hard to believe the attack that just occurred doesn't involve you," his father said, scratching his chin.

"Sir Lee, if whatever attacked these people were after me, don't you think it would've killed me too?" she asked.

"You're saying it's a coincidence?" Erevan asked, folding his arms. She shrugged again, and a roguish smirk formed on her lips.

Sir Lee shook his head. "I sympathize with your current plight, but I'm not going to put my son in danger to protect you from an enemy I can't even see."

"I can protect myself," Erevan said. "You've taught me how."

"From a common thug, yes," his father said, stepping forward to point at the crisscross slashes through the captain's body. "From whatever did this, I'm not so sure," he said, then turned to the girl. "Which is why I'm declining your offer, courier," he finished, before walking past her, motioning for Erevan to follow him.

"You'd go against your Magistrate's orders?" the courier asked, hurrying to follow Sir Lee, Erevan right next to her.

"I'm a mercenary, young courier, not one of her townguard captains. She doesn't *own* me," he said with a hint of disdain.

"You'd turn down a thousand gold?" the courier asked in disbelief, her pretty lips opening wide.

"Mother could use the coin," Erevan pointed out to his father. He didn't trust the courier, but opportunities like this didn't come around for people like him.

Sir Lee shook his head again. "It's not worth dying over. You'll have to find someone else to protect you. I suggest heading east and checking the Coral Coast for mercenaries if you can make it that far," Sir Lee said, picking up his pace.

The courier reached one of her gloved hands inside her cloak, pulling out a handful of red dust. The smell of cherry and cinnamon sifted through the air as she threw it forward. "Ventu!" she commanded, and the dust dissolved into a fierce gust of wind ripping up a long stretch of wheat from the ground several yards away in a howl.

Grain and leaves floated back down like dandelions on the breeze. Sir Lee stopped and turned to face the courier. "I believe you've misunderstood me. I don't need your protection, Sir Lee. I can do that myself," she said fearlessly. Then she pointed back to where the captain's dead body lay. "The man that brought me here to meet you is dead. All I'm asking for is a guide through a country I do not know."

"What courier doesn't know their neighboring lands?" Erevan questioned.

"I've told you already, I'm a *court* courier. I send and bring missives only to and from the royal court of Nyumbafro. That usually means inside my own country."

"So you work for pampered princesses?" Erevan asked, grunting. "As though we need people in fancy meetings telling us what to do."

The townmaster of Bogudos had used Isaiah's imprisonment as an opportunity to speak of how well the townguards were enforcing the law by providing security and removing *dangerous* things from the community. He failed to mention in that meeting that Bogudos had more crime than any other city in New Lanasall.

"Those meetings are about helping commoners," the courier argued.

"No, they're about discussing how to take more from us. Kings, Magistrates, Townmasters, doesn't matter what they call themselves, they're all the same. I've seen what they do to people like me," he said. "We'd be better off without them. You're a fool if you think they really care about us."

The courier narrowed her eyes, eyeing Erevan up and down, starting with his patched-up hood and ending on his tattered boots. "I wouldn't expect someone like you to understand that life."

Erevan leaned forward, glaring back. "Nor do I want to. Anyone who sits in a palace having a feast while their people starve doesn't deserve to lead."

The courier's nostrils flared. "Our people don't starve, unlike yours, *krishnak*."

"What did you call me—"

"Erevan, that's enough," his father said, stepping between the two of them.

"But she—"

"A man must know when to let things go," his father said, shooting him a sharp glance, before turning to the courier. Erevan settled for folding his arms and launching a scowl the courier's way. "We're headed east to the Cold Creek Bridge, it isn't far from here. Once there, we'll catch a boat ride from one of the ferrymen on the river that runs under it," Sir Lee said, before pausing and adding, "If you wish, you can travel with us, but only until we reach the bridge. There you'll have to find a ride on your own ferry," he finished, before walking forward.

"And how far will that ferry take me?" she asked, following him on one side, while Erevan trailed on the other.

"All the way east on the Raging River to Bogudos and then further northeast to Nyumbafro, if you have the coin," Sir Lee said.

"Is Bogudos a safe city to stop in?" she asked.

"If you don't mind backstabbers and murderers," Erevan said.

"And if I *do* mind?"

"Then you can get off the ferry at the Coral Coast," Erevan suggested.

"Is that a place with decent folk?" she asked.

"Hardly," Sir Lee grunted, adjusting his hat.

"Aren't there any other options?"

"You can try your luck crossing the Cold Creek Bridge alone into the Numino Forest on foot," Sir Lee said, trudging through the endless fields of wheat.

"No thank you, I don't tend to have the best luck," the courier said, following behind him. Erevan thought he caught something golden shining from inside the courier's cloak for a moment, but when he craned his neck for a better glimpse, she pulled the cloak tighter around herself, concealing everything. Erevan looked up to face her.

"You never told us what you're delivering."

The courier's roguish smirk returned. "If left to me, it's something that's going to make you a fortune."

~ Chapter 4 ~
The Apothecarist's Assistant

"**O**H NO, THAT THING IS WORTH A FORTUNE!" someone shouted as something crashed, waking Aireyal from her dazed slumber of never-ending wheat. She turned to find a pale, handsome face smiling at her. The boy who had visited her mother's study. He plucked a cracked bottle filled with leaves off the floor.

"Apologies, I didn't mean to wake you," he said, clearing his throat. "I'm not the best apothecarist, *clearly*." He motioned to the bottle with a chuckle.

Apothecarist? Did that mean this was the apothecary? Aireyal's eyes studied the room, which was better described as a hut. She was in a bed, but potions, plants, and oils filled wooden shelves on every wall and the crisp aroma of mint wafted in the air. Through the open windows, the sun glowed nearly at its peak.

"How did I get here?" Aireyal asked. Her memory was foggy, like a haze drifting over a field of wheat. *Wheat*. Why did she keep thinking about that?

"I carried you. You've been in and out all night. This is the first time we've spoken," he said, then paused. "Where are my manners? Nice to meet you, I'm Zale, the apothecarist's assistant," he said, offering his hand for a shake with a smile. *A perfect, dazzling smile.* Then he thought better of it and pulled his hand back as his eyes peered to her hand. Aireyal looked down, her hand was pink, fleshy, and slightly scorched.

She gasped. *That strange mirror.* It was all coming back to her. Why did her mother even have something like that? Why did it burn her? And how did it absorb an egg? Aireyal needed to talk to her mother.

"I've never seen anything like this," Zale said, staring at Aireyal's hand as he moved over to one of the tables filled both with potion bottles and a yellow bucket. "Scary powerful magic. I wonder where that mirror came from."

"I'd like to know too," Aireyal said. Zale's hands picked up several flasks of green jellies and liquids, examining them. "Which one is the aloe?" he murmured, thinking aloud.

"That one," Aireyal blurted out, surprising herself. Her finger pointed to the brightest green of the gels. She recognized it from her readings of *The Wonderous Webs of Willoworms (and their many uses)*. Willoworm aloe wasn't aloe at all but resembled the plant gel they were named after.

"Are you sure?" he asked, holding up the flask.

She nodded. "I read it in a book."

Zale's lips twisted into a smile. "You read a book on willoworm aloe? Most people only care about that stuff," he said, pointing to a jar of willoworm silk on the highest shelf.

"I read a lot of books," Aireyal said, looking down as her cheeks flushed. "I don't do much else."

Aireyal! Why would you admit that? Now he's going to think you're strange.

"You say that like it's a bad thing," Zale said, smiling his perfect smile, and her heart fluttered. "How else are you supposed to learn? Or as the saying goes, Aoi winne prudi fali, i aoi prinowalio."

The phrase translated to, *what do you know that you have not been taught?* A common proverb in Sylvan, the language of elves, found in ancient elvish books no one else her age bothered to open. And one of the few elvish sayings Aireyal knew. "You must read a lot too."

"A little," he said, giving her a wink that made her heart do another fluttery thing.

Pop!

Aireyal turned; a small, red shark was sprawled out, unmoving next to the yellow bucket atop the table. "Oh no," Zale said, picking the shark up and putting it inside the bucket. A splash of water followed. "Just because you can breathe air doesn't mean you should be out in it," Zale said to the shark, smiling.

"What is that?" Aireyal asked.

"A baby slipshark from the Felaseran Forest. One who needs another day here before he moves on to bigger waters. They can pass right through objects like this bucket here, hence the name. It's funny, I think, that magical creatures like this aren't limited by dust like we are. Perhaps we should take lessons from them," he said, chuckling. Then he turned back to Aireyal and brought the flask of green aloe over to her. Then he moved *closer.* "May I?" he asked, pointing to her hand. She winced at her withered fingers for a moment, before offering it cautiously to him. "Thank you," he said as he took her hand.

Aireyal turned away, hoping he didn't notice her face going red as he poured a bit of aloe onto her wounded hand, then rubbed it into her skin softly. It was cold but soothing all the same. She opened her mouth to say something, though she couldn't decide on what, so she said nothing at all. Zale stopped.

"I'm not hurting you, am I?" he asked.

"No, it feels good," Aireyal said, trying to pretend she didn't notice the part of her mind that hoped he kept holding her hand like this all day long. Then again, this didn't *officially* count as hand holding. She stole a glance as he worked diligently, his focused expression twisting his mouth up in the cutest way while he treated her.

"There we go," he said, letting go of her hand which was smoother than ever. Then he reached for a roll of soft bandages.

"Thank y—"

Pop! Pop!

The shark shifted *through* the bucket. Its head peeking past first, then its whole body as it landed in a flop onto the table. Aireyal leaned forward, wondering if her eyes had deceived her despite Zale's earlier words as he hopped up and picked the shark up again, placing it into the bucket. "Takes some getting used to, doesn't it?" he asked, laughing when he turned to her. Aireyal realized her eyes were wide and promptly closed them back to normal. "You're rather brave, you know," he said, coming back to wrap her hand up in the bandages.

Her cheeks went pink again. Though she wasn't sure if it was because a cute boy said that to her or because she knew it wasn't true. "Why do you say that?"

"You're letting me, of all people, heal you up," he said with a sheepish smile, finishing his wrapping, then walked off, picking up several more corked vials of willoworm aloe. He came back and handed them to her left, *uninjured* hand. "Rub this on your hand twice a day and your burns should get better in a couple of nights. Though, it might never heal back fully," he said, looking away like it was his fault. But Aireyal knew how magic worked. There was no *real healing magic.*

She remembered reading Darr's explanation on it, '*To heal a wound would be to reverse or accelerate time itself. But time magic is not possible and therefore neither is healing magic.*' *-page 71 of 'The Core of Magic, Volume IV: Mysteries and Myths'.*

The crashing ding of the school's bell tower brought Aireyal out of her thoughts. It was noon. Something scratched at the back of her mind. She was supposed to be somewhere at noon. *Your history lecture.*

"I'm going to be late." Aireyal realized the words hadn't come from her. Zale stood up, organizing things around the room. "Sorry, I wish I could help more, but I have to get to my lecture. I've heard Docent Tolk doesn't take kindly to a lack of punctuality," Zale said. Aireyal had heard the same. But she hardly cared about that right now, her mind was focused on something else.

"You're in the same history course as me?" Aireyal asked, hoping her voice didn't sound as anxious as her clammy hands felt. Then again, maybe that was because of the aloe.

"I guess I am, which means we're both late," he said, frowning. "We better hurry." Zale headed to the door and held it open. "After you." Aireyal gave him a small smile before rushing outside into the midday sun.

"It's not a far walk," she said, leading the way so she could hide her cheeks in case they went pink again.

Pop! Pop!

Zale sighed, running back to place the shark in its bucket once more.

"Won't it just slip out again in another minute or two?" Aireyal asked, looking back.

"Probably, thankfully he'll just lie there bored on the table while I'm gone. Still, as long as I'm around, it's only right I try to do my duty," he said, following Aireyal down the tall hill the apothecary hut was built on along a scenic stone path in the grass back towards Darr-Kamo's many buildings. It could've passed for an affluent town as opposed to a school; the golden bell tower, the glistening green grass, the grand architecture. The townguards on patrol around the school grounds seemed out of place though, protecting an area that had never seen trouble and likely never would. "It's all a bit much," Zale said, motioning to a series of perfectly trimmed hedges. "Or perhaps it seems overwhelming because this is my first year here."

"Really? It's my first year too!" Aireyal said more excitedly than she'd intended. Zale smiled though, and Aireyal blushed again, so she spun her head forward.

"What are you here to study? Are you a future artificer? Runereader? Or, wait… are you here to try to become a Grandmage like your mother?"

The words sent a chill down Aireyal's spine though she wasn't sure why. It was a reasonable thing to be expected of her. "Maybe one day. I have to become a Senate-Mage first," Aireyal said, and Zale paused for the slightest moment, before speeding up to walk beside her.

"You want to be involved in city politics?" he asked with what might have been a hint of disappointment.

"I want to help people," Aireyal corrected, more defensively than she intended. "Lanasall's laws need to change, our newest ones hurt more people than they help."

"Sorry, I don't know much about politics," Zale said quickly, raising his hands in alarm. The words revealed an accent so subtle, few people would probably ever notice. Zale spoke a hair quicker than most, his words fluttering for a fleeting moment like a leaf in the breeze. Aireyal looked at the pointed ears sticking through his sleek blond hair. It all made sense the more she thought about it.

"You're from the elven villages in the old Felaseran Forest up north," she said. He hesitated for a moment, staring at her and tilting his head.

"I'm surprised you know about them. There were hardly a dozen of us who lived in my village, if you can call it that. It's so small that map-makers don't bother acknowledging its existence," Zale said. "How about you?"

"I lived here in Longaiya all my life."

"Where the wealthiest people in Lanasall live. Doesn't this city have massive streets paved in gold?"

"There's only one golden street," Aireyal corrected, and Zale chuckled.

"That's one more than the rest of the world. I can't believe you all wasted that much gold on something so... pointless," he said, shaking his head.

"I don't approve of it. We could be using that gold to help many of the small towns that don't have much, or better yet to help New Lanasall. They've been struggling since that stupid treaty in Rifton. I've heard some of their people are falling dead, starving in the streets. Meanwhile here in Longaiya, I've been to giant banquets for three or four people because it looks nice, then all but a of couple plates of food are thrown away. It's despicable! Parliament shoul—" Aireyal caught herself, she hadn't meant to yell.

"I didn't realize you cared so much, few people in my hometown do," Zale said, tilting his head one way, then the other. "It sounds like you want to revolt against Parliament."

"Of course not, both the Parliament of the People and the Senate of Mages serve vital roles to our country, and we need them. I'd be honored to be in their position, and I'd help everyone I could, no matter who they were."

None of that will happen if you don't pass your courses here at Darr-Kamo first, that inner voice reminded her.

Zale halted. "I think this is it," he said, looking at an antique but refined fiery red building in front of them. "After you." He nodded to the open door where a couple dozen of their peer apprentice mages were seated in a square room, staring ahead at an old man with bushy grey eyebrows, balding hair, and a sour frown. He stood at a desk of pine wood as ancient and polished as himself. And the stack of papers atop it were high enough to have all of history written upon them.

Aireyal tiptoed inside, searching for an open seat, but the old man's neck craned her way like a vulture catching a morsel. "Miss Ando, I don't care who your mother is, strolling into my lecture late is unacceptable, is that clear?" he warned with a frown so deep it threatened to drop off his wrinkled face.

All the kids turned around to stare at Aireyal and she dreamed of a world where she could crawl to a corner and disappear. It was only made worse by them noticing she wasn't wearing her purple school uniform like the rest of them. Nor did she have on one of the school's pointy wide-brimmed hats many of the kids wore that went with the uniforms. She hadn't had time to change.

Aireyal's breaths quickened. *Where'd all the air go? And why must everyone stare?*

"Apologies, Docent Tolk, Aireyal's tardiness isn't her fault. She was receiving treatment at the apothecary," Zale said, pointing to Aireyal's bandaged hand.

The docent turned his preying gaze to Zale, then took a long look at one of the papers on his desk. "Mr. Zalerius Varron."

"I prefer to go by Zale, sir," he said courteously.

"And I prefer my apprentices to be at my lecture on time. What's your excuse for being late, Mr. Varron?"

"I was the one treating Aireyal," Zale said, and the docent ruffled his bushy eyebrows.

"Where's the apothecarist?"

"She's helping Docent Irwi to retrieve a shadow tiger from the Lagoona Jungle. They'll be back from their trip next week. I'm her assistant."

Docent Tolk's eyes narrowed, but he didn't argue further. Instead, he motioned to Aireyal, then to an open seat at the front of the room. Then to Zale, and a chair in the middle of the room. "Have a seat, apprentices. Make this the last time either of you are late to my lecture."

Aireyal and Zale nodded in unison, then hurried to their assigned seats. Aireyal dared to take a quick glance behind to Zale, and he gave her a smile. Then the docent cleared his throat ominously and Aireyal spun back, hoping no one noticed the tiny squeal she let out.

"Now, back to the lesson on the biggest historical event of our country," Docent Tolk said.

"Me coming to this school?" offered one of the boys near the back and several kids laughed.

Aireyal recognized the boy, Winston Ellisburg. He'd always lived in Longaiya like her, attending some of the fancy balls her mother made her go to. Docent Tolk, however, wasn't amused by Winston's comment. The docent's face soured again, like he'd swallowed a lemon whole.

"As I told Miss Ando, I don't care who your parents are, and I don't take kindly to my lecture being interrupted," Docent Tolk said, eyeing all the apprentices in the room until the place was quiet enough to hear the gentlest of autumn breezes outside. "Now, let's go over how our country changed forever with the creation of Parliament. Who can explain our history before and after that event?" The room went quiet. "No one?"

"Before Parliament, Grandmages and the Senate-Mages that worked under them made all the decisions for us," an attentive girl near the front said. Several kids glanced at Aireyal when the girl said *Grandmages*, and Aireyal squirmed in her chair. She'd probably get even more attention when she made it to her mother's lecture. "But now," the girl continued, "they only overlook magical concerns, and Parliament handles non-magical concerns for our country."

"Quite correct, but a Grandmage's power is not infinite. Not even Grandmage Ando, who governs the region here around Longaiya," Docent Tolk said, his frowning face pausing on Aireyal for a moment before looking around the rest of the room. "A seventh voice, the Archmage, steps in when those six don't agree on magical concerns that affect the country of Lanasall as a whole. But why am I telling you all this?" More silence. "Because of the Treaty of Rifton, which our Parliament signed to ally with Heritour. And why did this happen?"

Another kid near the front spoke up, "We had to work together to fight Nyumbafro who was building magical weapons secretly in the city of Rifton, so we stormed the city with Heritour. And Heritour has occupied Rifton ever since."

"Also correct. Now remember, each moment in history is shaped by the one before it and that moment then shapes the future," Docent Tolk said, pacing back and forth. "But there are multiple perspectives to every story. Who can tell me the result of the war?"

"Nyumbafro's borders were hard to penetrate, and the war lasted longer than anticipated," a kid said.

"And we took many casualties here in Lanasall," another offered up. "Mostly on the eastern border, where people decided they'd had enough of fighting, and split into a new country, New Lanasall. Then they called for a truce, ending the war."

"Quite correct," Docent Tolk said. "Though if Nyumbafro created more secret weapons, the fighting would surely begin again."

"What else can you expect from those drows," Winston said, and one or two kids gasped. "What? We were all thinking it."

"That is not appropriate language," the docent said, furrowing his eyebrows. The word *drow* referred to the people of Nyumbafro. And not in a particularly kind way; it was a derogatory term for dark-skinned elves. Aireyal had heard it before, eavesdropping on closed door meetings in Longaiya.

"Who cares? It's not like any of them are here," Winston said. "In addition, I heard they're strange looking with grey skin and practice dark magic in secret."

There was a grunt of agreement somewhere in the room, and the docent scowled in its direction, searching faces for the source.

"Perhaps it's time for a test!" Docent Tolk huffed, grabbing the giant stack of papers on his desk. "Maybe that'll teach you all some respect."

Several kids voiced their disapproval, including one who said, "But it's the first day of school." Aireyal's hands shook. *You're overreacting. Surely the docent is joking. He wouldn't really give us a test today*, she told herself.

The docent gave a satisfactory chuckle at the frightened faces around the room, and with that, Aireyal let out a breath she wasn't aware she held. *There's nothing to worry about, he was only trying to scare us.*

Thud. A piece of paper full of questions slammed down in front of her. She looked up to see the docent, and the sense of dread returned.

"Miss Ando," he said, smiling ever so slightly, then continued throughout the room handing out papers, delighted more by each new expression of horror he'd caused. When Docent Tolk made his way back to the front of the room, he spoke. "I hope you all did your summer readings. You have five minutes to answer the ten questions before you. Begin."

Only five minutes? Aireyal peered down at the quiz.

Question 1: The Treaty of Rifton was signed in what year? *This one is easy enough at least. It was nearly fifty years ago.* 754 A.S., otherwise known as, After Settlement of the western world. It was still hard to believe that the deceased parents of elderly elves living today were the ones who had settled the continent.

Question 2: What race of gnomes have recently gone extinct? *You know this too.* The crystallite gnomes. A shame, it was said their colored crystal skin was striking under sun and moonlight alike.

Maybe this test won't be so bad, she thought to herself, taking a deep breath. None of the questions were hard. Most concerned complicated political treaties between countries. *What a relief.*

When Aireyal finished her test and looked up, all the other kids were still staring at their papers. "I hope you aren't searching around hoping someone will give you answers, Miss Ando," the docent said.

"N-not at all, Docent Tolk," Aireyal stammered, itching to apologize though she'd done nothing wrong.

"Then put your head back down and finish your test," he said.

"But I already finished," she mumbled. The docent's eyes shot wide open.

Murmurs came from around the room. Docent Tolk glowered at her and walked over to inspect her test. His mouth fell open. "We haven't even gone over most of this, how have you gotten everything correct?" he demanded. She wasn't sure what to say. Telling him the test was easy seemed disrespectful somehow.

"I-I don't know, I guess I j-just read a lot," she stuttered, shrugging. Several kids giggled and the docent looked up to glare at her, then at the rest of the kids.

"Hand in your tests," he said.

"But it's only bee—" a kid tried to protest, only to be cut off by the docent.

"Hand them in."

A chorus of grumbles and softly murmured dissents followed. Nonetheless, the apprentices got up and handed their papers in. Several of them shot Aireyal dark looks suggesting it was her fault they hadn't got more time. It was punctuated by a, "Thanks a lot, Ando," from one girl and a, "You're the worst," from another as they walked past.

Aireyal shrunk down in her chair, wishing to disappear in a storm as frosty as their words. "Don't worry about what they think, you're brilliant," someone said, passing by to hand in their test. Zale. He gave her a wink that melted her before going back to sit down.

Docent Tolk flipped through the papers, shaking his head as he marked them with a quill, saying nothing except *wrong* every so often. Then he leered at everyone. "It seems Miss Ando is the only one who managed to get more than three answers right," he announced. Another chorus of complaints rang out from the kids. "Honestly, you should be ashamed of yourselves. Most of you put down New Lanasall for the eighth question. Are you seriously not aware they and Nyumbafro have similar laws to us regarding the illegal selling of dust? It was plainly stated on page one hundred and fifteen of your books."

One hundred and fifteen? They were only required to read the first ten pages for the lecture today. Granted, Aireyal had already read the whole book, but that wasn't the point. Surely, the docent hadn't expected them to read that much in one day. Part of Aireyal wanted to raise her hand and ask, but she'd already gained far more attention than she preferred today.

After a lifetime of scolding from Docent Tolk, he decided to hand their papers back and dismiss them. But not before leaving them with a question to answer in tomorrow's lecture. "What's worth more, life or choice?" *That's not much of a history concept.* "Dismissed," Docent Tolk said, gathering his papers and heading out. Kids shuffled from their seats in haste, funneling to the door behind him, except for one. Zale. He walked up to her, smiling, as she stood from her desk.

"How'd you know all the answers on the test?" he asked.

"I read a lot of books," she said, shrugging again and trying to hide her blushing cheeks by looking away.

"Stop saying that like it's a bad thing," Zale said, leaning over until those piercing, ocean blue eyes of his met hers. "I'm going to the library to study, do you want to come? Clearly, I could use some help," Zale said, pointing to his test. He'd only gotten one of the ten questions right.

Aireyal stood there for a moment. *He's asking to spend time with you... on purpose?* She spent several seconds, calming her trembling nerves enough to speak, "Y—" she started, only to have the crashing bell tower ring, signaling it was fifteen minutes to one o'clock. The same time her mother's lecture started. "I'd love to, but I have to get to my next lecture."

"I see," Zale said, his shoulders drooping. "I'll probably be there all day if you want to stop by."

"I will. I promise," she said. He smiled, and her heart did another of the stupid wavery things she was starting to hate... and like.

But right as warm, fuzzy feelings began building within her, they crumbled away, and her mind shifted back to where she was headed.

She would finally be able to get answers about the mirror, but it would be at her mother's lecture, *Introduction to Magic*. That meant Aireyal was going to have to do magic, *today*. She needed mystical help of major proportions.

Chapter 5

The Troll's Toll

MYSTICAL. ONE SIMPLE WORD WAS ALL THE courier had been willing to say. Whatever she was delivering was mystical, small enough to be hidden on her person, *and* apparently worth more money than Erevan had made in his life. Perhaps it was the thing he'd seen sparkling inside her cloak earlier.

No matter, they'd be parting ways soon. The vague outline of the Cold Creek Bridge appeared ahead as Erevan led the way through New Lanasall's countryside. His father and the courier trailed behind; the three of them passing more trees with every step.

The bridge was as rickety as Erevan remembered; worn wooden planks held together by moss-covered sinew stretching far into the distance. An empty wooden post with little holes pecked in it stood before the bridge. Below it, the Raging River flowed as violently as its namesake, threatening to claim the lives of any foolish enough to touch its water outside a boat.

Nestled alongside the river, a gloomily sweet tune whistled from the bridge's direction. Noticeably missing, however, were the sea shanties often sung by the ferrymen that rode their boats up and down the river. As were their boats. *As were the ferrymen.* It wasn't like them to miss a chance to earn a fare, especially on a sunny day like this. But even their salty sea stench was missing from the air.

"There's some kind of creature ahead," the courier said, squinting her big brown eyes which held a hint of hazel in their center. She stared straight at the bridge, but Erevan couldn't make out much more than a silhouette on its wooden planks yet. His eyes might've seen twice as far as a human's, but only half as far as an elf's.

"What do you see?" he asked as they moved closer toward it.

"I'm not sure, I've never seen anything like it," she said, concentrating so hard that her nose wrinkled. "The skin is green and scaly, a water-dweller possibly? It has yellow eyes and a beak like a bird, but it resembles some strange cross between a turtle and a man."

"Does it have something on its head? Like a mountain caved-in at its top?" Sir Lee asked. The courier turned to him, her eyes opening wide.

"Yes. You know of this creature?" she asked.

"Kappas. We cleared them from these lands years ago to provide safety for travelers. I can't imagine why they'd be back now, they're rather fearful of the ferrymen."

"Should we be concerned?"

"Probably not. It'll be fine, I'm sure," Sir Lee said.

Adventurers told tales of kappas but Erevan had never seen one with his own eyes until now. And the courier's description had been accurate. Rumor had it kappas were more mischievous jokesters than an actual threat. Though the word of adventurers in Bogudos wasn't always trustworthy.

The melody paused as they approached the kappa. Its webbed hands held tight to a reed flute. "Stay alert," Sir Lee said, looking behind them. Erevan turned as well, but there was nothing there.

"Day good travelers, pay Kappa toll for bridge cross," the kappa said with a long but careful bow, keeping its head pointed forward instead of tilting it down. Its voice came out in a series of croaks, like how a toad might sound if it spoke.

"You've no authority to collect tolls here," Sir Lee said, walking up next to Erevan. "Last I checked, this bridge was in New Lanasall territory." Erevan peered around, but there was still no sign of the ferrymen.

"Last Kappa checked, New Lanasall owes coin," the kappa croaked.

"Depends who you ask," Sir Lee said.

"You ask Kappa."

"We didn't ask you anything," Erevan noted.

"Kappa."

"We passed this way not three weeks ago, and there was no sign of you," Sir Lee said, moving his hand to the hilt of his sword. "Where are the ferrymen?"

"No pay, no pass," the kappa said.

"That's not an answer," Sir Lee growled.

"We aren't looking to go into the Numino Forest," Erevan pointed out to the creature. "We need a boat to travel along the river."

"No boat. Pay toll. Kappa."

"Why don't we just pay the creature and go across the bridge?" the courier asked.

"Pay and be on way, yes, Kappa."

Sir Lee glared at the kappa before turning to the courier. "Because the forest is filled from edge to edge with everything from giant snakes and murderous plants to reports of strange illusions. We need a boat," he said, a line of concern along his brow betraying his otherwise stoic expression.

"Then why'd you suggest the forest route to me earlier?" the courier asked.

"I'm not responsible for your life, or your choices, courier," Sir Lee said. "Besides, it's the principle of it all. This kappa doesn't own these lands. If we let it start collecting taxes, then what's to stop bandits or outlaws from doing the same?"

"The New Lanasall army, I'd presume," she answered.

"New Lanasall is a country of farmers. Mercenaries like my father are the army," Erevan said.

"Small army," the kappa said.

"Quiet, creature," Sir Lee said, before pulling Erevan and the courier several paces from the kappa until it was out of earshot of his whispers. "These kappas are opportunists and charlatans. As much as I don't want to get involved with their business, we need to find out what happened to the ferry crew. For all we know, these kappas could be responsible for—" Sir Lee stopped short, looking past them.

Erevan spun around. The kappa was gone. Erevan walked toward the bridge, his companions following. In the creature's stead, they found a cup for coin and a parchment note nailed in one of the many holes on the wooden post in front of the bridge's first step.

ALL TRAVELERS MUST PAY THE TROLL'S TOLL OF FIVE GOLD OR FACE AN EXCRUCIATING PENALTY.

The Troll's Toll. That didn't sound good. Erevan studied the bridge. The ragged planks were hardly wide enough for two people to walk across at a time. One false step would send them plummeting into the roaring river below, and it would take several minutes to cross by walking.

"Those words weren't written by the kappa. They don't speak like that," Sir Lee noted, wrinkled concern taking over more of his forehead.

"You think a troll wrote them?" Erevan asked.

"Trolls are too big to write that small," Sir Lee said.

"Then who—"

Zip! Instinct saved Erevan; he ducked back as a dart flew past his face into the wooden post. *So that's where all those holes came from.* Slime coated the edge of the dart.

"Poison," Sir Lee said. Erevan drew his sword and spun, searching the area.

"Stop, we'll pay," the courier said, also looking carefully. But another zipping dart answered her, and she jumped to the side to avoid it. "Fine." She slipped a small rock-handle torch from her cloak. She scratched across it with a stone in her other hand and sparks ignited, lighting the head of the torch. Then she reached back into her cloak, replacing the stone in her hand with a pouch o—

A moist hand snatched Erevan's leg and ripped him off his feet. He twisted as a kappa popped up from a grass-covered hole in the ground and stabbed at him with a thin, slime-coated spear.

Erevan sliced the spear in two with his sword and kicked the kappa back.

"Igno!" the courier shouted above him and flames erupted at the kappa from her torch. The creature croaked in fright, plunging back into its hole. Fire scorched the grass, but another kappa popped up from a different hole nearby with a reed flute in hand. *Zip!* It blew a dart from the flute, which flew at Erevan, and he rolled out of the way. When he looked back, the kappa was gone.

"We need to go forward," the courier said, stepping onto the bridge. It creaked under her foot. Not a good sign considering how little weight it seemed like she carried.

"We can take them," Erevan said, standing up and readying himself for a fight.

"Not worth the risk. We won't be riding the river," Sir Lee said, pointing to the bank where at least twenty kappas emerged from the waters, each of them armed.

"And there's that," the courier added, looking back the way they'd came. Erevan got his answer before he could ask. *The Mist.* It enveloped them from behind. The courier hurried along the bridge to avoid it, but the mist pushed forward onto the bridge surrounding everything as the planks bent and squeaked under the courier's soft footsteps.

"Careful, you don't know what's on the other side!" Sir Lee shouted.

"We can't let her go alone," Erevan said, chasing after her and ignoring his father yelling after him.

Faintly over the rushing river, a single monstrous bellow ricocheted behind them. Erevan turned his head back as he ran to see dozens of yellow eyes peppering the edges of the fog.

"Keep moving!" Sir Lee shouted, running behind Erevan. The bridge creaked under every step of the man's heavy armor, and he let out a curse.

A dart flew past Erevan's face, then something or someone thudded onto the bridge in the mist after them. *Creak.* The planks were ready to snap.

A vague shadow briefly appeared in the mist. A figure, maybe. Erevan squinted for a better look through the fog but burning in his nostrils stole his attention. The undeniable smell of smoke. It came from the mist ahead of him, which turned from milky white to grey. Erevan ran into the clouds anyway, coughing violently.

Where is this smoke coming from?

"AARGH!" Erevan spun to the terrible roar. With one colossal and impossibly light-footed step forward, a troll rose above his father's back. Eight feet of tough grey hide and a face that might've looked human if not for its enormous, eggplant-like nose, boils, and jagged toothed underbite.

Erevan ran to his father, who drew his sword. Drool trickled down the troll's crusted lips, and with one meaty hand, it held a club—no, a broken tree trunk.

"No more step," the troll bellowed as giant globs of spit spewed out with its rancid breath of rotten fish. Scratching its hairy chest, it ordered Sir Lee, "Leave shinies on bridge." But the man stood prepared to strike.

Erevan stopped at his side, drawing his own sword, though he wasn't sure it would matter. With one swipe of the tree trunk, the troll could knock him off the bridge into the roaring waters far below. "I told you to keep moving," his father barked at him.

"I'm not leaving you," Erevan snapped back before coughing on the fumes of smoke that mixed in with the mist surrounding them.

"Shut talk hole. Give bag," the troll boomed at Erevan, seemingly unaffected by the smoke and pointing to Erevan's traveling pack.

"I can't give you my pack, it has rations an—" Erevan coughed.

"Then me take," the troll growled, furrowing its single, shaggy brow and raising a hand. Yellow eyes appeared in the mist behind it. *Zip!* A dart flew at Erevan, and he narrowly dodged it, nearly bumping into his father on the skinny bridge.

Suddenly, Erevan was floating in the air. The troll had picked him up by his bag. Erevan smacked the troll with his right hand and swung wildly at it with the sword in his left. He cut both his bag off and the troll's hard grey skin. The troll roared in pain, dropping him as his father also cut into its hide. The troll punched at the man, but he sidestepped it and landed two more precise strikes with his black blade.

A loud thud to the face confirmed Erevan had fallen hard onto the bridge. *Snap.*

The plank he hit broke in two, sending Erevan plummeting. Or it would have. His father reached down and grabbed him, but their combined weight pulled his father down too.

Sir Lee grabbed onto a plank with his sword hand leaving them dangling over the watery abyss far below, but his hat fell down into the river. *Creak.* The plank wouldn't last long holding them both.

"Stupid boy kill self and friend," the troll cackled, watching Sir Lee try to pull Erevan up. It clutched Erevan's pack and walked back in the direction it came, laughing all the way, the yellow eyes disappearing into the mist alongside it.

Sir Lee groaned, pulling Erevan up. *Almost there.* Erevan latched onto the next plank with his left hand.

Snap.

The one that held Sir Lee broke and he fell.

"NO!" Erevan shouted, barely managing to grab his father's wrist with his right hand. The grip he had was awkward at best, but there was no way to fix it without letting go.

It was his turn to pull them to safety. And he'd have to do it with his off-hand. *Creak.* The planks were breaking.

Erevan put all his strength into pulling up his father, but he couldn't do it. He didn't have the leverage he needed to lift that much weight. But if he shifted, he might lose his father altogether.

"Erevan. A man must know when to let go."

"No!" Erevan shouted back. "I'll nev—"

"You can't pull me up like this," Sir Lee said. Erevan studied everything in sight. There had to be something. The bridge creaking around them? The smoky fog burning his lungs? His father's heavy armor? *The armor!* That was it!

"Your armor! I can pull you up if you can get it off," he said, but they'd have to do it quick, Erevan's arm strength was wearing thin.

"I think you might be right," his father said, loosening his armor. The sudden shift of all Sir Lee's weight almost forced him to slip through Erevan's hands. *Almost.*

But Sir Lee found a way to pull his armor off and it dropped away. Then Erevan pulled as hard as he could until at last Sir Lee made it back up onto the bridge, a task much easier now that the man was in a simple tunic and pants.

They didn't have a chance to celebrate. *CREAK! SNAP!* The bridge was collapsing within a few yards behind them.

Erevan led the way running forward with his father close behind. *SNAP! SNAP! SNAP!* Erevan's arms burned in pain and his lungs did too. The smoke was still there, albeit sparser now. Every step, the mist thinned until faint outlines of trees appeared. They were nearing the end of the bridge.

A figure was ahead. At first, he'd hoped it was the courier but soon realized it was far too large.

SNAP! SNAP!

They reached the other side of the bridge before watching its wooden planks fall to the currents below. There was no going back.

Erevan let out a much-needed breath, then turned back to what he had thought was a figure earlier. *Bodies.* A pile of charred kappas sprawled on the ground. Motionless. Dead. And with crisscross slashes through them. *Just like the people at the farm.* Scorch marks littered the grass, leading straight into the Numino Forest.

Sir Lee turned to Erevan, a grim look on his face. "I appreciate your help on the bridge, but next time, follow what I tell you."

"And leave you to fight a giant troll alone? I could nev—"

"I've faced trolls before. I had a plan to deal with the situation." Sir Lee paused and examined one of the scorch marks. "You told me you'd listen to what I said on the road. And from this moment on, that's what I'm going to expect."

"Yeah, but not if it means—"

"I'm not asking you. Consider it an order," his father said with a rare finality Erevan knew better than to challenge, then he walked cautiously toward the forest.

"Yes, sir," Erevan said, following him. On the ground of the forest's edge was a familiar dark cloak. The courier's. But she was nowhere to be seen. Instead, a kappa stood there, frozen solid, reaching out for a golden-rimmed hand mirror, wrapped partially in the courier's cloak on the ground. Strangely enough, the mirror didn't reflect the forest around them.

~ *Chapter 6* ~

A Curiously Courteous Conversation

T HE MIRROR. IT HAD SHOWN FIELDS OF WHEAT. Aireyal wasn't sure why that thought was etched into her mind as she walked into her mother's lecture hall, but she was going to ask when she got the chance. The couple of dozen other kids already inside turned and stared at Aireyal the moment she entered. Elvish eyes and ears rarely missed anything, and she was one of the only humans in the grand, circular room. At first, she expected them to comment on her lack of a school uniform, but they turned to look at her mother who stood at the room's center sipping tea, then turned back to Aireyal.

A series of whispers were exchanged between the kids, and Aireyal's mind raced. What were they saying? *They probably notice your freckles. Or they found out you can't do magic,* her inner voice said. She shook her head, then scurried around the freshly painted walls to a desk at the back of the room hoping when she sat down, everyone would look elsewhere.

They didn't. So she sunk in her chair wishing it would hide her, but the whispers continued. "Can you believe we're lucky enough to be taught by a Grandmage this year?" one of the louder kids asked another.

"I'm surprised she has time to teach at all," the other said. *She didn't.* That's why she'd be sharing time with Docent Stewart as their instructor. Aireyal had seen the documents over the summer of all the connections her mother had to use, just to be able to halfway teach for one year. And Aireyal knew why she did it. Her mother wanted to watch over her. The thought was as comforting as an undeserved trophy. She sighed and a couple of kids looked back at her, so she drooped deeper into her chair. Hopefully, no one talked to her and she c—

"How are you feeling?" her mother asked, taking a sip of tea and gazing directly at her. All the kids, most of which had glanced away, turned to stare at Aireyal again.

Why me? She trembled and some of the kids stared at her bandaged hand. *Look somewhere else, please.* But she knew the only way they would, is if she answered her mother's question. And that would require talking. Talking in front of a group of strangers, no less. Something she'd always avoided doing. And now, the anxiety of her inexperience clenched at her throat.

Aireyal opened her mouth to speak several times, but nothing came out. After a long awkward silence, she managed to mouth the words, "I'm nervous," to her mother. Several kids snickered.

"Nervous, you say?" her mother said aloud.

Mother! Aireyal buried her face in her hands. This couldn't have started off worse.

"What a wonderful way to begin our lesson on the first color of magic dust. Red. For today, we learn about *fire* and how to control it." Her mother's voice was infused with a certain vigor when she said the word *fire,* which made Aireyal peek an eye through her fingers. And there was something else too, a certain… "Passion!" her mother exclaimed. "It is the heart of your flame." She looked around, glancing at apprentice after apprentice. "If however, we choose to forgo this passion and instead cower in fear," she continued, her eyes back on Aireyal now. "Then we shall never light our flames at all."

The pity of witnessing Aireyal's shortcomings flickered in her mother's eyes, and Aireyal looked away, pretending not to notice the all too familiar setup in the room's center. A table with a candle and a red pouch on it. A pouch, filled with red fey dust.

Pretending not to notice all the kids watching her and whispering among themselves was much harder. Aireyal's stomach twisted so much she was ready to vomit. Thankfully, many of them turned away when a boy raised his hand.

"Grandmage Ando, my father said all I have to do is believe in myself to do magic, and that's always worked for me, is he right?"

Aireyal's mother smiled. "Believing in yourself is a big part. But I think it's more precise to say you *can't* do magic if you *don't* believe in yourself. Though there's plenty more to it."

Part of Aireyal wished there weren't a school rule against apprentice mages having their own bags of dust to practice magic at their leisure without an instructor present. She had a feeling she'd fare better *alone*, and away from all of the judgmental eyes. Then again, she might blow herself up. That is, *if* she could do magic.

"Young apprentices, my course can be quite easy. Don't speak out of turn, and we'll all get along fine," Grandmage Ando said, tapping a finger to her lips, the silky, sky blue sleeves of the dress she wore swishing as she did so. "It's my job to prepare you for your sparks test at the end of the year. If you don't pass it, you won't be back next year, so we'll be going over all the basics of magi—"

"It's not like the test is hard. I could do it with my eyes closed," a girl with a uniform dyed black along her sleeves and ruffles said snippily, and a few of the kids around her snickered. But she made the mistake of saying it just loud enough for the Grandmage to hear, and Aireyal's mother turned the girl's way.

"Then please, Morgana, come show us," Grandmage Ando invited, putting her tea down and motioning for the girl to join her in the center of the room.

"But—" Morgana started to protest, however, Grandmage Ando cut her off.

"With your eyes closed," she said, frowning, though her tone was as warm as ever.

Morgana got up, strutting to the center of the room, muttering something under her breath. She was tall and beautiful. *Really beautiful.* Like a princess from a fairytale. And the sweet melancholy scent of black lilac followed Morgana everywhere she walked. *You don't even belong in the same room as her,* Aireyal's inner voice whispered. Morgana had vivid violet eyes, perfectly flowing dark hair with a few defiantly dyed purple streaks in it to match her eyes, and no *stupid freckles*.

Grandmage Ando handed Morgana the red bag as she approached, then Morgana observed the candle before her, obviously trying to focus. The Grandmage gave her a firm look and Morgana squeezed her eyes shut to several kids' amusement. "Snob," one of them sneered.

"Anytime you're ready, Morgana," Grandmage Ando said.

Whoosh! A blast of red dust flew from Morgana's hand at the candle's flame. "Igno!" It brightened... *maybe*. And only for a split second, before going back to normal as the spicy-sweet smell of red dust coated the room.

"You have quite a bit of practicing to do. Next time, let's not allow our mouths to get ahead of our talent," the Grandmage said as cheerily as ever and several more of the kids laughed. But not Aireyal. She had always known her mother to be kind, forgiving, and patient. This was anything but. Was she like this with all her apprentices? Or was this because Morgana had spoken out of turn?

"Anyone else?" her mother asked as she motioned for Morgana to go back to her seat, which the girl did with a frown trying to decide if it wanted to be embarrassed or enraged. No one else dared to speak. "Good. Let's return to our lesson. Special treats for the apprentices that answer my questions," she said with another smile, reaching into her pocket. "First question, how do our feelings affect our elemental magic?"

She called on a boy whose hand shot up before a dozen others, and everyone turned to him. *They're all finally ignoring you.* Aireyal smiled at the thought as the boy answered her mother. "Each element requires you to harness a different emotion inside of you to use it, like fire with passion."

"Very good," her mother said, tossing a green-packaged candy to him from her pocket. An apple lollidrop. Aireyal's least favorite flavor, but she still watched bittersweetly. Her mother used to do the same with her when she was younger. Britaberry lollidrops were Aireyal's favorite. Hard-shelled, but chewy on the inside and sweeter than any other flavor, with slight sour sensations. Like lemons and strawberries blended together; the perfect fruit. Clever motivation for a small child, and from the looks on the boy's face, good motivation for sixteen-year-olds too. "Can anyone tell me the other five elements we control with red dust and the feelings that correspond with each one?" Grandmage Ando asked.

More hands shot up, and Aireyal's mother called on a girl near the middle of the room, though not before giving Aireyal a look that said, *raise your hand, you know this too.* But there was no way that was going to happen. Instead, Aireyal turned to the girl her mother had called on as she spoke, "Yes, Grandmage Ando, there's the feeling of calm serenity with water. Then there's freedom with wind, and hardiness with earth. Light requires hope and darkness needs fear."

"Wonderful," Grandmage Ando said, smiling, then she tossed a yellow-packaged lollidrop from her pocket to the girl. Lemon. One of the tastier flavors. The girl then raised her hand again, and the Grandmage nodded for her to speak.

"Grandmage Ando, everyone has an element they're best at using, their *primary*. But why is that? Are we born that way?"

"That is an excellent question. Would anyone like to answer?" she asked, looking directly at Aireyal. "I have a double treat for anyone who knows," she said, pulling two red-packaged lollidrops from her pocket. *Britaberry.* Aireyal's mouth started to water. *You know the answer, raise your hand.* But her arm didn't move.

There was no competition; every other kids' hands were down. Some of them followed the Grandmage's eyes to Aireyal. *They're staring anyway, just spit it out.* Aireyal closed her eyes for a moment. *You've put in the time to study this. You can do it.*

Aireyal opened her eyes and slowly raised her hand. "Yes," her mother said, and Aireyal's legs trembled at all the faces that turned to watch her.

She opened her mouth to answer, and her mother's face perked up.

Don't disappoint her.

"..."

Nothing came out. And hope drifted from her mother's face. Aireyal tried again, this time struggling to breathe. The room's air must've gotten thinner.

"..."

Still nothing.

Several kids laughed, highlighted by an, "Ugly and stupid," from the boy next to her. He said it just loud enough so Aireyal could hear, but quiet enough that her mother couldn't. Aireyal buried her face in her hands as fast as she could. Hopefully, it was before the tears came down, though everyone could still hear her crying. *What's wrong with you?*

"Your primary is determined by the emotion you control best. Which is why those who can't control their emotions, can't do magic," said one of the girl's voices from earlier. The words weren't directed at Aireyal, but they sure felt like it. Shame carved a home inside of her and nestled down comfortably.

"That's right, Morgana," her mother said. "But let's make a habit of speaking when called upon, shall we? That's already twice from you."

Aireyal didn't hear much from the rest of the lesson. She spent it telling... no, lying to herself, that everything would be fine. But she knew better. She was going to be expelled. And *soon*.

When her mother dismissed them all, she walked to Aireyal's desk, where she sat alone with her head in her arms. Thankfully, she'd stopped crying, but from the crumpled expression on her mother's face, her eyes must've still been puffy and red. "We need to talk," her mother said.

She was right. Though Aireyal had come here hoping to *ask her* things, not the other way around. She had more questions about the mirror than she could count. *Why did it show a field of crops? Why did it burn? How did it swallow an egg?* But what did her mother have to say?

"The headmistress wants a word with you." Her mother's hands tensed as she folded up scrolls. "She knows about your *condition*," she continued. "And unfortunately, she is not happy about it."

Aireyal tried asking her mother about the mirror on their long, slow walk to the headmistress's office, which was made longer and slower by Aireyal dragging her feet. Her mother, however, skidded the issue, giving her, *it's nothing too important* line. That was Mother for, *official Grandmage business you're too young to know about.*

Instead, her mother tried shifting the conversation back to Aireyal's struggles in the lecture and how she needed to *try counting to calm herself when she's feeling fretful because no matter how bad things got, it will all pass in time.* But Aireyal had no plans to give up so easily; she was going to find out more about the mirror despite her mother's secretiveness. And figuring out a way to do that was what she spent the rest of their walk thinking about, partly because she was genuinely curious, but also because it kept her mind off the reason they were walking in the first place. Or, it did, until they reached the intimidating silver doors of the headmistress's square office.

Inside, frowns lined the walls on the faces of former headmistresses and masters. Paintings. But disturbingly realistic. Aireyal kept peeking at them, convinced she'd seen several of their eyes move. Far creepier though, were two statues on either side of the door. Grey stone goblin gargoyles. Each with closed eyes, but hostile faces and open jaws. She half-expected them to come to lif—

"Miss Ando, am I boring you?" The headmistress's voice, sharp like the edges of a new book. Aireyal perked up in her seat and looked ahead to the towering, tidy desk before her, a hard contrast to her mother's unkempt study. Even the bookshelf behind the headmistress was full of polished awards and methodically ordered bags of dust.

The headmistress herself sat behind her desk in a tall thin chair that echoed her slender frame. Her posture was stiff enough to be one of the paintings on the wall and her cold, silver eyes, which matched the color of the room's walls, would've fit better on a ghost than an elf.

"Apologies, headmistress, I was only..." Aireyal trailed off. She couldn't exactly admit she was watching inanimate objects checking for life.

"Do you realize how serious your particular predicament is?" the headmistress inquired, smoothing wrinkles from her rich, velvety sleeves.

"I assure you she does, Mirvana," Aireyal's mother said. She sat casually next to Aireyal across from the headmistress at the desk.

"It is Headmistress Markado," the headmistress quickly corrected, eyes narrowed. Her finger pointed down to a silver plaque on her desk, inscribed with her official title.

"Very well, *headmistress*," her mother said, in her typical happy tone, but her eyes matched the headmistress's frosty glare. The stare down went on for several seconds before Headmistress Markado turned to Aireyal. *What is going on?* Did these two have some history she didn't know about?

"I am sure you already know but I'm going to tell you anyway, for I would be doing a disservice to you otherwise," the headmistress said, her face curling into its first smile thus far, but it took considerable effort to do so. "You do not belong at my school, silly little girl."

"Watch how you speak to my daughter, Mirvana," Aireyal's mother said, sitting up in her chair.

"Watch how you speak to mine. And it is headmistress to you," she corrected, *again*. "There's an old elvish saying, *krisiya floriya hylia, matuso*. It means, treat someone as delicately as a flower and they'll wilt as easily as one too," Headmistress Markado said, turning her attention back to Aireyal. "Miss Ando, do you want to know why I happened to let you attend Darr-Kamo?"

Yes, I would. Though Aireyal was terrified of what the answer might be. Her eyes darted to her mother, who gave a thin-lipped smile, then back to the headmistress.

"Your mother is arrogant and prideful. She believes that you and *you alone* should be granted something no one else in the history of this school has ever received. As you well know, every other apprentice who has walked these storied grounds could perform extraordinary magic for their age before they got here. You have done nothing except have admittedly historically exceptional written scores on your entrance exam," the headmistress said, *almost* sounding impressed. "Somehow, your mother thinks that should afford you until the sparks test at the end of the year to prove you have *some magical ability*," the headmistress said. There was a specific way in which she indifferently waved her hand when saying, *some magical ability*, that made Aireyal's left eye twitch.

"And you don't?" Aireyal asked. *You're about to be expelled.*

"No. But I am going to let you attend anyway," she said. *That's nice of her.* "So I can see you fail the sparks test." *Never mind.* "Then I will remove you from my school for the *magically gifted*. And the Grandmage here," she paused for a moment to look at Aireyal's mother, "who likes to stretch her legal powers as far as they can go, will finally get what she deserves."

The inevitability of the headmistress's tone slammed into Aireyal like a book to the face. This might've been worse than expulsion. She had to go through the school year with the most powerful person here rooting and possibly plotting, for her failure.

"I guarantee she'll pass," Aireyal's mother offered up. "And when she does, I don't ever want to see you bother her again."

The headmistress drummed her fingers on her desk. "Let us try to be realistic here. She won't pass. And what oh ever shall you do when she doesn't?"

"If I can't teach my own daughter magic, I'll retire!"

"You can't do that," Aireyal protested. For several, unbearably long seconds, the headmistress's office had less air in it than her mother's lecture room in Darr Hall. The headmistress smiled her frigid, dead smile.

"Yes, she can, though I do hope you can handle the pressure, young Miss Ando. The people that walk these grounds have to earn it," the headmistress said. Aireyal frowned. "Oh, don't look like that. I am not your enemy. Although, I am curious why you wanted to come here, despite knowing the requirements for this school."

"So I can protect people from those that would abuse their power," Aireyal answered, somehow managing to hold the headmistress's gaze, though her legs trembled. Thankfully, the headmistress couldn't see that from behind her tall desk.

"Abuse of power, you say? Like allowing a magicless girl to attend my school?" she pointed out. "If we followed the rules, you and I would not be having this conversation." She took a short breath, then straightened her posture even more, if it was possible. "I hope it's clear that news of your... *flaw* isn't to be shared with anyone. I am sure we would all hate for Parliament or the Senate to get involved because rumors started flying around, now wouldn't we? I cannot imagine what it would do to the school's reputation."

"Or my daughter's feelings?"

"I suppose that matters too," the headmistress said, dismissively waving another hand. "Now, we do have another matter to discuss while we're all here."

"This doesn't concern Aireyal," her mother said.

"She is the one who broke the mirror, is she not?"

She was? Vague memories of something shattering when Aireyal had gone unconscious in her mother's study came to mind.

"It was an accident," her mother said.

"Does that make the mirror any less broken? I expect it fixed by tomorrow."

"I already told you it will take me several weeks to repair."

"Not if you use Nodero's notes. I am sure he has quite a solution."

Who?

"I don't care if his methods could fix it with a snap of my fingers. I happen to have standards," her mother said tartly.

"And I happen to have deadlines. The world doesn't revolve around you, Mrs. Ando."

"That's Grandmage Ando to you," her mother corrected with a cheeky grin. The headmistress's only response was drumming her fingers against the desk.

"I need the mirror fixed by tomorrow. And you will do everything in your power to ensure that it is, *Grandmage*," she said, spewing the last word with utter disdain. "It is, after all, your responsibility to settle regional magical disputes like this one." *The mirror is a regional magical dispute? Why would politicians be arguing over the mirror?* "But you have also decided to teach at my school. Failure to do either could lead to your termination."

"You're so ready to be rid of me, aren't you?" her mother asked, smiling. The headmistress chose to turn her attention to a stack of paper on her desk instead of answering. Aireyal's mother scoffed. "Anything else?"

"The egg," Headmistress Markado said, flipping through the stack. Aireyal's mother tensed in her chair. "It needs to hatch soon."

"I'm working on that," her mother said. Were they talking about the black egg in her mother's room? Visions of it falling into the mirror and vanishing flooded Aireyal's mind. *She hasn't told the headmistress it's gone.* The realization tingled Aireyal's back and she jumped ever so slightly. Thankfully, the headmistress was too busy giving her mother a cold look to care about Aireyal. Being unnoticed sometimes had its benefits.

"You have been working on the egg for quite a while now," the headmistress said.

"It's a complicated matter."

"It certainly seems so when left in your hands. How complicated could it possibly be?"

"More than you know," Aireyal's mother said.

"The Senate expects a living, breathi—"

"I know what they expect."

"And I am sure you also know that your reputation as a Grandmage hangs in the balance based on your successes... or failures in these matters."

"Anything else?"

"No, I do believe that is all," the headmistress said, looking back and forth between Aireyal and her mother. "Well, well, this is going to be an interesting year for the Andos, is it not? I cannot wait to see how it all ends."

With an overly pleasant smile that was returned by the headmistress, Aireyal's mother rose from her chair and Aireyal quickly did the same, following her to the door. Aireyal took one last glance back as they left to see the headmistress still smiling at them. The smile of someone who knew they'd already won. "Good day, Mirvana," her mother said, closing the door before the headmistress could respond.

Aireyal's mother led her down the hall, wringing her hands together as she did so. Aireyal had *so* many questions. "Mother?"

"Not now, lollidrop."

"But—"

"This is one of the times I really need to focus on my work."

"You're always focused on your work, mother."

"I mean *really* focus, like… do you remember what Minister Boltus wrote in the letter he sent me asking for my approval and oversight on the application of new protective wards for all townguard barracks in the region?"

"You never let me see that letter. You said it was *nothing too important*," Aireyal noted. Her mother tapped a finger to her frowning face.

"That doesn't sound like something I'd say," she said. "We'll talk tomorrow, Aireyal, I promise. But there are a few things I need to research first." She forced another smile as though everything was fine. "Fixing this mirror is the most imperative thing in the world to me. I didn't tell you earlier because I didn't want you getting worked up, but it *might* be the key to helping you learn magic."

"Really?" Aireyal asked, pausing, eyes wide. Her mother nodded and leaned against the hallway wall.

"Then let me help you fix it," Aireyal offered.

"I don't want help," her mother said.

"I promise I won't get in your way. I can even look up this Nodero person's research if you don't want t—"

"I don't want your help Aireyal, and no one should be following his work," her mother said sternly, almost frowning before forcing another smile.

"Why not? Who is he?"

"Nodero *was* a foolish apothecarist known for fixing things. Magical things. He's been dead for twenty years."

An apothecarist?

"The headmistress made it seem like he was the best way to fix the mirror quickly," Aireyal said.

"She makes lots of things seem the way she wants them to."

"Do you have a plan to get it done by tomorrow?"

"Don't worry about that," her mother said in her most reassuring voice. But Aireyal knew better than to trust it. If her mother had a plan, she would have said so.

"She's going to try to remove you from the school if you don't have it fixed by tomor—"

"I know."

"So why not use Nodero's research if it can help? What's going on between you and the headmistress?"

"It's nothing too important," her mother said, smiling softly, but the bags under her eyes were big enough to fill with a mountain of dust. Aireyal frowned. Being treated like a child was bad enough. Being treated like a child so her mother could run herself into the ground was unacceptable. Arguing, however, was pointless; a lifetime of being raised by her mother had already proved that. The solution was simple. Aireyal would research how to fix the mirror herself. The faster she found the answer, the faster her mother could rest easy. And the faster she might finally learn magic.

The Library of Longaiya, the most extensive one in the western world, was right here on Darr-Kamo's grounds. And there was going to be a cute apothecarist's assistant waiting there for her. Perhaps they could work on fixing the mirror *together*.

~ Chapter 7 ~
Gnashing Gnomes

EREVAN AND SIR LEE ENTERED THE FOREST together, fresh pine scenting the air. Happy birds chirped high above, and little animals scurried along a path of colorful stones set into the ground leading through the center of trees before them. A pleasant sight. Too pleasant. Like the promises of the card game swindlers on the streets of Bogudos.

The scorch marks they'd seen by the bridge continued into the forest down the stone path for a while then split away, stopping between a set of trees where a single defiant beam of sunlight hit the forest floor. Erevan walked up to inspect it. The final scorch mark was here under the light. *But why? Maybe it—*

Something pulled him up and away before he could finish the thought.

"Erevan!" Sir Lee shouted, but he too was snatched. Thrashing vines ripped them in opposite directions. A few seconds later, Sir Lee disappeared behind endless branches and leaves.

Tree. Another tree. More trees. The vine yanked Erevan this way and that until he'd lost track of time, then, as abruptly as he was grabbed, the vine dropped him over an emerald green lake littered with slimy frogs and water lilies. He took a deep breath.

Splash! Erevan plummeted into the lake, then flailed for the surface, but the water was heavier and thicker than a bowl of tree sap. And his arm strength was still spent after pulling his father up on the bridge. So, he sank, staring up to the light at the lake's surface. *I need air.* His chest wavered and the more he held on, the more a pounding pain grew in his head. A consistent rhythm, like a clock counting down the moments until his death. Then his vision faded, and memories of his friend Isaiah's face jumped into his mind.

"Hold on, I'm coming, Isaiah!" Erevan leapt headfirst into a mud pool west of Bogudos. *Growl.* His gut reminded him it had been three days since his last meal, but an empty stomach wasn't going to make him lose his best friend at fourteen years old to a filthy swamp. *Alive at twenty-five.* That was the goal of the kids that grew up in the city. He had to free Isaiah's leg from the bottom of the thick mud befor—

"Erevan, be careful!" Tinny shouted, shivering at the edge of the pool. A nice sentiment. Though sentiments wouldn't save Isaiah.

"Grab my hand!" Erevan yelled to Isaiah, reaching out. Isaiah stretched, but a pair of giant mandibles emerged from the mud first. *SNAP! SNAP!*

Erevan ripped his hand back, and Tinny screamed. "Don't be a worry-wombat, we're fine," Isaiah assured, though his eyes suggested otherwise.

Mud flung as the creature in the muck rose. Erevan didn't wait for it to finish climbing. He yanked Isaiah toward Tinny, and they all tumbled into a tree.

Hssss!

"Run!"

Schling! A sword came down, cutting the head off the giant centipede creeping toward them. "Are you kids crazy? You have no business being out here until we finish clearing the area!"

Erevan rubbed his head; he must've looked guiltier than the time his mother caught him stealing her flowers to give to Selea. *Growl,* his stomach complained again. Tinny shuddered at the quivering centipede head before them. Isaiah hid his hands behind his back, scooting away. "We were just leaving," Isaiah said, nodding to Erevan and Tinny to follow him.

"Hold it. What do you have there?"

Isaiah didn't stop moving. "Dinner for the next week, old man," he said.

"I said hold it, by order of the law." The man grabbed him, but Isaiah ripped his arm free, though not before the item he carried was revealed, a jar filled with a sticky green substance. *Centipede ooze,* as Erevan called it. "Kid, you can't eat that."

Growl. "We're not eating it. We're gonna sell it," Erevan said.

"To whom, assassins? So they can make poisons?" the man demanded. "This city already has enough problems."

"We gotta eat somehow," Isaiah said, then he turned back to Erevan and Tinny. "Let's go, boys."

"I can't let you take that. It's against my code as a townguard," the man said.

"Then you might as well try to kill me here," Isaiah said. "I don't come up with plans this dangerous to walk away empty-handed. If I don't do this, my friends don't eat."

Growl. The townguard shook his head at Isaiah. "You need to come up with better plans then, kid," he said, offering three silver pieces to them with one hand and leaving the other out for the jar. "Let's make a trade."

Isaiah hesitated.

"C'mon Isaiah, it's a good deal," Erevan said. Isaiah eyed the guard for a long moment before handing the jar over in exchange for the coin. The townguard smiled.

"Stay out of trouble kids, you have your whole lives ahead of you," he said.

"Thank you, sir," Tinny said, before Isaiah pulled him and Erevan away and back towards the city. "That townguard was pretty nice, huh?"

"He's not always gonna be around," Isaiah said. "The only way to survive is to rely on ourselves. Just give me some time, I'll make the perfect plan."

"We'll follow you no matter what," Tinny said. "Isn't that right, Erevan?"

"Erevan? EREVAN!"

Hacking out water, Erevan sat up in a rush and his eyes fell on the courier. Her long black cloak laid on the grassy bank at her feet. Underneath was a thin layer of sleeveless, soft black leather embroidered with lion patterns. Under that was a top that was still dripping wet and sticking to her skin—

"It's rather rude to stare, you know," she said, grabbing her lightweight belt from the ground and fastening it around her waist.

Had he been staring? *Er...* "Sorry."

"So?" she asked, as though he'd forgotten something, wiping water off her face before checking the colored pouches on her belt, then below it on her pants leg where a dagger was holstered.

"So, what?" Erevan asked, shrugging.

"Aren't you going to thank me?" she asked, a hint of surprise in her voice... or was that irritation?

"For what?" Erevan asked, folding his arms.

"Saving your life. You're rather lucky I was nearby," she said, shaking off water before picking her cloak back up.

"Most people wouldn't ask for a thanks."

"Most people wouldn't be so ungrateful."

Erevan scoffed, looking away. An ash black egg lay on the ground before him.

"Don't touch my egg," she said, rushing over to pick it up.

"Where'd you get an egg from?" Erevan asked as she placed it into the blue pouch on her belt.

"Wouldn't you like to know?"

"Yes. That's why I asked," Erevan noted.

"Then you're going to be disappointed."

"Why?"

"Because I'm not going to tell you."

"Are you always this annoying?"

"Are you always this rude?" she asked, tying her cloak around her neck. It'd been ground length the last time he'd seen it. Now it was torn to barely past her knee.

"What happened to you?"

"I was attacked—" she started, and a chill of realization iced Erevan's mind.

"The kappas on the bridge. You burned them alive. That was brutal."

"That wasn't me."

Mist appeared at the bridge. Just like the farm. "Then it must've been the same creature that killed the captain and the farmer," Erevan said. The courier nodded. "What is it?"

"Pray you never find out," she warned.

"I don't trust prayers and faith. If Evlynna cared, why was I forced to steal coin while I starved on the street as a kid?"

"You're a criminal?"

Erevan ignored the prick of pain in his chest. Or was that embarrassment? *Of course not*, he told himself. "Someone like you wouldn't understand. You get to play dress up while hard-working people scrub the floors."

"Does that make me so bad?"

"The only ones worse are those that sit on the thrones above you," he said, and she glared at him.

"You love to complain. Why don't *you* try being a leader for once? What do you know about making decisions that affect other people's lives? It's not easy to turn away those in need of help because someone else needs it more."

"And how many more people wouldn't be in need at all if everything wasn't being hoarded by a small few?" Erevan snapped back. "I *have* been a leader. That coin I stole wasn't for me. It was to make sure my little brothers and sisters wouldn't die because all my mother could afford to buy was half a loaf a day of molded bread to split between us all!"

The courier's expression shifted. Her glare was gone, but her furrowed brows suggested she still wanted to argue. She opened her mouth to say something, but didn't, then she turned away to the grass and walked along the bank, scanning the ground as though she'd lost something.

"What are you looking for?"

"Something I dropped."

Obviously.

"Your little hand mirror?" he asked, recalling he and Sir Lee finding it outside the forest.

"Do you have it?" She stopped and turned to him, eyes wide.

"No, my father does," he said. Her shoulders sank. "Don't worry, it's safely wrapped up in your cloth, it's not going to break or anything. Well, I think it's already broken, it doesn't even show—"

"Your reflection? It's not supposed to."

"That's stupid. What's it supposed to show?"

"I doubt you'd like the truth," she said.

Erevan eyed her warily. "Let's just find my father, he'll know how to get out of this place. Then we can go our separate ways," he said.

"That's the first thing you've said that I agree with."

"Then it's a good thing we won't be together long. But for now, whether you like it or not, you're stuck with me," Erevan said, walking around the lake in the direction he thought the vines had thrown him from, checking for anything else that might grab at him. Unfortunately, everything looked suspicious. The now motionless vines, the colorful carnations, even the chubby-cheeked chipmunks could be covertly crooked.

Thick fish with thin scales slipped under the green lake's surface. They'd make for a good meal but fishing wasn't one of Erevan's strengths. He'd tried in the past, but lacked the patience necessary according to his father who'd promised to teach him when he was *ready to learn,* whatever that meant.

"I'm assuming you got split up from Sir Lee when that vine grabbed you and tossed you into the lake?"

"Very observant."

Her nostrils flared at his comment.

"Father, I'm over here!" Erevan called out.

"Yelling like that will let every single creature know where we are," she said, hurrying far away from a tree infested with spiders as big as Erevan's head, her face twisting into a disgusted frown.

"That's the plan," Erevan said.

"It's a bad plan."

"You sound scared."

"I'm not scared of anything," she said. "But what you're doing will attract the wrong kind of—"

Rustling leaves and chattering teeth. Erevan grabbed the hilt of his sword and spun around. *Maybe she had a point.* The rustling closed in until soft footsteps pattered the leaves underneath a nearby bush. It wasn't Sir Lee. The bush was hardly tall enough to hide a child.

"Come out of there!" Erevan ordered. The rustling stopped. Then it started again, faster this time and moving. Whatever was in the bush ran from them under shrubs and tall grass, though not the way it came. It might've been headed north, south, east, or west.

Keeping a sense of direction in the forest was no small task. Trees Erevan thought he may have passed before seemed to be in unfamiliar places. Flowers bloomed in odd spots. If they did find Sir Lee, getting out of the forest would become a challenge of its own. *A man must always carry a compass.* Erevan shook his head as his father's saying came back to him.

"Honestly, Erevan, what if that thing had been dangerous?"

He opened his mouth to respond then realized he didn't know what to call her.

"What's your name?"

"I go by this and that, depends on who you ask," she said, her mischievous smirk returning.

"I'm asking you," he said, frowning.

"I'm the greatest sorcerer that's ever lived," she said, raising her chin. He folded his arms. The chances of that being true were about the same as Nyumbafro and Heritour becoming allies. *None.* He didn't know much about magic, but he knew it took years of study and she was probably his age.

"I'm not calling you th—"

Another rustle from the same direction as the first, along with more chattering teeth. Erevan and the courier exchanged looks. This time, they hid behind one of the trees as the rustle approached. Whatever was coming couldn't be that dangerous if it was so small, right?

Murmurs came from the bushes; they might've resembled the voices of mice if they could talk. But while Erevan could hear them clearly, their words were gibberish.

"Igra morba asiasu!" one squeaked.

"Muca muca bowmani, acabeli!" another squealed.

The courier tapped him on the shoulder. "I think I know what they are," she whispered. He did too.

"Gnomes," Erevan whispered back. She blinked.

"How'd you know?"

"I've heard enough stories at The Lazy Lizard tavern in Bogudos of their squeaky little voices," Erevan said. "I'm more surprised you know about them. I thought Nyumbafroans spent all their time in underground caverns making weapons."

Her mouth dropped open. "We're not dwarves or goblins!" she hissed in a whisper. "Evidently, you foreigners know nothing about our country. We wouldn't have been making weapons if it weren't for Heritour."

"I'm pretty sure I heard that you all building weapons *caused* your war with them."

"You weren't there."

"Rifton was taken fifty years ago, were you?"

"No, but I know what happened. Heritour's prosperity since then isn't an accident. They were eyeing our city for years. Its location is perfect as a center for trade, coin an—"

"Loti moto buga!" a gnomish voice shouted in a series of squeaks.

"What are they saying?" Erevan wondered aloud.

"They're going to loot a body, I think," the courier said.

"You speak gnomish?!" Erevan said so noisily, it hardly counted as a whisper.

"It's mostly sylvan, although their dialect is hard to follow. Some of the words I can't recognize, and it seems you're having no better luck."

"I don't really speak any of that elvish stuff," Erevan said. The courier's brows wrinkled up.

"They didn't teach you in school?"

"There are no schools in Bogudos, that's why my mother wants to start one."

"Oh," she said, looking away at her boots.

"Listen, it doesn't matter. Let's just follow the gnomes. They might lead us to my father," Erevan said. Trailing a group of gnomes probably wasn't wise but thinking of a better idea could take too long.

What gnomes lacked in height, they made up for in viciousness, according to the word of travelers in Bogudos. Apparently, they did everything in groups. *Everything.* A fisherman claimed he'd once seen three dozen gnomes gang up to kill a single worm.

Looting, Erevan thought, remembering the courier's words as they snuck after the gnomes. No one looted bodies that were alive and well. So if his father was the body they were talking abou—

"Motini buga buga!" a gnomish voice shouted, interrupting Erevan's thoughts.

"Seen biggi bowmani etera!" another said.

"Motini biggi magi fali!" the first responded.

"What are they saying now?" Erevan asked in a whisper as they snuck hurriedly after the voices.

"Something about a forest sorcerer, maybe? I'm not sure," the courier responded, keeping her voice low too.

"Why are they so interested in this sorcerer?" Erevan asked, but the courier shushed him.

"That's what I'm trying to figure out," she said, her face so focused that her nose wrinkled.

More rustling came from every direction, all converging on the same point, a small clearing in the trees not far ahead. Inside was a grove where the rays of the sun shone, but little could be seen inside the clearing through the trees.

The gnomes they'd been tracking stopped their rustling, but the other gnomes were still closing in from every direction towards the grove, including from behind Erevan and the courier. There was nowhere to go. Moving forward meant walking into the clearing for all the gnomes to see. Staying put meant waiting to be found. The gnomes started shouting back and forth from every tree, and the clinking of many hundreds of teeth rattled through the forest.

"Biggi bowmani!" said a voice behind them.

"No kappa!" declared one on their left.

"Asi Asu!" squealed another above them in the trees.

"Monkas mi!" said the first.

"Polo kringiddy tuto!" said a fourth from… somewhere.

"Oh no," the courier said. "I think they know we're here." Erevan reached for the hilt of his sword but stopped when she grabbed his wrist. "There are too many of them to fight. We're going to have to talk our way out of this."

"Whosa Usa!" a gnome's voice squeaked at them. A strange woodsman once said those words on a trip selling logs in Bogudos. *Who are you?* That's what the words meant. Erevan considered them; he didn't want to lie to the gnomes, but saying he was from New Lanasall seemed like a bad idea too. According to complicated political treaties between countries that he hardly knew, foreign countries weren't supposed to enter the gnome's forest uninvited.

"Igra mogi babu era tera," spoke an unusually soothing voice. The courier's voice.

What does that mean? Erevan wondered.

"Ima ima bo bo, maki sey wa!" a gnome responded.

And what does that mean? These gnomes keep yelling, that's probably not a good sign.

"Asi Asu!" said another gnome.

And they keep saying that. Are they about to attack?

"Usala bogo, meri meri motaza," the courier said back to them.

"Motaza!" several gnomes repeated and laughed. Whatever she said made her raise her hands in an embarrassed apology.

"Motasa," she corrected with an unsure smile.

"Can you tell me what's going on already? I feel like I'm about to be ambushed," Erevan said.

The courier tossed up her hands. "Calm down, Erevan, it's not like they're going to swoop down upon us... at least, not without reason."

"Hmm." Erevan raised an eyebrow. "Swooping would be bad."

"Listen, I'm trying to keep us from getting shot by all the archers above," the courier said. Erevan peeked up; nothing was there except clumps of leaves sliding on branches in the breeze. Wait. The gnomes were covering themselves with leaves and flowers to avoid detection.

It would be quite effective too, if not for the gnome waddling about on an oak tree branch inside the ridiculous cover of a rose bush. Erevan covered his mouth to avoid chuckling, though he knew he should feel more in danger than he did with however many armed gnomes surrounded him. Perhaps being taken lightly was why they were such a formidable force. Good thing his father wasn't here to give him a lecture about underestimating enemies.

Chattering again. First from above, then the right, left, and even behind. Then it started again, in the same order, but the sound was ever so subtly different. Like bigger teeth were grinding. Then a third time, with even larger crunching. Above once more, and the other sides coming after. A call, Erevan realized. Then a response. It wasn't merely racketing noise; the gnomes were communicating. Then at once, they stopped.

"Asa baba! Biggi magi! Cari! No taki!" said a gnome from above.

The courier turned to Erevan. "They're going to let us check around the body, but don't touch it."

"They're going to shoot at us if we do?"

"Actually, they're saying there's a spell on it. If you touch it, you'll be blown up," she said, walking forward to the clearing.

"Noted," Erevan said, following her.

"Afilla," the courier said up to the trees with a slight curtsy before focusing her attention forward.

"What's that mean?"

"Thank you," she said. "These gnomes were gracious enough to let us pass through their fores—"

She gasped when they reached the edge of the clearing. Several motionless gnome bodies were sprawled out with scorch marks beneath them. And in the center of the clearing was a much taller body. Sir Lee's, however, was nowhere to be found. The body here was an elven man's.

His age was hard to tell. Elves may have reached physical maturity the same time as humans, but once they were adults, their appearance withered away four times slower. Erevan remembered the first time he'd met the elvish apothecarist in Bogudos who barely looked thirty, but she claimed to be sixty-one.

Whether the elf before him now was thirty, sixty, or eighty, Erevan had no clue. And whether the elf was alive was even harder to say. His sleek, white hair, pale face, and tunic were dirtied in bloody soil. On his belt were pouches like those the courier carried on her own. Except his were white with swirls.

"This must be the elf sorcerer they were talking about," Erevan said. The courier nodded carefully, as though she expected the elf to rise from his half-dead state.

A whistle flew through the trees. The gnomes around them scattered.

"Biggi magi!" several of them cried, fleeing. *That doesn't sound good.*

"I'm such a fool," the courier gasped. "How did I not understand it before? They were talking about her."

Before Erevan got a chance to ask who *her* was, footsteps approached, and an out of season spring breeze blew by.

"She probably won't hurt us," the courier said. *Probably.* Through the trees came a short lady using a branch taller than her for a walking stick.

"Hello, Erevan," she said, smiling.

~ Chapter 8 ~
Lanasall Law

"HELLO ZALE," AIREYAL SAID. SHE WAS SUPPOSED to be here at the Library of Longaiya for Nodero. But when she pushed through its massive doors into a chorus of quiet conversations, her legs didn't walk to the librarian's lavish limestone desk for help finding his research. Nor did they bring her to the grandiose bookshelves filled with the inviting smell of fresh pages containing tales, truths, and triumphs.

Her legs headed straight for the boy with the piercing blue eyes. He was sitting down reading a shimmering book. Its cover, a laughing mouth with a tongue of ever-changing colors. People stood on it giggling as though the tongue itself was a road.

"I assume a book that shines must be special," she said, making her way over to his table. Zale looked up, smiling, and somehow, seeing that made Aireyal feel a little less like her entire future was doomed.

"Quite the opposite," he said, showing her the book's cover. It was titled, *Flint's Flashy Foolery*. "It's a book of jokes."

Aireyal grinned slyly. "I thought you were coming to the library to study."

Zale lifted his hands in surrender with an even bigger smile. "I must admit, you've caught me on one of my extended breaks," he said, chuckling. Aireyal gave a small laugh.

"What's your favorite joke in the book?"

Zale's eyes lit up. "I'm glad you asked," he said, turning the pages. "What did the hundred-year-old tree say to Docent Tolk?" he asked on the verge of more chuckling. Aireyal shrugged. "Wow, I thought I was the stiff one," he said, and they both laughed again.

"That's not in there." Aireyal giggled.

"Of course it is," Zale protested in jest, still flipping through the book. "I just can't remember the exact page," he said before cracking a smile, then laughed some more. Aireyal laughed with him until she snorted, then her whole face went red. Zale laughed harder after hearing her snort, and Aireyal's face dropped to a canyon of a frown.

Someone nearby shushed them. An old man who resembled a grey parrot. Zale quieted to a moderate chuckle that ceased altogether when he saw Aireyal's frowning face. "I can't believe I let you hear that," she murmured, looking away.

"What do you mean? That's the most adorable laugh I've ever heard," Zale said, and her face went redder than it already was. *Adorable? Really?* She smiled, peeking at him as he pushed a chair out for her to sit in. "So, what brings you to the Library of Longaiya?" he asked.

"To be honest, I came looking for some research, but since you're here, I suppose I could help you study history before my next lecture. That is, if you have time. It seems like you're pretty busy right now," she said, nodding toward his joke book. He chuckled again. *Why isn't he hard to talk to?* she wondered.

"Please, don't stop your search on my account, I'll join you," Zale said, closing the book and folding it under his arm, then he hopped from his seat and pushed the chairs in. "Lead the way. Though, any help in history would be more than appreciated. I don't know how I'm going to survive that course, never mind three full years at this school," he said, following her as she walked toward the bookshelves.

She knew the feeling.

"What's the hardest part for you?" she asked as she started sifting through the book section on magical remedies.

"Everything."

"Well then, let's start at the beginning."

"Of history?"

"I meant Docent Tolk's course," Aireyal said, giggling as softly and under control as possible.

"Oh, good. We'd be here for hours talking about The Divine Tree," Zale said.

The Divine Tree, Aireyal hadn't heard that term since her mother made her study the world's faiths. There was an anthology of ancient texts known as *The Anima*. Aireyal could still recall all the reading she'd done on the subject, *'Many elves, especially those in the northern forest villages of Lanasall, believe in a tree that takes root between this world and the next and is supposedly the source of all magic. Their beliefs are backed by lots of historical evidence, but no proof.' -Faliana Yuneva, page 777 of 'Walking by Faith'.*

"You believe in The Divine Tree?" Aireyal asked. It made sense considering he was from the northern Felaseran Forest of Lanasall, the place elves first came to when they settled the western world.

"Shouldn't everyone?" Zale asked.

"I think people should believe in whatever they want," she said, looking through a second row of books after finding nothing useful in the first.

Zale looked down at his own book's cover where the tongue shimmered from red to gold. "Fitting, considering this country's words of promise. Lanasall, land for all. Do you think the elves that started this country believed those words?"

It was hard to say. When humans arrived at the western world in droves from the east, elves invited them to live in Lanasall. And some humans did, which is why Lanasall's population was mostly split half and half between elves and humans now. But most humans settled on the southeastern shores of the continent and created the country of Heritour that was still their home today. "I'm not sure, why do you ask?"

"No reason," Zale said, shrugging, still staring at the book's cover.

People don't ask things for no reason. "You're thinking about the disparity of this country, aren't you? The golden street," Aireyal said, moving on to a third row of books.

"And the people who must've worked to build it. I wonder what they thought of it."

"You don't know?" Aireyal asked, and Zale shook his head. It had been a rather noteworthy event when it happened. At least, in the city of Longaiya it had, perhaps word never reached the northern forests. "The people who built the road hated it. They claim they were promised a thousand gold by Parliament to pave the road, but that's not what they received when they finished. It led to several months of public protests against Parliament."

Aha. Aireyal picked up *Famous Fixes from Fabulous Minds* and started scanning through it.

"What did the workers get instead?" Zale asked.

"The Senate of Mages got involved. The Grandmage more specifically," Aireyal said. It was all rather intriguing considering most Grandmages only got involved with *magical* disputes in their regions.

"Wait, the Grandmage. Your mother?"

"No, the Grandmage of this region before her. This all happened years ago. An agreement was signed in secret after that between Parliament and the workers. No one knows what they got in the end."

"Were the workers happy about it?"

"Didn't seem like it," Aireyal said, frowning and placing the book down, which had nothing on Nodero or anything mirror related. "But things like that happen all the time here in Longaiya," she said, walking to another section of the library, *Magical Items and Objects,* looking for information on magical mirrors.

"Someone should do something to stop that."

"I'm trying to," Aireyal mumbled. *It's the whole reason you're here at Darr-Kamo, though it probably won't end well,* her unnecessary and unasked for inner voice noted. "If I become a Senate-Mage and get to settle magical disputes within cities, I have a plan to help normal working people. A way everyone can live happily and believe whatever they want." *That is if you can get your plan classified as a magical one.*

Zale frowned. "Everyone believing in different things is dangerous. It's the reason people go to war."

"Ilizabeth Kamo said you can't make everyone agree on one thing." Aireyal recalled the words of their school's founder. *'To live in a world devoid of difference is neither possible nor a possibility to strive for in creating a clean and perfect world. For what is utopia without uniqueness? That is a thought I hope every Member of Parliament studies. For she who trains to learn, trains to lead.'*

"You mean you shouldn't," Zale said, responding to Aireyal's point.

"Both. Even if you could, that would be taking away people's free will," she said, hauling *Guna's Guide to Mystical Mirrors* off the shelf.

"Is that a bad thing if it saves their life?" Zale asked. That sounded awfully familiar. "I think that's the kind of question the docent wants us to answer," he said. Docent Tolk, that's where she'd heard it before. "What do you think?"

"About what?" Aireyal flipped through her book, seeing mirrors that showed viewers their worst enemy, mirrors that showed false beauty, and mirrors that did a hundred other things that weren't important right now.

"What's worth more, life or choice?" Zale asked, watching her as though she had the answer.

"I don't know," Aireyal said, shrugging. To live without choice was slavery. But what did choice mean if you were dead? Both options were dreadful, and she frowned, wishing they went back to talking about jokes. No wonder Zale was taking *extended* breaks from studying.

"I have a feeling it'll be on the next test," Zale said with a shake of his head. He was probably right. And if their first day was any indication, the next test could be tomorrow. What answer were they supposed to give if it was?

"How is there any right answer to that?!" Aireyal slammed the book back down, flinching; she hadn't meant to do that, or yell. The parrot man appeared around the corner and shushed her again. She gave him an apologetic look and walked to another section of books, the one on apothecaries.

"I don't know either," Zale shrugged. "That's why I'm asking you."

"I'm a terrible study partner then, because I'm just as lost," she said, and Zale cracked a smile that turned into a chuckle, and it wasn't long before Aireyal did the same. She picked up *Important Apothecarists and their Impact*, opening it up. *Surely, this will be it.*

"I've had enough of trying to answer that question for now, we can always come back to it later."

"Excuse me, mister," a small voice said nervously as a tiny hand tugged on the bottom of Zale's tunic. A boy, no older than seven or eight stood there with his feet pointed inward.

"Mister?" Zale repeated. Then he craned his neck forward like an elderly man and spoke with the voice to match it. "I won't be a mister until I look like this. Now, what can I do for you, little fellow?" he asked, reaching for his back, feigning pain.

The boy laughed for a few moments then spoke, most of his nervousness gone, "It's just that I was looking for that book you have but couldn't find it anywhere."

Zale stopped his performance and peered at the joke book in his hands. "I'm afraid this is the only one they have."

"Oh," the boy said, drooping his head. "Sorry to bother you," he muttered, turning to leave.

"Why don't you hold onto it instead? I bet you're funnier than me anyway." Zale offered the book with a smile. The boy turned back with an excited hop.

"Really?!"

"Of course," Zale said.

"Thank you!" The boy took the book and ran off to a table where a lady sat. "Look what he gave me!" he said, pointing back to Zale. The lady glanced over and gave Zale a smile of thanks, which he returned with a smile of his own and a wave to both her and the boy.

"That was kind of you," Aireyal said, smiling as she flipped through the book in her own hands.

"Eh, anyone would've done the same," he said, clearing his throat. "In the meantime, you've been searching for something this whole time. What are you looking for?"

Aireyal hesitated for a moment, then against her better judgement asked, "Have you ever heard of an apothecary named Nodero?"

Zale's eye's slimmed with the air of suspicion one had when reading the accomplishments under the statue of Jumol Gomou, Lanasall's worst prime minister in history. Zale gave her a slow nod, then asked, "What in Sithrel's fur could you possibly want to know about him?"

"Sithrel's fur?" Aireyal repeated, unfamiliar with the expression.

"The elven god of mischief."

"Elves worship some furry god?"

"Not just Sithrel, there are plenty of gods in The Astral Realm. There's Fenrir, Aviana, Windego…" Zale said. *The Astral Realm.* That place was mentioned in *The Anima*, though its existence had basically already been proven false. Not that she

was going to mention that to Zale, who was still naming gods. "...
Galuon, Wuko—"

"Wait, what about the tree?"

"The Divine Tree isn't a god," Zale said, laughing.

Aireyal rubbed her forehead. "This is complicated."

"Aren't all faiths?"

Aireyal sighed. "I just want to know about Nodero," she said,
placing down the book, which had nothing on him.

"Right, sorry. It's just that I don't know all of the details about
him, and I doubt you'll find much in this library even though he
was rather praised during his day," Zale said.

"What about his research?" she asked, and Zale's face tightened
almost as much as Aireyal's did when her mother forced her to
attend crowded balls.

"Most people don't go searching for Nodero's research. I thought
you wanted to be a Senate-Mage, not a historian."

"How can we create good policies if we don't look to the past
to see how bad ones failed?"

"I've heard that before," Zale said.

"It's a quote from Yanda Oligar."

"He's one of the wealthiest people in this city, isn't he?" Zale
asked, and Aireyal nodded.

"Yanda is the most famous economic mind in the western world.
He's saved Lanasall more coin than anyone else in over two hundred
years," Aireyal said with a smile. "I was in awe when I first read
about him."

"You seem to really appreciate his work. I hope you get to meet
him one day."

"I already have. He came to meet my mother and I over the summer about my essay proposing changes to our system of taxation. It was all about creating a way for everyone to make enough to eat and have shelter, no matter who they are."

"That must've been a great essay," Zale said, raising his eyebrows. Aireyal blushed.

"You're giving me too much praise," she said, hiding her cheeks in her hands.

"You're giving yourself too little," Zale countered. "What did Oligar have to say about it?"

Aireyal spoke her next words in a mutter. "He said it was the most innovative economic essay he'd ever read... and surprisingly feasible."

"Aireyal, that's remarkable," Zale said, but she shrugged, shrinking. "Why are you so down about it?"

"It's complicated," she mumbled.

"What's that supposed to mean?"

"Parliament doesn't approve of my plan. They said it requires too much reliance on magic."

"What about the Senate of Mages?"

"Same thing," Aireyal said, submerging further down.

"What do you say?"

"I think they're all worried because too many of their powerful supporters would lose a little more money than they'd like. They'd still be wealthy, just less wealthy. And Parliament has bashed my essay in economic hearings so much that the public thinks it's a foolish idea."

"Why not go around them? Your mother's a Grandmage. Can't she help?"

Aireyal shook her head. "Grandmages look over entire regions of the country. The Senate has already passed a law stopping sudden economic changes in large areas like that, not to mention Parliament has to co-sign all magical related changes after the Scourge of Mableton."

"They must really hate your plan," Zale said, and she nodded solemnly. "So, you need a normal Senate-Mage, someone over a smaller section, like a city," he said, and Aireyal nodded again.

"Before they make a law stopping them too," she murmured. "But I've already tried asking every Senate-Mage I could."

"What happened?"

"They're all terrified to go against popular opinion. It would end their careers."

"Sounds like things would be better off if the Senate and Parliament didn't exist," Zale said.

"We need laws and authority. Without them we're left only with chaos."

"That's another quote, isn't it?" Zale asked. Aireyal shook her head.

"That one is all me," she said, and he flashed his dazzling smile, making her heart melt like ice in summer. She looked away to keep from losing focus. "I have to become a Senate-Mage, that way, I can make the changes myself. Even if they block this plan, I'll come up with another one."

Zale laughed. Aireyal turned back; he was beaming at her. "I like the way you think," he said, and her whole stomach flipped. "And I'm happy to help however I can. So, what exactly are you trying to find out about Nodero?"

"I need to fix something."

"Using Nodero's methods?" he asked, then he leaned in and dropped his voice to a whisper. "Is this about that mirror in your mother's study that broke?"

Aireyal nodded. "She's going to get into a lot of trouble if I don't help her by tonight and it's all my fault. I have to fix it."

"Then you'll have to wait until the library closes."

"Why?"

"So I can show you the real library. The secret one."

Chapter 9

The Fern of the Forest

EREVAN DIDN'T KEEP HIS NAME A SECRET, *like some people*, but that didn't mean everyone knew it. "Who are you?" he asked the little stranger standing before him and the courier. Pink flower petals crowned the lady's hair, and she wore a dress of leaves carrying the sweet aroma of berries with it. A bag the color of fresh soil adorned her shoulder.

"My name is not important to know, I am merely the fern that helps this grove grow," she replied. *Fern.* That was close enough to a name. Erevan was getting tired of using titles.

"You called me by name, how do you know me?" he asked.

"The fern knows all things, she has outlived many kings," Fern said with a majestic tap of her head.

She's not going to answer everything in riddles and rhymes, is she?

"Do you know how to get out of this forest?" Erevan asked.

"The fern knows all thing—"

"Great, how do we get out?" Erevan asked, cutting her off. She looked far into the distance as if in deep thought.

"Not sure—"

"But you just said—"

"Forget it, Erevan, she's undeniably mad," the courier said.

"And yet as two in a lot, asking for help from the fern I am not," Fern said, gliding over to the courier and looking her up and down.

"That's not a denial," the courier murmured under her breath.

"If out the grove you seek, first you must help the weak," Fern riddled, then she stepped over the elf's body on the ground and sat on his other side. She waved her walking stick a few times, then reached in her bag and pulled out a handful of blue leaves.

"You don't intend to help him, do you?" the courier asked. "He killed countless kappas just outside the forest, and he tried to kill me too."

Wait. What? "This elf attacked you?" Erevan asked. *Did that mean he was the one who summoned the mist and the creature within?*

"And now he's here defenseless," the courier said, watching the elf with dangerous eyes.

"What happens outside the forest is not the fern's concern, death is something he has yet to earn," she said, patting the leaves down on the elf. Whether the leaves were being used only to cover the wound or to provide some magical aid, Erevan couldn't see from where he stood.

"Choosing to save the life of a murderer is quite the contradiction," the courier pointed out.

"The fern protects all life. No matter the strife."

"You're crazy," the courier said. "I'm ending this now." She pulled the dagger from her belt.

"Harm him now you will not, his end doesn't come at this spot."

A trembling howl swirled through the trees. Soil and earth shook and leaves floated from the forest floor. Then vines came to life, slithering the courier's way. Even the sunlight seemed to dim, all while Fern glared at the courier.

"I don't think crossing her is a good idea," Erevan warned. The courier nodded, sheathing her dagger. Fern rose from the elf's side and held out some of her blue leaves to Erevan.

"The fern shall help you, as the fern helped him too."

"What're these for?" he asked, taking the leaves with a thankful nod.

"The feathers of azure can mend, many a broken bone of your friend," she said, though upon feeling them in his own hands, Erevan was still pretty sure they were leaves and not feathers. But Fern's words turned his attention to the courier. *She has broken bones? Maybe that's why she's so grumpy.* But the courier looked back at him and shrugged. If Fern wasn't talking about her...

"You mean my father? Is he hurt?" Erevan asked.

"Sometimes the one you wish to find, is there only if you'd look behind."

"Please, no more riddles, I have to know if he—"

"It's no riddle." Erevan turned. Sir Lee was walking up behind him. Erevan smiled, then frowned. Sir Lee was limping. "I figured those gnomes were running from something fearsome," the man said, glancing back and forth between Erevan and the courier. "Didn't expect to find you two." He tried to grin but winced in pain instead. There were several cuts through his tunic around his chest, along with the limp.

He would've been fine if he had his armor. Erevan gritted his teeth. *This is my fault.*

"What happened?" Erevan asked.

"This place happened," Sir Lee said, limping forward.

"Looks like you came out on top," the courier said.

"Hardly," Sir Lee said with a grunt. He struggled over and sat down, leaning back into a tree trunk, his knee bruised.

"These can help," Erevan said, running over with the leaves and placing them on his father's wound like Fern had done with the elf.

"He needs a proper healer, not some flower-headed wild woodslady's remedies," the courier said, watching Fern out the corner of her eye. Surprisingly, Fern nodded in agreement.

"These won't save him?" Erevan asked. He received his answer as the leaves dissolved into the wound above his father's knee and the bruise healed. They *were* working. "Do you have any more leaves?" Erevan asked, looking at the cuts around his father's chest.

"For another the need is dire, the one who is born of fire," Fern said, peering at Sir Lee's wounds then walked away from him, toward the elven man.

"You've already healed the elf," Erevan protested, but Fern didn't stop at the elf. She walked past him to the courier and held out her hands, pointing to the courier's blue pouch. *The same one the egg is stored in.* The courier pulled away.

"Without the feather's prize, the child soon dies," Fern said, motioning again. The courier reached for her pouch, then stopped. "Worry not for this gift will be swift, then back into your hands she shall shift," Fern assured. *She. The egg is a she?* Surely, Fern couldn't know that.

The courier slowly opened her pouch and handed the egg over. Fern took it with a smile. She wrapped the egg with leaves from her bag. Then as before with Sir Lee, the leaves dissolved, and the eggshell beamed. Still black but reflecting all light that touched it as though it were made of glass.

"Warmth and sunlight she needs, it is in the cold that she bleeds," Fern said, then handed the egg back to the courier. Another grimace sounded out. Sir Lee. Erevan turned to see him holding his chest.

"Please, do you have any more leaves?" Erevan asked.

"Not for the three of you, there is other pain the fern must undo," she said, walking away.

"My father still needs help," Erevan pleaded.

"Seek another's aid, somewhere beyond this glade," Fern said, without so much as turning around.

"But—"

"It's fine, Erevan. We'll make for the Coral Coast, it's not far," Sir Lee said.

"The stone path shows the way, all others will lead you astray," Fern said, passing behind a tree but she never appeared on the other side. Erevan moved over and examined the area, but there was no sign of Fern, or the pale elf for that matter. All that was left was the sweet smell of berries on the breeze.

"Where'd she go?" Erevan asked, turning to his companions, but they both looked back at him shaking their heads.

"There's the path she spoke of," the courier said, pointing to the ground. Stones of varying colors set into the forest floor, leading through the trees. The same kind they'd seen at the forest's entrance. Erevan nodded, then helped his father to his feet. He tried to determine if he was grateful for the help Fern had given them or annoyed she hadn't done more. In the end, he decided that above all, he was glad to be rid of her endless rhymes.

"Do you think you can make it all the way to the Coral Coast?" Erevan asked his father.

"I'll manage," he said, grunting forward along the stone path, his limp all but gone. But the cuts on his chest remained.

"And what exactly is this place we're going to?" the courier asked, following behind them.

"*We're?*" Erevan repeated. "Did you just add yourself to our party? What happened to going our separate ways?"

"Trust me, being away from you sounds delightful, but this coral place is where you all told me to go anyway, and we may as well stay together in this treacherous forest. So, like it or not, you're stuck with me."

"No thanks, I'd rather have to deal with whatever's in that mist," Erevan said.

"Don't worry, nothing is after you, krishnak," the courier assured.

"I know, it's after *you*. And you're following me, that's the issue," he said as something rustled in the trees above.

Erevan glanced up and the movement stopped at once. Bundles of leaves, however, sat on the wrong trees. Gnomes. And they whispered their gibberish language amongst themselves. Erevan looked back to see the courier listening in attentively with her elvish ears.

"Not all the gnomes are friendly," she said in a low voice. "Some of them are waiting for us to drop our guards."

"Anything out here will lose our trail once we're all safely inside the gated walls of the coast," Sir Lee said, looking up as well, but the gnomes didn't move. "Personally, I'd rather avoid fighting before then when I can get these wounds looked at, and staying together to watch each other's backs is a good way to do that."

"Are you saying she can come with us?" Erevan asked, frowning at his father. "You sounded a lot different by the farm."

"As did you," his father said, looking at him too, and the rustling started again, as did the chattering of teeth.

"That was before I spent time with her," Erevan said, not bothering to look up again.

"That's some way to talk about the person who saved your life," the courier said, nostrils flaring.

"Saved? You're exaggerating," Erevan said, shaking his head.

"You were literally drowning."

"I was going to be fine."

"Then next time you're dying, don't call me."

"I didn't call you the first time."

"Aha! So you admit you *were* dying."

"You're hearing things, I—" Erevan was cut off by his father.

"My chest pain is less noticeable now—"

"Oh, that's good—" Erevan started.

"Only because the headache I've gotten from listening to you two bicker is worse," he said, kneading his temples with both hands.

"Very funny, old man," Erevan said sarcastically.

"Apologies, Sir Lee," the courier said. "But please, I would like to know about this coast place we're headed to."

"The Coral Coast," Erevan said, exchanging a grim look with Sir Lee as they walked along the stone path.

"Why are you two looking like that?"

"Because the Coral Coast is full of thieving pirates and dust trading drug lords," Sir Lee said, pulling out his pipe.

"Didn't you say that about the other place too?" she asked.

"No, my hometown of Bogudos is full of backstabbers and murderers, it's much more respectable," Erevan said. Sir Lee chewed on his pipe, nodding in agreement.

"Are all the cities in New Lanasall horrid?" the courier asked, tossing her hands up.

"Mostly, but the Coral Coast is likely the worst," Erevan said.

"Then shouldn't we go somewhere else?" she asked.

"There is nowhere else. Pirates are the only people crazy enough to build a town near this forest," Erevan said as a thump landed above. He peered up and the gnomes froze in place again. *Do they think we don't notice them?* he wondered, looking back down.

"And it has a port," Sir Lee added to Erevan's point about the coast. "One that would make our lives much easier. Traveling by river would shorten our journey and the coast is our last chance to do so. It'll all be fine, I'm sure."

"Pirates are going to give us a boat?" the courier asked, blinking several times.

"You can get anything you want in that town if you've enough coin," Sir Lee said.

"You seem to know the place well. Were you a pirate, Sir Lee?" The courier asked suspiciously.

"No, I was born and raised in Heritour."

The courier's eyes squinted to match her voice's suspicion; no doubt due to her people's issues with Heritour. "And now you live in New Lanasall?"

"Correct."

"Care to share why?"

"Not at the moment."

"Secretive, are we?" The courier asked, squinting harder.

"You're one to talk," Erevan said, thinking of how many questions she'd avoided thus far. She opened her mouth several times, seemingly trying to come up with an insulting reply. Eventually, she gave up and said something else entirely.

"Let's hope we're going the right way," she said at last.

Their walk was in silence for most of the rest of the day, other than the gnomes following them above as they winded along the stone path through the trees. Erevan's stomach grumbled a few times, but all they passed were poisonous-looking mushrooms. He was hungry, but not yet hungry enough to coin flip life and death. *Stupid troll, stole our food.* He wasn't going to taste a real meal again until they made it to the coast.

The courier, meanwhile, was more concerned about getting her mirror back from Sir Lee, which she did. Sir Lee spent his time warning them of what to expect at the Coral Coast. Apparently, the town was mostly run by two pirate gangs. *The blah blah blahs and the other guys,* Erevan hadn't paid much attention, his father's lectures were too long. As the sun set, Sir Lee stopped.

"The path is getting too dark to see. Let's set up camp for the night," he said.

"Shouldn't we go all the way to the coast?" Erevan asked.

"We've made good progress today, we'll reach the coast in the morning," Sir Lee said.

"If we aren't eaten in our sleep," the courier murmured.

"As much as I hate to admit it, I kind of agree with her," Erevan said, listening. The chattering gnomes were joined by growls, slithers, and a host of other ruffles as darkness came. The courier blinked at Erevan, more shocked by his statement than travelers seeing thieves in Bogudos steal in broad daylight.

"You wish to take your chances drifting from the path instead?" Sir Lee asked.

The stone path shows the way, all others will lead you astray. Fern's words repeated in Erevan's mind.

"On second thought, let's stay here for the night," Erevan said.

"And wait for death to come to us? Do you realize how important my mission is?" the courier snipped.

"No, I don't, because you won't tell me anything," Erevan snapped back.

"Enough," Sir Lee said, before the courier could respond. "I'll admit I'm not keen on staying the night either but continuing on could be as bad if not worse."

"I—" Erevan started, but Sir Lee spoke over him.

"The decision is final. We'll keep turns watching and alert each other if anything happens."

"You sound like you're expecting trouble," Erevan said.

"Hopefully, trouble leaves us alone when the sun goes down."

Chapter 10

Nodero's Notes

AS THE SUN'S LAST RAYS DISAPPEARED OVER THE horizon, Aireyal finished her last lecture of the day and headed to the library. Its outside torches were quickly becoming the only visible light as Zale walked out with the rest of the people ushered outside at the library's closing. The librarian locked its doors with an iron key, telling Aireyal to, "Say hello to your mother for me."

The lady then pulled out a pouch and tossed a single handful of blue dust on the door's handle, reciting the magical word, *Clostro.* A simple but effective spell. The refreshing smell of the ocean filled the air as blue dust clamped onto the door handle, pulled by an invisible force, then it vanished from view and the librarian headed off. But not before she made it perfectly clear that the library was now *closed*.

Aireyal took another look at the door. She couldn't see it, but she knew the dust was still there, she'd read about it many times before, '*Blue fey dust is for defensive magic. As opposed to red dust, which is more offensive. If an elemental spell is created from red dust, then an equal or greater amount of blue dust can stop that spell in its tracks. Blue dust can also disarm hexes and charms made from green dust. In addition, blue dust itself can be used to form protective wards keeping an object or place safe from magical interference.*' -*Antoni Darr, co-founder of Darr-Kamo, page 50 of 'The Core of Magic, Volume II: Arcane Abjurations'.*

Zale led Aireyal off in the direction of The Banquet Hall for supper at a snail's pace until the librarian was out of sight, then he turned to Aireyal. "Now we can return," Zale said, taking her back towards the library. Zale hadn't explained his plan yet, saying, *you'll understand when we get there.* Aireyal had tried and failed earlier as Zale had predicted, to find more information on Nodero in the library. It was as though Lanasall wanted him erased completely from the annals of history.

"Ready?" he asked when they reached the library's front doors again.

"Ready for what?" Aireyal asked, an arrow of anxiety pricking her skin. Zale took several long looks to make sure they were alone before pulling out a red pouch. "Is that what I think it is?" she asked. He answered with a smile before digging into the pouch and pulling out two handfuls of red fey dust.

"We aren't supposed to have that outside of our lectures," Aireyal said, wringing her hands together.

"We aren't supposed to go into the library after hours either." Zale tossed dust up into the torches above. "Igno," he said in a confident whisper and the fire scorched to life. Flames came down at the door handle and a series of red and blue sparks flashed around the door handle for a few seconds, until the blue sparks dissipated, and the door handle melted away. Then Zale pushed the door open and bowed before Aireyal cheekily.

"Are you crazy?! I didn't realize this was your plan!" she said in a furious, shouting whisper.

Zale chuckled. "My plan? You're the one that wanted to see illegal documents," he said, pointing a playfully accusatory finger in her direction.

Illegal?

Dread washed over her like ice to her core. "Why didn't you tell me Nodero's notes were illegal before?!"

"I assumed you knew," he said, looking at her curiously. She shook her head.

"That's why I asked you so many questions."

"Oh, sorry," he said, shrugging. They stood for a long moment in silence. "So, we're not going in?"

Aireyal groaned. They were so close. And she needed to see those notes. *Tonight.* If she didn't get them there was no telling what the headmistress would do to her mother. She sighed. Then against her better judgement, tiptoed inside.

Her footsteps echoed down its long halls. There wasn't a soul in the area. *Yet.* Aireyal had an inevitable feeling they'd be spotted before the night was through.

"So, this is the *real* library? It looks the same to me," she said, inspecting the rows of enormous shelves stacked full of books. It was more ominous with the light of the moon creeping through the tall glass windows, but it was undoubtedly the same place.

"Follow me," Zale said, trotting off, and she let out another sigh. *Aireyal, what have you gotten yourself into?*

Every step forward made her legs tremble more than the last, but they did make it over to the librarian's limestone desk without being discovered or triggering a blaring, magical alarm. *Yet.*

Zale began snatching books from the bookshelf behind the desk and placing them on the floor. "What are you doing?" Aireyal asked. If there was a pattern to his pulling, it was far too chaotic to tell.

"You'll see," he said. "Trust me."

A sea of tomes surrounded their feet when he finished removing books from the shelf. Zale stood there, tapping his chin in silence.

"What was the point of that?" Aireyal asked.

"Huh, it seems I've made a mistake."

"You what?!" she said in another shouting whisper. *This whole thing was a mistake.* She never should'v—

"I'm joking," Zale said, laughing, then he pushed a nearly imperceptible dark spot on the back of the bookshelf. *Rumble.* The stone floor beside them shifted, revealing a staircase heading down into darkness. A cold draft of air blew up, chilling Aireyal's bones.

"I'm assuming that creepy, unlit staircase leads to—"

"The *real* library."

"Right. Of course it does," Aireyal said, sighing.

"Did you want to go first? Or would you rather I lead the way?" Zale asked, visibly trying not to laugh more. Aireyal stared down the tunnel and could've sworn a rat scurried along it. That was all she needed to know. She was absolutely, by no means, under any circumstances, going in first.

"After you."

Zale happily led the way, walking down the steps with exaggerated arm-pumping. His absurdity was almost enough to bring a small smile to Aireyal's lips. *Almost.* Heading through darkness was still terrifying. The steps curved and curled, then went straight, then curved again until any sense of direction was long gone. The only sound was that of their footsteps, save the occasional squeak of small animals that Aireyal pretended weren't there.

"How is it you know of this place?" Aireyal asked, her voice echoing along the walls. *How long is this tunnel?*

"The library's architecture is elven," Zale said, though that didn't really answer her question.

"So?"

"Elves hide all sorts of things in their structures. I'm surprised you haven't read about it in a book," he said, and though she couldn't see his face, Aireyal had a feeling he was smiling. Thankfully, it was too dark for him to see her blushing.

"I never said I knew everything. Besides, you made this staircase appear because of a bookshelf, not the building itself," she noted.

"Fair point. To tell the truth, there's a library built like this one not far from where I grew up. Same secret passage and everything."

She would've thought he was joking if not for how serious he sounded. Perhaps she needed to do some research on the architect behind the library too.

Their path curled again, and as they came around the bend, there was finally some light. For the first time, Aireyal realized how close they were forced together in the tunnel. Her shoulders nearly brushed up against Zale's, and when he looked over at her, her breaths quickened.

"Almost there," he said, excitement beaming in his eyes.

Dim red light overtook the darkness as they came into a room where twelve candles illuminated twelve bookcases that stood tall. *Are these candles always lit?* The bookcases were made of iron maybe, or some other type of metal and reflected the color of blood around the room. Aireyal's stomach twisted in ways that couldn't have been healthy.

"Welcome to the *real* library," Zale announced, spreading his arms out like he was giving a presentation. He picked up a journal. "This one's titled, *Why Lanasall Should Burn to the Ground* by Count Dario. Seems like a cheery fellow." Aireyal had heard of the count before, an outcasted Senate-Mage that swore revenge against the whole country. Zale picked up another book. "*Blood Magic: Performing the Impossible,*" he said. Then he picked up an abnormally large tome. "*The Life, the Death and the Life of Kalio, the Necromancer and His Techniques.*" She'd heard of him too. He was from a far-off land and had supposedly raised armies of the dead to do his evil bidding. She looked again at the hundreds of books in the room. Were they all filled with accounts of horrible people and deeds?

"Don't worry, Nodero's notes are probably here somewhere," Zale said, noticing her scanning the shelves.

"Wait. What do you mean *probably*?"

"I've never actually been down here," he said with a shrug. She glared at him.

"You broke in, then dragged me all the way down into this creepy place without knowing?" she fussed. Her cheeks burned, but Zale smiled, which only made her heat up more. Then he laughed and she was fairly sure her face exploded.

"I'm joking again. It's right over there," he said, pointing to the top row of one of the bookshelves. Part of her wanted to yell at him and part of her wanted to laugh with him. She decided on continuing to frown and stomped over to the bookshelf.

It was… higher than she thought.

"I might need some help," she mumbled almost silently.

"I'm an elf, but even our ears aren't quite that good. What did you say?" Zale asked, walking over.

"I'm too short," she whispered, again in the teeniest tiniest voice.

"Huh?"

She pointed up at the notes, unable to admit the truth to his ears. He looked up at them, then down at her, then up again. A grin crawled across his lips.

"Ah, I see," he said, holding back a laugh and plucking the notes from the shelf.

"We shall never speak of this moment."

"You do realize we're breaking at least twenty school rules right now. I don't plan on telling anyone about tonight," Zale said, handing her the rolls of parchment. He had a point. They were breaking *a lot* of rules.

"You're risking so much to help me."

"Risk assumes we have a chance of getting caught," Zale said, smiling. Aireyal frowned. They hadn't been caught. *Yet.*

"Seriously, Zale, thank you," she said, and it might've been the crimson light, but she thought she noticed the slightest tinge of red in his cheeks.

"I'm happy to help," he said, then he cleared his throat and wandered off, fiddling with some of the books on the shelves.

Aireyal watched him for a long moment before unrolling the parchment in her hands, which was blood red under the candlelight. She scanned title after title of experiments before finding what she needed.

Solution for Shattered Glass

Experiment #1, Day 1, 782 A.S.

Glass subject is unresponsive to the poisons of various animals found on the northern coast, no fix for broken glass yet, but if I can fix metals for him, then this should not take long...

Subject? What an odd thing to call a piece of glass.

Experiment #22, Day 37, 783 A.S.

Glass subject is responsive only to Webori, rather lucky considering how common it is. Taleri continues to prove lethal in large doses, still no fix for shattering, this has already taken far longer than expected. Thankfully other more successful experiments have eased his patience with me...

Who is he working for?

Experiment #66, Day 213, 788 A.S.

Glass subject is responsive when pouring a mixture of 1/2 cup of Webori, 3 ounces of Hulgi weed and 1 baby blood hawk heart, all mixed with the blue faerie dust, of course. I believe this is it, a fix has been found. More tests must be done to check for the solution's dual purpose, of course. Subjects have been difficult to come by, however, since my time no longer working at the monastery. Perhaps samples could be provided to drow seeking revenge in exchange for their recording of test results. I remain curious of its lethality on human subjects. Using it to rehabilitate gnomes for more torture before their deaths bores me. I'd prefer to see them die quickly...

Aireyal gasped.

"What's wrong?" Zale asked, coming over. She shook her head, grabbing her stomach which was queasier than a sickened maggot.

Crystallite gnomes. *That's why the glass was referred to as a subject.* Nodero was far worse than she'd imagined. "He was killing living, breathing beings. I-I thought…" she trailed off. "You said people praised him. Did they know what he was doing?"

Zale nodded. "I suppose it's because he saved a lot of elven lives with some of his experiments," Zale said with a shrug. "He's responsible for the creation of some invaluable remedies."

"But he took lives too. It didn't even seem like he thought twice about it. The crystallite gnomes are gone now. I can't believe this is what happened to them. He's a horrible person!" she yelled. There was a pain in her hands, and she realized she had squeezed them into fists so tight that her nails dug into her skin. Her right hand was in pain, but she grit her teeth to ignore it. Zale might've felt responsible if he knew, considering he'd bandaged her up earlier today. His eyes still studied her though, his expression as dark and solemn as the blood red room around them.

"There's more to the story Aireyal," he said. "Nodero was locked away—"

"Good."

"Hold on, let me finish," Zale said, frowning. "He was locked away at birth. No mother or father, no chance to have any morals instilled in him. Only science and magic."

"Who would lock away a child?" she asked, forcibly keeping herself from squeezing her hands again. "That's barbaric."

Zale sighed. "Nodero came from somewhere far away. Wherever it is, it's not on any map here. We don't even know how he got here. But what we do know is that he spent his youth in the service of someone he called a tyrant," Zale said. "That so-called tyrant was the one who locked Nodero up, only keeping him alive to do those experiments."

"Where was this?" Aireyal asked.

Zale shrugged. "Unclear, the accounts are inconsistent. Most people assume it happened deep in the Felaseran Forest," Zale said, shrugging shamefully.

Zale's people. The Felaseran elves didn't answer to Parliament like the rest of Lanasall did, that much Aireyal knew. She hadn't read much on elven history, but if it was this bleak, she wasn't sure she wanted to.

"The day Nodero chose not to do an experiment was the same day he was sentenced to death," Zale said, and Aireyal's anger went from sizzled to stunned. She stood there, jaw agape, unsure of what to say. "Remember Docent Tolk's question? Takes on quite the meaning from Nodero's perspective, doesn't it? What's worth more, life or choice?" he asked.

Aireyal shook the nerves creeping along her skin. She hated that question. "Whatever the reasoning, what Nodero did was still wrong. An entire race is extinct because of him. We have laws and rules for a reason."

"We're going against school rules right now, in a place we aren't allowed to be, so that you can read illegal notes."

"That's not even close to the same thing. I'm breaking the rules for a good reason."

"I'm sure that's how Nodero felt," Zale said, raising a pacifying hand. "Look, I don't mean to argue with you and I'm not going to pretend to be the wisest person alive. All I'm saying is, it's hard to know what you'll do in a situation until you're in it."

Aireyal frowned. She wasn't sure if she agreed or disagreed with his point. What she did know is that she'd had enough of this cursed room and the notes within it. She rolled the parchment back up and tossed it to the highest shelf. "Let's go."

They didn't talk on the way back. Her head kept going back to what Nodero had done, and every now and then it shifted to wondering what her actions would've been in his position.

She didn't have an answer. Eventually, the light of the moon shimmered off the walls. They were close to the surface. Aireyal sighed. There was something she needed to ask Zale. The question she should've already asked but was terrified of what he might say.

"This wasn't your first time in the *real* library. Why have you been there before?"

Silence. Zale stepped back up onto the library's main floor.

"Zale?" Aireyal insisted, hurrying up the steps behind him.

"Rather sloppy to leave this staircase exposed for all to see, don't you think?" a cold voice asked.

Aireyal spun to see a hooded figure shrouded in a dark blue cloak. From her physique and voice, Aireyal could tell it was a young lady, or perhaps even a girl her age. The light of the moon bounced off a crescent brooch at her neck, encrusted with red, blue, and green gems.

"Who are you?" Aireyal asked.

"A lovely little shadow. Noxa!" she said, then everything faded to darkness.

~ Chapter 11 ~
Wizards, Witches, & Warlocks

DARKNESS COVERED THE SKY LITTERED BY STARS above the trees as Erevan awoke to a ravenous growl. He scanned the trees around their campsite for some hungry beast before realizing what it was. His own stomach. *When was the last time I ate? Breakfast?* And now they had no rations. *Thanks, troll.* Hopefully, the Coral Coast wasn't too far away.

"Nothing ever comes easy for Erevan. He's had to scrap for everything he has. Clothes, coin, food." His father's voice. Erevan shifted his head over to the campfire, where Sir Lee and the courier sat engaged in conversation, so far unaware of Erevan waking up. "He was the oldest. Many days he had to find his own. My wife and

I had too many mouths to feed, especially when I was too injured from a job to work anymore for a while."

"So, where did he eat? At his friends' homes?" she asked.

Sir Lee sneered. "The group he ran around with, Tinny, Isaiah, and Selea, they didn't have homes. Tinny's parents had less than we did. It was no wonder that boy was always so frail. Selea, she didn't know her parents, same as Erevan. I think that's why they bonded so close. And Isaiah, the clever one. That kid didn't make it. Shame too, always had a stupid grin on his face when I saw him, like he was happy just to be alive." Everything his father said was true, not that it was any concern of the courier's. Erevan could still recall many of the plans Isaiah hatched that got them into trouble.

"What happened to Isaiah?" the courier asked. Erevan wished she wasn't snooping around his past, especially when she was so secretive herself. But he refused to be part of the conversation. Too many painful memories. He closed his eyes to fall back to sleep, but it was no use.

"Isaiah and Erevan wanted to find a way to get food for all the orphans in the neighborhood. They came up with a plan to steal coin from a known dust trader," Sir Lee said.

Three Little Thieves.

That had been the name of Isaiah's plan that went wrong that day. But despite what happened to him, he still managed to save Selea.

"Why would they try to steal from a licensed trader?" the courier asked. "That's foolish."

"He wasn't licensed, few people in Bogudos are. A dust trading license is expensive, not to mention the fees in taxes you have to pay to the Magistrate. Which means other sellers are far cheaper."

"I thought selling dust without a license was illegal in your country," the courier said to Sir Lee.

"It is. Not that stealing is allowed either," Sir Lee said, sighing, sounding as disappointed in Erevan's actions as he had been years ago. "And things went bad for Erevan and his friends. He's never been quite the pickpocket his little brother Scoti is around the house." *Scoti's little talent isn't a good one for a kid to have.* "The trader reported their theft to a townguard and claimed the kids were the one's selling it."

"But if he was a known illegal trader, shouldn't something have happened to him too?" the courier asked.

Sir Lee sighed again. "If only it were that simple. He was a man of no morals, ruining many lives in the community, but he wasn't a fool. My suspicion is the townguard that day was paid off to give a false report, and in the end, Erevan's friend Isaiah was the one who took all the punishment."

Liars. The only thing as bad as terrible leaders, Erevan thought to himself.

"Punished how? What happened to him?" the courier asked.

"It isn't my place to say."

"You can't stop the story there!" the courier grumbled. "Maybe I'll ask Erevan about it," she said nosily.

Mind your own business.

"Bad idea," Sir Lee said.

"Why?"

"Erevan blames himself for what happened to his friend."

Because it was my fault.

Silence. It lasted for a few minutes before the courier got up, walked to her belongings, and laid down. Several more minutes passed before Erevan sat up, yawning loudly as though he was just waking up now. His father was by the fire, half watching the surrounding trees, half reading the map sprawled on his knee. Erevan walked over.

"You should be resting, we've got a long hike ahead of us tomorrow," his father said.

Long hike. That means they weren't close. Sigh.

"Don't tell me that, I'm hungry," Erevan groaned, and his father chuckled. "Are you deciding our path for tomorrow?"

"I'm deciding our path for the whole trip," Sir Lee said. "If we sail straight out from the coast tomorrow, we can make it to Bogudos in less than a fortnight, as long as the winds are kind to us."

"That's not bad," Erevan said.

Sir Lee nodded. "Much better than on foot, we'd be on the road for a month."

"It's that much longer?" He knew traveling on land was slower, but that seemed excessive. His father nodded again, showing him the map.

"We'd have to travel through goblin territory near the Otenbul Mountains before we made it back to Bogudos. It would be beyond dangerous. They patrol their borders armed with fire arrows."

"Speaking of danger, I'm surprised the gnomes have left us alone tonight," Erevan said, scanning the trees above for any strange looking bushes.

"Perhaps they fear anyone they think might be a friend to that strange druid." *Fern.* Strange was the right word for her. A rustle sent Erevan spinning around, but it was only the courier adjusting herself uneasily on the ground, eyes wide open and watching the forest.

"You should get some rest," Erevan said to her.

"Isn't that what you're supposed to be doing?" she countered. He scowled.

"Why are you always so combative? You're the most irritating person I've ever met," Erevan said, folding his arms.

"The feeling's mutual," she said, turning her back to him. Erevan turned to his father.

"Can you believe her?"

"You aren't doing yourself any favors, son."

"It's not my fault she finds issue with the smallest things."

"*She* is right here," the courier said, rolling back to face Erevan. "Don't talk about me like I'm not."

"I'm sorry, I must've forgotten your name… oh wait, that's right, you never told me."

"I only give my name to people I trust."

"See?" Erevan said, turning back to Sir Lee, who sighed.

"If you kids are going to stay up arguing, I'll get some rest," he said, closing his eyes and leaning back into a tree trunk. He didn't appear the slightest bit uncomfortable, even with rough bark scratching into his back. *Unbelievable.*

"You two look nothing alike. He's not your real father, is he?"

"So, you won't answer my questions, but I'm expected to answer yours?" Erevan asked, turning to her, arms still folded.

"Fair," she said, sitting up, the hint of a smile on the corner of her lips. "Let's play a game." She reached into her things and pulled out a deck of cards, each one with a colored *W* on its back. "Wizards, Witches, and Warlocks. Are you familiar?" Erevan smiled and moved over to sit next to her on the forest floor. He'd learned how to play from an infamous bandit who also happened to be the best card player in the city of Bogudos. The game was quite popular with scoundrels in seedy taverns. "If you win, I'll answer your question. If I win, you answer mine," the courier offered.

This is my chance to finally learn her name. "I'm game. But I have to warn you, I'm pretty good."

"I've heard it's a game of chance," she said.

"Only losers think it's about luck."

"You think it's about skill?" she asked. He nodded.

"Better player wins," he said as she shuffled the cards. She placed them down with a confident thud.

"Deal."

He tossed five cards to each of them, then looked at his hand. A good one.

The game was simple. Thirty cards to a deck. Ten Wizards, Ten Witches, Ten Warlocks. Wizard cards were black, witches were white, and warlocks were grey. Each card had a number, from one to ten. The higher the number, the stronger the card.

Each turn your opponent played a card. And you had to play one of the same suite. If they played a wizard card, you had to play a wizard as well. Whichever card had the higher number won *and* took points away from the loser. Points of which each player only had ten. Falling to zero points lost you the game. But none of that was what made the game interesting.

"Your move first. Are we playing by New Lanasall rules? Or Nyumbafro rules?" she asked.

"What's the difference?"

"In Nyumbafro you only start with five points. I like it that way. *Sudden death.*"

"Fine by me," Erevan said. "You'll lose either way." He took another look at his hand. He had the Ten of Wizards. The Nine and Seven of Witches. And the Nine and Three of Warlocks. One weak card, the rest were strong.

He started off by playing the Nine of Warlocks.

"Oh, that's a pretty good card," she said. She only had one warlock card in her hand. She'd have to play that one. She tossed it down. The Six of Warlocks. "Looks like I lose three points," she said, refusing to glance his way, turning instead to a faint squirrel-like scampering sound in the distance. She only had two more points by her rules. He could win on the next turn.

They both drew a card from the deck to bring their hands back to five cards. Erevan picked up the Eight of Witches. Another good card. He grinned.

"You're smiling. That's not a good sign for me," she said.

No, it's not. "Your move." Erevan watched her fumble through her cards with the indecisiveness of a child before a plate of spinach. *Her draw must've been bad.* She looked up to him then back to her cards. "Any day now."

"Sorry, I just..."

"Not used to losing, are you?" he asked, grinning wider. She shook her head. "Don't worry, we all have to lose sometimes."

She sighed. "True." The courier finally decided on a card. She placed down the Ten of Warlocks. Wait. *Ten?* All he had was the Three of Warlocks. And he'd have to play it. Which meant he'd lose seven points. And he only had five because of her stupid rules. "Your turn, Erevan," she said, a smirk sprouting on her face. He reluctantly dropped his card down. "Oh, would you look at that, seems like I won. Good game."

"Pure luck, you only won because of these ridiculous rules."

"Hmm, I seem to recall someone saying only *losers* complain about luck," she said, putting extra emphasis on the word, *losers.*

"If only I could remember who that person had been." She looked up into the sky, sarcastically scratching her head in deep thought.

"We're playing again. Regular rules this time. We didn't even get to the fun part of the game."

"Ah yes, round three. I'm not sure you'll last that long with me," she giggled. Erevan grabbed the deck, shuffling it in a frenzy. "Also, you lost. You have to answer my question. Rules are rules."

"Fine," he grumbled. "What's your question?"

"Sir Lee. Is he your birth father?"

"No."

"Then why do you call him your father?"

Erevan dropped the deck down on the ground. "You already got your answer. Next game, regular rules this time."

"Guess I'll have to win again," she said, smirking. *That isn't going to happen.* "How about we up the stakes? Winner gets to ask two questions."

"Fine by me," Erevan said. That meant he could ask her name and what her mission was all about. She dealt the cards. His hand was… awful. Five and Four of Wizards this time. Five and Three of Witches. And this time he had the Two of Warlocks.

"I shuffled, your move," he said loudly, trying to fake confidence in his voice.

"Indeed it is," she said, placing down the Ten of Witches. *You can't be serious.* Erevan dropped his Five of Witches. *Five points lost already. Five more to go.* Coming back wouldn't be easy, but it was more than possible. He just needed a good draw. Erevan reached over to pick up a card.

Five of Warlocks. *How unfortunate.* Hopefully, she didn't have any other strong cards.

"Your move, Erevan."

"I know," he snapped. She grinned.

"So grumpy."

He glared, then peered at his hand. He settled on playing the Five of Wizards. All he needed to do was make it to turn three and he'd be able to do that as long as she didn't hav—

The Ten of Wizards. She placed it down, her grin widening. "Good game."

"I had a bad hand."

"I'm sure you were just unlucky, Erevan," she said, unable to keep herself from laughing.

"You cheated, didn't you?" Erevan pointed an accusative finger at her. She held a hand over her chest, pretending to be offended.

"I can't believe you think so little of me," she said, smirking, and still giggling like a thief whose crimes couldn't be proved.

"You did."

"I don't know what you're talking about," she said, laughing harder. "You shuffled the deck and watched me deal right before your eyes. When could I possibly have had time to cheat?"

"I—" he didn't have a good answer, so he folded his arms and grumbled.

"Fair's fair. Now my question. Why do you call Lee your father if he's not your real one?"

"*Sir* Lee," Erevan corrected. "He earned that title before he left Heritour. Unlike the people you're around, he had to work for what he got. He and his parents labored endlessly as servants to the royals of Heritour and they were rewarded with barely enough food to survive until the day his parents died. My father refused that fate. And he is my *real* father as far as I'm concerned. Whoever my birth father was didn't care enough to keep me."

The courier flinched. "And your birth mother?"

"Same thing."

"Oh. I'm sorry to hear that," she said, and for the first time, there was kindness in her voice.

"It's fine."

The courier's eyes were full of the all too familiar pity he got when people learned his story, not that he wanted any of it. Maybe her pity was more so because she knew as he did that one of his parents was probably an elf from Nyumbafro. Where his human parent was from, though, was as much a mystery to the courier as it was to him. "At least they left you with Sir Lee," the courier said.

"They *left* me in the middle of the street as a baby," he spat with such venom that she jumped a hair. "But the lady I consider my *real* mother brought me to her orphanage, and that's the only reason I'm alive."

It stung. Even all these years later. Worse than a wasp's sting, more like a needle, a fine one, jagged and permanently piercing his pride. A reminder that no matter what he did in life, there were at least two people that believed they were better off pretending he didn't exist.

"That's awful. I'm sorry for asking. You don't have to talk about it anymore if you don't want to," she said. *I don't.* He didn't even like thinking about it. And so, they sat in silence. The birds and bugs chirping were all that could be heard in the forest around them. Until at last, she spoke again. "Erevan?"

"Yeah?"

"You can call me, Nya," she said, then paused like she was trying to decide whether she wanted to say something else. "It's late, I'm going to get some rest," was what she finally settled on. Then she laid back and closed her eyes.

"Goodnight, Nya."

~ Chapter 12 ~
Morgana's Meddlesome Moment

"GOOD MORNING, AIREYAL," SAID A WINTRY voice as the dark syrupy fragrance of black lilac flowers invaded Aireyal's nostrils. Vigorous, violet eyes stared unblinking at Aireyal as she awoke. She recognized them alongside the stylish additions made to the school uniform worn by the princessy elf girl before her. *Morgana.*

She sat at a desk the color of midnight, complete with dark oils, floral perfumes, a giant *working* mirror, and other things to make one look gorgeous. Not that Morgana needed any help; she had the face of someone sculpted by a divine entity.

Heart-shaped lips and fair, flawless skin to go with her thin frame. Aireyal made the mistake of peering down to find Morgana's bust was fuller than most grown ladies. Aireyal sighed quietly, and her face might've warped to a little frown. Thankfully, Morgana had turned back to scribble at her desk with a quill.

They were in a pristine white room complete with two of everything; wardrobes, windows, bookshelves, and beds. A black bed on the other side of the room had already been made and the one Aireyal found herself in was yellow. "You look lost," Morgana said, surveying her.

"Where are we?"

"The girl's dormitorium. In our room," Morgana said, her tone mostly neutral, but there was some emotion in it Aireyal couldn't quite place.

"*Our?*" Aireyal repeated, inspecting their surroundings. One bookshelf had dozens of novels and study tomes her mother gave her. *The Adventures of Allia,* her all-time favorite, sat there with a tea stain on its spine. Aireyal still remembered the day she accidentally bumped into her mother and got drenched from above, leading to her smelling like minty herbs the rest of the day.

"Yes, *our*, unfortunately," Morgana said, that flicker of something in her tone again. Something negative. *Disappointment.* That was it. *She hates you already.* "I had a glimmer of hope yesterday that I would have this room all to myself."

"Sorry to disappoint you?"

Morgana gave a half shrug, dropping her quill and picking up a comb. "I am not angry, just curious," she said, running the comb through her ravishing raven hair.

"About?"

"Where you were last night." *The library. Nodero's notes. The girl with the brooch.* It all came back in such a flash that Aireyal's head throbbed. She had blacked out again. How did she even get here? Aireyal gazed through one of the painted glass windows as though it had the answers. "Are you ignoring me?" Morgana asked.

Aireyal jumped. Annoyance tweaked Morgana's thin eyebrows. *You can't tell her.*

"I-I was—" Aireyal started shakily, only for Morgana to raise a hand.

"Let me stop you there. You look like you are about to lie."

How does she know?

"I was at my mother's study yesterday. There was some research I needed to do for her," Aireyal said. It wasn't precisely a lie. Misleading? Sure. But not a—

Morgana's eyes narrowed to snake-like slits. "What secret are you hiding?" Aireyal's back tensed and she forcibly straightened it, surely only making herself look guiltier.

"I-I c—" she started in a stutter.

"Your mother carried you here early this morning, mumbling about how you should have listened to her. I may have been half asleep, but I heard that part clearly." Morgana placed down her comb and grabbed two blinding, black earrings. Aireyal's mind whirled. Her mother brought her here? *How did she even know to come to the library? What happened?* "Where were you?" Morgana asked again. Her inescapable elvish eyes all but peering through Aireyal's soul.

"I'd rather not say," Aireyal said, scooting away from her, though they were already half a room apart. "Why do you care so much anyway?"

"Because there was a..." Morgana trailed off, giving another half shrug. "It doesn't matter, I have a way to find out every single secret you have," she said, checking her new earrings in the mirror.

A modish match with her uniform. Then she got up and left the room, her heeled shoes clicking down the hall.

Aireyal gulped. She didn't need any more enemies. *You should leave before she gets back.* Aireyal hopped out of her bed and snuck a peek down the marble hallway which housed detailed paintings of famous ladies who'd formerly been apprentices at Darr-Kamo along the wall.

Morgana was nearly out of sight and heading down the steps already. *How does she walk so fast in those shoes?* The bell tower rang, signaling it was already the fifth hour past sunrise. *Breakfast time.* Which meant her history lecture was soon. *Zale.* Maybe he'd have some answers about last night.

Aireyal spun back to her room where several purple school uniforms hung in the wardrobe next to her bed as did a few purple cloak-like overcoats. A pointy wide-brimmed Darr-Kamo approved hat also sat inside, but not much else. The other wardrobe, by Morgana's bed, was noticeably fuller with a collection of breathtaking dresses. They were worthy of admiration, but Aireyal didn't have time to dawdle.

Her feet brought her to the washroom not a minute later where a few other girls scurried around, frantic about starting their day so late. Aireyal waited until they'd all finished their baths and left before she washed off. The mere thought of being naked around other people was enough to kill her. Thankfully, she wouldn't have to be today.

She unbandaged her injured hand, putting on more aloe. It was still pink and scorched, but most of the unbearable pain was gone. *Zale really knows what he's doing.* She'd have to thank him when she saw him later.

Aireyal finished her warm bath and headed to her history lecture, arriving just in time to hear Docent Tolk ramble on about how Lanasall's Parliament had changed over the years.

The topic would've been interesting, but today, Aireyal was too busy searching for Zale, who'd yet to arrive. Docent Tolk went on and on, telling them about the current prime minister's alleged bloody rise to power. But she barely heard a word he said.

Is Zale hurt? Did that hooded girl with the brooch last night do something to him? Aireyal's stomach kneaded over like dough in the hands of a baker. She needed to find him. *But where could he be?*

Aireyal considered swinging by the library before her mother's lecture, then thought better of it. If word had gotten out they were snooping around last night, there was no telling what the librarian's punishment would be for all the rules they'd broken.

She needed to find out what happened last night. And the best way to do that was to ask her mother. Aireyal bolted out as soon as Docent Tolk dismissed them and sped into her mother's lecture before everyone else showed up. Everyone except for Morgana, that is, who grinned when her eyes met Aireyal's, as if to say *you can't hide from me.*

"Hello, Aireyal." The tone was cross, but surprisingly, it didn't come from Morgana. Aireyal turned to see her mother's eternally bright smile replaced with a deep frown.

Oh no. She had a lot of explaining to do about last night. "I—"

"Save it," her mother said, placing the tea in her hand down next to several green pouches on the center table. Then she glanced at Morgana before turning back to Aireyal. "We'll talk after the lecture."

The other apprentices filed into Darr Hall not long after, but not before Aireyal slipped to her seat in the back corner where the sunlight from outside didn't shine. Most of the kids didn't notice her as they talked and laughed amongst each other before the lecture started. That, at least, brought a smile to Aireyal, who hid her face under her wide-brimmed, pointed school hat.

This is the best seat here.

Then Morgana hopped up from where she was sitting and plopped down in the chair next to Aireyal.

This is the worst seat here.

"Hello, Airy," Morgana said, smiling in the most condescending way possible, the same way a princess might look when telling her servant she was allowed to dust the royal jewelry, but not have it.

Airy? Whatever. Aireyal peeked at Morgana from the corner of her eye, ignoring her wobbling insides. Morgana said nothing more, she just smiled. And that only made Aireyal tremble more. *What does she have planned?*

Aireyal's mother cleared her throat at the room's center. "Good afternoon, apprentices. Yesterday, we went over the first of the three fey dusts. Today, we'll go over another. Green," she said as brightly as ever, then her eyes darted over to Aireyal and her expression shifted. "I hope we all spent our evenings productively last night doing the reading as instructed. I'd hate to hear any of you were *distracted* with other pursuits."

Aireyal looked down, pretending to write something with her quill.

"Would anyone care to explain how green dust is used?" her mother asked. Aireyal peeked up to see her twirling a Britaberry lollidrop in her hand.

Don't take the bait. Not that she didn't know the answer, Antoni Darr had outlined it in *Volume III of The Core of Magic.*

Morgana's hand rose, but thankfully Aireyal's mother called on a girl with fair, blemish-free skin on the other side of the room, Priscilla Hornbuckle. She was one of the main kids who snickered with her nasally laugh at Aireyal yesterday, and practically every day before. They had always gone to the same schools, and Priscilla constantly made fun of Aireyal's freckles. Though Aireyal had never told her mother; being a Grandmage meant she had enough to worry about without adding Aireyal's juvenile troubles to the list.

"Green dust affects emotions and moods. You can make someone happy, angry, sad, or whatever you want. Apothecarists use it to make people feel better when they are recovering," Priscilla said in a sweet but coldly sinister voice. Or maybe it just sounded that way to Aireyal.

Grandmage Ando gave a tiny nod. "Yes, that's part of it," she said, tossing Priscilla a candy. "But I'm really asking about *how* it's administered," she said, and Morgana's arm shot up again, though the Grandmage wasn't looking her way, so she called on a boy instead. Morgana let out a quiet, frustrated sigh.

"This might be wrong," the boy started. "But aren't you supposed to use it when people aren't paying attention for it to work?"

"If you don't want them to know you're manipulating their emotions, then yes. Which is why it's used for hexes," her mother said, the cordial but unimpressed expression on her face showing she was looking for a different answer. "It is, however, considered quite unbecoming to manipulate emotions without consent."

"But isn't it used to keep people from lying when testifying at political hearings?" another kid asked. Grandmage Ando nodded.

Ilizabeth Kamo had argued against the morality of forcing the truth out of people, but Parliament had found success with it, like when it helped to solve the mysteries of the Scourge of Mableton, and they hadn't looked back since. "Can we learn how to do that?" the kid asked.

The Grandmage chuckled. "It takes many years of training to know how to delicately weave someone's emotions enough to make them tell you the truth against their will. I believe there's only two people at this entire school who have mastered that skill."

"Who?"

"One is our illustrious headmistress. The other, of course, is me," she said, smiling. "Now, apprentices, the answer I hoped you all would give me is that it's important that green fey dust is used one on one," she said, and a series of *ohs* and one or two *I knew that's* came from the apprentices. "Are there any pairs of you feeling adventurous enough to try it in front of everyone?"

No one raised their hand. Except for Morgana. She was brave. Having your emotions played with in front of all your peers seemed terrifying. Aireyal's mother tapped her pointer fingers together, looking at Morgana, "Do you have a partner?" she asked.

"I was hoping Aireyal would join me," Morgana said.

WHAT?!

Aireyal's heart plummeted to the floor. *Say no.* Her chest tightened and the room started getting smaller. It had to be. Closing in until she'd be crushed. *That's your imagination. Just breathe like your mother told you, you're fine.* Aireyal looked up at her mother; the fire in her stare was gone, a soft twinkle replacing it. Breathing became difficult. *You have to use words,* Aireyal told herself. *Say you're happy to stay right where you are.*

Aireyal shut her eyes and opened her mouth, hoping something would spurt out this time. "I'm happy to…" she trailed off. She could feel all the eyes on her. Watching. Waiting. Whispering.

You have to say more. People will thi—

A hand was already helping her up out of her seat. Her eyes cracked open; Morgana was pushing her to the middle of the room. *Say something now, or it'll be too late.*

But Aireyal's mouth didn't move. It took all her focus to keep her shaky legs from giving out. She wished she were an elf so she could hear everything the kids were gossiping about as she walked. Then again, they were probably pointing out how short and ugly she was compared to Morgana, whose confident strut made Aireyal's wobbling appear even more absurd.

The Grandmage gave Aireyal a look that seemed to say, *are you sure about this*, as she reached the room's center, and Aireyal's left eye twitched. Or perhaps it was her whole body that was shaking, but she stood up anyway, deciding to stare at the pouches of green dust on the table instead of the room full of eyes trained her way.

"Morgana, you volunteered, so let's see what you can do," the Grandmage said, handing Morgana one of the pouches. "Try the spell *tranquilla* to calm your partner's nerves. It helps make them more open to other emotional changes."

Morgana nodded, then she sprinkled green dust in the air. "Tranquilla," she said, and the dust dissolved around Aireyal, leaving behind the smell of fresh mint and soil.

Sunsets, cozy beds, and fireplaces. If those were a feeling, Aireyal felt them. The comfort eased its way through her like a smooth liquid, and for the first time in her life, she wasn't worried about the room of people staring at her. Or Priscilla snickering at her freckles. Or anything else. *Is this how other people feel all the time?* The thought was bittersweet; the dust wouldn't last forever.

"Grandmage, may I try something?" Morgana asked. Aireyal's mother looked at her, trying to hide a smile. *Is she... proud of Morgana?* Aireyal was filled with the shame of a thousand disappointments. *Why wouldn't she be? She deserves a better daughter than me.*

"Go ahead," Grandmage Ando said to Morgana, watching as the girl sprinkled more dust in the air. "Verita."

Did I hear her right? There's no w—

"Where were you last night?"

"I was in the library with Zale." Aireyal clasped her hands over her mouth.

How does she know how to do truth spells?

Morgana turned to look at Aireyal's mother, whose jaw dropped.

"I am quite the talent, aren't I?" Morgana said, giving a half shrug and an ostentatious wink.

~ Chapter 13 ~
Coral Coast Corsairs

RELENTLESS RAIN AND ENDLESS WIND WERE matched only by the growl of Erevan's empty stomach as he marched forward in the evening, shrugging it all off. Nya was a step behind him, her hood as soaked as his and Sir Lee several steps behind her. Cool, damp air sailed through the lantern-lit town before them, past the broad wooden walls surrounding it and into Erevan's ears in a spooky whistle. On the edge of the town, a rotted sycamore sign stood. Sketched poorly, by blade from the looks of it, read, *The Coral Coast*.

"Are you sure this is a good idea?" Nya asked, her eyes fixated on the many shambled buildings before them.

"I never said it was," Sir Lee grunted with a puff of his pipe. Nya's face twisted. "It'll be fine, I'm sure," he said with a reassuring grin as Erevan's feet came to a splashing halt before the town's massive front gate. He knocked on it, only for the gate to creak. Several moments passed and the Raging River roared nearby between gaps in the shrieking breeze.

Then a small hole popped open in the middle of the gate and an inquisitive eye peeped through.

"State yer bizness," wheezed a man behind the gate.

"We're looking for passage on a ship to Bogudos," Sir Lee said.

"And food," Erevan added, his stomach growling again. Marching through the forest with no rations wasn't pleasant and the smell of juicy meat was being cooked somewhere on the other side of the gate.

"Bogudos?" the man repeated, coughing. His eye slipped away from its hole. He hacked a few times; then there was a nasty *splat*. A few moments later, the eye returned to its hole. "What ye be lookin' ta go there for?"

"It's home," Sir Lee said.

"Then ye lot be in a worse spot than the rest of these buccaneers," the man replied.

"We could also use a healer if there's one around," Erevan added.

"Depends on what ye be lookin' ta get cured."

"A few cuts and scratches, nothing serious," Sir Lee answered.

"Cuts an' scratches from what?" the man asked.

"We ran into some trouble in the Numino Forest," Erevan said.

"Don' ye know better than ta be goin' there?"

"That's exactly what I was telling this one, but he insisted," Nya said, butting in with an agreeable nod, pointing at Erevan.

"Stupid boy," the man coughed.

"Hold on a—" Erevan started, before Nya gave him a pat on the back and took a step in front of him.

"I'm trying to keep him from getting himself killed," she said, shaking her head. "Surely there's someone here that'll help my noble cause."

"Try the potion master, lil' dwarven fella, shop's near the center of town," he said, and Erevan's stomach growled yet again, this time *loudly*. "If ye be needin' food an' lodgin' from the comin' storm, there's the Tiny Tortoise Tavern. Got an inn attached it does. The place be right up the road," he said in another cough.

"Are you sick?" Erevan asked.

"Fit of scurvy, notin' more. Half the town gots it," he said, and a squeaky creak churned through the rain as he pulled the gate open. "Welcome ta the Coral Coast."

Part of the town was quite literally built over the river, with planks forming a series of intersecting piers as walkways to get around above the water. Buildings all over town were built right on top of the wooden piers, and the water rushed only a few yards underneath. *Hopefully, these planks are sturdier than the Cold Creek Bridge's,* Erevan thought.

On the far side of town, a massive structure built in the shape of a ship stood menacingly in the rain with the overcast sky behind it. Erevan trudged forward anyway, keeping an eye out for the potion master's shop, Nya and Sir Lee alongside him.

Protruding up between the planks that held the town above water were a series of colorful coral in every shape imaginable from circles and stars to sea serpents. Precisely crafted, as though by the hand of an artist.

The people that walked amongst them, however, seemed to care little, passing by without so much as a turn of the head. Perhaps the town of coughing, hacking pirates was simply too used to such a sight. Then again, it appeared some of the pirates were dead on the street. Or perhaps they were drunk, it was hard to tell, many were passed out with a bottle in hand.

There were two main crews. One wore blue bandanas with swirling waves on their heads and the other, red ones on their arms with sharks. And there was *a lot* of coughing. Half the town seemed to have been a good estimate. Many of them begging for their thirst to be quenched.

"Scurvy looks horrible," Erevan said, watching a man cough up a glob of phlegm.

"They don't have scurvy... well, they might," Sir Lee said, reconsidering his words.

"But the guard at the door said—"

"Pirates blame everything on scurvy. It doesn't make you cough. Something else has afflicted this town, keep your distance from them," Sir Lee warned. Erevan nodded, though the delicious, luring smell of cooked beef grabbed his attention.

Shouts and sword clashes rang from one of the buildings they passed. The wooden sign hanging over its door had a cup of overflowing ale twice the size of the tortoise next to it, who admired the drink's size. The Tiny Tortoise Tavern. A body flew through the tavern's swinging doors, crashing outside.

"AND STAY OUT!" a massive voice boomed from inside.

"Are we sure we want to stay at that place?" Nya asked, hurrying past the tavern.

We. This time Erevan didn't point it out; his father did. "You intend to stay with us?"

Erevan looked back, dreaming of when he'd get his hands on tasty meat.

"Only in this town, of course. Then we can part ways on separate ships if that's what you want," she responded, but her eyes were looking at Erevan.

Is that what I want?

He tried to tell himself that staying with her was a good decision for the reward in gold at the end. And that *was* true. There might've been another reason, but he refused to think about it.

"We'll see what the future holds when it comes," Sir Lee said.

About halfway through town, they came before something that was more run-down hut than building, with faded painting that simply read, *The Potion Master's Shop*.

Nya blinked, "Not too creative a name." Silky smoke billowed from the hut's stone chimney, vanishing into the gloomy sky. Toadstools and weeds covered the wilted grass around the house, emitting a foul stench. If death had a home, this was it.

They stopped before its decayed wooden door, complete with an eyehole in the center crusted with fungus. Nya looked at Erevan, a frown curled at her lips. "Maybe we should go somewhere else."

"But we're already here," Erevan said, then he knocked on the door. Clatters. Then cursing. Then heavy steps thudded toward the door. The eyehole filled with a great yellow eye and a rumble hummed low in the air.

"What do you stupid kids think you're doing, get away from my door!" a hardy voice yelled. Erevan and Nya exchanged looks. "I have half a mind to cut you down with my axe!"

"Maybe you were right," Erevan said, and Nya nodded. They turned together, running as the door opened but they only made it five steps before they were trampled into the ground from behind.

Erevan let out an *oof* as his face hit the dirt, and Nya let out an *ow*.

"Oi! Get off them you half-blind beasts!" the hardy voice growled. Heavy feet stomped on Erevan's back for a moment or two longer before stepping off. "Don't mind them, they have the intelligence of a six-year-old barbarian. They're just territorial." Erevan stood up to see five creatures. Sharp teeth, scaly skin, and long grey snouts with spikes going from their tip to their tail. They were the size of a wolf, though they felt like they weighed as much as a brick house. Baby rhinogators.

"Go on!" said the voice, and several large slabs of meat were tossed past the creatures who chased after the easy meal. *Meat!* But it was raw. Erevan turned and found a sturdy dwarf with a singed beard. He wore a coat speckled with burn marks and had a copper monocle over his left eye. "Shadow tiger meat. Their natural rivals," the dwarf informed, stroking his beard as though he was proud to have such knowledge. Erevan doubted a water-dwelling creature like a rhinogator would care about a cat, but he didn't question it. "I don't get visitors often, you lot must be desperate, who's dying?"

"No death, just a few flesh wounds," Sir Lee said. Somehow, he'd managed to go untrampled. *Lucky.* "Sir Lee," he said, introducing himself and extending his arm for a handshake.

"*The* Sir Lee? Bless my beard, I've heard stories of your feat slaying Thurss, the three-headed ogre with the Sword of Silence," the dwarf said, then he looked at his own hands, both ridden with ash. He wiped one on his coat, cleaning it from disgusting to dirty, then merrily shook Sir Lee's hand. "Ziggli Thickbeard, at your service."

"That tale is an exaggeration, I assure you," Sir Lee said. Erevan frowned, he'd never heard of this story before, though it was impossible to know all the ventures his father had gone on over the years.

"Regardless, you're a welcome sight. Most people that come here think they're dying of scurvy," Ziggli grumbled with a shake of his head.

"If it isn't scurvy, what's wrong with them?" Nya asked.

"That's what I'm researching," Ziggli said. "I believe it's something to do with the coral that grows here. It's got magical properties and has a peculiar reaction to dust."

"What kind of reaction? The deadly kind?" Erevan asked.

"If you fish in the waters under town, you'll see," Ziggli said, eyeing the planks they stood on.

"I don't know how to fish," Erevan admitted, glancing at his father for a moment, who scratched his beard with a thoughtful, but otherwise unreadable, calm-faced expression.

"What matters is, I'm on the verge of a breakthrough," Ziggli said.

"If the coral is making them sick, why do you live here?" Erevan asked.

"I never said the coral made them sick. It's doing something else entirely. Those fools are sick from drinking salty water and from inhaling the dust they pilfer and sell. Tricky thing that dust, as popular as a drug as it is for magic."

Particularly shady people in Bogudos spoke of the Coral Coast being the hub of the illegal dust trade in New Lanasall. Pirates rode out onto the Raging River from here selling dust to any who would buy. Bogudos was one of their more frequent spots, and the city didn't have many people using it for spells. Another excuse for the townguards to rough up folk on the streets, claiming to be searching for drug dealers.

"Whatever the case, come in out the rain and have a sit-down. I won't charge your month's earnings unless you've been sent into the sky by one of those pirates' new exploding weapons, cinder bombs they call them. It's a pain to clean up," the dwarf said, motioning to the door. Sir Lee nodded thankfully and followed him in. Erevan and Nya looked back at the rhinogators feasting in the streets behind them before heading inside.

The pungent smell of dead plants stuck to the air. Dried leaves, toadstools, and steaming potions of various odors, all of them horrid, were housed on a long table near the door. And coral, mostly *dead* coral, filled every inch of the hut that those didn't. Erevan brought his hands up to cover his nose. Nya took a step back out of the house. Ziggli looked back before adding, "Er, I forgot how sensitive the noses of elves were."

"Why don't you two go back and get us a room at the inn?" Sir Lee said. "I'll come along when I'm done here. And see if there's word of when the next ship's heading out," he said. Erevan nodded happily, already thinking about food again, and headed off with Nya.

Soaking rain picked up to a storm as they passed coughing pirates on their way. Many of them ran for shelter from the docks on the town's eastern edge where great galleon ships meant for the open sea, were now anchored down in the brutal weather.

By the time Erevan and Nya returned to the tavern, the shouting inside had mellowed to moderate hollering and… singing? Music blasted them alongside the salty scent of the sea as they walked inside. A trio of blue bandana pirates stood atop a platform, one with a lute, one with a small drum, and the other with a surprisingly melodic voice.

'Fill the barrels high, there's an endless supply
Drink up all yer ale, before yer dead in jail
There be monsters in the sea, so come an' sail wit' me...'

Erevan's attention was taken by the unmistakable slice of a blade. The knife impaled the center of one of the wooden tables, and next to the blade was a stack of cards. *Wizards, Witches, and Warlocks.* Two men engaged in a game, one wearing a red bandana, the other blue, both sweaty, and on the edge of violence. Shadows danced dangerously around their faces from the smoky candle on the table. A crowd of onlookers cheered from behind either of them, many of whom held coins in their hands. *Gamblers.* Erevan walked up to one who wore the water-worn boots of a veteran of the seas.

"My friend and I are looking for passage to Bogudos. Do you know if anyone's setting sail out of here soon?"

"Ye might as well be gettin' comfortable boy, no ship'll be leaving port 'til the storm passes," he said, looking Erevan up and down. "Even the ferrymen ain't passed this way lately, and they sail through any weather."

"'Sides, our c-crews don't take outsiders wi-with 'em u-unless you've plenty of coin to offer," said another in a series of coughs.

Coin. Erevan had lost everything he had to the troll on the bridge. "I don't have any coin," Erevan admitted and Nya took several steps away from the man as someone whispered *scurvy* under their breath.

"Then I be thinking ye kids wandered to the wrong place," the first man said, turning back to the game at hand.

"All we want is a ship," Erevan said.

"Then you're definitely in the wrong place," boomed a voice behind them. Erevan turned to see a one-eyed bugbear eyeing him. A thick, hairy goblinoid creature with tan skin, sharp claws, and a bear-like nose; he stood nearly seven feet tall in an undersized apron. The bartender. His left eye shrouded in mystery behind an eye patch. "If you aren't here to buy something, then get out," the bugbear groaned. Erevan pretended not to hear his gut's complaints as meat sizzled on the stove.

"Couldn't you at least point us in the right direction?" Erevan asked.

The bugbear answered by raising a meaty finger and pointing towards the door.

"Who be wantin' next?" the red bandana card player challenged.

"Erevan, I've got this," Nya said, walking to the table of pirates. "I'll play if we can get passage on the next ship out of here," she said. A round of laughter filled the room.

"And if I be the one claiming victory?" asked the card-playing pirate sitting down. He rubbed a hand across two long scars under his eye.

"Don't worry, you won't," Nya said.

The man let out a raspy laugh. Nya's familiar smirk crossed her face. Erevan watched as the cards were shuffled, cut, and handed out. The pirate grinned at his hand. *This was a bad idea.* "You don't have to do this," Erevan said to Nya.

"It be t-too late to back out now," coughed a pirate in the crowd.

Another pirate scooched away from him. "Scurvy," he said, looking disapprovingly at the first.

"Why does everyone here say that?" Erevan asked no one in particular.

"'Cause it be true," said one who didn't cough, pointing to his leg. "I used to be an adventuring lad like ye 'til I gots scurvy on me knee."

Erevan raised a suspicious eyebrow. Someone chuckled and he turned to see the crowd behind Nya shaking their heads at her hand. The Six of Wizards. The Two, Three, and Four of Witches. And the Two of Warlocks. *Bad luck.*

Nya tried to keep a confident look on her face, but it wavered as she slipped her Six of Wizards down onto the table. The pirate responded with the Ten of Wizards. *Four of her ten points lost already.* There was a roar of laughter from the crowd as they both drew their next cards. The One of Witches for Nya. *Horrible luck.*

"My move, girly," the pirate snickered. She scowled back at him.

"Don't call me that," she said as the pirate placed down The Nine of Witches. Another wave of cackling circled the crowd. The pirate smiled wide, showing golden capped teeth. She threw down her Four of Witches. Five more points gone.

She only has one point left. She's going to lose.

"Turn three," Nya said, drawing the Five of Witches. "You know the rules." This was where the game got interesting. Every three rounds, the losing player got to swap one card with their opponent. But they weren't allowed to see the card they were swapping for. Though, almost any card was better than the ones Nya had.

The pirate pushed his cards face-down to Nya, letting her choose one. All of them Witch cards. She took one, swapping it for her own One of Witches. She received the Eight of Witches in return. *Finally, a decent card.*

"My turn," she said, playing the Eight of Witches she'd just gotten.

"Unlucky," the pirate said, playing the Ten of Witches with a smile. *Nya lost.* "Good game, girly." A roar of approval sounded from the crowd around them. Nya stared ahead, her face stunned in disbelief. "Now, 'bout the reward," the pirate said, grinning. Nya glared at him.

"You cheated!" she shouted. His grin dissolved into a deadly frown.

"Say that again an' you'll see this here dagger ain't for show," the pirate warned, grabbing the knife from the center of the table. "Now, why don't you empty your pockets, *girly.*"

Nya's brows furrowed as she reached into one of the pouches around her waist. She pulled out a handful of red dust.

"I don't think that's a good idea," Erevan said, stepping towards her cautiously.

"He cheated."

Woosh!

The dagger flew from the man's hand, straight at her head. Erevan reached out with his left hand to catch it, but the blade cut into the center of his palm. For a moment, Erevan wished he was fully human so he didn't feel every bit of skin torn apart like sliced thread. He fell to the ground, reeling as blood trickled down his fingers. It was too painful to even know for sure if he'd screamed.

Nya stood up and threw red dust at the candle in the middle of the table. "Igno!" she shouted, and the flame erupted, spiraling toward the pirate. He lurched out the way and several of the red bandana men behind him drew sabres from their hips.

"THAT'LL BE QUITE ENOUGH, GAVLIN!" boomed a voice. The bugbear stomped over with a snarl. "IF YOU CAN'T PLAY WITHOUT KILLING SOMEONE, YOU CAN GO ELSEWHERE!" the bugbear yelled at the pirate, pointing to the door, before snatching Erevan off the floor. The bartender's one good eye flicked back and forth between Erevan and Nya. "AS FOR YOU TWO, IF YOU'RE HERE TO CAUSE TROUBLE INSTEAD OF BUYING SOMETHING, YOU CAN LEAVE TOO!"

"We'll be waiting, *drow*," Gavlin said to Nya, picking up his cards as he and his crew exited the tavern. *Drow*, the slur of choice against the elves of Nyumbafro. Nya's nostrils flared.

"I'm on my way!" she shouted back at Gavlin, taking a step toward the door before Erevan caught her arm with his good hand.

"Don't. Those guys make a living by robbing and raiding," he said, grimacing through clenched teeth. She looked down at him and her eyes widened seeing the knife wedged in his hand.

"Look at your h—"

"I'm aware," he said, refusing to peer at it again himself. She reached down and grabbed the knife's hilt.

"This might hurt," Nya warned.

"Wai—"

Rip!

Erevan winced. A moment later, he lost all feeling in his hand. All feeling *except* for the pain, that is.

"No bleeding out on my floor. You can do that outside," the bugbear grunted.

"But they're waiting for us out there. He's in no condition to defend himself," Nya argued.

"Not my problem. You're the one who chose to mess with the crimson corsairs," the bugbear said, watching the blood drip from Erevan's fingers.

"How could you be so heartless?"

"I run a business, not a church. If you want to stay, cough up coin for a room."

"How much?" Erevan managed to ask through gritted teeth.

"For you? One gold piece a night."

"But The Lazy Lizard in Bogudos only charges one silver," Erevan protested. He hadn't tasted the food here yet, but it couldn't be good enough to justify being ten times the price of The Lazy Lizard.

"Does this look like Bogudos to you?" Several pirates nearby cackled. "Pay the price or get out."

"With prices this high, you'd think the place would look better," Erevan grumbled, noticing a wall stained with dried food. "Where's all this money going?" The bugbear leaned in close enough to Erevan that his musty breath replaced the smell of ale in the room.

"The *Magistrate* and her townguard dogs might be afraid to come here and force their taxes on this town, but the pirates take more than their share in protection fees," the bugbear growled, spitting at the floor on the word, *Magistrate*.

"Erevan?" Sir Lee's voice. Erevan turned to see his father striding toward them, his traveling bag overstuffed. He turned a quick eye to the trio of musicians, who'd never stopped singing, before looking back to Erevan. "What happened?" he asked, pointing to Erevan's hand.

"You're the one responsible for these kids?" the bugbear asked. Sir Lee nodded. "They need to get out or pay for a room and take their ruckus up there," he said, pointing to stairs that led up to another floor.

"I have coin. How much is it?" Sir Lee asked, digging in his bag.

"One gold apiece," the bugbear repeated. Sir Lee scratched his chin in disapproval but didn't argue. Erevan considered saying something, then his empty stomach reminded him staying quiet was probably the only way to get a meal. *An overpriced meal.*

"And we need food," Erevan said. Sir Lee looked at him, as did the bartender.

"You're thinking about food when your hand is in that condition?" Sir Lee asked.

"I've been thinking about food since yesterday. I can't believe you aren't," Erevan said as his father shook his head.

"You aren't going to get your mother's cooking here in a tavern," Sir Lee warned.

"I can live with that," Erevan said, and not just because he was hungry.

Sir Lee handed the bartender several coins in exchange for a key with the number *four* engraved into it and a small boneless chunk of seared beef. "Would you help Erevan up there?" Sir Lee asked Nya, who nodded as he passed her the keys. Erevan took the meat from his father with his good hand and started chomping away. Somewhere in the back of his mind, Erevan's younger self reminded him to never pass up a meal because he didn't know when the next one would come.

"There's a washroom upstairs with clean water. I don't want him bleeding over my floor," the bugbear grumbled, pushing Erevan up the first few steps.

Again, he stopped himself from saying something back; the bugbear was ready to throw him out on the streets as is.

Erevan devoured the beef by the time he and Nya made it up to the second floor. It helped him get his mind off the pain of his hand... for a moment. Ahead of them was a hallway of ten numbered doors, and at the end of the hall was an open room with a tub of water inside. "Let's get you cleaned up," Nya said, carrying the frown of someone who knew their mistake got someone else hurt. Erevan had carried that look before himself. Maybe he still did.

Nya grabbed a rag and a bar of soap as soon as they entered and dipped them in the water. Then she sat on the floor and motioned for his hand, avoiding eye contact. "It's not your fault, you know," Erevan said as she ran the rag softly along his hand.

"Huh?"

"My hand getting cut," he clarified.

"Who said it was my fault?" she asked. "I had the situation quite controlled."

Erevan would've laughed at the ridiculousness of the statement had he not still been feeling the pain of being recently impaled. "Strange, I seem to remember a dagger being flung at your face. A dagger that would've hit you if not for the likes of a certain someone," he reminded her, pointing at himself.

"Honestly, Erevan, you shouldn't have done that, you could've gotten yourself seriously hurt," Nya said, shaking her head.

"I did get hurt!" He motioned to the long gash running across his left palm. "Most people thank those that save their life, you know. At least that's what a girl once told me," he said, smirking. She glared back at him. Or, tried to. Her mouth twisted into a smile and her nose did its cute wrinkling thing, so she looked away. *Wait, cute?*

"Let's just get you cleaned up," she said, rinsing the rag off, then running it over his hand again. Her touch was gentle and warm, but cautious all the same, like the orphans he grew up with who were afraid to get too close to anyone.

"Thank you," he said. Nya looked up for a moment, her eyes slightly wider than usual before they flitted back down.

"I'm not doing much, it's only water."

"I still appreciate it," Erevan said. She didn't respond, but he thought he caught the hint of another smile on her face.

She dried his hand with a second rag, then wrapped it around his hand. "There, good as new." Her words were an overly optimistic exaggeration, but he did feel better. Most of the bleeding had stopped, and the pain was much more manageable. He was lucky he hadn't been cut deeper. "Let's see how run-down our room is," she said, hopping up and heading to door number four.

Run-down, didn't begin to describe it. There were several holes in the wall the size of fists. And Erevan had a feeling that's exactly what had caused them; it was a town of pirates after all. The room smelled of old ale, and a rat sat casually in the corner squeaking at them. An irritated squeak, like they'd just intruded on his personal property. Erevan shrugged. "It's better than the places in Bogudos."

"You're joking."

"This place has two beds *and* a fireplace," he said, going over and jumping into one of the beds. It *crunched*. Definitely not a sound a bed should make, but Erevan pretended not to notice. A frown from Nya indicated she heard it too, though she also chose silence. Instead, she sat near the dormant fireplace, rubbing wood in it together until she got a flicker of flame. "I could get some fresh wood if you're cold—" Erevan started, but Nya was already tossing red dust into it.

"Igno!" The fireplace lit up. "I got it," she said with a smile before taking her egg out its pouch and placing it near the open fireplace. It had kept the sheen it received from Fern. "That lady in the forest said it needed warmth."

"What's inside?" Erevan asked.

Crash! The whole room shook, and they both jumped up, only to realize the sound came from the room next door. Had someone been slammed against the wall?

"Who do you think d—" Erevan started, turning to Nya, then his eye caught the egg rolling, headed straight for the fireplace. "Nya!"

But it was too late. It bowled right into the flames. *CRACK!* Nya spun around to see the egg's shell swallowed by fire. Whatever poor creature was inside was going to be burned alive.

~ *Chapter 14* ~
A Risky Remedy

AIREYAL'S FACE BURNED WITH EMBARRASSMENT as her mother paced back and forth in her study, which was more unkempt than last time. Papers and books tossed this way and that, clumped in unorganized groups around its rounded walls. Morgana's little display in the lecture led to everyone laughing at Aireyal. Thankfully, they all assumed she had snuck out to the library at night for *kissing,* not for finding illegal research. Not that she liked being known for that either, all the kids had made smooching sounds at her for the remainder of the lesson. Aireyal groaned.

"I hope you know your level of frustration doesn't come close to mine."

And then there was that problem. Aireyal forced herself to look up and face her mother. "S—

"What were you thinking?" her mother demanded.

"So—" Aireyal started, only to be cut off again.

"You realize you could've gotten yourself injured, right?"

"Sor—"

"Do you know how bad this looks on me?"

"SORRY!" Aireyal shouted. Her mother stopped pacing to stare her down, and Aireyal flinched.

"Don't raise your voice at me, young lady," her mother said.

"You won't let me talk," Aireyal protested.

"Because I don't want to hear anything you have to say right now."

"Then why'd you ask me three questions?"

"Don't get clever with me. How could you ever think—"

"That's another question," Aireyal mumbled. Her mother straightened up and gave her a leer fierce enough to stop a charging bull. "Sorry," Aireyal said, looking down. "I was only trying to help."

"Help? What are you talking about?"

"I went to the library to find Nodero's notes. Which I did and I—"

"You what? I told you specifically not to do that," her mother said.

"No, you told me you didn't want help," Aireyal mumbled.

"You knew what I meant."

"And I knew that you needed to fix the mirror. If you had let me help, I never would've gone out on my own. You've always overworked yourself, putting all that sugar in your tea to keep you awake. I remember all the nights when I was little that I was scared because you didn't come home, and you were in your office, working through paper after paper all night instead," Aireyal said, and her mother's expression softened to a feather. Aireyal caught herself before she mentioned how her father had stayed up through those nights; her mother wouldn't want to talk about him.

"I'm sorry, Aireyal. Sometimes being a Grandmage means putting in more hours than I wish it did. If I could've been there to comfort you through the hard nights, I would have."

"I was fine, mother. It was you I was worried about. Just like I am now," she said, and her mother gave her the wearisome smile of a much older lady.

"Aireyal, there is a reason I'm not asking for your help." She paused and took a deep breath, fumbling with a paper on her desk, before folding and placing it in a drawer. "Some things are too dangerous for children."

"I'm not a child."

"Yes, you are."

"I can help, if only you'd let me—"

"No."

"Let me show y—"

"No! I don't even know what *I'm* doing here," her mother said, flinging a hand towards the broken mirror on the table.

"That's fine."

"What do you mean that's fine, do you understa—"

"I know the remedy to fix the mirror... at least I think I do," Aireyal mumbled. Her mother's eyes popped open.

"What?!"

"I figured it out from Nodero's notes," Aireyal said. "That's what I've been trying to tell you. You mix one half cup of webori, three ounces of hulgi weed, a baby blood hawk heart, and blue dust. Then pour it right onto the mirror and it'll be fixed," Aireyal said. *Hopefully.*

Her mother paused, tapping a finger to her lip, contemplating. "That sounds like it could work. You're sure those measurements are right?" Aireyal nodded, and her mother turned away to the window, thinking out loud. "Webori. What else should I expect from Nodero? Where am I supposed to find that?"

"The notes said it was a resource in high supply," Aireyal said, and her mother turned back to her.

"It is. In the Felaseran Forest. Webori is the name for willoworm silk in sylvan. We don't have any."

"We do," Aireyal said, smiling. *Zale had shown her at the apothecary.* Her face dropped. She still didn't know where Zale was. "I need to know what happened last night."

Her mother placed her hands on her hips. "The guards noticed the library's *ward broken* doors when they passed by on their patrol and reported it to the librarian who found you unconscious on the floor. Apparently, the stairs to the Crypt of Infamy were open as well. Thankfully, nothing was missing, so I convinced her not to tell the headmistress. I..." her mother trailed off, shaking her head. *The Crypt of Infamy.* That must've been the name of that creepy room. "How did you get past those wards? Did you finally learn how to..." *Do magic?* Her mother's face was rather hopeful for someone questioning their child who'd broken a bunch of rules.

"No, that was—" Aireyal stopped herself.

"That *Zale* boy you were with?" A particularly negative emphasis was in her mother's tone when she said, *Zale.* Aireyal nodded, wishing she could shrink to the size of a mouse. "Where is he?"

"I don't know. He disappeared last night after..." *Is it a good idea to tell her about—*

"After what?"

Aireyal squirmed. "There was someone else in the library. I couldn't see her face, but she wore a crescent moon brooch. It had a big white gemstone in it surrounded by red, blue, and green gems," Aireyal said, and her mother's face wrinkled.

"You're sure?" she asked.

"You know her, don't you? What's going on?"

"It's nothing too important."

"Don't do this to me. Let me help," Aireyal pleaded.

"Forget about her," her mother said. Aireyal let out the frustrated breath of someone realizing the mountain they'd just climbed was only a hill. If her mother wouldn't tell her about the girl, she'd just have to figure it out on her own. "What we need to focus on is this willoworm silk," her mother continued. "You said you knew how to get some."

"It's at the apothecary."

"Why don't you see if the apothecarist can lend you some silk and hulgi weed. I'm going to get the other ingredients going for the remedy."

"You have the heart of a blood hawk lying around?"

"Long story. You get to it," her mother said, nearly shoving her out of the door.

Aireyal ignored everyone and everything she passed. The apprentices talking about an upcoming dance. The docents yelling at the apprentices for loitering. The creepy rock goblin statues around the grounds that were more disturbing than the ones in the headmistress's office. By the time Aireyal burst inside the apothecary hut, she was completely out of breath, gasping in the fragrant scents of herbs and potions lining the walls and tables.

The apothecarist was once again nowhere to be seen. Aireyal's skin crawled like fire beetles at who she found instead.

"Morgana?" She was sitting down in a chair, giggling next to Zale, who sat in the bed, *shirtless*. Aireyal's eyes narrowed before she could even think. "You're here?" She wasn't even sure which one of them she was asking.

Morgana answered. "I knew you couldn't resist coming to check on him, Airy."

Airy. Whatever. "How did you even know he'd be here?"

"I asked around. Found out he was the apothecarist's assistant and figured this was the best place to check," Morgana said. "He's a cute one, isn't he." She gave Zale a tiny pat on the head, and Aireyal's eye twitched. Morgana got up and smiled. *What game is she playing at?*

Morgana walked to the door but stopped when she passed Aireyal and leaned in to whisper, "Let me know next time you two are going on an adventure, I would love to join." Then she slithered out the room. *What?* Aireyal turned her attention to Zale.

"What was that about?" she asked. Zale shrugged.

"She showed up to talk."

"About what?"

"You, mostly," he said with another shrug. Aireyal took a deep breath. She had so many questions, but she also came here for a reason.

Aireyal opened her mouth to ask about the silk, then stopped as she glanced down at his body. Her eyes studied every inch she could see of his lean, toned muscles as fast as they could. *He must work hard to get them like that.* She would've stared longer, but he was wrapped in bandages all over. Each of them covering a different bruise.

"You're hurt," she said, frowning.

"A little," he said, far too fast, trying to sit up… unsuccessfully. She hadn't noticed until now how stiff he was. He made it halfway up again before grimacing and laying back down. "On second thought, it might hurt the tiniest bit more than a little," he said, painfully forcing a smile.

Aireyal's frown deepened. "Did that brooch girl do that to you?"

"What brooch girl?"

"The one last night," she said, but his face was blanker than an empty page. "She was wearing a weird crescent moon brooch," Aireyal continued, but his face showed no recollection at all.

"Are you sure? I'm quite sure it was just us last night," Zale said. *How could he not remember? Did she knock him out first?* Aireyal tried recalling what happened, but her memory of last night was fuzzy. Maybe she'd dreamed of the girl.

"If it wasn't her, then how'd you end up with all those bruises?" Aireyal asked, pausing. "How'd you even get here?"

Zale's eyebrows curled, and he sat thinking for a long moment before saying, "I'm not sure. I think I remember slipping and falling," he said. Was that really what happened? Had he fallen back down the steps to the crypt? *Maybe there is no brooch girl.* She must've been going crazy. No. Her mother knew something about the girl. *But she's not going to tell me. I'm going to have to find out some other way.* However, she had other concerns for now.

"Is there any hulgi weed here I could use?" she asked.

"Yeah, right on that table," he said, pointing to a small bag. Aireyal walked over and picked up the lightweight herb.

"And do you still have that willoworm silk?"

"Sure, it's on the top shelf there," he said, pointing up to a jar on the shelf next to him. The silk hung inside resembling curtains of spiderwebs. "Do you need it for something?"

Aireyal nodded. "It's... pretty important," she said after a pause. *Would Mother be mad if I told him?*

"Then take as much as you need. Actually, take the whole jar," he said.

"Are you sure? Won't the apothecarist be angry?" Aireyal asked. Then again, this was her second time here and she still hadn't seen the lady. She was beginning to wonder whether the apothecarist was even real.

"I'll tell her I lost it, go ahead," he said, motioning to the jar again.

"Why are you always so nice to me?" Aireyal asked, walking over to the shelf. She wished there were something to give him in return for his help, but what?

"I'm paying you back for all the times you've helped me with history," he joked. She cracked a smile. They hadn't studied a single page yet.

She turned her attention to the shelf. "Oh, that's a problem." The jar was on the *top* shelf.

"Say no more," Zale said, pushing himself out of bed and hobbling up. His right leg was bandaged in cloth and had a deep purple bruise.

"No, Zale, you can't—"

"It's nothing," he said, limping over. It clearly *wasn't* nothing. Aireyal started forward to gently push him back towards the bed, then stopped. He was *shirtless*. Her heart wouldn't survive touching him like that.

She let out a breath to re-focus. "This is all my fault. If I hadn't made you go with me last nigh—"

"Aireyal. You didn't make me do anything. I happily chose to go with you," he said, his eyes locking onto hers. *Pump, pump.* "Despite the state I'm in, I enjoyed spending last night with you, and I'd do it all over again," he said, then plucked the jar down and handed it to her, leaning on the shelf for support. His piercing eyes locked onto hers for a long moment, then another, and then a third before Aireyal finally found words to say.

"Thank you." It wasn't enough, but it was all she could give him for now. "I suppose I should get going."

"And I should get some rest," he said, clearing his throat.

But neither of them moved.

"I almost forgot," said a snippy voice out of nowhere, making Aireyal jump a mile out of her skin. She spun to find Morgana standing leisurely at the door. "The whole reason I came here was for those herbs," she said, then she glided to a shelf and picked up a small, green box that smelled of mint.

"How long have you been standing there?" Aireyal demanded, her face burning up.

Morgana smiled. "Not long."

Liar. "What do you need those herbs for?" Aireyal asked.

"Fashion purposes, of course. What else could they possibly be for?" Morgana gave a quick raise of her eyebrows, then she snaked back out the room. Aireyal groaned. She didn't have time for Morgana's antics. She needed to get back to her mother.

"I'll see you later," Aireyal said, giving Zale a smile that he returned. "And please, get more rest for—" she stopped her lips before they could embarrass her by saying, *me,* "your health," she said instead.

"I will, I promise," he said, giving her another smile, then she headed out with an extra little bounce in her step.

For a while, at least. After what felt like her hundredth slog through the school grounds in the past two days, Aireyal realized, if nothing else, this year at Darr-Kamo was going to make her fit. That is, if she made it through the year. *You do not belong at my school.* The headmistress's words echoed in her mind. Yet another problem to overcome.

At some point, she'd *actually* have to do magic. And she was getting the sinking feeling it would be sooner than later. What would everyone say if they learned the truth about her? What would Zale say?

She pushed the thought out of her mind as she reached her mother's study, hoping she'd never have to answer that question. A sickening draft hit Aireyal when she opened the doors. A mix of sweat, old flesh, and some other moldy thing. Her mother was half paying attention to a dark red brew in a flask she mixed with a large wooden spoon. Beside it on her desk sat the mirror, with its shards placed roughly back into place. And beside that stood a tall, strong-armed townguard, pointing to a map of what looked like New Lanasall, and Aireyal's mother nodded along to where he indicated.

"Oh, Aireyal, you're back," her mother said, looking up, and giving the townguard a tap on the shoulder. He promptly rolled up the map. Probably, *official Grandmage business.* Aireyal decided not to ask. "Let me finish this, Borris," her mother said, motioning to the brew.

"Of course, June, I'll see you again soon," he said, giving both Aireyal's mother and Aireyal pleasant smiles before heading out the room. *June?* No one called the Grandmage by her first name.

"I see you found the ingredients," Aireyal's mother said to her. "No troubles at the apothecary then, I assume?"

"Not really."

"What's that mean?"

"Morgana was there, though I don't know why, she was being cryptic," Aireyal said, and her mother shook her head.

"That girl is just like her mother."

"Her mother?"

"Mirvana."

Oh. Aireyal stood there stunned, mostly at herself for not realizing it yesterday. They had the same sharp voice. The same bitter expressions. Both of their names even started with M. Of course Morgana was the headmistress's daughter.

"Would you mind passing it to me?" Aireyal's mother asked, pointing to the ingredients in Aireyal's hands like it was at least the second time she'd done so. Aireyal nodded as her mother spoke again, "Let's see if the notorious Nodero knows what he's talking about."

"Knew," Aireyal corrected, handing her mother the hulgi weed and willoworm silk. "He's dead now."

"Right you are," she said, opening the jar of silk and measuring it with a spoon. "I hope you didn't touch this stuff. It's poisonous. Seeps right through the skin. It would kill you in a matter of hours if untreated." *That would've been nice to know earlier.* Good thing she hadn't touched it. "To be honest, I'm surprised we have any at the school," she said, mixing the silk and hulgi weed into the rest of her concoction. *Hiss.* Bubbles erupted but her mother kept mixing until the whole thing turned a clear but gross snot-like color.

"Will it work?"

"I hope so," her mother said, pausing. "Nodero was a lunatic and he tended to write the wrong measurements in his experiments. Those who try to reproduce his work sometimes yield other things entirely," she said, then took a deep breath before pouring the brew onto the mirror. Another *hiss.*

Smoke rose and her mother took a step back. The fog rose, filling up the room. Aireyal stood motionless while her mother grabbed a handful of red dust from the table with one hand and blue dust in the other. She tossed the red dust first. "Ventu!" It glittered in the air, then vanished. A swirling gust took its place. *Woosh!*

The smoke followed the gust's direction, heading to the corner of the room in a thick cloud. Then her mother tossed blue dust at it. "Countru!" A moment later, the cloud dispersed in sparkling specks of sapphire.

Aireyal let out a breath she hadn't realized she'd been holding. "You used the red dust to guide it all to one spot, then the blue dust to stop it. That was smart."

"I'm a Grandmage for a reason," her mother said, smiling. But it quickly turned to a frown. "What I don't understand is where that smoke came from in the first place. Yet another mystery of Mirvana's mirror, I suppose."

Mirvana's mirror? "This mirror belongs to the headmistress? That's why she wants it fixed so badly?"

Her mother nodded. "She'll be using it tomorrow, I'm sure." *What in the western world could the headmistress be using the mirror for?* As vain as the lady seemed to be, it didn't show reflections. All Aireyal had seen in it were fields of wheat. "Looks like we've done it," her mother said, leaning toward the mirror.

Aireyal peered over too. The mirror had been restored to its original state. No, *better*. It was clearer now. The mirror revealed a run-down room where a wooden wall was littered with holes.

"What exactly is the mirror showing?" Aireyal asked.

"Not what, but where," her mother corrected. "This is one of the Frostfire Mirrors," she said hesitantly, clearly still deciding how much she wanted to share. "What you see is the location of another mirror."

"And where is that?"

"I think that's precisely what Mirvana plans to find out."

"How's she going to do that?"

"Do you remember the egg?" her mother asked. Aireyal's stomach turned, waiting to be scolded. "Things can go through one mirror and come out of the other."

Aireyal's eyes opened wide. "You're saying wherever the other mirror is, the egg is there too?" she asked. Her mother nodded again. "How is that even possible?"

"I wish I knew," her mother said. "The magic that powers them is ancient. And powerful. And *dangerous*," she continued with a thin-lipped frown. "The whole situation is rather complicated, even more so with the egg."

"The headmistress said the Senate was expecting the egg. What kind of creature is inside of that thing?"

"If I'm right, it's something that shouldn't exist," she said, then paused, shaking her head. She looked at Aireyal, then turned away, wringing her hands together, then she looked back and sighed. "You can never speak of what I'm about to tell you."

Chapter 15

Perilous Pirates Pursuit

"**E**REVAN! LISTEN CLOSE TO WHAT I'M ABOUT TO tell you," Nya said as red dust flew from her hands into the fireplace. "Igno!" It swirled into a flaming tornado around the egg. She managed to keep the egg from burning, *for now*. The inferno was relatively controlled, but that didn't stop it from being a whirlwind of fire, shooting embers into a wooden room. She tossed more dust into it, "Igno!" the flames stabilized, *for a moment*. "Erevan, grab a bucket of water from the washroom," she said, straining, her eyes focused on the fireplace. "I need you to put this out while I hold it away from the egg."

He sprinted to the washroom and grabbed a bucket. *Zing!* Pain shot up his left arm. He'd forgotten about his injury in the rush of fire and smoke. Erevan settled for picking the bucket up with his right hand and swooped it in the tub, filling it with water. Then he ran back, spilling water along the hall.

"Watch out!" he said as he entered the room, thrusting water out and at the fireplace. But aiming with only one hand wasn't easy. Most of the water splashed around the fireplace, not in it. Some even sprinkled Nya, making her lose concentration on her spell and the fire engulfed the egg.

"Igra morta, asi asu!" Nya snapped at Erevan. Whatever that meant, her tone assured it wasn't a compliment. Erevan ran back to the washroom and filled another bucket. Then he raced back to Nya's side, suffering the pain of clenching the bucket with both hands this time and drenching the fireplace.

Sss. The fire died in an enthusiastic hiss. Clouds of smoke billowed out and filled the room. Erevan stepped back and peered forward. Dust singed his nose, and he coughed. Memories of his lungs burning on the Cold Creek Bridge came back. Nya hacked next to him, and they both stumbled from the room.

Crack.

"The egg," Nya wheezed out, covering her face in her hands. Erevan looked towards the fireplace, but the smoke was too thick to see through. Thankfully, some of the smoke dispersed through the hand-sized holes in the wall. As it cleared, Nya gasped, staring at the fireplace. "Oh no."

After a few more moments of the smoke thinning, Erevan saw pieces of eggshells lying in the fireplace; a mound of ash in the center. Whatever was in that poor egg had been burned to a crisp. What an awful way for a baby to d—

Grrr, growled a tiny voice. Erevan looked down; a night-black lizard stared up at him with eyes as red as raspberries. Or… lizard wasn't the right word, this creature had wings. Tiny little wings. But wings, nonetheless. *It can't be.*

"It's a drag—"

Nya's hand flew over his mouth and she put a finger to her lips. Then she reached down and scooped the baby up with one hand and pulled Erevan back into the room with the other. She shut the door behind them and leaned back on it, her signature smirk wide on her face. "That's a dragon," he said, unable to believe his own words.

"*She's* a dragon," Nya corrected in a whisper, beaming down at the creature. The dragon was nearly half a foot long head to tail, with a head much too big for her skinny neck and eyes equally oversized for her scaly black head. One half of the eggshell sat like a round helmet atop her head with two teeny horns protruding through it. "You're so cute," Nya said, poking her in the cheek. The dragon gave another, *grr*, though it was hardly fierce, more a mildly drowsy kitten than ferocious beast.

"This is the important thing you're trying to get back to Nyumbafro, isn't it?" Erevan asked. But Nya was too busy poking the dragon in the cheek and giggling to listen. "Nya."

"Huh?" *Knock. Knock.* Someone at the door. Nya searched the room anxiously, then ran to one of the beds and wrapped the dragon in a blanket before she motioned toward the door. "Whoever that is, tell them to go away," she whispered.

Erevan walked over and cracked the door ajar a bit. "Oh," he said, opening it up.

"That's the opposite of what I—" Nya hissed, then stopped. "Oh," she said too as Sir Lee strolled into the room. He looked at the smoking fireplace, then back and forth at the two of them, stroking his beard.

Grr. Sir Lee peered over to the poorly concealed lump in the bed. "As much as I'd rather not, I suppose I have to ask, what's going on here?"

Nya hopped up and shut the door behind him. The dragon popped her eggshell-helmeted head up from the covers and tilted it to study Sir Lee. She blinked several times, cocked her head straight, then tilted it again.

"I'm assuming that came from the egg?" Sir Lee asked. Erevan nodded.

"She's a dragon," Erevan said.

Sir Lee sighed regretfully. "If Evlynna lives, she does so only to curse me. This trip just got a whole lot harder," he said, rubbing his temples.

"But she's adorable," Nya said, walking back over and scratching the dragon under the chin. It gave an approving purr.

"And defenseless," Sir Lee said, lowering his voice. "Not to mention every pirate in town will want to steal it to sell."

"That's going to make getting passage out of here rather difficult," Erevan said.

"Then why don't we walk to Bogudos?" Nya suggested, now making goofy faces at the dragon. She watched Nya inquisitively, jumping every so often and ducking under the bed sheets at Nya's scarier faces.

"Because it's far," Sir Lee said dryly.

"Not to mention dangerous," Erevan added. "The first weeks of travel are fine. But going on foot eventually means a journey up the Otenbul Mountains and by the goblin's central city of Gozzo," he said. "Besides, we should still take the river once we get to Bogudos. It's much easier to get to Nyumbafro on a boat headed northeast past Kugoz. That is, unless you want to go straight through the city of Rifton, which I suppose would be quicker."

"That city is Heritourian territory now. Me going there could cause political... problems," Nya said, pausing.

"I know Heritourians and Nyumbafroans don't like each other, but is it really that serious?" Erevan asked.

"Yes," his father answered. "If the Rifton townguards suspect someone's from Nyumbafro, it turns into a nasty process of identification."

"Is that why you've always told me not to go there?" Erevan asked, shaking his head. "Why can't anyone ever assume that people they don't know aren't out to get them?"

"Says the one with preconceived notions of every leader in the world," Nya pointed out smugly.

"I'm just saying, it isn't that hard to get along."

"Yes, it is. Heritour is terrified of us. And fear breeds hate," Nya said. "That's why their treaty states we aren't even allowed back in *our own* city. They think we'll use every magical discovery and advancement we make for the purpose of destroying them. But we're not violent. At least, not without being provoked."

"So, the rumors of all the weapons your people create are false?" Erevan asked.

"Oh, they're quite true. But we wouldn't do any of it if Heritour didn't want to kill every elf they saw."

"Heritour is allied with Lanasall. They don't try to kill the wood elves over there," he noted.

"That's because the Felaseran Forest doesn't sit next to Heritour's boundaries like my country does. If it weren't for the jungles filled with dangerous animals on the border between Heritour and

Nyumbafro, we would've already been invaded. Thankfully, there are only so many places to cross safely into Nyumbafro, it's much easier to defend that way. And defending is all we've ever tried to do."

"That's not what I've been told. I want to hear a Heritourian's side of the story," Erevan said.

"There's no point. They're liars."

"Now who has the preconceived notions?"

"Honestly, it doesn't matter, we need to focus on getting to Bogudos," Sir Lee said.

"Can't we walk from here and go around the Otenbul Mountains?" Nya asked, sticking her tongue out at the dragon. The dragon made a cackling sound, then stuck her own long forked tongue out.

"Did she just laugh?" Erevan asked, watching the dragon as it tried to mimic a series of faces Nya made. Some, the dragon had more success with than others.

"They're intelligent creatures," Nya said casually as though it was common information.

"How would you know? They've been extinct for over three hundred years."

"Apparently not," Sir Lee noted.

"Neither of you have answered my question. Why can't we go around these mountains?" Nya asked.

"Because on the other side of the mountains is the Raging River," Erevan said.

"I mean the west side of the mountains, not the east, obviously."

"And go through the town of Garolek?" Erevan asked, scratching his head.

"Isn't that one of your bigger towns?"

"Garolek is a ghost town," Erevan said.

"That sounds perfect, nobody will bother us," Nya said.

"No, I mean, there are rumors of undead. No one who goes to Garolek has returned in years."

"Oh, come now, Erevan," she said, finally turning from the dragon to look at Sir Lee. "There aren't actually ghosts there, right?"

"Doesn't matter, the path is the same," Sir Lee said, pulling out his map to show Nya. "Those goblin-filled mountains curve around near the town of Garolek, and the little monsters shoot everything in sight."

"Maybe the goblins are killing everyone that goes into Garolek," Nya said. Erevan looked at his father. "What?"

"He's been there," Erevan said.

"You have?" she asked Sir Lee.

He grunted, pulling his pipe out. "Long time ago. Wouldn't advise going back."

"So, all three of our ways forward are bad then?" Nya slouched her shoulders in defeat. "We either risk fighting a whole pirate crew over this little girl," she said, scratching under the dragon's chin again, to which it gave another purring hum. "Or goblins rain arrows down on us in the mountains. Then Garolek is..." She looked to Sir Lee, who puffed smoke from his pipe but remained silent. "A complete unknown."

"I'm afraid this may be where we part ways," Sir Lee said to her. "I won't risk my life for that dragon. Erevan and I will take the first boat from this town when the storm passes."

Nya's eyes dropped in disappointment. "There aren't any smaller boats that the three of us can crew?" she asked.

"Across the Raging River? No. The currents would tear any small boat to pieces, and it doesn't settle until much further down," Sir Lee said, surveying the rain.

Nya looked back and forth between him and Erevan. "I'm not sure how to say this but, I don't know the roads of this country well enough to travel them myself."

"I believe the words you're looking for are, *I need help*," Erevan said. He expected a glare, but she nodded instead. Erevan's face lit up. She needed them. *And I need her... to help Isaiah. Helping her is the key to freeing him.*

"I don't think that's going to happen, son," his father said, looking at him as though he had a key to Erevan's thoughts. And perhaps he did.

"I have to try," Erevan said, then he turned to Nya. "I'll get you to Nyumbafro if you're serious about the gold you offered."

"I am," she said. *One thousand gold. That was more than enough to save Isaiah.*

"Son—" his father started, but Erevan shook his head.

"I have to do this," he said, and his father sighed, but Erevan continued, "You can't change my mind. If you want to go back home, that's fine, but I'm bringing Nya to Nyumbafro."

"You're as stubborn as your mother. And she'd never let me leave you to do something so foolish alone," Sir Lee said, then he sighed again. "Stay put, I need to ask around. And don't let anyone see that thing," he said, pointing to the dragon, then headed out the door.

Asking around, it turned out, took hours, that turned into days, that turned into weeks with the unending storm. Erevan and Nya stayed in the room for the most part, while Sir Lee went out each day, returning late with bad news. Or rather, *no news*. Which was the same as bad news.

Nya took kindly to her role protecting the dragon, who she named Ashe, sneaking her little pieces of meat up from the tavern and treating every knock, thud, and bang outside the door as coming doom. Erevan spent his time losing to Nya in Wizards, Witches, and Warlocks; and practicing his swordsmanship... against air. Thankfully, his hand had nearly healed, but they couldn't stay here forever. They'd run out of coin to spend at some point.

On this particular night, the rain had stopped, *momentarily*. But the sun was already down, and Sir Lee had yet to return.

"I don't think Sir Lee's going to find another way out of this place," Nya said, lying on her bed, staring up at the ceiling. Ashe was curled up in a scaly little ball, sleeping on Nya's chest, something the dragon had quickly grown fond of doing. Erevan didn't want to admit it, but he had a feeling Nya was right.

"Would you take the path through the mountains, or Garolek, if you had to?" Erevan asked, peering out the window, where a few remains of Ashe's dinner were on the sill. Erevan looked out to the potion master's shop where his father had headed to, its chimney puffing out smoke.

"I was going to ask you that same question," Nya said.

"Me?" he asked, turning to her.

"I figure you know these lands better than me."

"Barely. I spent my whole life in Bogudos."

"Until now, that is. What made you leave?"

"My mother," Erevan said.

"She kicked you out?"

Erevan laughed, shaking his head. "She wants my father to let me join him as a mercenary, but he says I'm not ready. That's why we were in New Longaiya when we first met you. We had just finished escorting a merchant there."

"You two are spending a long time away from home. Will your mother and little siblings be safe? From what you've told me, Bogudos can be perilous."

"My mother's older brother, my Uncle Acric, is in town. He hunts some of the wildlife that migrate the country, Berrydeer mostly. The herds pass the outskirts of Bogudos this time of year for a few weeks. He'll head after them when they do, but we should be back in Bogudos by then if we leave soon."

"And if you don't get delayed any further," Nya added. Erevan nodded. "Your mother must be rather kind to run an orphanage," Nya said, then opened her mouth to say something else, but closed it. She paused for a moment, dismissing some idea from her head, then spoke. "I'm surprised she wants you to be a mercenary, it's a dangerous life."

"My father's getting older. He won't admit it, but he has to take more breaks between each job every year. He can't keep it up forever, and he needs someone to watch his back on the job."

"A man his age shouldn't be working so hard."

"We've needed the coin," Erevan said. "But thanks to you, things will be different when we finish this job. He won't have to work anymore if he doesn't want to." Erevan smiled again. "We'll even have enough for all these taxes."

"Your country really is poor," she said, chuckling. "It's rather ironic, really."

"How so?"

"The farmers of your lands here in New Lanasall made much of their trade with my people in Mikiwamoto, or Rifton as you all now call it, since Heritour has taken it," Nya said. "But since you all called for a truce, becoming an independent country and ended your war with my people, Heritour has turned their trade routes westward, back to your homeland of Lanasall. And that's where Mikiwamoto's riches now flow. Here in New Lanasall you're running out of coin as a result."

"How do you know all this?" Erevan asked.

"I'm a courier, remember? Your Magistrate and I had a lengthy conversation. It's a shame she's so power hungry."

"Says the one who lives under a king."

"At least he doesn't take the people's money with insane tax laws."

"He doesn't have to, he's a king."

"A king that looks out for his people."

"Those in power pretend to be kind by giving people just enough so they need them, but never enough for them to be content on their own. That's not what they want."

"It's different in Nyumbafro," Nya said. "Our king is a good man."

"Is he? Is that why he sent you on a mission that appears destined for your death?" Erevan asked, and Nya's expression faltered.

She turned away. "You don't know what you're talking about," she said.

"I don't have to live there to know your king lives better than your farmers, or *you* for that matter. And what right does he have to do so?"

"I…" Nya trailed off, then shrugged. "I hadn't really thought about that," she said, looking down. "What do you think makes a good leader?"

"One that sits at the same table as the common folk. Shares the food, the coin, all the resources. Even weapons."

"Fae dust?"

"Well, maybe not that. We can't all do magic like you."

"Don't say that," she said, turning back and curling her lip in disgust.

"I'm serious, it's t—"

"No, I mean, *that* word."

"What word? *Can't?*"

"The *M* one. No self-respecting elf uses that word," Nya said, frowning.

"You mean mag—"

She interrupted him before he could finish. "Don't say it."

"Why?"

"That word is an insult to our people. We are not magicians. We are sorcerers."

"They're the same thing, aren't they?"

"No," she said. "A magician does party tricks for children. We sorcerers are the *source* of arcane power. If you can use fae dust, you are a sorcerer."

"Well, I can't use dust," Erevan noted.

"Yes, you can. It's your birthright as an elf. Come here, I'll show you," she said, placing the napping baby dragon down on the bed, then rushing over to the fireplace.

"You're going to teach me mag—" he caught himself this time.

"Sorcery," she corrected, sitting down. "It's not as hard as you think."

BOOM! Erevan spun and his eyes scanned the town through the window to find the potion master's shop ablaze. He hopped up without another thought.

"What was that?" Nya asked, standing up.

"The potion shop. I have to make sure my father is safe," Erevan said, hurrying to grab his traveling bag. He needed to get there, *fast*.

"I'm coming with you," Nya said.

"You have to keep an eye on Ashe—" Erevan started, only to see Nya already placing the sleeping baby dragon in her bag.

"She can come with us. Let's go," she said. Erevan nodded, leading the way out the room, the tavern, and down the plankboard streets, ignoring strange looks and coughs from the pirates along the way.

Half the potion master's shop was burned down by the time they arrived, and it reeked of overcooked fungi. The baby rhinogators ran about cluelessly outside the now collapsed front door.

"Father!" Erevan screamed as loud as he could.

"Sir Lee!" Nya shouted after him, both of them nearly out of breath from running.

No answer.

"I'm going inside," Erevan said, starting forward.

"Are you insane? The whole building is coming down," Nya said, grabbing his arm.

Erevan walked to the shop anyway. "I have to save him."

"You don't even know if he's in there."

"I can't just stand here."

"You shouldn't kill yourself either. Think," she said. "It's a fire. We can't go inside until it's doused."

"Where are we going to get water from? We don't have time to run back to the washroom," Erevan said.

Nya pointed down. Oh, right. The town was on the river.

"The problem is accessing i—" Nya started, frowning at the planks, but Erevan was already unsheathing his sword. He quickly cut a hole in one of the planks. "Ah, a sword, I suppose that works," Nya said.

"Now what?" Erevan asked. "We don't have a bucket t—"

Nya was already pulling out her pouch, pouring red dust into her hands, "Aquo!" she shouted, tossing the dust into the hole he'd made. A gush of water came up and flew at the fire, sizzling a few of the flames.

Erevan nodded, impressed. "Ah, sorcery, I suppose that works too."

Nya smirked, but only briefly, "Unfortunately, there's a lot more fire than I have dust for. But maybe I can clear enough for us to see if anyone's insid—"

"Oi! You don't have to," said a hardy voice. Erevan turned to find Ziggli, the potion master, rushing to them. Sir Lee was at his side, both ridden with soot and carrying buckets of water.

"You're alive!" Erevan said.

"But my work is burning. Decades of study," Ziggli grumbled, pushing past Erevan and tossing water at his shop. *Hiss.* Some of the fire dissipated, but the task was futile. Four hand buckets of water weren't nearly enough to stop a flaming house. Though that didn't keep the dwarf from fighting his way inside.

"Ziggli, you won't be able to save it all, just get the research from—" Sir Lee started, only for a raspy voice to shout out to them.

"So, ye finally decided ta show yerself." Erevan looked down the street to see a familiar face walking their way. Two, long, clawed scars streaked under a pirate's eye. Gavlin, the card playing pirate from their first day in the Coral Coast. He strode their way with half a dozen crewmates behind him. All of them armed with sabres and wearing red shark bandanas. Nya stepped forward, glaring.

"This isn't the best time," Erevan said, pointing to the burning house.

"Shut it, *drow*," Gavlin said, pulling something out of his pocket. A ball bearing a painted skull and crossbones with a candlewick sticking up from it. He lit it on a nearby flaming piece of debris. "Here's a present for ye," he said, throwing it at Erevan and Nya. They jumped away, but not before the explosion.

Boom! Erevan flew several feet in the air, then slammed to the ground. *Those must be the cinder bombs.* There was a bit of smoke, but no fire. The collision with the ground hurt more than the exploding fragments of the ball itself.

"Erevan! Erevan! Erevan!" Sir Lee called out several times, or... maybe only once. A pirate said something and so did someone else, but it all melded into one endless echo and Erevan's vision faded in and out from white.

When his hearing and sight returned, Nya was still on the ground next to him. Ashe wiggled out her bag, screeching, and Erevan picked her up.

"Time to leave this cursed town," Sir Lee said. He was engaged with Gavlin blade to blade. The pirate couldn't land a single blow on him, but a host of his fellow corsairs closed in to ensure it wouldn't be a fair fight. The nearest of them took a swipe at Sir Lee's head. He ducked it, then ran the pirate through before spinning to block a strike from Gavlin.

"I'll cover us, start running," Nya groaned. She got up, holding her hands over her ears. "Can you keep her safe?" she asked Erevan, nodding to Ashe.

"I won't let them hurt her," Erevan promised. Though perhaps his pledge was premature. Two more pirates popped out from an alley, running at him.

"Ventu!" A handful of red dust flew past Erevan. It dissolved into the air, then a howling vortex of wind blasted the pirates, knocking them off their feet. Erevan looked back at Nya. "I told you, I'll cover us. Let's go!" she said, pointing to the gates of the town.

"Father!" Erevan called. Sir Lee cut down Gavlin, but a dozen other pirates came his way and he backed up.

Another handful of red dust flew past Erevan's face. This time landing mostly in one of the buckets of water before dissolving. "Aquo!" Nya shouted. Water rose from the bucket and flew out between Sir Lee and his pursuers. Several of them slipped and fell, giving Sir Lee the chance to turn and run.

Swirling light grabbed Erevan's attention. He looked back to see the dust Nya had tossed at the bucket had landed on some of the coral protruding through the planks too. The coral beamed as though a small sun was held inside. And the light spread to all the other coral nearby. It was *compelling*. It was *mesmerizing*. It wa—

"Watch out!" Sir Lee said, snapping Erevan's mind back.

"This'll fetch a nice price," a voice said behind Erevan. A hand pulled Ashe but she bit into it. Erevan spun to see a pirate yelping and pulling back his bleeding hand.

"Leave the baby out of this," Erevan said, punching the pirate square in the jaw with his right hand. The pirate fell to the ground, but more of his kind were on the way. "Why are there so many?"

"Just run!" Nya said, sprinting down the street. He groaned but followed.

The remaining pirates were several dozen yards behind. Or... they would've been if the pirates weren't calling to their comrades ahead to give chase too. Soon enough, half the town was after them.

So much for getting a ride on a pirate ship.

Nya ducked into alley after alley to avoid the gangs, and Erevan stayed right behind her. The gates of the town were getting close. It wouldn't be long befor—

Boom! Another cinder bomb. Erevan wasn't sure what happened next. But the moment after that, he was blinking in and out, white blurring his vision and his ears ringing again.

What he could see was that they had made it out of the town's gates. They'd been blown out of the town, literally. But it wasn't over. More cinder bombs were in the air.

Boom! Boom! Boom!

Erevan scuttled forward as fast as he could, cradling Ashe.

BOOM!

A bomb landed behind him, sending them forward and rolling across the ground.

More bombs came, but they all fell short. The pirates had blasted him out of their own range. Erevan took a deep breath before rising to his feet. Somehow, he'd managed to only take a couple of small scrapes.

His father looked to be fine as well. But Nya was still on the ground. Her pack several feet away from her with its contents sprawled along the soft, grassy ground. "Nya?" Erevan rushed to her. She cupped her ears and groaned. "We have to get out of here before they catch up," he said, helping her up.

"Please, stop shouting," she whimpered. But he wasn't. Erevan looked closer; blood trickled from her ear.

"Nya needs help," he said, turning to his father.

"No time," Sir Lee said, tossing her things back into her pack. But he stopped when his hands picked up a note with a strange symbol on it. Erevan looked over.

Dear stranger,

If you would return what is mine as soon as possible, I would be forever grateful.

Mirvana Markado, Headmistress of Darr-Kamo

~ Chapter 16 ~

The Light in the Lake

ARR-KAMO WAS FULL OF SURPRISES, BUT AIREYAL had spent the last three weeks unable to believe what her mother had told her. A dragon. They had all been hunted down in the dragon wars when the entire western world had been scorched. Lanasall even made a dragon killing law to make sure of it.

'All dragons that touch or fly over Lanasall soil are to either be killed on sight or reported to the local townguards immediately.'
-Lanasall Law #51, 410 A.S.

How could one have survived? Where had it come from? And if there was an egg, that meant there were parents somewhere.

Aireyal wanted to ask her mother every question that came to mind, but she'd been gone on *official Grandmage business* at the Senate since the day she told Aireyal about the dragon. And Aireyal had already tried the library for answers. *The normal one.* Avoiding the librarian along the way. As much as she needed help finding the right book, Aireyal knew better than to ask after her little stunt the first night of school. And she dared not check the Crypt of Infamy again. If her mother found out she'd gone back, that bit of dragon knowledge would be the last secret she ever told Aireyal. Then again, Aireyal didn't have many options left.

Some of the books Aireyal searched were so big she couldn't even lift them off the shelf. Thankfully, the friendly townguard with burly arms she'd seen in her mother's study was searching the library himself. She helped him find a few of the books he was looking for, those on high society etiquette, which seemed an odd thing for a townguard to research. But in turn, he helped Aireyal carry the most massive tomes she had to a table for studying.

The historical books she did find, supported what she already knew. Or, thought she knew. No dragon had been sighted in nearly four hundred years. There were books based on rumors as well, discussing everything from fables of people becoming dragons to how a knight gained the power of fire from a dragon long ago. The latter had little proof of happening, though that didn't stop bard's tales that grew the knight's popularity. Sir Falsius was his name, and a fitting one at that.

Aireyal picked up *Accounts of the Fall of Quartztown,* which detailed one of the last dragon sightings in Lanasall.

'It came in the night. They warned us, but we didn't listen. My father was born here, and my father's father and his father before him. The Mal's have lived in Quartztown through droughts, storms, and wars. This was our home. I wasn't going to let an overgrown

lizard take it from me. Or, so I thought. It came in the night. First, were the roars, then red filled the sky. They aren't mindless beasts, they're cunning and cruel. My son was eaten before my eyes, then I swear on Evlynna's name, the dragon cackled at me before flying off. I'll never forget the small hole I left in its wing. I'll find that dragon one day and kill it. I'll come in the night.' -Treaton Mal, surviving farmer, page 41 of 'Accounts of the Fall of Quartztown'.

None of this answered the questions Aireyal had. The worst part was she couldn't say anything to anyone. Her mother made that *excruciatingly* clear. But there had to be a book on dragons somewhere that could tell her…

She didn't even know what she was looking for. Rumors of living dragons? Information on dragon eggs? The Frostfire Mirrors?

Aireyal ripped through page after page, day after day, getting more frustrated with each new failed attempt at finding information. She even managed to check through some books written in elvish, the basics of which she was starting to pick up on in her Sylvan language lectures. But it was to no avail.

She gave up her search after a while, looking instead through books on jewelry, hoping to find something about the brooch worn by the girl that night she'd been in the crypt. *Adie's All-Encompassing Anthology of Adornments and Accessories, Modern Looks for Balls and Festivities, Felaseran Fashion: Bracelets, Brooches, and other Baubles…* Every page of every book was useless, so she went back to searching for anything dragon-related.

The next book she opened, *Dragons and Dungeons*, was more vague rules of a game than historical fact. She slammed it shut, realizing it was another dead end, smashing her once burned finger in it in the process. Thankfully, she was *mostly* healed now.

"Oh my, what did that book do to you?"

Aireyal's head snapped up. Zale's blue eyes greeted her from the other side of the bookshelf. He looked nothing like he had in the apothecary a few weeks ago. Not even a lingering bruise. And his hair was perfectly styled as always. *What does it feel like?* she wondered.

"Hello there."

"Sorry, I—" she said.

"I think the book is the one that needs the apology," he said, smiling. She tried not to laugh, placing it back on the shelf. This wasn't the time for jokes, she needed to find... something. Aireyal forced herself to adopt her *serious face.* Flat-line lips, unblinking eyes, and slightly creased eyebrows. Actually, she might've looked more angry than serious. "Oof, my joke was that bad, huh?" Zale asked, still grinning.

Her mouth started curling upwards. *No, stop that.* "I'm trying my best to be focused right now," she said.

"But I like it so much better when you smile," Zale said. Her heart did that weird flutter as he slipped to her side of the bookshelf. "What's wrong?"

"I—" she started, unsure what to say. *I can't find a useful book about dragons. I still know nothing about this girl with the brooch that attacked us. The headmistress will be using the mirror for... something.* "There's... a lot," she said, frowning again.

"Can I help?"

No. Not unless I told you one of the many things I'm not supposed to, like the fact that DRAGONS STILL EXIST!

"I'm not sure," she said softly, wringing her hands together. Zale frowned, then his eyes lit up and a big smile came over his face.

"Follow me, I want to show you something," he said, leading the way out of the row of books.

"Not another library, I hope."

Zale chuckled. "No books, I promise. You seem not to like them today anyway," he said, and the corners of his mouth twisted up in the cute way he probably didn't even realize they did. A tiny grin crept onto Aireyal's face as she followed him out the library. A grin she couldn't get rid of no matter how hard she tried.

"Where are we going?" she asked, trailing behind him.

"You'll see."

Maybe telling Zale everything would help. Even if it didn't lead to any clues, Aireyal knew she'd feel better afterward. Hoarding secrets was exhausting. But her mother had finally begun to trust her. If she found out Aireyal had gone off and told everything she learned so soon, her mother might never trust her with information like this again.

The secret that weighed heaviest on her shoulders, however, was the most personal of them all. *What would Zale say if he knew you were magicless?* the inner voice, which hadn't bothered her in a while, crept up to ask. It would be a relief to have someone she could talk to about it that wasn't her mother, but would he accept her? The uncertainty wobbled Aireyal's legs as they walked. *It's too risky,* she told herself.

Where was he taking her anyway?

Zale brought Aireyal this direction and that, past the school's bell tower and the stone maze near it, past Sybill Observatory, and on still until they were in a part of the school grounds she'd never seen before. There was no one in sight, and only one building was ahead, which was better described as a cabin. Around which, grass so tall it reached her shoulders grew, and before it was a lake that shimmered under the afternoon sun.

Throughout the lawn stood a dozen or so fenced-in areas, each holding animals inside. Bluebeard bunnies bounced in one, their sea-colored fur forming silly beards under their chin. Aireyal laughed, imagining them as tiny old men inspecting the world around them.

"I figured you'd like this place," Zale said, smiling. "It's where they hold lectures on animals," he said as Aireyal ran up to the bunnies' fence. "Here, put out your hands." Zale reached in, picking one up. The bunny squeaked, its nose twitching as Zale laid it in her arms. The pillowy fur fluffed into poofy clumps in her hands.

"Are you sure we're allowed to be doing this?"

"Of course, would I ever do anything against school rules?" he asked, giving her an innocent wink. Aireyal giggled.

"You? Never," she said, and he laughed. "What are we supposed to do if we get caught?"

"Caught what, petting bunnies? I can't imagine the punishment for that is too severe," he joked, and she laughed herself into a snort. Zale smiled, but she looked away, blushing. "How many times will I have to tell you your laugh is adorable before you believe it?"

"At least a hundred more times," she said sarcastically. Zale nodded, then cupped his hands around his mouth, shouting.

"Your laugh is adorable! Your laugh is adorable! Your l—"

"Stop," Aireyal said, snorting again. "What if someone hears you?"

"I wouldn't mind at all," he said, looking into the bunny pen. "But no one comes here anyway."

Aireyal gave a final pet to the one in her arms, then placed it back softly. It gave a happy squeak, then scurried off to its friends.

Aireyal turned her attention to the next pen. This one housed four flaming red birds taller than her with magnificent tails. Flamicocks. *The pompous bird,* according to a book she'd read, *Animals of the Kahamian League.*

SQUAWK! The closest bird strolled to the edge of its fence and flapped its wings and tail. He flickered an assortment of colors in the sunlight, from red to orange, yellow and pink. Then the bird stood there for a moment as though waiting for applause with his chest feathers puffed out and beak held high. Any moment, a royal band of bird trumpeters would surely appear and mark the grand event of *The Fantastic Flamicock* blessing them with his presence.

"Ah yes, you're very impressive, Sir Bird," Zale said, giving an exaggerated bow. He nudged Aireyal and she joined in with a curtsy, giggling the whole time. The bird gave a magniloquent nod, then pranced off. "You should see them with Docent Irwi, they love competing for her attention."

Hmm. Zale seemed to know a lot about animals. Maybe it was worth asking him about the drag—

No. You can't tell him.

Then again, perhaps she didn't have to. She could be more discreet. "What's your favorite animal with scales?" she asked.

Zale tilted his head. "That's an oddly specific question," he said. *Honestly, Aireyal, of all the things you could've asked, why that?* "I suppose I'd have to say the frigi snake," he answered.

"I've never heard of those."

"They live around the river and lakes where I grew up," Zale said. *Makes sense,* Aireyal thought. She didn't know much about the Felaseran Forest's native animals. "Tree badgers attack the snakes to keep them away because they're afraid, but the snakes feed on toxic bugs that would poison the water supply if the snakes didn't eat them. Without those snakes, the badgers would die," he said, looking out at the pens. "It's admirable, I think, staying where you aren't wanted to protect those who fear you."

"The snakes probably just stayed for the food," Aireyal noted, and Zale shrugged.

"Maybe. But I like to think of them as little guardians," he said, smiling. "I used to hide their homes so they could keep the badgers safe from themselves." Zale turned to her. "What about you? What's your favorite scaly creature?"

"Dragons," she said, trying to shift the conversation to her original purpose.

Zale tilted his head again, staring at her. "That... is not what I expected you to say," he said, chuckling.

"Why not?"

"You're not exactly fearsome, you're too sm—" Zale's lips started to form the word *small* until Aireyal narrowed her eyes. "Smart."

"Oh really? And what do you know of a dragon's intelligence?"

"Nothing. Same as everyone else," he admitted with a shrug. *So much for that.* Aireyal sighed, looking over to the next pen, but nothing was inside. "That's where the shadow tiger is," Zale said.

"It's empty." Aireyal looked around hesitantly.

"Don't worry, shadow tigers only eat large prey, they aren't interested in us."

"Yes, that makes me feel much better about it being out its pen," Aireyal said, still examining the area from outside, and Zale laughed.

"I'm pretty sure it's in there, they can render themselves invisible under the sun," he said, squinting inside.

"What? How?" Aireyal asked. Zale shrugged.

"Something about controlling how their fur reacts to rays of light. Helps them hunt. They need it because their other senses aren't that sharp."

"Where'd you learn that?"

"Animal Studies and Remedies. It's required for all future apothecarists."

"And you're sure the docent isn't going to catch us out here and be upset?"

"She can't. Docent Irwi is out today at the tailor. The rhinogator needs a new leash. Then after that, she has to make a trip to the icy waters of the Pengu Sea. She's bringing back some black and white birds that I think you'll love. They're called Gabigwens." Zale said, leading her over to a pen at the edge of the lake. A six-foot-long rhinogator bathed under the sun in its pen. It seemed to either barely notice them, or barely care enough to acknowledge them. The leash holding it to a thin wood pole did indeed look beyond the point of needing replacement.

Pop. Aireyal turned to see bubbles forming at the top of the lake. "What's in there?" she asked.

"Nothing interesting. Just a bunch of fish," Zale said, feigning a yawn.

"Fish *are* interesting," Aireyal said. She bent over the lake, trying to get a better view of the fish, but the sun's glare on the water blocked almost everything.

"There's a better way to see them, you know," Zale said. She leaned further toward the lake, straining her eyes.

"HowAHH—"

Aireyal screamed as she went plummeting forward into the lake. "ZALE!" He'd pushed her forward. Then he jumped in behind her, laughing.

"I told you there was a better way," he said as Aireyal flailed about.

"That's not funny, I can't swim!" The words weren't entirely true, her mother *had* shown her how multiple times, but knowing how and doing were two different things. Aireyal kept flapping around in panic for several more seconds until she realized she wasn't drowning.

"Don't worry, I've got you," Zale said. He was holding her hands. She went stiff and her face ignited as red as a tomato. "Do you trust me?"

"I would've said yes before you pushed me into a lake," she grumbled. He laughed.

"You want to see what's down there, right?"

"Not if it'll kill me."

"I'm not going to let anything happen to you. Hold tight," he said. She could do that. *Happily.* Her palms were sweating now, or maybe that was water. "Here we go."

Splash! Aireyal closed her eyes as they plunged under the lake's surface. Something slick brushed her cheek and her eyes popped open. Fish of every shape and color swam around them. The sun's rays glittered along their scales in a beam of light at the lake's center, like a lighthouse pointing down from above. Reflections danced over the sandy floor beneath them, creating illuminating circles. It was a painting in motion.

Aireyal looked back at Zale, and he gave her a wide smile. All her earlier worries faded away.

"Th—" Aireyal started to say, then remembered where they were. *You're an idiot.* She could feel water filling her lungs. But before she knew it, her head was bursting back up through the rays of the sun and above the lake's surface.

"You can't talk underwater," Zale said as she coughed.

"I know, I'm just stupid."

"No, you aren't. You're the smartest person I know." She froze and looked up at him. His perfect smile. Those dreamy blue eyes. She leaned closer to him. And his hold on her was getting tighter. *Pump, pump.* And he leaned in too. Until…

He was snatched out of her hand and pulled down into the lake. "Zale!"

Aireyal dove after him. She reached out and grabbed his hand. But all that did was get her pulled down along with him. Whatever dragged them down was impossible to see at the speed they were moving.

Aireyal's heart thrashed so hard she could barely concentrate enough to hold Zale. *Count, and calm down,* she told herself. *Just like mother told you.* One. Tw—But it didn't help much; her hand was slipping. She was going to lose him. *Focu*— A fierce roar shook from below.

A large furry paw snatched Zale's leg as they were pulled out of the sun's light. *The shadow tiger. They can swim?*

The fish hurried away as a figure emerged above them. Aireyal looked up, the rhinogator's sharp-toothed snout was inches above her head. She cowered and froze, but the creature swam past her, rushing toward the furry claw.

The tiger released Zale and swam to the light, disappearing again. The rhinogator stopped in the water, its head snapping back and forth. Aireyal went stiff. *What have you gotten yourself into?*

Another paw grasped at her, and she nearly lost her breath again. Or, no. Not a paw. Zale's hand. He pointed up to the surface urgently. *He's right, we have to move. Now.*

His grip on her tightened and he led them up. But right before they reached fresh air, something pushed her back down into the depths. This time, she felt the furry paw. The tiger was protecting the surface, while the rhinogator searched the waters for something. The tiger?

The light. The tiger was invisible under it. They had to get away from the sun's rays. Aireyal kicked as hard as she could, fighting to change the angle of their descent. But the tiger was too strong. She yanked at Zale, getting his attention. Then she pointed away from the beam of light in the lake's center surrounding them. He nodded, then fought and kicked with her.

A single claw appeared on her shoulder as they were pulled down but away from the light. The whole paw came into sight next, then the creature's arm and finally its great, terrible head. Gold and black fur billowed in the water around bright red eyes and fangs the size of thick daggers. Gills protruded from its cheeks, and the tiger let out another roar.

Just as Aireyal thought she'd die for sure, something rammed into the tiger.

The rhinogator.

The moment the tiger's grip was ripped away, Zale pulled her to the surface. She didn't care what happened in the waters below. She just wanted to live.

Aireyal shot up above the lake and gasped for air, flailing about.

"Ow!" Zale said as she smacked him accidentally. "I'm trying to help."

"Sorry." Aireyal ceased her flapping so he could guide them to the shore. She listened instead to the waters, preparing for one of the creatures to burst up from below, but neither did.

"There's no need to apologize," Zale said. "You saved us."

"Me? I didn't do anything."

Is he confused? she thought, looking down as he helped her up onto the bank of the lake and they sped away.

"Aireyal, I would've never thought to go deeper into the water and out of the light. That was your idea, and it was brilliant. I was just going to keep rushing for the surface, it probably would've ended with us sliced up."

Maybe he was right. "But you're still the one who led us out the waters, don't disregard how much you did."

"I'm not. I'm making sure you don't disregard yourself," he said, and she looked up at him. Zale cleared his throat. "Just remember, next time we're about to drown or be carved into pieces underwater, you can save us," he joked.

Aireyal smiled, but resisted the urge to laugh as they walked, leaving a trail of water along the ground. She was headed right to her room for dry clothes, where it was safe.

"Why is that tiger even at a school?" she demanded, frustrated at... well, she wasn't sure who. The docent over animal studies, perhaps? Whoever told her tigers should be brought around people? Actually, the headmistress was probably a good person to blame. Signing off on having deadly animals around seemed like something she'd do with a smirk on her face.

"Shadow tigers' sight, smell, and even hearing out of water is rather weak," Zale said, answering her. "So they aren't much of a threat... I think. Besides, it's only supposed to be here for three more weeks," he continued. "It's staying here while it's injured. It'll be returned to the jungle once it's healthy again."

"Looked plenty healthy to me," Aireyal grumbled. "But I doubt it'll make it to three weeks with that rhinogator after it."

"Those two wrestle, but they aren't going to kill each other."

"Then I'm not going to be able to sleep for the next three weeks."

Zale laughed. "Sorry, I promise I'm not planning ways to get you killed," he said, trying to smile, but it faded. "My hope was to get you to forget whatever was upsetting you earlier. Even if only for a little bit." Zale kicked the dirt and Aireyal's stomach did the thing where it dropped like a rock off a cliff. He didn't deserve to feel bad for being thoughtful. *Even if we did almost die.*

"What you did was really sweet. Thank you," she said, and Zale gave her one of his beautiful, *real* smiles.

He was going to kiss you earlier by the lake, she told herself.

No, he wasn't, the inner voice argued back.

Yes, he was... maybe, some other part said.

Aireyal pushed the thoughts from her mind before a fourth opinion spoke up and confused her more. She did feel better after her time with Zale, but she was no closer to finding anything about dragons than she was at the library. A frown worked its way onto her face as she tried to come up with a plan as they walked.

"You know you could tell me anything, right?" Zale said when they reached the door of her room as minty grass and other scents wafted down the marble hall. "Sometimes, sharing the load can lift a weight off your shoulders."

I wish I could.

But she'd promised her mother not to speak of the dragon or the mirror. They weren't even things Aireyal was supposed to know.

And she'd already talked to him about the girl with the brooch. There was only one secret she had left. One she really shouldn't share. Aireyal grabbed her door's handle, then stopped.

"I can't do magic." The words slipped right out her mouth. Her eyes widened to the size of the sun and Zale's did too. *Are you crazy? Why would you say that?!*

"What do you mean you can't do magic?" he asked, tilting his head. This was a big mistake. But it also felt good to get it out. *You can't tell him the truth. Say it was a joke. Lie.*

"I'm magicless." *No. This is such a bad idea.*

"But you're at Darr-Kamo."

"I know I—it's complicated."

He stared at her, either in disbelief, confusion, or disgust, and Aireyal looked down at the floor. "Are you angry?"

"What? No. Why would I be angry with you?"

"I don't know," Aireyal said, shrugging.

"How many people know?"

"Just you, and my mother. You can't tell anyone."

"I won't."

Aireyal took a long deep breath and her eyes shifted to the door. Staying outside with Zale sounded much better than going inside, though. So, she stood there, hand on the door, waiting for any excuse not to go in.

Crash! Something fell inside. Aireyal sprung the door open. Morgana stood right there picking up a book from the floor. She turned to Aireyal.

"Wait until everyone hears about your secret."

~ *Chapter 17* ~
# Training & Treaties

SECRETS. NYA HAD TOO MANY OF THEM. THE LETTER. The mirror. The dragon. Her mission. Erevan couldn't help but wonder about them despite his more pressing concerns. According to Sir Lee, Darr-Kamo was an expensive school for magic in Longaiya, the capital of Lanasall.

How all of that tied into the Magistrate of New Lanasall and a secret deal with Nyumbafro, neither Erevan nor his father understood. Sir Lee warned Nya that he wouldn't come to her defense if they ran into trouble without knowing the full story about why she was carrying a strange letter from a school.

They'd asked her about it several times during their journey toward Garolek and the Otenbul Mountains, where they'd stopped now at the final fork in the rocky road, only for her to deflect questions in her typical, frustrating ways. For some reason, Erevan smiled slightly, thinking back on it.

Sorry, I didn't quite hear you, Erevan. My ears aren't what they used to be, she had said.

Her ears, however, had long since stopped bleeding. She'd even managed to hear far off chatter from a traveler's lodge along the road they'd stopped at to resupply and eat the same time Erevan heard it. If her hearing had been damaged by the bombs, he couldn't tell.

Erevan's hand had also healed to the point that not even a scar was visible anymore. Thankfully, elves recovered a good bit quicker than humans. That was at least one of the reasons elves lived so long, or so people said. Their increased senses meant they felt injuries and illnesses more agonizingly than humans, but at least if they survived, they didn't have to spend weeks visiting an apothecary.

Erevan's eyes flicked over to where Nya sat now, Ashe sleeping next to her by a boulder where the mountain trail began. The dragon still had half an eggshell covering her head; Nya had tried to toss it away, but Ashe managed to sneak off and plant it back on her head at some point. Erevan grinned, and thought he caught the beginning of a smile on Nya's face too, but a soft thump on the head brought him back to his *pressing concerns.*

"Ow," Erevan said, looking up at the pommel his father had just bopped him with. "Was that necessary?" he asked.

"Every time your opponent is distracted, you must do what?" his father quizzed, pacing between where the green forested grassland they'd traveled met with the grey pebbles of the mountain path.

"Strike," Erevan answered, rubbing his forehead. Nya giggled off to the side, and he considered glaring her way. Then Erevan took another look at the pommel of his father's sword and thought better of it.

"A man must take advantage of his opponent's weakness in battle," his father said.

Just how many things must a man do?

"What must a girl do?" Nya asked. Erevan carefully peeked her way, but only out the corner of his eye.

"She should learn to fight too," Sir Lee said, turning to her.

Nya patted the pouch of dust on her belt and smirked. "I have all I need right here."

"And when that runs o—"

Erevan took the opportunity to sweep his father's legs from under him, bringing the man to the ground. Then he brought his blade to the man's neck. His father raised an eyebrow and Erevan shrugged, pulling his sword away. "You were distracted."

Sir Lee chuckled. "Good. You finally pass."

Erevan shook his head. "That doesn't count. I'd rather beat you at your best. Where's the honor in winning an unfair fight?"

"There is less honor in dying due to your own stubbornness," Sir Lee said, getting up. He peered out to the sky. "Take a look, son," he continued, pointing at one of the blood hawks above. "Do you know how they eat?"

"They eat field mice," Erevan answered.

"Ah, I'm not asking you what they eat, but how," Sir Lee corrected.

"They swoop down and grab the mountain mice in their claws."

"That's right." Sir Lee nodded. "Turn around and look down," Sir Lee said. Erevan turned, a few dark brown mice scuttered in the trees behind them.

"I don't get it."

"The woodland mice used to live out here too, but they moved after the blood hawks arrived. Now, they prosper in the trees, while their kin at the base of these mountains are almost all gone."

"The hawks have the advantage in the field."

"Exactly."

"But why don't the mountain mice leave and live in the woods like the others?"

"Good question. Why do you insist on fighting enemies at their strongest?" his father asked, giving him a pat on the shoulder before taking a break to eat some of the meat he'd made at their campfire. Then the man stared at the sign at the road's fork as though it would change if he looked long enough.

$$= | \text{\textsf{I}} | \text{\textsf{III}} | \rightleftharpoons | \text{\textsf{III}} | \rightharpoonup | \text{\textsf{II}}$$
$$\rightleftharpoons | \text{\textbackslash} | \rightharpoonup | \text{\textsf{I}} | \rightarrow | \text{\textbackslash} | \text{\textsf{III}}$$

Goblin. Those were the crude scratches of their symbols. Erevan couldn't read it, but he didn't have to. The path on the right led up the Otenbul Mountains to Gozzo. That meant the left one would take them towards Garolek.

Erevan looked over to Nya, who snickered. "What's so funny?"

"Oh, nothing," she said, then she turned to his father. "That was an interesting lesson, Sir Lee. I particularly liked the part about the small-minded nuisance trying to get himself killed."

"Themselves," Erevan corrected. "Shows how much you listened, there's more than one mountain mouse."

Nya smiled. "I was talking about you."

Erevan gave her a glare, but his lips betrayed him, grinning. "And yet you're following me around day after day."

"Only to make sure you don't get yourself into too much trouble *and* because I still need to teach you sorcery."

"Is that your citizen's duty?" Erevan asked, amused.

"Yes. An elf that doesn't know sorcery is hardly an elf at all," she said, hopping up and opening one of her pouches of dust. "Hold out your hands," she said, pouring out a spoonful-sized portion of red dust into his hand when he did, then doing the same for herself. It smelled like cinnamon-covered cherries. "Now listen, sorcery is not as hard as it looks."

"Of course not. You just toss dust in the air and yell words in elvish, easy."

Nya laughed. "Not quite. The first step is to gather your feelings."

"You sound like my mother when she's teaching people to pray," he said, snickering.

"Pay attention, Erevan. Each element responds to a different emotion," she said, then looked at Sir Lee's campfire. "For fire, it's about *passion*. Let that emotion overwhelm you. I like to think of the people I care deeply about. Then I throw the dust and say…" She tossed the dust in her hand into the flames. "Igno!"

Sizzle! A few flames spun into the shape of a small bird for a moment, before calming back down.

"Can you make it cook too?" Sir Lee asked, chewing on a bit of salted pork. Nya grinned, before looking to Erevan.

"So, red dust controls fire?" he asked.

"Red dust controls *all* elemental sorcery," Nya said, then she pointed to two of the other pouches of dust on her belt. "Blue dust is mostly for nullifying someone else's sorcery. And green dust can influence the mind itself. But don't worry about any of that for now, just focus on trying to do what I showed you."

Erevan nodded, then closed his eyes and thought of his family back in Bogudos. Their smiling faces. Everyone eating dinner at their far too small table. Then he thought of his friends; Tinny, Selea… Isaiah. All the stupid trouble they'd gotten into over the years. All the trouble they planned to get into later.

"I see you're smiling," Nya said. Erevan opened his eyes; she was right. "Hold onto that feeling you have. Now, throw the dust in the flames and say Ig—"

"Igno!" Erevan shouted, tossing the dust forward.

Sizzle! A flicker of fire shot up, roasting the back part of his father's lunch before settling again.

"Well, would you look at that," Sir Lee said, stroking his scruffy beard.

"First try," Erevan said, smiling. "I always thought it would be hard."

"It's easy because you have a great teacher," Nya said, her chin raised high. "Not to mention, the dust can feel your elven ancestry. All we have to do is speak to it," she said.

"You talk about dust like it's alive," Erevan said.

"Because it is," Nya said, pouring another spoonful into his hand. Erevan peered at it. *The dust is alive? That doesn't sound right.* Then again, Nya seemed like she knew what she was talking about. "It grows right here on this earth."

"I thought dust came from rocks," Erevan said, scratching his head.

"It comes from rare red, green and blue crystals that form in caves around the western world. They sell for absurdly steep prices as jewelry, but when you crush the crystals, you're left with fae dust. You should know this, the land across the river from your hometown is ripe with them."

If Rifton is full of crystals, that explains the constant illegal dust trade on the other side of the Raging River in Bogudos, and why Heritour, a country full of non-magical humans, wanted control of the city in the first place.

"Try the wind next," Nya said.

"What emotion do I need this time?"

"*Freedom.* The wind only answers the call of those that are carefree. You must let go of everything."

"That sounds simple enough," Erevan said, closing his eyes. "The word is Venti, right?"

Nya giggled. "Ventu," she corrected.

"Close enough."

"Close won't count. You need to say the whole word *correctly.* One of the easiest ways to make a sorcerer useless is to keep them from speaking. The dust must hear you, don't forget that. Now, focus on being carefree," she said, scrunching up her face seriously. He nodded, closing his eyes as her nose wrinkled in the cute way it always did.

Let go of everything. He took several deep breaths. *Don't worry about Garolek or Otenbul. Forget about becoming a mercenary. Let go of helping the family. Stop thinking of Nya—what?* Erevan shook his head. *Why did that thought just come into my mind?*

He opened his eyes and tossed dust into the air. "Ventu!" *Did it work?* The wind might've swerved.

"No good. Strange, I thought you'd get that one. You must be holding onto something," Nya said.

"I'm not holding onto anything. Maybe your dust is broken."

She scowled at him and tossed dust into the air. "Ventu!" The wind sliced sharply for a moment. "My dust is fine, thank you very much," she said, turning her nose up. "Clearly, you're just a hot-headed fire primary."

"A what? Primary?"

"Your primary is the element you're most comfortable using. For you, that would be fire."

"How do you know I'm not a water primary?"

Nya laughed. "Because our emotions are a giveaway. Water primaries are calm and peaceful. Earth primaries are stern and steadfast."

"What're you trying to say about me?" he asked.

"That you don't know how to wait. Hothead."

"Let me have some more dust. I'll show you."

"I can't. I'm fresh out," she said, playfully shrugging.

"No, you aren't," Erevan said, laughing. He reached over to her pouch, but she hopped back, running away, watching him and giggling. He chased after her until she tripped over her pack on the ground and everything in it went flying out onto the grass.

"Ow," she said, falling to the ground, still giggling.

"Haha! That's what you get," Erevan said, pointing down at her.

Nya slipped her foot under his and tripped him the same way he'd done to his father earlier. Erevan landed face first in the grass next to her and she giggled harder. "And that's what you get for laughing at me," she said. He faked an annoyed face. It lasted a couple seconds before he started laughing right with her.

Grrrrr. Ashe grumbled half-asleep between baby dragon snores.

"That's a problem," Sir Lee said.

"It's not so b—" Erevan started, sitting up, then he realized what his father was talking about. The mirror, sprawled out on the grass.

Erevan's eyebrows shot up. There was a face inside the mirror, staring right back at him, eyes wide. An elf lady with pinned-up hair.

"What is it?" Nya asked, getting up. "Oh no." The lady said something, but Erevan couldn't hear her. "She doesn't know the mirrors don't share sound," Nya said, blinking in surprise.

The lady said a couple more things. Then when they still didn't respond, her eyes opened wide again. She placed a finger up to the mirror, motioning for them to wait, then pulled out a quill and wrote hastily. A few moments later, her hand was stuffing a letter at the mirror. Then a letter came through the mirror and fell on the grass before them. Erevan picked it up,

Dear strangers of Nyumbatro,

Due to the inelegance of one of our apprentice mages, it seems my egg has made its way to you. I would happily exchange something for its safe return.

Mirvana Markado, Headmistress of Darr-Kamo

"That's not going to happen," Nya said, looking over Erevan's shoulder at the letter. *The egg. It came from this lady?* Erevan tried to ponder the thought, but his mind kept wandering elsewhere.

He glanced up at his father and asked, "Where did you say Darr-Kamo was again?"

"The city of Longaiya, hundreds of miles away from here in the home country," Sir Lee said as he got up from his place at the fire to come read the letter. Then he looked at Nya, his jaw clenched. "It's time you tell us what exactly that thing is," he said, nodding to the mirror, where the lady watched the three of them. Nya's pleading eyes found Erevan and she groaned, but he folded his arms. His father was right.

"It's a long story," she said, sighing.

"We have time," Sir Lee said. Nya took another deep breath.

"It's called the Frostfire Mirror, and it's an ancient artifact with incredible capabilities made by unbelievably abominable people to do impossibly deplorable things. I am trying to keep it from falling back into their hands."

Erevan looked at her, unamused. "I don't think I've ever heard someone use so many words to say so little. But if this thing is so dangerous, why not destroy it?" he asked.

"I'll get to that, I told you it was a long story," she said, glaring at him for his interruption. "It all began long ago, when the mirror was forged by creatures that no longer inhabit this realm a—"

"Can you give the shortened story, please?" Erevan asked as another letter passed through the mirror. Nya pointed to the letter.

"What you see before you *is* the short story. There's more than one mirror. You put something through one, and it comes out another," she said.

"That's it?" Erevan asked, scratching his head. "That doesn't sound like some powerful artifact to me," he continued as his father picked the newest letter up. "What would happen if I put my hand through it?"

"I wouldn't suggest it," Nya said. Erevan leaned over his father's shoulder to see what the letter said.

I am willing to offer a substantial reward to you for the egg's safe return in the amount of three thousand gold pieces.

Erevan's eyes popped open. "That's a fortune!"

"And apparently, it'll mean giving the dragon back to its rightful owner," Sir Lee said.

Nya grabbed Ashe from her nap and held her tight. "You can't give Ashe to her. That lady will kill her."

"What are you talking about?" Erevan asked.

"Don't you know anything about anything? Lanasall kills off every mystical creature they consider a threat. It's part of the treaty they signed with Heritour. The same treaty where they vowed not to use sorcery against Heritour for any reason and to share all their research. The same treaty my people refused to sign, and it got us nothing but blood," she seethed.

"How do you know all this?" Erevan asked.

"I'm in the royal court every day. It's common knowledge there," she said.

"That doesn't change our situation," Sir Lee said, shaking his head.

Nya glared at him. "I don't need coin, and I'm not trading Ashe for anything," she said. The lady seemed to get the message and wrote down another note, staring the whole time at Ashe. *She knows it's not just an egg anymore.* Then the lady tossed the note through the mirror along with her quill.

What do you want for the dragon?

Nya snatched the quill and the note and scribbled something in elvish. Then she tossed it back to the lady, whose eyes widened.

"What did you tell her?" Erevan asked, but another note came rushing through the mirror a moment later. Erevan grabbed it.

In accordance with the Treaty of Rifton, the breeding or housing of dragons is considered an act of war. If you will not return the beast, it is your duty to kill it.

Nya gasped, reading the note over Erevan's shoulder, then she leaned forward to the mirror and mouthed the word, *never.* The lady in the mirror once again got the message, narrowing her eyes, then Nya snatched the mirror from Erevan and shoved it into her bag.

"Negotiations are over," she said.

"Shouldn't we get a say in this?" Erevan asked.

"No," she snapped. Erevan looked to his father, who shrugged. "I need to get Ashe to Nyumbafro where she'll be safe."

"That lady thinks we're already there," Erevan said.

"I don't care what she thinks," Nya said.

"I won't lay my life down for this cause," Sir Lee warned Nya. "I hope you understand your plan may cause more problems for your people than you realize."

"There are enough people telling me what to do back home, Sir Lee, I don't need your unsolicited advice too," Nya said. He gave her a shrug that seemed to say, *if that's what you want, kid*, then he turned back to the sign at the fork in the road, once again looking between Otenbul and Garolek.

"I've chosen," he said, lighting his pipe. "It's time I visit that cursed town again."

~ *Chapter 18* ~
Parliament's Power

THIS YEAR WAS CURSED. HORROR DIDN'T BEGIN TO describe what Aireyal knew her expression was. How could she have been so stupid? Spitting out her secret right in front of a door. She told Zale she would handle the situation, then she dragged Morgana into their room and locked the door. Aireyal scanned the whole room; windows, wardrobes, beds, searching fruitlessly with suspicious eye flicks for someone hiding. She'd already warned Morgana twenty times not to say anything. The fox-like grin on Morgana's face, however, suggested she was more amused than threatened.

"You can't tell anyone," Aireyal reiterated for the twenty-first time to Morgana, who, *hmm'd*, then picked up two pouches from the floor. The contents of one flickered blue, and the other green under the sunlight beaming in from the closed glass windows before Morgana hid the pouches deep in her wardrobe. "Are those pouches of dust?"

"Maybe."

"We aren't allowed to have those outside of our lectures, where'd you even get—"

"I have my sources, Airy," Morgana said, smiling. *Airy. That's not my name.* Aireyal huffed out a frustrated breath, but that only made Morgana's smile widen.

She's trying to mess with your head. Stay focused.

"What are you using that dust for?"

"Hexing you, of course," Morgana said flatly. Aireyal gasped. It all made sense. *'By first setting a magical ward with blue dust, then enchanting it with an emotional green dust charm, you can create a hex. Hexes are invisible, silent traps used to alter the emotions or mental state of the first person who touches them' -Olia Mungus, page 22 of 'Simple Magical Protections for your Home'.*

"You created another truth spell," Aireyal said. That's why she had told Zale her secret so freely.

Or did you tell him because you wanted to?

"I was a bit worried Zale might touch the door first when I heard you two outside," Morgana said, going over to her desk to scribble something down. "Thankfully, everything went better than I could have hoped."

"Why would you even do something like this?"

"I only wanted to hear more about your trip to the library. I thought it was odd you two chose that of all places for late-night romance," Morgana said.

Aireyal blushed. *Why does Morgana care anyway? Does she know where we went? Was there a book she thinks we—*

"Tell me what happened that night, and my lips will be sealed about your little secret. Deal?"

What choice do I have? Aireyal opened her mouth, then hesitated. *Her hex could still be on me, I might not even be able to lie.*

Knock. Knock.

"Who is it?" Aireyal demanded. *Someone to punish Morgana like she deserved?* she thought hopefully, knowing it couldn't be true. Perhaps news of her being magicless already spread. But how? Morgana was locked in the room with her. The only other person who knew was Zale, but he would never tell... *would he?*

"Note from the headmistress," a voice outside said. Aireyal's blood froze, her eye twitched, and her inner voice whispered, *The headmistress found out your secret's been exposed.* And so quickly. Aireyal's legs wobbled, and she stumbled to her bookshelf, grabbing it to avoid falling. This was going to be her last day at Darr-Kamo.

I can't keep letting that voice frighten me, she told herself. Even if her fears were true, worrying wouldn't change anything.

Morgana got up and answered the door. A snot-nosed boy on the other side straightened up his posture when he saw her. Aireyal recognized him as one of the boys who made fun of her stammering regularly in her mother's lectures. "Hello, Morgana," he said, giving his best smile, which was as awkward as a horse walking on two legs.

"Who is the note for?" Morgana asked.

"Ando," he said, sounding disappointed. The boy looked over at Aireyal as though she were some gangly, unwanted creature. Then he turned his attention back to Morgana and beamed. He handed Morgana the envelope with an over-the-top bow.

"Thank you," she said, shutting the door, but he held it cracked open with his foot.

"Morgana, I'm sure you know the school dance is coming up in a few weeks. Did you want to go with me?" he asked, trying to stand up tall. "I heard Tyus already asked to be your escort."

"He did. Unfortunately, for both of you, I am not interested in the boys in my magic lectures," she said, then closed the door in his face. *How rude.*

Flop. Morgana tossed the letter onto a bookshelf and Aireyal cringed. She stared at the angry letters written upon the envelope.

"Are you not going to open it?" Morgana asked, somehow managing to have snuck behind her.

"Not with you peering over my shoulder," Aireyal said, picking the letter up and squirming away. She opened it, holding it away from Morgana's prying gaze.

Miss Ando,

Your unexpected role in what may become a historic event has increased even further. Your presence has been requested along with my own on the Parliament floor today—

Aireyal dropped the letter. Parliament? They wanted to talk to her? Oh no. This was about her being magicless, wasn't it? Her heart stopped for several beats. Forget the whole school knowing. The entire country was going to learn her secret.

"Wow, you are going to speak to our Parliament, what an honor," Morgana said, in a tone that might have been sarcastic as she picked the letter up and read it.

Aireyal didn't just have to show up. She had to *speak* in front of every member of Parliament in the country. Not to mention the massive crowd of angry citizens that would also be watching. *How? You can't even speak in front of your own peers.*

A tornado of nausea spun in her stomach. *Why is it always my stomach?* she wondered, giving it a rub to prevent vomit from rising.

"You must be excited to meet all those lawmakers."

"I'd rather be given a slow, painful death," Aireyal groaned.

Morgana scoffed, reading the end of the letter. "Lucky you, apparently, she will be watching your back." *The headmistress?* Aireyal let out a hysterical laugh. *Watch my back with a knife, perhaps,* she thought, looking back to the letter's end.

Wishing you the best as always,

Headmistress Markado

She actually had the audacity to write that. "I need to talk to my mother."

"You do not have time," Morgana said.

"What do you mean?"

"The letter. Did you not read it? You are skipping the rest of your lectures for the day. I am supposed to take you out to my mother now," Morgana said, pausing and observing Aireyal. "Though, you might want to change out of those wet clothes before we go." *Wet?* Aireyal looked down. Oh. *The lake.* Rushing to her wardrobe, she grabbed the first thing she could. "You are going to wear that?" Morgana questioned. Aireyal's face went red.

"Should I not?" she asked.

"Do what you want," Morgana said, giving a half shrug. Aireyal tossed the clothes back into the wardrobe and grabbed a different pair. Morgana gave a groan that suggested the choice was equally unacceptable. Aireyal tossed it back too and grabbed a school uniform. Morgana sighed in *slight* disappointment.

Good enough.

Aireyal glanced up at Morgana. "Aren't you going to look away?"

Morgana gave a roll of the eyes so exaggerated, getting her pupils to come back around deserved an award. She did, however, turn and walk to the door. "Why don't we get back to our chat earlier," Morgana said, as though Aireyal didn't have enough problems to deal with. "Do we have a deal?"

"I'm not telling you anything. I don't care anymore," Aireyal said, struggling to slip into her new clothes before meeting Morgana at the door. If the truth was coming out either way, she wasn't going to give Morgana the satisfaction of coercing anything else out of her.

"As you wish," Morgana said, leading the way into the hall. Aireyal dragged her feet behind her. *Rather fitting Morgana is the one to usher me to my demise. Maybe I should leave my dignity in this room too.*

It didn't take long to notice they weren't walking in the direction of the headmistress's office. Instead, they were headed for the school's front entrance, though halfway there, they were stopped. "Hey, Morgana." Winston Ellisburg, the arrogant boy from Aireyal's history lecture. "I was thinking you and I could go to the dance together," he said.

They were perfect for each other. And not just because of their personalities. Winston was handsome. At least, that's what a lot of kids said. It was probably true. Refined features, straight cropped hair, and taller than most of the other boys. Even his school uniform was devoid of the spots and stains other kids had acquired over time.

"How many times do I have to say *no*, Winston?" Morgana said, pushing past him, but he grabbed her shoulder.

"However many times it takes for you to start saying, *yes*," he said, grinning.

"Get your hand off me," Morgana said, smacking his arm down.

Winston raised his hands in amused apology, chuckling. "Sorry, I didn't realize you couldn't handle a little jest."

"It wasn't funny."

"Not to you, clearly," he said, then he glanced over to Aireyal. "You're awfully quiet, aren't you, Ando? Don't be afraid of Morgana, I'll handle her for you."

"Leave her alone," Morgana said. Winston's eyebrows raised, but not more than Aireyal's. "She's not interested in being part of your games."

"Morgana, you wound me," Winston said, faking a stab in the chest. "We're all pieces in someone else's game, are we not?" he continued, giving Morgana a smile, "But, I assure you my games are quite fun."

"Let's go, Aireyal," Morgana said, then she stormed down the hall. Aireyal followed. *What just happened?* "One of these days, I am going to send him out a window," Morgana said. And not in a joking tone.

"You shouldn't say things like that. Violence never ends anything, it only makes the coming backlash worse, that's what Ilizabeth Kamo said. And Winston said he was only joking anyway."

Morgana frowned at Aireyal in... disbelief? Disgust? Disappointment? "What is it like to live in a world where you are allowed to be so naïve?"

"I'm not naïve. I've read plenty of books," Aireyal countered.

Morgana laughed. "I'm wasting my breath on you, aren't I." It wasn't a question. Morgana was thinking aloud.

What does she know, she hates everyone, Aireyal thought until she remembered the one person Morgana didn't seem to hate at all. *Zale.* They'd been in the apothecary together. *Smiling. Laughing.* Aireyal's stomach knotted into a rope.

That doesn't mean anything. Quickened heartbeats betrayed Aireyal, though, and she stole a glance at Morgana. *I'm not interested in the boys in my magic lectures,* Morgana's words. They made more sense now; Zale wasn't in their magic lectures. A needle of despair drained all life from Aireyal. Today couldn't get any worse.

"Here we are," someone's voice said, Morgana's probably. Aireyal looked up to an open carriage door. The headmistress waited inside, an empty seat across from her lined in ghastly black cloth. *Today just got worse.*

"Miss Ando, would you care to join me?" the headmistress asked, her cold, calculating smile etched across her lips. *I may as well, my life's doomed anyway.* Aireyal slunk into the seat. The door slammed shut behind her so ominously, the horses were surely pulling her to her death. Then again, their muffled neighing sounded more like rattling bones than horse. Perhaps the headmistress rode around in a carriage pulled by undead skeletons; it seemed fitting enough. In *The Adventures of Allia*, the Witch of the Wilderwood had similar steeds, and she ate young girls whole.

The air is thinning again. Aireyal gasped. Everything was going dark. *Is this carriage some kind of trap?* She gasped again, searching for something sucking her breath away. But there was nothing. *It's in your head. Just count and calm down, like mother taught you.* One. *This will pass.* Two. *This will pass.* Thr—

"Miss Ando?" The headmistress stared at Aireyal as though she'd been calling her name for some time. "You look dreadful."

Thanks. Aireyal slumped her shoulders and peered out the window. Darr-Kamo was already a dot in the distance. They couldn't have been traveling that long, could they? How fast was the carriage moving?

"Your mother told me you struggle in front of crowds," the headmistress said with what could've been mistaken for concern in her voice. Of course, that wasn't possible. "She wanted me to tell you she will be there today, though it may be a challenge to find her amongst all the people."

The thought of her mother watching her be torn to shreds on the Parliament floor was as comforting as it was dispiriting. Did the crowds still throw rotten vegetables at people they disliked? It had been outlawed years ago, but there were stories of flinging sessions when someone said or did something particularly unpopular.

"She also told me you plan to become a Senate-Mage one day. I assume you are aware of how the hearing will go?" the headmistress asked. Aireyal turned to her. The lady's face was creased with the same stress lines that usually adorned her mother's face.

Aireyal nodded. She'd read more books than she could count on the subject, *'Those presenting testimonies before Parliament will answer all questions the Members of Parliament have for them fully and truthfully. Failure to do so will lead to lengthy imprisonment, or possibly death.' -Jumol Gomou, former prime minister, page 270 of 'Becoming the Leader of Lanasall'.*

"Good," the headmistress said. "Then as you know, the prime minister will be the one asking you questions. He is the most powerful person in the western world. Well, he and the Archmage. She might be there too. In any case, I highly suggest you answer his questions quickly and politely. He is a short old man, with an oversensitive ego. If he gets the smallest hint he is being trifled with, he will do his best to make your life miserable." Something in her tone suggested she had experience with that exact thing.

There were stories of the prime minister's temper. He'd once burned down an allied Member of Parliament's house who had voted against him on an issue. Well, allegedly, of course. Unfortunately, the Member of Parliament in question hadn't survived to tell the story, nor had there been any recoverable evidence. Sweat began trickling along Aireyal's palms.

"I promised your mother I would not let anything happen to you today," the headmistress said with what could've passed for a warm smile on someone else's face.

Since when are you and my mother friends?

"You should be fine though. I doubt they will ask you more than one or two questions. Your entire presence here today is a formality. It's a bit absurd you have to be here at all..." *Wait.* Aireyal stopped paying attention. *Was it not the headmistress's plan to have her expelled today?*

Screech. The carriage pulled to a stop.

"Well, well, we are here," the headmistress said, gazing out the window. *Already?* "One last thing. I hope you aren't as silent in there as you have been on this ride. Parliament tends to assume quiet people are guilty."

With that, the door to the carriage swung open and two men offered their hands to help them down. When Aireyal hesitated, one of them gave her an aggressive nudge onto a hedge-lined path. At the end of it stood a massive square building of stone. The Home of Parliament. Next door, there was a smaller but more exquisite building, and its spiraling crystal-like exterior sparkled under the sun. The Poliagou, the official name in Sylvan of The Senate Building. Even now, Senate-Mages walked around it, most of them elves. But that's not where Aireyal was going today.

She turned back to The Home of Parliament. Silky golden drapes hung from four massive columns towering before its closed doors. Chatter from inside could be heard as Aireyal was forced along the hedge-lined path towards it by the man behind her. People stood on the other sides of the hedges, eyeing her with accusatory stares. *I'm doomed.*

Many of them held signs of protests. *Equal Wages for All, Purge Palo, Re-unite our Country,* there was a sign for every side of every political issue. And mixed in the crowd were beggars. Ragged clothes, unkempt hair, and smelly. Like days upon weeks of unwashed dirt and sweat. Aireyal reached a hand up to cover her nose.

"Look at her, she thinks she's better than us!" one of them shouted, pointing at Aireyal. She dropped her hand. And her head. These were people who couldn't afford to eat. People who weren't born to a life of silky clothes and fancy balls in Longaiya. People she was supposed to become a Senate-Mage to help.

"Don't mind them," the headmistress said to Aireyal. "They would rather stand here and complain that other people should solve their problems than get up and change things for themselves. That is exactly the type of person you should avoid becoming."

The words almost sounded like advice, but surely that wasn't something the headmistress was capable of, and Aireyal wasn't a fan of what she was insinuating anyway.

Each step summoned more dread than the last until Aireyal's feet moved up the stone stairs and to the door. Now that she was here, she thought of turning around, but a hand pushed her ahead to a screaming chorus of sound.

The headmistress said something that Aireyal didn't quite catch as the doors of The Home of Parliament blasted open before her. The shouting of citizens and officials filled the room. Stairs led down past ten long rows of seats. Nine of which were filled with common folk.

Some were dressed in farmer's work clothes, some had fresh ash adorning their skin, blacksmiths perhaps, and others still carried the pompous sneers of tax collectors. Every kind of working person she could think of was in sight, filling all four sides of the room. There were hundreds of people, and they all stopped their screaming at once. To look at her.

Aireyal's legs lost their ability to function. She moved forward only due to the constant nudges of the man behind her, passing down row after row of seats. Each row was filled with slightly more dignified-looking people than the one above it, all the way to the last row, which housed Lanasall officials. Aireyal scanned the row for her mother on one side, then another. A third, and finally the fourth. If she was here, it was impossible to find her.

Aireyal was prodded forward more until, at last, they reached the marble floor of the building where the Members of Parliament dressed in rich, decorated robes watched her approach, most of them human. Roughly half of them sat on red cushioned chairs on one side of the floor. And nearly the same amount mirrored them on the opposite side in blue seats. There were a few green and yellow seats mixed in as well. Nevertheless, most held expressions of stiff, forced politeness—the type one had when pretending bad news was good.

At the far end of the floor were two unassuming chairs. They sat before a tall platform with three decorated chairs, a jewel or two away from being considered thrones. The middle and most extravagant chair sat behind a podium adorned in glimmering gold.

That chair housed none other than Prime Minister Palo, who was hardly half the size of the chair. He could've been mistaken for a child pretending to be a king in his oversized golden robes, if not for his white beard and wrinkles. It was almost a comedic sight, but unlike the other Members of Parliament, he didn't fake a polite smile. Instead, he scowled ahead at Aireyal as though he was appalled. Or... no, his eyes were trained on the person next to her. The headmistress.

"Mirvana Markado, Headmistress of Darr-Kamo. And Aireyal Ando, apprentice mage at Darr-Kamo," announced one of the men behind them in an unnecessarily loud voice. Aireyal's eye twitched at the mention of her name. "The Parliament of the People has requested your testimonies due to your role in recent events. Please head forward to your seats." Aireyal was shoved ahead once again before her legs had the chance to decide whether or not they wanted to move.

Fervent yelling from the crowd began again as she and the headmistress were brought to the meekly chairs at the end of the floor. Indiscernible whispers traded back and forth from the Members of Parliament on either side as they passed. Sweat trickled down Aireyal's face. Her legs gave out the moment she reached the chair, and she collapsed into it. The headmistress slipped into the one next to her, somehow managing to make the chair appear more impressive than it was. *Her perfect posture, perhaps?*

"Every word that comes from your mouth today will be recorded by scribe and is expected to be true, as is in accordance with Lanasall law," barked the man from behind her. "Lies and apparent misleadings shall be punished to the fullest extent of that law..."

Apparent misleadings. That sounded vague enough to execute anyone of Parliament's choosing. *Or burn down their hous—*

"Verita!" A cloud of green dust blasted Aireyal in the face and she spent the rest of the man's speech coughing. *Truth spell. Do they think we'd be foolish enough to lie to Parliament?*

The man behind Aireyal must have left at some point, because the crowd cheered as the prime minister rose from his seat and stood on a box behind his podium. The podium itself wasn't tall, but he scarcely managed to get his chin over it.

"Mirvana Markado," he said, and the chattering of both the crowd and the Members of Parliament died at once. "You stand before Parliament making an accusation of the highest order," he said, his voice deeper than Aireyal had expected. "What do you have to say for yourself?"

The headmistress rose from her chair. "You have heard many rumors of this girl, I am sure. But I doubt you realize just how serious her crimes are," she said, not an ounce of cheekiness to be found in her tone.

Crimes? Aireyal's mouth dropped in horror. The headmistress was going to sit right next to her and condemn her to some unspeakably awful fate. Aireyal tried opening her mouth to object but no words came out.

"What proof do you have of your claims?" the prime minister demanded, an annoyed vein bulging on his head as though he'd already heard enough from the headmistress. Perhaps he was on Aireyal's side.

"This," the headmistress said, holding up a note. "Written by her own hand," she continued, offering up the note to the prime minister, and he seized it instantly. *What was on that paper?* "That is proof she has taken the last living dragon to Nyumbafro." The crowd gasped and shouted back and forth in an endless frenzy. *Wait, what? Dragon? Nyumbafro? What was going on?* "Nyumbafro is trying to get their hands on every tool of war they can. We all know it. And we all know they are not doing so to keep the peace." The prime minister glowered at the headmistress as she continued. "We know how Heritour will respond to these transgressions, how will you, Prime Minister Palo?"

"I will assess the nature of this letter. You may be seated," the prime minister said to the headmistress, who did as asked, looking rather pleased with herself. The crowd quarreled in an uproar as did the Members of Parliament.

"Read the letter aloud!" shouted one of the Members of Parliament from the blue side.

"What's it say, Prime Minister Palo?" asked another from the red side.

"Give me a moment," the prime minister said, reading through whatever was on the note agitatedly.

Against her better judgement, Aireyal leaned over to the headmistress and whispered, "I'm not in trouble?"

The headmistress creased her eyebrows looking back, "Why would you be?" she whispered.

"I thought this whole thing was about me not being able to do… you know…" Aireyal waved her hand in a way that she hoped resembled someone throwing dust, but the headmistress just looked at her as though she'd lost her mind.

"Did Morgana not give you the letter? It explained everything that is happening today."

The letter. The one she absolutely did *not* fully read. "I sort of… glanced through it," Aireyal admitted. The headmistress sighed.

"Your ability to focus on things that matter is uncannily like your mother's," she said, and not in the tone of a compliment.

The crowd gasped again. Apparently, the prime minister had voiced some shocking revelation, but Aireyal's head was swimming with far too many questions to listen. "If this whole thing is about some other girl, why am I here?" she asked the headmistress.

"I explained that in the letter," she whispered, curtly. "You are here to help m—"

"Aireyal Ando." The prime minister's voice was stern and unwavering. "Can you confirm Mirvana Markado's words?" he asked, giving the slightest of head shakes, suggesting she say, *no.* Aireyal looked over at the headmistress, who nodded, then back at the prime minister. *What in the western world am I agreeing to?* Aireyal slowly opened her mouth. "Choose your words carefully. We wouldn't want any *apparent misleadings,*" he said, putting extra emphasis on the last two words. Aireyal gulped. Maybe it was best not to speak at all. But... *Parliament assumes quiet people are guilty.*

Count. She needed to count before she forgot how to breathe. One. *This will pass.* Two. *This will pass.* Three. *T—*

"Aireyal Ando?!" The prime minister's voice sent a chill down her back.

"W-what am I-I agreeing to again?" she stuttered in a mouse-sized squeak.

"That the words written by Mirvana Markado in her letter to us yesterday are indeed true," he boomed back. "Are you the cause of the egg's disappearance, or not? This is your last chance to defend yourself."

Something told her saying *yes* was the wrong answer. But saying *no* would be a lie. And that seemed like a bad idea considering the truth spell she was under. "I am, b-but it was an accid—" she didn't get to finish the word.

"Very well, you may be seated," he said, and the crowd started shouting again. Aireyal's knees gave out and she fell into her chair, turning to the headmistress whose face was half-pleased, half-concerned. "I believe that is all the information needed to make a decision, yes?" the prime minister asked, his eyes peering over the other Members of Parliament. *Is that really all they are going to ask me?*

"I call for an adjournment to deliberate on these findings," said the man sitting in the chair right of the prime minister's on the platform. Minister Boltus. Prime Minister Palo glowered at Minister Boltus before turning for a moment to the chair on the left, which was empty.

"Delay this if you'd like, but you will come to a decision when we reconvene," Prime Minister Palo said, pointing a finger at Minister Boltus, who frowned back at him. Then the prime minister looked out to the crowd. "We will begin again in one hour's time," he said, then his gaze turned upon the headmistress. And Aireyal. "You two have played your part and are dismissed. I hope to never see either of you again."

Another shiver slithered down Aireyal's spine as she turned to the headmistress, who smiled at the prime minister. "What happens now?" Aireyal asked.

"For us, we go back to Darr-Kamo. For them, they vote," she said.

"Vote on what?"

"Whether or not Lanasall is going to support a war."

~ *Chapter 19* ~

The Ghost Town of Garolek

H AD HE BEEN TOLD GAROLEK WAS WAR-TORN,
Erevan would've believed it. But that wasn't the case. The
wars of the past hadn't come this far beyond the borders; the
rusted armor and crunched bone littering the grassless ground
here were the remains of adventurers. Those foolish enough to
go searching for treasure where they shouldn't, according to his
father. *How much did his past experience affect those words?*

"Why'd it take you so long to decide on coming back here?"
Nya asked Sir Lee. But he gave no answer as they walked into town,
passing a wooden sign that stood in solitude, where it read in faded,
carved letters,

WE WELCOME YOU TO GAROLEK.

The walk into town didn't summon a welcoming party, however. Nor did it bring the shady eyes of pirates, the far-off whispers of goblins in the mountains above, or any other deadly foe.

Quiet was an understatement. Silent was more accurate. Even the dead plants in the ground were afraid to shift in the wind, unlike the stench of rotted carcasses, which followed Erevan's nose through the town, though everything here was long since deceased.

"Sir Lee?" Nya inquired again, but the man remained silent. Nya frowned.

"Don't worry, he's never told me the full story either," Erevan said, turning to his father, who grunted. The man had told the younger kids at the orphanage even less, though that hadn't stopped little Scoti from taking their father's journal when he wasn't looking, hoping to find stories of grand adventures.

"Because of what it reminds me of," Sir Lee said, taking a long pause before he spoke again, "I once had a young soldier like you in my company," he went on, looking at Erevan. "He refused to ever leave a soul behind."

"Sounds like a good man," Erevan said.

"There was a rainy night many years ago," his father continued, ignoring his comment. "Thunder and lightning littered the sky. A dozen of us were tasked with clearing beasts from the outskirts of this town by the Magistrate."

"You were a townguard?" Nya asked.

"No, we were mercenaries, paid poorly by the little tax money the country could offer us. But at least it was for a noble cause, the people of Garolek were in danger."

"In danger from what?" Erevan asked.

"Dread wolves," his father said. Adventurers in The Lazy Lizard tavern in Bogudos spoke of dread wolves from time to time. Like typical wolves, but bigger, fiercer, and far more clever. Erevan remembered a thief who claimed their howls sounded like a whistle of shadow. "While traveling up the mountain, one of our men slipped in the rain. He fell onto hard rock and injured his ankle so bad he couldn't walk."

"Let me guess, it was the young soldier?" Erevan asked. He had a feeling he knew exactly where his father was going with the story.

"No, but while the rest of the company went out to deal with the beasts, the young soldier stayed with his injured comrade to make sure he survived the night."

"Like I said, sounds like a good man." The story had taken a welcome turn from his father's usual grim accounts of battle.

"At first, the night moved on without trouble. But when midnight came, a howl echoed on the mountain and with the rest of their party gone, the two soldiers drew their weapons. A sword for the young man and a bow for his injured comrade. Dread wolves came upon them with bared fangs and sharp claws. Metal gleamed under moonlight that night. The young soldier defended his companion, vowing never to leave his side. Dread wolf after dread wolf they fought off. The injured companion fired arrows through the night, downing the beasts, until at last they left him be."

"Did their company return the next day?" Erevan asked.

"Indeed they did," Sir Lee said.

"It all worked out then. That young soldier was fearless, loyal an—"

"That young soldier was my best friend. I was the one who slipped in the rain and couldn't walk. He died that night protecting me. Unable to let go of his honor. He saved my life but left his pregnant wife alone in the world to fend for herself."

"That's not a very happy story."

"Few stories with swords are."

Nya's eyes dropped.

She probably regrets bringing it all up. Nya looked off to the wooden shacks that lined either side of the street; visible remains of the goblins that once lived here, they'd probably fall if a strong enough gust blew by. Newer buildings of stone they passed as they moved deeper into town were proof New Lanasall had taken over Garolek. But they were barren too.

"Where'd everyone go?" Nya asked, peering into the window of a house. A long-winding creak answered her, cutting through the air like a knife. Erevan spun, searching the area, but the sound seemed to come from everywhere and nowhere, all at once. Suddenly, it stopped. They exchanged looks.

"I think it best not to disturb whatever evil holds this town," Sir Lee whispered. "Let us move quickly and be rid of this place."

"Are you sure we shouldn't turn back and take the mountain pass?" Nya asked, whispering low as well.

"If there were a safe trail through the mountains, Garolek would have never been taken," he said in a voice even lower than hers.

"From your story of vicious dread wolves, this route doesn't sound much better," she noted.

"It's not. But at least dread wolves have to get close to kill you."

"That's a comforting thought, I'd love having my limbs eaten off," Nya grumbled.

"We'll be fine, they don't come out until midnight, we should be through town by then," Sir Lee said.

Snap! Erevan stepped on a twig. Another creak, this time from right behind them. They turned in unison yet again, only to find an empty town. A squeal came from Nya's bag. A moment later, Ashe peeked her eggshell-covered head up to look around.

"Don't worry, little one," Erevan whispered, patting her snout. Ashe did her purring thing, then after a couple more suspicious glances around, she slipped back down into Nya's bag. Nya smiled brightly at Erevan. It wasn't the mischievous smirk he was used to; it was something warmer and more welcoming.

The sun set slowly behind them on the horizon, its light fading far in the distance behind the endless trees of the Numino Forest. "Nightfall will be here soon, let's move," Sir Lee whispered.

"Maybe there's nothing to worry about. It might've been the wind," Erevan said, shrugging.

"If it were only wind, the goblins would have returned," Sir Lee said, eyeing the area as they walked, passing empty home after empty home until they came to a circular market plaza. Abandoned shops withered by the hands of time lined its edges, blocking the last moments of sunlight and in the center stood a cracked stone well. It protruded several feet above the ground and was wide enough for Erevan to be concerned about tripping and falling inside of it.

Beside the well was a defaced statue of Evlynna. The god of good... or so her worshippers said. Evlynna's believers considered her the mother of all creation and a caring and loving guardian to all with a good heart. She would supposedly reward those who did good deeds and punish the wicked. It sounded nice, but Erevan wasn't convinced.

"Someone isn't a believer," Nya said, and Erevan turned to her, wondering for a moment if she'd read his mind. But her hands traced along the statue's head, where a crisscrossed *X* had been carved through Evlynna's face. A shivering thought cut through Erevan's mind, then he shook his head. *It can't be.*

Another swirl of wind sliced past, but nothing was around again. "This is the center of town," his father whispered as the last of the day's light waned. Erevan peered down into the well. Cold air drifted up past him. If there was water inside, it couldn't be seen.

He picked up a stone and dropped it into the well. There was no splash. But no hard crash either. Either the rock had disappeared, or it landed silently. His head popped back up when a howl rang in the air. A howl that could only be described as the night itself.

Nya took a startled step back, stared into the darkness, and reached for a bag of dust.

"I'm going to need help, there are at least a dozen wolves," she said. Slanted yellow eyes appeared not long after, prowling towards them in the darkness. Erevan drew his sword and turned to Sir Lee, who did the same. Nya lit her rock-handled torch, holding its orange glow out into the pale moonlight.

"I thought you said they wouldn't come until midnight," Erevan said to his father.

"I'm not always right, son," he said, examining the eyes coming their way.

"Let's go straight through them," Erevan suggested. "We can carve a path and get out."

"We don't know how many there are," his father said.

"Nya said it's only a dozen, we can take them," Erevan said as the stench of dead flesh grew in the air.

"I said *at least* a dozen. I can't be sure, it's dark," she corrected. Shadows surrounded them as the crescent moon lit up the circle around the well and little else. A crack or crevice between the long shadows of the buildings here and there got some light, but it was hardly enough to see anything meaningful.

"If we run into the dark, we'll never see them coming. Staying by the light near the well is our best chance," Sir Lee said.

"And wait for wave after wave of bloodthirsty wolves to come at us?" Erevan argued. "We have a torch, we should use it and run."

"A torch isn't nearly as much light as th—" Another howl pierced the air, cutting off Sir Lee, this time from right on the outskirts of the circle, and the yellow eyes began circling their perimeter. "Everyone, back-to-back, watch the edges," Sir Lee commanded. Erevan and Nya did as he said, each of them watching a third of the plaza around the well, waiting for one of the wolves to dare to step forward.

A mangled face of luminous fur was the first, carrying the wicked feeling of lifelessness about it. The wolf's coat was translucent and glistened under the moon. There were enough cuts along its body for it to already be dead. And perhaps it was.

"That's not good," Erevan said. Sir Lee and Nya turned his way. The wolf was the size of a small horse and it circled them, yet its paws carried it almost silently. The wolf's head snapped back and forth between them as though assessing who to strike first, and ghoulish foam seethed from its barred fangs.

"That's no mere dread wolf," Sir Lee said, and for the shortest of moments, angst filled his father's eyes, while the creature seemed almost to form a crude grin at his remark.

Can it understand us?

"What's he waiting on?" Nya asked as the wolf continued to walk around them. "Something's no—AHH!" Erevan spun around.

Another ghostly wolf, one with arrows filling its back, dragged Nya away. Her torch clattered to the ground as the beast's fangs dug deep into her belt. It had snuck behind them while the other circled.

Erevan leapt after it, sword at the ready. He swung at the wolf's neck, but unlike the arrows in its back, Erevan's sword went through the beast, its ghostly fur wavering unharmed as though tickled by a breeze.

"Our blades are no use here," Sir Lee said from behind him.

Nya squirmed, ripping the belt free of her waist, rolling further from Erevan in the process. The wolf threw Nya's belt down from its jaws and chased her. Nya ran, only to head towards the many yellow eyes still surrounding them in the shadows of the plaza's perimeter, as the wolves now walked into the moonlight. Even without counting, it was clear there were far *more* than a dozen. Each of them battle-torn in ways that should've led to their death. Spears through the neck, sides split in half, heads detached, and yet they all continued on.

Erevan ran forward and reached into the dust pouch on Nya's discarded belt. *I won't let her die like this.* "Igno!" he shouted, throwing dust onto the torch's fire. Flames flew up, but not nearly as many as he attempted to command. Erevan tried hurdling them at the wolf running after Nya, and most of the flames did, but some curled out of his control, flinging back at him. Erevan jumped away to avoid burning himself.

Sorcery isn't as easy as I thought.

A howl of pain punctured the night as the fire singed the ghoulish hide of the wolf that had snagged Nya. The wolf shivered, ethereal wisps dripping from its body in place of blood. Nya took the chance to scramble toward Erevan. But the wolves watching from the perimeter closed in, snarling from every direction. *I have to get them away from her.*

Erevan grabbed more dust. "Ig—" he stopped. He couldn't afford to burn Nya. But there was something else he could do. *Let everything go… but*—Erevan shook his head and took a deep breath. "Ventu!" A pathetic breeze blew out, doing nothing but blowing Nya's belt of dust away from him. *Oh no.*

Nya reached out for it, but the wolf closest to her dove forward, gripping the belt in its jaws, then it threw the belt into darkness. Nya took the chance to make it back to Erevan at the center of the plaza.

"Thanks," she said.

"Thank me when we last the night."

A shout came from behind and Erevan turned to find his father evading jaws and claws from several wolves around him.

"What do we do?" Nya asked, still stepping back. She stopped when her foot hit the stone of the well. Erevan spun around.

The well.

"Jump in!" Erevan shouted.

"Are you crazy? We don't know how far down it goes!" Nya yelled back, gazing into its black abyss.

"What I do know is that we can't fight all these things in the dark," Erevan said. "It's too big of an advantage for them," he continued, recalling his father's advice about the mice and hawks. "We all need to get out of here."

Nya gave a long look at the well, her face twisting this way and that as she considered their options.

"Sir Lee, what do you think?" she asked. But the wolves didn't give him a chance to answer. The creatures bounded forward at once.

"Let's go!" Erevan said, grabbing her. He stepped up onto the stone and jumped into the well, pulling her with him. Nya screamed, but Erevan could hardly hear her. He was falling too fast and everything around them went dark.

~ Chapter 20 ~
Aireyal's Altruism

DARKNESS HAD OVERTAKEN THE SKY BY THE TIME Darr-Kamo was in sight. Aireyal had woken up this day with a series of questions, most of which were still unanswered, only to have even more now. She considered asking the headmistress about more than one of them, but the throbbing headache in her skull advised her not to. Perhaps she'd ask her mother. They needed to talk.

As the carriage pulled up to the school, the headmistress said something to Aireyal that she didn't quite catch. Her attention had been stolen by a tall boy with pale blond hair. Zale. He was waiting in front of the school, along with a host of other apprentices and docents. Was a welcoming committee necessary? And why did they all have to stare?

The moment the carriage's door opened; Zale rushed to it. "I wanted you to know, I didn't tell anyone," he said, his eyes drooping in pity.

Tell anyone what?

"The magicless girl returns!" Priscilla Hornbuckle shouted from behind him, snickering just as crudely as she did in their magic lectures, and a chorus of kids laughed around her.

They know?

"How does it feel to be the most useless person to ever attend this school?" asked another kid. An even louder series of laughs ensued.

"You're a disgrace, Ando," spat a third.

How did they find out a—Morgana. A wave of emotions slammed into Aireyal, and she wasn't sure which one she should feel. Anger, at Morgana for telling everyone her secret? Fear, of what else they now knew? Shame, that every insult thrown her way by the crowd of ruthless kids was true? What she did know was that water cascaded down her face. *Was it raining?* She looked up at the sky. Dark and devoid of any warmth, just like her. But there was no rain. *What's hitting my face?*

She felt Zale's hand wipe under her eye. *Tears.* Rolling down her face like ripples in the sea. Someone wrapped a warm arm around her and helped her trembling legs forward before she fell. Then again, perhaps being left on the ground so everyone could berate her with their worst remarks would be better. They might be enough to sink her deep into the ground where she'd never be seen again. Yes, that would be best.

Aireyal's eyes blurred, stained with tears, and burned like they'd been set ablaze. Her chest thumped, sobbing. People said things around her, but she couldn't hear them.

You don't belong here, that inner voice reminded her. *You never did. At least now it's over. You won't have to worry about secrets or magic or anything. You can go home and be a useless disgrace.*

"Miss Ando, pull yourself together." The headmistress's voice snapped Aireyal back to the present. But instead of its usual cold tone, there was something fiery in it. "And wipe your nose while you're at it. You look like a troll."

A handkerchief landed on Aireyal's face. *A troll.* It wasn't her fault she didn't look like Morgana. Her sadness boiled into a brew of hostility. Morgana had told everyone; she was sure of it.

Aireyal blew her nose, and an unspeakable amount of snot gushed into it. Her face went as red as a cherry when her tear-stained eyes locked with Zale's, snot dribbling down her face. *I can't believe I let him see me like this.*

It was only now she realized she was sitting in her room with four sets of eyes staring at her. The headmistress, who shook her head in… disappointment? Zale, whose eyes were filled with more pity than she could bear to see. Her mother, whose face was covered in so many worried wrinkles that she looked twenty years older. And Morgana, behind everyone, huddled in one of the room's corners.

"We need to figure out how the whole school found out about your flaw," the headmistress said. "Darr-Kamo will never be viewed the same. Thankfully, Parliament and the Senate are now both busy with another matter at the moment."

Aireyal's mother folded her arms. "Reputation? That's what you're concerned with?"

"And finding out who spread this rumor, of course. They will be punished to the fullest extent my powers can go," she said, turning furiously to Zale. *She thought he did it? He would never.*

"It wasn't Zale," Aireyal nearly shouted, and the headmistress spun to her instead.

"Then I implore you to enlighten us all. Who was it?" *Oh, you're going to love hearing this,* Aireyal thought, then out of the corner of her eye, she saw Morgana shrink like a frightened turtle behind the headmistress. *Is she scared? Surely her own mother wouldn't do anything too harsh to her. Would she?* "Who was it?" the headmistress repeated, staring Aireyal down, a dangerous tone etched into her voice.

"I-I don't know," Aireyal stuttered, but the headmistress held her gaze for several moments longer. The scowl on her face was enough to say what didn't need to be spoken. *She doesn't believe me.*

"Very well, Miss Ando, I will find out on my own. I hope for your sake you are telling me the truth," the lady said, then she stalked out the room.

"Don't mind her," Aireyal's mother said, placing a hand on Aireyal's shoulder. "I won't let her do anything to you as long as I'm around."

"Thanks," Aireyal said, forcing a smile. "I'm a little weary after everything at Parliament today though. I'm going to rest a bit." And by *rest,* she meant, talk to Morgana, *alone,* not that her mother needed to know that.

Her mother tried to hide the concern on her face with a smile herself. "I'll talk to you later then, lollidrop. Rest well," she said, giving Aireyal a light squeeze, then she left the room.

Zale gave Aireyal a sad smile. "I'm sorry about today," he said, kicking the floor softly.

"It's not your fault," Aireyal said, forcing a smile for him too. But the gesture only made his face drop.

"I'm going to take a walk, maybe get lost in that stone maze west of the bell tower for a while. If you want to talk, come and find me," he said before turning and sharing an awkward look with Morgana. *Huh?* Then he hurried out the door, closing it and leaving Aireyal and Morgana alone.

Aireyal's eyes slid over to meet Morgana's.

"I thought you were going to tell them all it was me," Morgana said.

"So, it *was* you," Aireyal hissed. She'd already known it, but the admission still narrowed her eyes to a glare.

"Calm down, I didn't tell anyone."

Wait, what? She didn't? Aireyal shook her head. "You're lying."

"No, I am not," Morgana said. She sounded... honest. *But no one else knows.* Except Zale. *He wouldn't.* Would he? *No. It wasn't him. She's lying. Or her mother is. The headmistress could've done it. But that doesn't make any sens-*

"Aireyal?" The sudden sound of Morgana's voice made her jump. She stared at Aireyal as though she was waiting on an answer. When she didn't get one, Morgana raised an eyebrow. "You do that a lot."

"Do what?"

"Drift."

"Drift where?"

"You tell me," Morgana said, looking down at her. *Wait, down?* Aireyal realized she was sitting on her bed. *When did that happen?* "You didn't hear what I asked, did you?"

"No," Aireyal admitted in a mumble.

"I asked why you didn't tell them it was me. You obviously thought it was, and they would have believed you."

"I don't know."

Morgana's eyes narrowed. "What do you want?"

"Huh?"

"People always want something. They don't do things for free," Morgana said.

"Then consider this a first, because I don't want anything."

Morgana's face almost let its guard down for a moment before she narrowed her eyes further. "No one has ever helped me without wanting something in return. Why did you do it?"

"Because you looked terrified," Aireyal said, the image of Morgana's face cowering in the corner of the room still fresh on her mind. "I was afraid for you."

"Why? We are not friends." Morgana moved to her desk, lit one of the candles on it and picked up a quill to scribble away.

"That doesn't mean we have to be enemies."

"Of course we do. Do you know what our mothers would do if we weren't?" Morgana asked, peering up at her mirror to see Aireyal's reflection.

"Just because they don't like each other for whatever reason doesn—"

Morgana stopped Aireyal with a suspicious frown. "For whatever reason? Like your mother being selected to be a Grandmage over mine."

Aireyal's eyes opened wide. "Is that what happened?" she exclaimed. Morgana blinked several times.

"I mean, that's part of—" Morgana paused. "She never told you?"

Shaking her head, Aireyal looked down. Her head ached with a sense of… sorrow? Or perhaps it was betrayal she felt? Aireyal's mother always wanted Aireyal to share everything with her, but she refused to do the same back.

Aireyal's eyes drifted back up to Morgana. "You realize we don't have to be our mothers, right?" she said, and Morgana frowned.

"I am not like them. They are not good people."

"My mother isn't lik—"

"Your mother is just like mine," Morgana said. "Have you not been paying attention in our lectures? She hated me from the very first day when she forced me to try to do magic with my eyes closed. And do you know what my mother said to me when I ran to her like a fool afterward?" A pained smile came across her lips. "How dare you embarrass me and the Markado name on your first day."

"That's awful."

Morgana laughed, but there was no amusement in it. "That's nothing. If she were like that my whole life, it would have been a wonderful change."

"What has she done to you?"

"What has she not?" Morgana scoffed. "Do you want to know how I first learned magic?" she asked, slicing her quill through a word on the page.

I'm not sure I do. "Yes," Aireyal said anyway.

"I was eight at the time. My mother was already disappointed in me. She had done her first magic in half the time as most people. A six-year-old *prodigy.*" Morgana looked at the candles on her desk. "One night, she handed me some dust and said, *I hope for your sake, you get it this time.* Then she lit a candle in front of me." Morgana reenacted the moment of lighting a candle as if she were her mother.

"You figured out how to do fire magic like that?" Aireyal asked, then Morgana stopped her reenactment, startled, as though she hadn't realized what she'd been doing.

"No. My mother tried to burn my face with that candle's flame."

Aireyal gasped, and the wounds of Morgana's past shredded her vicariously. "That's horrid," she said, but Morgana gave one of her half shrugs as though it was a common event.

"There was no water in the room, so I threw the dust to the only thing I saw. The shadows. I believe that is the reason I am a dark primary. I learned magic because I was terrified of what would happen if I did not."

"So, you didn't get hurt in the end?"

"Not that time. The darkness extinguished the light. It is the only thing I have trusted since."

Not that time. The words repeated in Aireyal's head as she watched Morgana's eyes start to glisten, but they managed to hold back their tears, for now. "What your mother did to you was wrong. I'm so sorry," Aireyal said, getting up and walking over to Morgana to… she wasn't sure. Give her a hug?

It didn't matter, because Morgana stood from her desk and shied away, moving to the other side of the room. "I did not tell you that story because I want pity. It's fine."

Aireyal stopped, eyeing the space between them. "It is *not* fine. You're hurting. There's nothing to be ashamed of. You shouldn't have to live with her i—"

"I don't. I live with you now. And in three years, we will be finished with school, and I will never have to see her again," she said, giving another half shrug of indifference. This time, a single tear betrayed her and rolled down her cheek.

"Morgana, I'm so sorry," Aireyal said, ready to cry with her.

"Don't." Morgana held a finger up as though to stop Aireyal's tears from coming down.

"You can't keep all this in, it'll consume you," Aireyal said. "I'm sure my mother w—"

"No. Don't tell anyone, especially not her."

"Morgana, the only way to get through this is if you open up."

"I know that. I will talk when I am ready… to whom I am ready to talk with." The solemnness in her voice dropped Aireyal's heart like a book to the floor.

Ding. Dong. Ding.

The supper bell rang. Morgana headed for the door, then she paused when she noticed Aireyal didn't move. "You're not coming?"

Aireyal shuddered at the thought of walking into The Banquet Hall, where Priscilla Hornbuckle and all the other apprentices would be ready and waiting to laugh at her all over again. "Maybe in the morning? I'd rather avoid seeing everyone right now," Aireyal said. Morgana's lips morphed like they wanted to say the word, *sorry,* but didn't know how.

"Oh. Right," she said instead, looking away from Aireyal's eyes. "Do you want to learn?"

"Excuse me?" Aireyal asked.

"Do you want to learn magic?" Morgana clarified, and Aireyal laughed.

"I haven't been able to learn from my mother, and she's a Grandmage."

"It's a good thing I am not your mother then, isn't it?" Morgana said, and if Aireyal didn't know any better, she might've thought the edge of Morgana's lips curled into a smile. "Why don't we wake up early tomorrow?"

"Sure," Aireyal said before her mind finished registering the words. A hopeful tingle zipped through her, though it was foolish. *There's no way this will work.* But something felt like maybe… just maybe, there was a chance, as Morgana headed west down the hallway.

West. That's where Zale had gone. They needed to talk. Morgana didn't seem like she was lying. Which could only mean—

Aireyal shook her head, thinking and waiting several minutes in her room as apprentices shuffled through the halls headed to supper. Then she slipped out, taking care to avoid everyone on her way to the stone maze.

The sight of it was far more sinister after sundown than it had been when she passed it on the way to her tarot reading lecture. A cool fog of darkness had overtaken the maze. And a hazy, shadowed figure stood at its entrance. But Aireyal couldn't make much out other than the person's elf ears from where she was.

"Zale?" Aireyal called out, walking toward the maze, but the shadow didn't answer. Instead, it walked inside, disappearing into the dark grey labyrinth, and the night.

That's got to be him, right? Everyone else is at supper.

The maze creaked the moment Aireyal stepped into it, sending a shiver down her spine. *Don't worry, it was probably only a squirrel.* She took a deep breath, then against her better judgement, walked into the maze.

~ *Chapter 21* ~
The Outskirts of Otenbul

EREVAN TOOK A DEEP BREATH. HE WASN'T DEAD. At least, he didn't think so. Death wasn't this soft. Wherever he was, it was pitch black, but it felt like bunches of old tattered cloth that he had landed on. They were riddled with holes, probably the work of rats from the size of them.

"Erevan," Nya's voice growled beside him. "You could've killed us."

"I knew we'd be fine," he said in his most assuring voice. When he'd dropped the stone down the well earlier and didn't hear a clank, he figured jumping down was safe. Of course, it was more a guess than a sure thing, but Nya didn't need to know that.

Snarl. Erevan looked up. His father's silhouette flashed under the moon's light, peering down the well. Then a wolf vaulted over the well at his father and he dove out of sight. A bone-shattering crunch followed, then a shout and a curse.

"Jump into the well!" Erevan shouted up. More snarls answered him. He couldn't let his father die like this. Erevan felt around at the stone walls, trying to climb back up, but it was too smooth to get a good grip and too wide to plant both hands against the wall. The only way he could help his father was to get him down. "JUMP!"

Another silhouette appeared at the top of the well, a snapping, flaming one. It hopped down to them, falling fast. Then it separated into two. Both Sir Lee and a wolf set ablaze were coming down. Before Erevan could consider moving out their way, his father crashed into him, and whatever strength the cloth had left gave out. They fell until Erevan's face smashed into the ground below, dirt filling his mouth. Jaws snapped, then there was a column of fire, and finally another howling whimper and a thud. A cloud of dust extinguished what was left of the flame, and spectral wisps faded up into the air, leaving them in darkness.

"About time you died," Sir Lee said.

His voice, the scurrying about of what might've been large rats, and the occasional howl from the undead wolves above the well, were the only sounds louder than their breathing. "Erevan?"

"I'm fine. You?"

"Small bite on the hand, I've had worse."

"Nya?"

"This is awful."

"She's fine," Sir Lee said, fiddling with something in his camping bag. "Now, how about some light."

Sir Lee's torch illuminated the area. Erevan found himself staring into the mouth of a spider the size of a grown man.

"AH!" Nya screamed.

The spider didn't move. "It's dead," Sir Lee said, lowering the flame to shine in front of a dagger carved from mountain stone that pierced through the spider's center. From the look of the wound, it had been dead for a while. It was only now under the light that Erevan realized it wasn't cloth, but spider webs that'd been holding them up in the well and it covered all their clothes.

"I don't care if it's dead, it's scar—creepy," Nya said, quickly correcting herself and moving away from the giant spider.

"Careful there, Nya," Erevan said, snickering. "You don't want us thinking you're afraid without your dust on hand."

She looked down, eyes slightly wide at the reminder her belt was gone, then she fought to straighten her expression. "Don't be silly. I've already told you, I'm not afraid of anything. Fear is for the weak-minded."

"Tell that to the girl whose screams I still hear ringing in my head," Sir Lee grumbled, rubbing his ear. Erevan started to laugh at the remark, then stopped. His father's hand injury was far more than the man claimed.

"You're missing a finger," Erevan said. It was his pointer finger to be exact. Sir Lee looked at his hand and let out a curse.

"A man must know there's always a price for battle," he said, leaning his head back against the cobwebbed wall and fumbling in his pack, eventually pulling out his pipe. The torch played the role of his lighter. He let out a puff of smoke and closed his eyes.

"You're taking a nap?" Nya asked, her mouth dropping.

"Do you know a better place for one?" Sir Lee asked, his eyes remaining shut.

"Oh, I don't know, how about anywhere not next to the giant spider!"

"But it gives the place so much character," Sir Lee said, grinning slightly.

"Unbelievable." Nya dropped her pack and walked off down the tunnel.

"Careful, that knife in the spider is goblin craftsmanship. These caverns must lead into the Otenbul Mountains," Sir Lee warned.

"I'll be fine."

Erevan considered following her, but he needed to look at his father's hand first. The torchlight wasn't much, but it was enough for his eyes to see. Blood trickled out from the fingerless hole, running down the man's hand.

"I'm gonna bandage that," Erevan said, fumbling through his pack for cloth.

"You should keep an eye on her."

"She said she'll be fine."

"You believe her?" his father asked, scratching his beard. Erevan hesitated. *Maybe he has a point.*

"Let's make this quick." Erevan wrapped the cloth tightly around his father's wound. "Holding your sword isn't going to be easy anymore."

"I'll manage," Sir Lee said, exhaling smoke to the side as he looked up the well. "Good thinking coming down here. How'd you know we weren't jumping to our deaths?"

"*Know*, might not be the best word to describe it."

"How about guess then?"

"Yeah, that's more accurate," Erevan said, and his father's eyebrow raised slightly. "I just tried to follow your teachings," Erevan said, only for his father's eyebrow to raise higher.

"Then I think you've misheard what I've said, despite those big pointy ears of yours."

Erevan laughed, and a moment later, his father did too. "You have to admit, I'm learning a little."

"You're learning a lot, son," he said, and Erevan grinned wide. "I never thought bringing you on the road would be a good idea, but you've always figured things out better by doing rather than listening, and I suppose this is no different."

"Does that mean when we get back home, I can start joining you on your mercenary jobs?"

His father gave another exhale of smoke. "I'll think about it. We can start by teaching you how to fish," he said, and Erevan's grin grew across his whole face. "There's still plenty you have to learn. But I can show you when the time's right."

For the first time ever, Erevan looked forward to his father's lectures. In the past, he'd begun tagging along just to spend time with the man, because his father was never one for idle chatter. Though while his words at times were few, his lessons were many. "Between what I'm going to learn from you and the sorcery Nya's going to show me, I'll be able to do anything," Erevan said, then there was a long pause.

"She's a nice girl, son," his father said, and Erevan felt his face warm up a little.

"What's that supposed to mean?"

"That you don't always involve yourself with the best people," Sir Lee said. Erevan actually knew exactly what he meant but had no interest in having *that* discussion again.

"Being nice is one thing, but Nya is used to watching servants do all the work while she sits back and watches. I'm not sure that makes her the best person."

"I've never heard her say that," Sir Lee noted. "Be careful not to make assumptions about people. You know where I was raised. If you didn't know me, what would you think if I told you I served in the king's castle in my youth."

"That's different, you were born into that," Erevan protested. "You didn't have a choice."

"Are you certain she does?"

A scream from Nya echoed down the tunnel. Erevan turned and ran into the darkness.

"Are you hurt?" he called out. Her footsteps hurried toward him.

"Something crawled on my shoulder."

"But are you hurt?" Erevan asked again. He felt a soft punch in his arm. How she managed to aim a blow perfectly in the pitch-black tunnel was beyond him.

"No, but it's—I'm… never mind," she said, walking back into the flickering light of Sir Lee's torch.

"You know you can admit you're scared, right? I won't think less of you because of it," Erevan said, following her.

"How many times must I tell you, I'm not scared of anything."

Erevan shrugged. "If you keep saying it, you might convince yourself. But everyone's afraid of something."

"What are you afraid of, Erevan?" she asked, turning to face him. He paused for a moment.

"Not finding our way out of these caverns for one. And I'm afraid of what might happen to my mother and little siblings back home while I'm gone. I'm afraid for my friend Isaiah, and I worry about not getting you to Nyumbafro."

Her eyes widened for a moment. "You're worried about me?"

"You deserve to see your home again. I can't imagine never making it back to Bogudos."

Nya paused for a long time before speaking. "You're always welcome to visit me if you'd like."

"Me, in the court of kings?" Erevan dismissed the thought with a laugh. "I'm not interested in feeding royals grapes off a platter."

"I told you, our king isn't like that, I've met him."

"You'd be surprised, most of them know how to put on a good show for the people," Erevan said, shaking his head. "Trust me, behind closed doors, everyone holding that much power is the same, and I hate all of them."

A long pause ensued, and the skittering of bugs and whistles of wind through the caves filled Erevan's ears until Nya spoke, "I was in the room when our king signed the document into law that made the selling of dust illegal in Nyumbafro for commoners. He said he did it to stop pirates from frequenting our cities, and I believed him... I still want to believe him," Nya said, pausing again for a moment. "But he and the princess laughed about it when someone mentioned less... *fortunate* kids in our cities sold dust too. Kids who needed coin anyway they could get it to survive. Kids like y..." she trailed off, looking down from his eyes.

"This is exactly what I've been telling you. You can't trust them. And the only thing worse than royals, are royals that lie."

Nya's head drooped further. "I stood by silently when the king signed that law," she said, staring down at her boots. "I hope you don't hate me for that. It's just that, me speaking against him wouldn't do anything. I don't have that kind of power... I don't think I want to." Nya's voice was filled with more terror than when she was dragged away by the undead wolf.

"Don't blame yourself." Perhaps she was more like him than he'd thought. "Blame the king," Erevan said, looking over to his father, who'd dozed off; the man's torch firmly planted in the dirt next to him.

"I don't think we should rest here, there's no telling where we are," Nya said, scanning the cobwebbed cavern walls. The tunnels were tall and wide enough for a spider three times her size to fit through.

"We're right under Garolek. The problem is where these caverns lead," Erevan said.

"To the goblins."

Erevan nodded. "Rumor has it the city of Gozzo is where the goblins breed the most vicious dread wolves for mounts."

"All the more reason we should leave. What if a patrol of goblins comes down here?" she asked.

"Into the lair of giant spiders? I doubt it."

"What if a giant spider comes?"

"I'll stab it."

"But it's—"

"A bug."

"A *big* bug," Nya muttered under her breath. "What if it stings us in our sleep?"

"It's a spider, not a scorpion," Erevan said, laughing. "They bite."

"That doesn't make me feel any better."

Erevan pointed to the giant dead spider impaled on the wall. "Don't worry, they're huge, they'd make plenty of sound crawling up to kill us."

"Again, not making me feel better," Nya groaned. "For all we know, they might move silently like those wolves," she said. The hairs on the back of Erevan's neck stood up as he thought back to the beasts. If the ears of an elf could hardly hear them, who could?

Nya looked up the well. The howling from before was absent. "Do you think they circled around and entered the tunnels?"

"Possibly," he said. Nya fiddled with her pack, giving a few pats on the head to Ashe, who snored the night away. "Is she always asleep?"

"Feels that way, doesn't it? I'm glad she can find peace here. Between the wolves, the pirates, and the forest, I'm surprised we're still alive." Nya paused. "I hope we make it." She closed her hands into tight fists when they trembled.

"What are you so afraid of?"

It took her a long time to speak as the shadows formed from the torch's light danced upon the webbed walls. "I'm not allowed to be afraid of anything. Too many people are counting on me."

"Where'd you come up with such a crazy idea?"

"My father," Nya said. Erevan shook his head.

"If I ever saw him, I'd let him know he's a fool for telling you that."

"That wouldn't be wise," she said, smiling.

"I suppose he's a great sorcerer like yourself?"

"Great people do tend to have lots of similarities."

"Does that mean he's scared of spiders too?" Erevan asked, grinning. Nya punched him playfully in the arm again.

"Don't laugh too much. I get to meet your mother first," she said, giving her signature smirk. "I can't wait to tell her all the times I've had to save you on our adventure."

"Once."

"I recall saving you more than once."

"Your memory is foggy. I've been the one saving you," Erevan said, and she blinked several times.

"Name one."

"How about when that wolf grabbed you by the hood, and I burned it to free you?" he said. She shook her head.

"You mean when you lost my belt to it? Oh yes, I'm sure people would toss coins your way for such monster hunting services," she said sarcastically, and he laughed.

"I also saved you by pulling you down the well with me," Erevan said.

"Pulling people to safety should absolutely not count in our scores," she countered, trying to put on a serious face, but it just made her nose wrinkle instead.

"Then I suppose the time you pulled me out of that lake in the forest doesn't count either."

"Did I say *our*? I meant *your* scores specifically," she said, and they both laughed until they couldn't anymore.

Their debate went back and forth as the torch slowly died, and Erevan took every chance he could to glance at Nya's beautiful brown face under its warm light, loving every moment of her stubborn cleverness. When the light went out, she rested her head on his shoulder.

"There is something I'm afraid of," she said softly. "Something I should've already told you."

"It's about the mirror, isn't it?" he asked, and she shuddered.

"Sort of."

"What i—"

A loud yawn cut him off as his father stirred and rose to his feet. "We should move," he said, lighting another torch. "Let's try to find our way out and *not* into Otenbul," he said, heading down the cavern. Erevan looked at Nya.

"What was it you were going to say?"

She watched his father closely. "I'll tell you later."

The caverns were endless. Every step forward, the walls closed in more until they were forced to walk shoulder to shoulder. Erevan's boots were wrapped in webs by the time they came into a large open room. Every inch of the rounded wall was covered in spider eggs, as was much of the floor before them.

"If this is the breeding ground, the mother must be close," Sir Lee said.

Erevan looked to the other side of the room. A fork. Two tunnels; one leading left, the other right. Both with goblin symbols carved into the rock above them.

$$\rightleftharpoons \Big| \searrow \Big| \Rightarrow \Big| \text{I} \Big| - \Big| \searrow \Big| \text{III} \qquad \text{II} \Big| \text{III} \Big| \text{U} \Big| \diagup \Big| \equiv$$

"I don't suppose either of you miraculously learned goblin tonight?" Erevan asked, staring at the markings hopelessly.

"We go right," Sir Lee said. Both Erevan and Nya looked at him, raising their eyebrows.

"The last time we were at a fork, the right passage led to the Otenbul Mountains," Nya pointed out.

"Yes, and this time it doesn't," Sir Lee said. "I think."

"Since when can you read goblin?" Erevan asked.

"I can't. But I stared at the last sign long enough that I believe I know the symbol they use for Otenbul."

"And if you're wrong?" Nya asked.

"We'll probably die," he said dryly.

"Fifty percent chance of death? Good odds," Erevan said.

Suddenly, Nya jumped. "Something crawled on my leg!" she shrieked, bumping into Erevan, who bumped into Sir Lee. Before

Erevan could even apologize, the torch slipped from his father's hand and fell to the ground.

First, one egg lit up, then another, and soon flames spread along the webs, burning all the eggs in their path. It set off a chain that swelled, scorching everything in sight and filling both their noses and the room in smoke. "We need to—" A hideous screech from one of the tunnels cut Nya off. Soon after, red eyes appeared in the left tunnel, followed by eight great legs crawling out of it.

Nya didn't say another word, she just sprinted straight for the tunnel on the right. Sir Lee and Erevan followed, leaving the torch behind, and entering the darkness. The screeching didn't stop. It got louder, and it was answered by more screeches. Scurrying and scratching surrounded them. Nya screamed ahead, but it was too dark to see what happened to her.

"Nya!" Erevan shouted out.

"I'm fine!" she said. "Something grasped my shoulder. I think they're tunneling toward us."

From the sounds of the scratching, she was probably right. *Crack!* Rocky debris fell on Erevan, followed by a moist, hairy leg that stroked his neck as he passed by. The scurrying behind them was getting closer. Eight legs, it seemed, were faster than two.

"I see a light!" Nya shouted. But Erevan saw nothing ahead of them. Not for another few seconds of running, at least. Then the pale moon's glow wrapped around Nya's silhouette. The entrance grew and grew until finally, they ran, then crawled their way up and out while scraping hairy legs pulled at rocks, closing the tunnel behind them, and clouding everything with dust and debris.

Nya gasped for air, turning to Erevan. "Are you two—" she started, then stopped. "Where's Sir Lee?" Erevan looked back. But he was nowhere in sight.

"Worry not about him," a voice said. They spun to see a familiar sight as the dust cleared. A milky mist surrounded them; and walking towards them was a knight, fully adorned in decorated white armor that glistened under the moonlight. His ivory sword was already drawn. "You have your own problem, princess."

~ Chapter 22 ~
Grimstone Goblins

NOT KNOWING WHERE YOU WERE GOING WAS A problem. Not knowing where you were going on a cold, cloudy night, in a creepy, creaking, cricket-filled maze was a much worse predicament. Especially when it felt like you were being followed.

Left, right, left. Aireyal's footsteps pounded against the earthy ground of the maze. The slick, ten-foot-high stone walls on either side of her had some tiny holes, dug by some nearly-finger-sized rodent or bug. They were big enough to peek through, and see more stone walls, but far too small to fit through. The only way to go was forward.

So, she walked, almost ran, following the maze, which was a straight line for the most part. But every so often was a *T* shaped crossroads. Each of them forced her to make a choice, left or right. She made the decision for the eleventh time already, but still didn't see any sign of Zale. Or anyone else, that is, until now.

Footsteps patted the ground on the other side of one of the stone walls. Aireyal peered through a hole and shivered. *The girl with the brooch.* She was a good way away, circling through the maze herself, but it was her. The girl's dark hair spilled out of her blue hood under the dim moonlight, but that's all that could be seen. Aireyal took a step closer towards the wall and the girl turned her way, brandishing a jagged dagger that was dripping with something. There wasn't enough light to see, but Aireyal had a good guess what it was. Blood.

Aireyal jumped back and started down the maze, palms sweating, the girl's footsteps on the other side. *She's a killer. Run!*

Whose blood was that?

It might be Z—

No, don't think like that.

Another intersection stopped Aireyal's path. This time, one of the stone goblin statues she'd seen around the school grounds was placed before her, crouched on a pedestal. She looked down both the left and right paths; they were each blocked by statues on stone platforms as well. *Why would someone put these things here?*

It didn't matter. She needed to get by. But there was no way to squeeze through, not so much as an inch stood between the statues and the stony walls. And sharp spikes protruding all over the statues' bodies meant that climbing over them would only lead to lacerations, not that Aireyal was athletic or flexible enough to get over them anyway. This was clearly meant to be a dead end. She'd have to push one of the statues forward down the path in front of her. If she could. These were statues of stone, not feathers.

Footsteps somewhere nearby gave Aireyal extra motivation. She steadied herself, then pushed against the statue on the left as hard as she could.

It didn't budge.

"Exclio, magitori mota!" creaked a rocky voice.

Aireyal's heart leapt out of her chest. She snapped her head up to see the statue before her, blinking open magenta eyes.

"You're alive?" Aireyal asked, astonished.

"Ecretee macca," the statue said, in what must've been some kind of Sylvan phrase. She had learned a few things in Docent Eldmer's lecture, but far from the whole language.

"I can't understand you."

"I said, I was having an excellent nap. How rude of you to try pushing me from my perch," he grumbled.

"Sorry, but I need to get through the maze. There's someone after me," Aireyal said, peering through one of the holes in the wall. The footsteps had quieted, and the girl was gone from the other side. Though that was only more terrifying.

"Elf children and their games, always chasing through our home for play," said another hard stony voice. A lady's. Aireyal spun to see the stone goblin guarding the right passage had awakened, staring her down with bright aquamarine eyes.

"I'm not an elf, and this is no game. I'm in grave danger, please let me through," Aireyal pleaded, only to have the third goblin before her, which guarded no passage, come to life, blinking open yellow eyes.

"You look funny," he said to Aireyal in the squeaky voice of a child. *Is this goblin a baby?* They all resembled old stone people. Their craggy skin emphasized by big bulbous noses and flat rocky teeth.

"And he woke me from my peaceful nap," the first barked, pointing at Aireyal.

"I'm a she," Aireyal corrected.

"All elves look the same to me," he said.

"I told you I'm not an elf," she said, giving a soft stomp to the ground. "I'm human. And all you goblins look the same to me."

"Goblins? We are grimstone gnomes, thank you very much," huffed the child.

"Everyone at the school thinks you're goblins. You should correct them."

"Shall we correct all the other things elves have wrong too?" grumbled the first gnome.

"Don't mind that one. He doesn't get good sleep anyway," said the lady gnome, frowning at the first.

"You lie," said the first, glowering back at the second.

A branch snapping in the far too close distance sent Aireyal's blood to ice.

"Can I please get by one of you?" she pleaded to the left and right gnomes who still stood atop their perches, blocking the paths.

"Which way do you want to go?" asked the third, childish gnome.

"I don't care," Aireyal said.

"You should," he squeaked back.

"Why?"

"Because one way will bring you doom, while the other goes to the end of the maze."

"Which one is which?"

"I can't tell you," he squeaked.

"Why not?" Aireyal asked, huffing out a frustrated breath.

"Because I don't know," the child said. "Only they do," he pointed to the other two gnomes.

Another branch snapped somewhere, even *closer* this time.

"Please. Which way leads me out of this cursed maze?" Aireyal asked, turning back and forth between the first and second gnomes.

"This way!" exclaimed the first, his magenta eyes blinking, the hint of a grin creeping on his face. He stepped down off his pedestal and motioned for Aireyal to hop over it and go down his path.

"Thank y—" Aireyal started, then the second gnome shouted out.

"Don't listen to him, he only tells lies! I am always honest and true."

"I've never told a tale in my life," grunted the first. "I say you're the liar."

Aireyal turned back and forth between the two, then she looked to the third.

"Which of them is the liar?"

The third gnome scanned the others with his big yellow eyes for seconds that felt like days. He gave a long screeching scratch of his stony chin then turned back to her.

"I can't seem to remember."

Ugh. She didn't have time for this. Aireyal looked at the second gnome, then pointed at the first.

"He told me his path led out of the maze because he's not a liar, didn't he?" Aireyal asked.

"No?" the gnome answered, rubbing her head.

Another snap. Aireyal looked down the path behind her. *The girl with the brooch.* She was walking Aireyal's way.

Without another thought, Aireyal ran down the first gnome's path.

"Wait, that's the wrong way!" cried the second gnome, but Aireyal didn't care.

She just ran. Right, left, left. Thankfully, no more gnomes were blocking her path at the intersections. She ran and ran, listening for footsteps behind her. Right, left, right, left. At some point, the girl seemed to have followed another way. *Unless those were someone else's footsteps.*

Zale might've still been in the maze somewhere and she needed to find him before the girl caught up to one of them. Left, right, right. A dead end. No. A door? It was built into the maze out of the same rock as the walls.

On either side of it stood two more gnomes. Both already awake. The one on the right had black eyes that twinkled like the night's sky. The one on the left had pearly white eyes that swirled like a cloud.

"Oh drat, it came this way," said the one on the left, watching Aireyal as she approached. A high-pitched male voice, like waterdrops splashing on marble. "Whatever you do, don't open the door," he said to Aireyal.

"But it's the only way forward," she pointed out.

"Don't open the door!" he screamed.

"Open it! Don't listen to him!" the other shouted louder. A girl's voice, thick but smooth, like mud.

"Please keep your voices down," Aireyal whispered.

"Why?!" they asked, *loudly*, in unison.

"There's someone here, she might kill me if she finds me."

"A good thing too, if you planned to open this door," said the left gnome.

Aireyal scowled at him. "What happens if I open the door?"

"Good things," said the one on the right.

"Horrible things, death to us all," said the one on the left.

Ugh. Why couldn't anything in this maze be simple? How could anyone ever make it through? Had the girl with the brooch already been this way?

"Did either of you see a girl?" Aireyal asked.

"What's a girl?" asked the one on the right.

"A bunny, you simplestone," said the one on the left.

"No, a girl is someone like me," Aireyal corrected.

"Oh, then yes," said the right one.

"You have seen one? When?" Aireyal asked.

"Right now. You're standing right in front of me."

Aireyal resisted the urge to stomp her foot. "That's not what I—"

A twig snapped.

"Someone's there," the left gnome said, pointing behind Aireyal, "That could be who you're looking for."

Aireyal turned to see the girl with the brooch fast approaching mere yards away. Aireyal spun back to the door and barreled forward.

Boom!

Aireyal flew in the air and pieces of rocky debris scraped her shoulder. She thudded face-first on the ground and got a taste of rock, tumbling forward. She groaned, rose from the ground, and looked at the path behind her. *What sent me flying?*

There were no answers. Just a blasted, broken door. And no sign of the girl. *For now.*

The end of the maze must be close. She didn't know if that was actually true, but the thought made her feel better, so she went with it as she lumbered ahead. Right, left, left. Another dead end, but this time, there was no right or left path. And there was no door. Instead, a single gnome blocked the end of the path.

Behind it, she could see Darr-Kamo's torches in the distance, past the lawn separating the maze from the school. This *was* it. All she had to do was get past and she was free.

"You there," said the gnome. Her voice came out like gravel as she watched Aireyal approach with shimmering grey eyes of sorrow and a great frown. Her chin rested on the palm of her hand as though in deep thought. "Tell me you aren't as stupid as you look."

What a way to greet someone. "I didn't realize I looked stupid."

"You do," the gnome confirmed as though she was doing Aireyal a great service. "You're welcome. You know, not everyone would be kind enough to tell you."

"Thanks?"

"You're supposed to say thanks before I say you're welcome, stupid," the gnome said, shaking her head.

"Clearly you don't like me much. Would you mind moving so I could get by?"

"No. I'm comfortable," the gnome said.

Crunch. Another twig snapped on the ground. Aireyal spun, expecting to see the girl right behind her, but there was no one there, *for now.*

"There must be something I can do to convince you to move," Aireyal said, turning back to the gnome in desperation.

"Not unless you can help me with this riddle. The other gnomes think I'm stupid like you because I can't figure it out."

"What's the riddle?" Aireyal asked, ignoring the, *stupid like you*, remark.

"A ship that continues to sail on both good day and ill. When built well, it weathers the worst storms with a duo's goodwill," the gnome said with a hopeless sigh. "It makes no sense. Any boat big enough to sail through terrible storms needs more than two crew members. You don't have to sail the seas to know that."

Crunch. A dead leaf broke under someone's foot. Aireyal turned around to see nothing again. But the girl with the brooch was close, she could feel it. *Focus.* Aireyal spun back to face the gnome. *Figure out the riddle, think of ships.* She took a deep breath. Galleons, galleys—

Crunch. The girl was getting closer. *Stop thinking about that.* Ships. Sloop? Brigantine? The gnome was right, there weren't any ships that… wait. It was so obvious.

"A friendship."

Crunch. She was here. Aireyal turned to see the brooch shimmering under the moon's light. As was the knife in the girl's hand. "That sounds right, maybe you aren't as stupid as you look. Go on through," the gnome said, not even acknowledging the girl with the brooch as Aireyal spun back to see the gnome hopping down off its stone perch.

Aireyal charged, jumped over the rocky slab, and ran out the maze. The school's doors invited her across the lawn. The torches beside them a guiding beacon to her. She looked back at the maze. The girl with the brooch had already emerged, and she was gaining on Aireyal. But she wouldn't catch up in time. Aireyal turned back. She ran up the steps to the school, then yanked at the door handle.

Locked.

Aireyal banged on the door, but it was no use. No one was around. She spun again to see the girl with the brooch standing right behind her, knife in hand. There was nowhere to go.

"Where'd you hide it, Aireyal?" her cold voice asked.

She knows my name? Something in her voice was familiar, but hard to place, like she was trying to sound like someone else.

"Hide what?"

"The egg. Where is it?" the girl demanded. Her free hand, gloved in blue, reached into her cloak and pulled out none other than the Frostfire Mirror. *How did she get that? Who is she?* The girl pointed her knife at Aireyal.

"I don't know where it's a—"

The knife flew in a blur, stopping inches from Aireyal's neck as the blade's steel flashed under the torches' light. "Don't pretend you don't know. I'm not going to let them steal from it."

"Steal? I don't know what you're talking about," Aireyal said.

"I've heard enough lies." The girl cut Aireyal across the cheek. The pain stung worse than anything she had ever known and Aireyal let out a scream to match it. Her skin was peeling off inch by inch. The knife wasn't normal metal. Warm blood slid down Aireyal's face. "The next lie will be the last."

Aireyal needed to move. Needed to run. Needed to do something. But her body was frozen stiff. *Don't panic! Breathe!* she told herself, but it was useless. She either couldn't or wouldn't move.

"Igno!" A bolt of fire came from one of the torches behind her and burned the girl's hood. She screamed, dropping the mirror in the grass so she could pat away the flames. Aireyal caught a glimpse of her impeccable fair skin, but the girl covered her face with one hand and reached into her cloak.

"Noxa!" the girl shouted, and shadows enveloped her. A moment later, she was gone, and the mirror was all that remained.

"Aireyal!" a voice yelled. Zale. He ran over, clenching tight to a fistful of red dust. *He was the one that ignited the flames.* Zale sprinted so fast that he nearly toppled into her. "I heard you in the maze, but I got stuck and lost and everything else in there. Someone was smart enough to blow part of the maze up, though." *Me?* "I'm so glad I made it before..." he panted, reaching to hug her, then he stopped himself halfway. "Sorry," he said, his face red. *Probably from running so far.*

"Don't be. I'm fairly sure I'd be dead right now if not for you," Aireyal said, and he smiled his perfect smile at her. Then she realized she was panting herself. And her heart was pumping, but whether it was from almost being stabbed to death, or something else, she wasn't sure.

She did like the thought of being in his arms right now.

Zale's smile faded. "Your cheek."

Oh no. Aireyal could feel the blood oozing out. "I must look horrible." She turned away.

"Not a chance," he said, and she looked back at him. They held each other's gaze for a moment before Aireyal glanced away once again. "I promise I'll fix whatever she did to you." Hearing that felt good, as did knowing that he too saw the girl with the brooch this time. "Seems like you've made quite the enemy here."

Aireyal's gaze flicked over to the mirror lying in the grass. "I'm not sure that girl has to be our enemy."

~ *Chapter 23* ~
Crescent Crusader

"HE'S OUR ENEMY, EREVAN," NYA SAID, STARING down the armored knight before them. A milk-white bone helmet with two protruding horns covered the knight's face. Holes on the helmet's front that were undoubtedly meant for eyes, instead were filled with barely visible trails of white smoke rising in their place and fading into the air right above the helmet.

The mist surrounded the three of them, though it was much thinner than before, and there was something oddly familiar about the knight's figure.

Erevan's head swirled with questions. Questions he wanted answered, *now*. But the snow-white sword drawn in his face required his full attention. He stood with his own blade at the ready, between Nya and the mysterious warrior lit by the crescent moon which speckled through the mist, while the dark outlines of the valley they stood in were faint beyond it.

"Hand it here, and my mercy will spare the life of your servant boy," the knight said, in a flowery, rapid-speaking accent, resonating hollowly from his helmet.

"I'm not a servant," Erevan said, tightening the grip on his sword. The knight was clad completely in white, from his armor to the bags tied loosely around his belt. Dust, probably.

"You're young for a royal guard," the knight said.

"Nya, would you mind telling me what's going on?"

"Nya?" the knight repeated. "Krisosollo whosayule," he said to her in what must've been elvish.

"Aoi i prudi needo nolar iyno," she said back, standing several yards behind Erevan. The knight gave a hollow chuckle.

"What are you two saying?"

"Are you so uncultured that you cannot speak the language of your kin? Too many centuries toiling with humans on this forsaken rock," the knight said.

"What are you talking about?" Erevan asked. "Nya w—" the knight's blade was at Erevan's neck in a flash. Erevan hopped back and raised his sword.

"If nothing else, call the princess by her true name," the knight said.

Princess. True name. How many lies had Nya told him? Erevan wanted to turn and ask her a thousand questions, but he wasn't going to take his eye off the knight for a second. Erevan studied the knight carefully, then realization hit him. The bags of dust he carried. Erevan had seen them before. *They're the same ones as the elf from the Numino Forest. The one that Fern healed. Maybe the mist carried no monster within. It might've been him all along.*

"He doesn't know my name," Nya said to the knight.

"Then allow me to inform him. Servant boy, get on your knees and bow before Princess Niysidialana."

"I told you, I'm not a servant," Erevan said, clenching hard on his sword again. The knight stepped back and took on a flawless stance, prepared to pounce in an instant.

"Prove it," he said, and lunged forward.

"Wait!" Nya shouted. The knight stopped at once. "Don't hurt him, we can make a deal."

"Riynebu," he said in his flowery accent.

"Aoi mira faliyno, sala aoi so crusozo," she answered, but her voice lacked its typical confident tone. Was she worried? Afraid? He needed to know what they were saying.

"Can you two at least speak in common tongue?"

"Hali," the knight said to Nya, not so much as glancing Erevan's way.

"What are you talking about?!" Erevan asked, much louder this time.

"We're discussing the terms of a deal," Nya said.

"What terms? A deal for what? The mirror? The dragon?"

"So, the child is here as well," the knight said in his slithering echo of a voice. *I shouldn't have said that.*

"Erevan, let me do the talking," Nya hissed in his ear.

"Maybe I would, if you'd explain what's going on instead of speaking a different language."

"Listen. What you see before us is one of the so-called crescent crusaders or white spectres, as the dwarves say. He's here for the mirror, and for information. Information he thinks he can force out of me."

"I won't let him."

"You are but a leaf before a whirlwind. You lack the roots to stop me," the spectre said, then dashed at alarming speed to Erevan.

He barely saw the spectre's gleaming blade slice through the air. Instinct saved him. A swift block stopped the sword inches from Erevan's neck. He hopped back a step to disengage.

"Nya, you should get out of here."

"And go where, Erevan?"

He took a quick glance around. She had a point, there was nothing but rocky hills around them. And he didn't get a chance to answer her anyway. Instinct again. Erevan sidestepped a blow before he could think. Most of it. He'd been nicked in the gut. Erevan returned it with a strike of his own. *Sidestepped?* He'd hardly seen the knight move. That wasn't a good sign.

"You don't have to do this alone. Get me his dust pouch," Nya said. The spectre's pouch was only held to his waistbelt by a string. Stealing it was possible. But the spectre was so qui—

Erevan's head ducked without a thought, dodging another strike. Maybe his father's endless training was more useful than he knew.

Erevan fought the urge to check the tunnel next to them. His father was still down ther—

Another strike. This time he was nicked on the top of his shoulder. *I can't get distracted.* A flurry of strikes came next. Erevan narrowly deflected or dodged all the strikes. Or... *almost* all the strikes. The sword was only one weapon. "Ventu!" the spectre said, stepping back.

Erevan hadn't even seen him reach for the dust, but a sharp, singing, gust of wind, cut him in a dozen places. Arms, legs, chest.

Then an armored elbow met his gut. Erevan fell to his knees. He grabbed at the knight, but a foot followed to his back, sending him crashing to the ground.

The taste of crumbling dirt filled his mouth, mixing with the blood forming on his tongue. It was worth it though. Erevan smiled. His hand squeezed on his sword's grip. But even tighter with his other hand, which now held a white bag of dust.

"Catch!" he said, tossing it back to Nya.

She snagged it, and confidence returned to her voice. "Now it's my turn," she said, opening it.

Erevan hated to admit it, but he needed her help. He'd never faced anyone or anything like the spectre before. *Our advantage is two on one. If we don't use it, we'll die.*

"Oh no, this dust is blue," Nya said, fumbling with the pouch.

"Is that bad?"

"A little. It means all I can do is keep it a fair swordfight," she said, pouring some into her hand.

"Do not challenge me in a show of sorcery, *girl*," the spectre warned.

"I'm the greatest sorcerer that's ever lived. It won't be a challenge."

The spectre's hand moved like lightning, grabbing dust from his pouch and throwing it at Nya. "Ventu!"

She tossed blue dust at the gale of wind. "Countru!"

The wind settled and shimmering flecks of blue scattered in the air. Both Nya and the spectre reached for their pouches again.

This was Erevan's chance, while the spectre was distracted. He sliced straight across the spectre's chest. Blood spilled everywhere.

The spectre reached for his smallest bag of dust, but he staggered and fell back into the mist before he could do anything else.

"You did it," Nya said.

"We did it," Erevan corrected, turning to her.

Nya smirked. "You're going to have to start paying me for keeping you alive," she said, chuckling out a sigh of relief. Erevan laughed too. Then stopped. The spectre's silhouette appeared in the mist, moving toward them.

"Don't. You've lost. You'll kill yourself shifting around with that much blood loss," Erevan warned. But as the spectre emerged, his skin was undamaged as though he'd never been cut. "That's impossible."

"All things are possible through the divine," the spectre said, brushing dirt off his armor.

Erevan readied his stance. "You sound sure for someone who should be dead." He charged forward. If he had to kill the spectre twice, he would.

Suddenly, the mist thickened, and the spectre faded into it, though not enough for Erevan to completely lose sight of him. They clashed swords, but the spectre reached for his dust. He threw it at the ground.

"Terru!"

The ground shifted and Erevan sunk into it as though it were loose sand, then it encased his ankles. He couldn't move. The knight sliced at his knee.

"I've got you," Nya called from right behind Erevan. Her hand clasped tightly onto his, then dust flew out. "Countru!" The grip on Erevan's boots was released just in time for him to leap out of the way of the spectre's swing. "I'd almost lost you in here," Nya said as the mist swirled.

"Stay close, I need you," Erevan said, squeezing her hand, then he let it go to start his own assault at the knight. But every swing he sent the spectre's way was blocked. *I can't hit him.*

The spectre was at least as skilled a swordsman as his father. How was he supposed to win if he couldn't land a blow? Fighting on instinct wasn't going to work. He needed a plan. But he didn't have time, the spectre's blade was closing in again.

The spectre swung unusually wildly, and Erevan dodged it with ease. *That was sloppy of him.* The spectre's other hand came through the mist in a fist full of blood. No, not blood. Red dust.

"Ventu!" A punch at the speed of a storm crashed into Erevan's face. *Crack.* Searing pain flowed into his jaw. "Ventu!" Another blast of wind, sharp as blades. This time to the stomach, sending Erevan to the ground. Bloody dirt filled his mouth for the second time. But his gut was worse. He had to hold both hands over his stomach to stop the bleeding.

It was obvious what the spectre was doing. Closing the distance with his spells, hitting Erevan before Nya could counter him.

Erevan tried to rise off the ground, but a foot to the back kicked him back down. The spectre's sword came down next. Cold steel on the back of Erevan's neck like sharpened ice. He considered trying to roll out the way, but it was risky. If the spectre reacted quicker than him, he was *dead.* There would be no second chances. Erevan caught a glimpse of Nya's face and wished he didn't. Her eyes were wide in horror, then fury took over them.

"Get off him," she said, her dagger at the ready.

"Alrio," the spectre said to her, and his blade pressed deeper into Erevan's skin.

"No!" she yelled, putting her dagger away and grabbing the pack off her back. "Don't hurt him, please," she pleaded, opening her bag.

I can't sit here and do nothing, Erevan thought. Something rumbled inside him or perhaps beneath him. But he couldn't move. Couldn't fight. He was useless. No. He still had his mind. *Think.*

Nya stepped back and pulled the Frostfire Mirror out her bag with one hand and Ashe out with the other. The dragon was miraculously still half-asleep.

"Aoi mira trastulele bugazo," the spectre said to Nya.

"Let him go first," she ordered.

"This isn't a negotiation. I'm giving you a command. Follow it before I lose my patience and sever his neck."

Erevan's eyes scanned the ground around him. *Is there anything I can use? Anything I c—*

Another rumble. Right next to him. Something or someone was pushing at the boulders blocking the underground passage near his foot. It could be his father. *Or a giant spider.*

"Even if I die, I'm not giving you what you want," Nya said, then she gave a long look to Ashe, before dropping the little dragon into the mirror.

"Krishnak!" the spectre snarled, then he rose his blade above Erevan's head, preparing to swing down.

It's worth the risk. With all the strength he had left, Erevan pushed against the rocks over the tunnel with both feet. Something else pushed it from below and a moment later, his father emerged with a grunt, spider webs covering him from head to toe.

Shling. Sir Lee parried the incoming strike from the spectre. Then he took a step forward, attacking, and the spectre mirrored him with a defensive parry. They traded several more times, each clash ending equally. As they did, the mist thinned.

Faultless footsteps made their swordsmanship appear more art than war. Black blade against white. It might've been mistaken for a dance if not for the men's eyes. Focused and fierce.

"They've done well choosing you to protect her," the spectre said.

Erevan tried to rise, but blood spilled from his stomach and his vision went dizzy. *Bad idea.* He laid back down, watching Nya pull her dagger out once again.

"Stay back," Sir Lee ordered her. "If you get too close, I can't protect you."

"I thought you said you wouldn't die for me," she said.

"I don't plan on dying anytime soon," he said, readying his sword stance.

The spectre readied his own. "It is a wicked thing indeed that you fight against the divine's purpose. The crusade could have used a man of your skill."

"I'd never join a cause that attacks children," Sir Lee spat.

"You misunderstand. The crusade fights to end violence, not let it endure."

Sir Lee stood unmoved by the words and the spectre shrugged.

"They fought well," the spectre continued, waving a hand at Erevan and Nya. "But all who stand against the empire shall fall like crumbled stone on the mountain. You are no exception," he said to Sir Lee, then he reached into his pouch of dust.

The spectre sprang forward. But Sir Lee was ready. Another equally matched exchange until...

"Ventu!" The spectre landed a punch of wind against Sir Lee's shoulder, knocking him off balance. Then a vicious sword strike against Sir Lee's leg, bringing him to one knee. "Vent—" the spectre tried to say, but Sir Lee reached up and blocked the man's mouth with his hand. The spectre sliced down with his sword for a killing blow anyway. A mistake.

Sir Lee stabbed up, straight and true at the spectre's heart. A perfect thrust. Then he pulled his sword out and prepared another strike for the head. But before he could swing, the spectre dropped to the ground, pouring dust in his hand.

"Luxa!" the spectre shouted hoarsely. Blinding light filled Erevan's vision and he squeezed his eyes shut. Dangerous seconds passed. When the light wore off, he opened his eyes to his father walking to him.

"We need to get that wound of yours bandaged," Sir Lee said, pulling cloth from his web-coated traveling bag.

"But the spec—"

"Probably bleeding out, same as you," his father said, waving Erevan off.

"You don't understand, I cut him clean across the chest before and he got up unharmed."

"It doesn't matter for now. He's gone."

Footsteps came from behind them and Erevan turned, reaching for his sword. But it was Nya.

"Roll Erevan over for me," Sir Lee said to her.

"Is that really the best idea?" Nya asked.

"It'll be fine, I'm sure," Sir Lee dismissed with another wave.

"Every time you say that, something bad happens," Nya said.

"Nonsense." He motioned again for her to roll Erevan over.

Nya held softly to Erevan's sides. "Ready?" she asked him.

"No."

She turned him anyway.

"AGHH!" It was as though he'd been sliced again. But his father was already wrapping him up to slow the bleeding.

"He'll make it, right?" Nya asked.

"It's bloody, but not as bad as it looks. If we keep him patched up, he'll be fine," Sir Lee said. "C'mon son, up we go." He brought Erevan's arm over his shoulder and stood him up, letting Erevan lean on him for support. But his father's knee buckled under him—a lasting remnant of the blow from the spectre. But that wasn't all. There were vicious spider bites across his father's leg too.

"It seems this night has taken a toll on all of us," Nya said. Or no… *Princess Niysidialana*. The thought frustrated Erevan more every time it entered his mind. *She lied to me.*

"Do we have everything?" Sir Lee asked, taking a last look around the area.

"I think so," Nya said.

"You've still got the mirror?" Sir Lee asked. She nodded. "And the dragon?" Nya gave him the guiltiest grimace Erevan had ever seen. "He took the dragon?"

Nya shook her head. "I wasn't going to let that happen."

"Where is it now?" Sir Lee asked.

"I sent Ashe back through the mirror."

~ *Chapter 24* ~

Challenging Choices

S CARLET RED EYES PEEKED OUT THE MIRROR AT
Aireyal. "Is that…" Zale trailed off, tilting his head.

"A dragon," Aireyal finished for him. The night-black scales
before her were the same shade as the egg she'd seen in her mother's
study weeks ago. The creature looked up at her, eyes wide in
confusion or… fear, perhaps? It shivered as its eggshell-covered
head darted around, taking in its surroundings on the lawn outside
the doors of Darr-Kamo. Then it let out a cry. "You poor thing,"
Aireyal said, reaching down to pick it up. The dragon cowered,
closing its eyes. But Aireyal's touch gave it enough comfort to nudge
its head against her palm.

"I just saw a dragon crawl out of that mirror," Zale said, staring in disbelief as he studied the dragon alongside Aireyal.

"She's beautiful," Aireyal said, then she looked to Zale. "There's a lot I need to fill you in on. And I need to find my mother." She cradled the dragon up in her arms.

"At this hour?"

Aireyal laughed. "My mother never stops working, she sleeps in her study. Let's go, I'll tell you everything on the way."

"Should we bring this?" Zale asked, reaching for the mirror.

"No, don't touch it, it'l—"

Zale picked it up without issue. No searing pain, no passing out, no scorched hand.

"How did you…" she wasn't sure what to ask. Part of her wanted to reach over and grab the mirror to see if it would still burn her, but she flinched at the memory of the blistering pain. The more she found out, the less she understood. Perhaps her mother could make sense of it all.

Regardless, Aireyal was done with secrets; they weren't worth the stress. As they walked, she told Zale everything she knew. It didn't feel fair not to after all that had just happened. The mirror. The dragon. She told him all she could remember, even her trip to Parliament earlier today, which felt like a lifetime ago. But she also made it clear that these secrets were *not* to be shared unless her mother approved.

Knock. Knock. Aireyal's knuckles tapped against her mother's study as she and Zale discussed the girl with the brooch. "Who do you think she is?" Zale asked.

"I don't know," Aireyal said, listening for her mother. Silence.

"There's one other thing I wanted to ask you about. We never talked about what you told me earlier today."

Aireyal cringed. She hadn't forgotten she'd told him she was magicless, but she had sort of hoped that he would, even though someone had spread the knowledge so the whole school knew. Someone who didn't appear to be Morgana.

"What is it you want to know?" Aireyal asked, a slight tremble rocking her hands.

"I just… if you don't pass the sparks test at the end of the year here at school, they won't let you back," he said. It wasn't a question. But she knew what he meant to ask; he was simply too kind to say it. *You aren't going to be able to pass the test, are you?* He stared at her in pity as though trying to find a way to help her. But there was nothing he could do, and they both knew that.

"I'll figure it out when the time comes," Aireyal said, hoping she sounded more confident than her shaking hands felt. The expression on Zale's face, however, suggested otherwise. "Regardless, I have to choose to do what I believe in," she said, knocking again on her mother's door, eager for a reason to discuss something else.

"Even if that means people are going to make it hard on you?"

"No change worth fighting for comes easy, that's what Ilizabeth Kamo said."

Zale smiled at her. "I love it when you talk like that," he said, and she blushed.

Suddenly, the door opened. Aireyal's mother's eyes popped the moment she saw her.

"Aireyal? Why are you here at this hour o—"

Grr.

Her mother's eyes flicked down to see the dragon in Aireyal's arms growling. "Is that—"

"A dragon," Aireyal said, turning slightly, hoping her mother didn't notice her red cheeks.

"And Mirvana's mirror," her mother said, looking at Zale. "Where'd you get that?" She glanced between the two of them, then she leaned forward to Aireyal. "What happened to your face?"

"The girl with the brooch. And she's the one that had the mirror," Aireyal said, and her mother's face paled. "Who is she?"

"If I knew, I couldn't tell you."

"Does that mean you know?" Aireyal asked, letting out a frustrated sigh.

"It means exactly what I said," her mother replied. "If there were something you could help with, I'd let you know."

Would you? I had to sneak into the Crypt of Infamy for answers before you let me help you with the mirror at all. But saying that aloud would be pointless; her mother always thought she knew best. "How did that girl end up with the headmistress's mirror?" Aireyal asked instead. *I'll have to find out the girl with the brooch's identity on my own.*

"That is what I need to figure out," her mother said, tapping a finger to her lips. "Mirvana's been keeping that mirror in her office which is heavily warded. I should know, I've placed some of them myself. And we're the only two who know how to get…" her mother trailed off.

"How to get what? Inside?" Aireyal asked, but her mother didn't answer. Instead her face remained focused on whatever she was contemplating. Then she shook her head and looked up at Aireyal and Zale.

"Come inside, quickly. And shut the door," Aireyal's mother said to them. They did as asked, while her mother rolled up a series of maps and official-looking documents spread incoherently across her table. *Iglio mata ugi magi oto Nyumbafro…* was all Aireyal could read on one, before her mother packed it away. *Magic items of Nyumbafro,* Aireyal was sure that's part of what it said, though a couple of words she was still shaky on. Her Sylvan was improving thanks to her lectures with Docent Eldmer, but it was far from perfect.

"What are those for?" Aireyal asked, pointing to the papers her mother stashed away.

"Nothing too important," her mother said before turning her eyes to Zale. "You can put the mirror down here," she said, pointing to the table, and it might've been Aireyal's imagination, but she thought she saw her mother's eyes narrow slightly. *She doesn't like him.*

Zale hurried to the table and placed down the mirror. "Apologies, Grandmage Ando. I—"

"It appears the mirror has no effect on you. Interesting," Aireyal's mother said, drumming her fingers together.

Zale gave a dumbfounded shrug. "Maybe it's not dangerous anymore," he said.

"Headmistress Markado and I will be the judge of that when I bring her the mirror tomorrow," Grandmage Ando said to him. "What you've seen today is not to be shared with anyone, is that clear?" Her tone was dangerous, threatening even. *She hates him.*

"I won't say a word," Zale said, nodding to the dragon. "I'd never do anything that would hurt Aireyal *or* get her in trouble."

"Is that so?" the Grandmage asked, watching Zale like a hawk. He stood perfectly still as though hoping to go invisible. Aireyal knew the feeling well, though it was never her mother making her feel that way.

Grr. Aireyal breathed a sigh of relief as the dragon stole her mother's attention. She moved over to Aireyal to inspect the baby and big red eyes blinked back.

"She's so cute, I think I'll call her Scarlet," Aireyal said, scratching behind the dragon's ear. Scarlet gave a purr in response.

"Don't get too attached," her mother said.

"What's that supposed to mean?" Aireyal asked.

"That it's our duty as citizens of Lanasall to either end her life or send her to someone who will."

Aireyal gasped. "But she's just a baby," she said. Scarlet's eye's twinkled, frightened, like she knew what they were talking about. *That can't be right.* The dragon had only been an egg when school started a month ago. *Unless time moves differently inside the mirror.*

"Most dragons grew up and became rampaging beasts. Some were rather peaceful, but many of them burned down entire towns unprovoked," her mother said. "Or so the stories go. Of course, even the oldest elves haven't seen a dragon egg since they were young." Aireyal's mother tapped a thoughtful finger to her lip, watching the dragon. "This one's egg was given to me to see if I could identify its origin. But before I got the chance to try, a certain clumsy girl knocked it into the Frostfire Mirror."

"Sorry."

Her mother smiled. "Don't worry, you've saved the dragon's life, for now."

"But she'll die if we keep her here."

Her mother nodded. "Probably. It is the law for a reason. Dragons are capable of terrible destruction."

"But you said yourself not all of them are like that."

"I did."

"So, you're saying we should kill a baby even though she might not be dangerous?"

"She *will* be dangerous. Whether or not she'll be violent is the question."

"But what if she's peaceful? It wouldn't be right to kill her now. She hasn't done anything."

"I'm not the one you need to convince," her mother said, raising a hand.

"Then I'll convince Parliament or the Senate or whoever I need to," Aireyal said, giving a soft, determined stomp to the floor. Her mother laughed and patted her on the head like she was a small child.

"Oh, Aireyal, I don't think they'll change the law on the word of one girl."

Aireyal thought back to her time at Parliament. Her mother had a point. "Then what am I supposed to do?"

Her mother looked to Zale. "Thank you for escorting Aireyal here, but I think it's best for you to head back to the boy's dormitorium before you're caught out after curfew," she said, ushering him out the door before he could respond.

"I'll see you later," Aireyal tried to say to him, but the door was already shut. She turned to her mother and frowned. "Why'd you do that?"

The lady tapped a quieting finger to her mouth then pulled Aireyal to the other side of the room. "The mirror on that table will send the dragon back without anyone ever knowing except the two of us. The second option, is bringing it to the townguards, where they'll no doubt execute it."

"Are you saying I should break the law?"

"I'm saying, I'm going to let you make your own decision."

Aireyal couldn't let a baby be executed. It wasn't right, no matter what the future held. But Scarlet had looked so scared coming through the mirror. Whatever was on the other side had to be dangerous. If she chose to crawl away, it was because she was in peril.

"There is a third option," her mother said, moving over to examine Scarlet. "Aireyal, do you know why all these wonderous magical creatures are dead?"

"Because of the law," Aireyal answered, but her mother shook her head.

"Killing a dragon gives its slayer magical power."

Aireyal hesitated. "That's just folklor—"

"It's true. People don't believe it because they haven't seen it. It hasn't happened in many hundreds of years, but it is true all the same." There wasn't a shred of doubt in her mother's voice. The girl with the brooch suggested someone wanted to steal from the dragon. Was this what she meant?

"Why are you telling me this?" Aireyal asked.

"This is your chance to do magic like you've always wanted," her mother said, smiling.

Vomit slithered up Aireyal's throat. "By murdering a baby? I can't do that," she said, taking a step back.

"Aireyal, what you can't do is pass this up," her mother said.

"It's a living, breathing creature."

"That's going to die soon anyway, you may as well get something from it."

Aireyal's mouth dropped. Who was this lady standing before her? This couldn't be her mother; she wasn't like this. *Was she?* "How can you be so heartless?"

"I'm doing this for you, don't you understand? Sometimes sacrifices must be made. It will be quick and painles—"

"I won't do it!" Aireyal shouted so loud, she flinched. Disappointment consumed her mother's eyes. Silence. A long silence. "I have been trying to learn magic my entire life. I studied every single page of every book you have ever given me. Reading them over and over until they burned into my memory. And I remember each lesson you've given me since I was a little girl. I won't cheat now, especially not at the cost of a life. I will earn my magic."

"I'm not sure that's possible."

Aireyal's heart broke in two. Her throat dried and tears welled in her eyes, but she fought them back as best she could. Those weren't the words the mother she knew would speak. It sounded like something Headmistress Markado would say.

"Maybe it's time I found a new teacher," Aireyal said, and her mother's face twisted in what might have been a look of betrayal. Aireyal didn't care. She turned from her mother's room and stormed out.

"Good morning." Aireyal awoke the next day in her room to Morgana's perfect face, lit by candlelight. The sun had yet to rise. *How can anyone wake up and look like that?* "Let's have some fun,"

Morgana said, but the grin on her face terrified Aireyal. *What have I gotten myself into?*

"What are we doing?" Aireyal asked, sitting up in bed, as Morgana pulled something from her pocket.

"Magic," she said, showing off a pouch of what must've been fey dust.

"Where are you getting all this dust?"

"My mother's office. Don't worry, she will never know," Morgana said, pouring a mountain of green dust into her hand. *Her mother's office.* The same place the girl with the brooch stole the mirror from. Aireyal's skin crawled. Did that mean… no. *Morgana wouldn't have put a knife to my face… probably.* "Ready to learn?" Morgana asked, grinning, and she didn't give Aireyal a chance to say no. Morgana tossed dust into the air. "Fides," she said, and the dust dissolved.

A rush hit Aireyal, something warm and powerful. She raised her chin and stopped slouching her shoulders, not by choice really, it was like she'd been commanded. "I know that spell, it gives confidence," Aireyal said, surprising herself with how certain her voice sounded. "Thank you."

Morgana waved Aireyal's appreciation off. "The spell should last for a few hours, which is more than enough time for what we need," Morgana said. "Your turn now." She handed the bag to Aireyal.

"You want me to cast something on you?"

Morgana nodded. "I think the reason you haven't been able to do magic is a lack of faith in yourself. There should be nothing holding you back now."

Aireyal took a deep breath. *I can, and I will do this. Right now.* Aireyal grabbed a handful of dust and sprinkled it into the air.

"Felix," she said. She could picture the spell clearer than ever in her head. Happiness. Morgana smiling big and wide... but it wasn't real.

In reality, Morgana frowned at her expectantly, then peered down. Aireyal's eyes followed hers to find all the dust. Not dissolved at all. Instead, it had fallen right down onto the bed. *I failed again.* She felt her very future drop like a boulder off a cliff. There was nothing to feel, except for defeat. But the mix of forced confidence within her gave a gross feeling of division. She still believed she could do it, even though she now knew she couldn't.

It was depressingly confident delusion. Or perhaps that wasn't an emotion from the dust at all. Maybe that was her own denial kicking in. Regardless, it stung worse than it ever had before, because this time she knew there was only one reason she failed. *I can't do magic.* Slowly, she looked up at Morgana, fighting the wave of untampered emotions swelling inside.

"Why didn't it work?" Morgana asked, her brows creasing together.

"Because I'm magicless."

"You cannot be. Your mother is a Grandmage. It's in your blood," Morgana said, taking a breath before opening her mouth to speak again. She was right. The bloodlines of Grandmages were considered so gifted magically that it was impossible for their children to be magicless. But after hearing what her mother had said last night, Aireyal couldn't help but wonder if everything she knew was a lie.

Did the first humans capable of magic only gain such a power by murdering dragons? Why were almost all elves able to do magic? *The Anima* and other texts focused on gods and faith had their opinions on the matter, but many of them contradicted each other.

The only way Aireyal could know anything for sure would be to hear it from someone who'd been there. *Someone ancient.* But did anyone like that even exist?

Was that even something worth worrying about? She needed to learn how to do magic. There had only been one person ever recorded as being magicless who eventually learned magic after the age of sixteen and that w—

"Aireyal, are you even listening to me?"

"Huh? Oh, sorry," Aireyal said. She didn't have time to worry about any of that other stuff now, she needed to focus.

"You *can* do this," Morgana assured.

"It doesn't feel like it," Aireyal said, smiling confidently. She despised the false feelings within; they were a betrayal of her true self.

They sat there silently for who knows how long; the crimson crickets and early morning birds of the fields outside were the only sounds in the candle-lit darkness.

"There is another way," Morgana finally said in a hushed tone. "A much easier way."

"I've tried everything, trust me."

"Oh, I doubt you have tried this. You are too good-mannered," Morgana said, biting her own thumb. Aireyal didn't like where this was going. "Blood magic."

Aireyal gasped. Blood magic was something she'd expect from the girl with the b—*stop thinking like that. It's not her... probably.* "You shouldn't do that, it's illegal. Where'd you even learn blood magic?"

Morgana scoffed. "Who do you think taught me?" The answer was obvious. *Her mother, the headmistress.* "Blood magic is illegal because the Senate of Mages is afraid. They don't want common folk doing magic without going to one of their precious schools to learn it. It is the same reason it is illegal to sell dust without attending one of these schools. It is all about power, Aireyal."

"It's illegal because mixing dust into your bloodstream makes you addicted. Those laws are in place for the people's protection. Without it, pirates would transport dust everywhere. I've read all about it."

Morgana sneered. "Who do you think approves the distribution of those books?" Morgana asked. Aireyal frowned. "Aoi winne prudi fali, i aoi prinowalio." *What do you know that you have not been taught?* Zale had said the same thing to her a few weeks back. "If you want to do magic as bad as you say, th—"

"I'm not doing blood magic," Aireyal said with such finality that she wondered if it was her speaking at all. She wished people would stop suggesting these kinds of shortcuts. "I'll figure magic out without cheating."

Morgana nodded. "I won't suggest it again. But do know, all magic is cheating, Aireyal. The sooner you understand that, the sooner you will be able to accept the truth. I hope that helps you."

Aireyal didn't know what she meant by the *truth*. And she wasn't going to ask to find out. Their session ended there.

Aireyal sat in thought while Morgana fiddled around with perfumes and combs at her mirror as though improving her appearance was possible.

Can I afford not taking a shortcut? Aireyal asked herself. Becoming a mage was bigger than her. The visit to Parliament was indication enough of that. The people of Lanasall needed help, even if the wealthy citizens around the school grounds of Darr-Kamo didn't. *Maybe I'm being too prideful, maybe it's worth it.*

Her mind didn't stop pondering those thoughts until after the sun rose. Aireyal skipped breakfast. She told Morgana it was because she didn't want to listen to a crowd of kids tease her about being magicless. Which was true… in part. But she knew why she was at the place she chose to go instead. She needed to talk with a certain someone. And so, she sat patiently outside the apothecary.

Aireyal's heart fluttered when someone headed her way. Then it sank. "Who are you?" she asked more rudely than intended. The little lady blinked several times, clearly aware of Aireyal's tone.

"I'm Casilda, the apothecarist, and you're standing in front of my door." *So, she's a real person after all.* Casilda carried a massive basket of leaves, both big and small in one arm, and a set of keys in the other.

Aireyal moved out of her way. "Sorry, I didn't mean to—" Casilda shot her a perceptive smile, as though she knew some dark secret of Aireyal's, then Casilda brushed a few stray black hairs off her almond skin before unlocking the door.

"I'm guessing you were expecting to see a different face this morning, eh, little chicata?" she asked in a sweet, rhythmic voice, guiding Aireyal into the apothecary's herbal scents.

"Uh…" Aireyal trailed off, feeling her cheeks warming up. She didn't know what *chicata* meant, but she certainly understood the rest of what the lady was saying. Casilda chuckled.

"Don't worry, he'll be along any moment," she said, scurrying to a table and placing down her basket of leaves. "When Zale knocked on my door the day before school started and asked if he could be my assistant, I wasn't sure what to expect. I don't normally accept first years, but he told me he wanted to learn to heal people so he could make the world a better place. Though, I'm sure you already knew that," Casilda said, smiling. "Aireyal, Aireyal, Aireyal. That's all he talks about," she said, smiling as she sorted leaves on the table. "Do you see that over there?" Casilda asked, pointing to another table in the hut. Twenty or so slimy square-shaped blue fruits lay on it. Five of them were diced into tiny pieces.

"What are those?"

"Goobafruits. One of Zale's assignments yesterday. He was supposed to dice them all up, so we could make an elixir for a boy who got sick from a camobug bite." She gave Aireyal another knowing look. "As you can see, they're not all diced." Casilda smiled again, then mimicked the voice of a young man. "Can I take a break? I want to make a bracelet for Aireyal. I promise I'll come back and finish," she said, then laughed. "Haven't seen him since."

"He made a bracelet for me?" Aireyal asked, ignoring everything else. Casilda put a hand over her mouth for a moment.

"I shouldn't speak so much. It's supposed to be a gift for you, little chicata. Probably so he can ask to be your escort to the—" Casilda stopped, using her hand to pinch her lips together. "I am talking *too* much."

Zale was going to ask her to the dance? Aireyal's heart pumped faster and a grin crept onto her face. Then it dropped like a stone. *I don't know how to dance.* She'd make a fool of herself if she went. It was better to stay in her room, surrounded by books. She couldn't trip and embarrass herself reading in bed... actually, she *had* done that befor—

"Aireyal? You're here?"

Aireyal spun. Zale was standing at the door. "Hello."

"Your cheek," he said, nearly stumbling to rush over to her. "I promised I'd fix it," he said, running a finger over her scar. Her whole body melted. "Sorry," he said, retracting his hand.

"I don't mind," she said, probably a little too quickly, because Casilda chuckled again. Maybe the scar wasn't so bad if it meant she got extra attention from his hands.

"I need to grab the rest of my kael and amimo leaves from the garden," Casilda said, picking up her basket. "Running some sana ointment over that scar should be a nice remedy," Casilda said with a nod, then she scurried out. Aireyal's palms started to sweat.

"Right," Zale said, his gorgeous eyes lingering on Aireyal for one more long moment before he ran over to a shelf. He rummaged through several jars before returning with a pink cream-filled one. He scooped some out then pointed to the scar on her face. "May I?" he asked, and she nodded.

Pump, pump. Zale's touch was softer than dough but somehow as firm and steady as the ground beneath her, and his thumb lingered on her cheek long after the cream had been rubbed onto her scar. *Pump, pump.* Not a single part of her wanted him to move away. There was a longing in his eyes like he wanted to lean in closer to her.

Yes, please do.

"Aireyal, I have something for you." *A kiss?* His hand finally slipped from her cheek. He reached in his pocket and pulled out a silver charm bracelet adorned with little baubles. They were in the shape of something. Letters. A-I-R-E-Y-A-L. And in between each letter was another kind of bauble. She squinted. Tiny little books. "I know it's not the best. I wanted to make it from gold, but I couldn't aff—"

"It's perfect," she said, beaming, and his mouth twisted up in the little way she adored.

"You like it?" he asked, and his cheeks flushed a bit.

"I love it," Aireyal said, grinning ear to ear. "And I'll happily wear it every day," she said, offering her wrist to him. Tingles came down her arm when he held onto it. Then Zale slid the bracelet on so slowly that she had to wonder why. *Is he savoring the moment? I hope so.*

"I'm not sure if you heard about it but…" he started, then his whole face went red. *Is he nervous?* "I uh, there's this dance thing I guess and—"

"I want to go with you." The words left her mouth before she could stop them. Perhaps the confidence spell from Morgana was still going.

Something changed in Zale's face. *Relief?* "I was so sure somebody had already asked you and—" he stopped as she let out a snort.

"Why would anybody ask me?"

"Because you're smart, caring, kind, and beautiful."

Aireyal scoffed. "I am not beautiful."

"You are to me." There wasn't even the tiniest bit of doubt in his words. *He meant that.* Then he ran his thumb over her cheek again. Warmth, sunlight, and all the other feelings of heat sped up her heartbeat. Every time she thought it couldn't go any faster, it did. *Pump, pump.*

"Kiss me." Aireyal froze. She hadn't meant to say that out loud. But she *did* want it to happen. And when he started leaning in, she relaxed right into his arms. *Pump! Pump!*

Aireyal stood up on her tiptoes and closed her eyes. Then she leaned into him and. Waited... Aireyal opened her eyes. Zale had leaned away. Oh no. *What did I do wrong?*

"I-I want to, so bad, but..." Zale said, trailing off. Aireyal's eyes flitted around, studying his face. Zale's eyes flicked away, then he stepped back and dropped his head. "I'm so sorry. I never should've... I should go," he said, giving the floor a soft kick.

"Oh, I see..." They stood there for the longest few seconds of Aireyal's life. Then Zale turned and walked away. "I guess I'll see you at the dance," she mumbled, but he either didn't hear her, or decided not to respond.

~ Chapter 25 ~
The Lazy Lizard

EREVAN HADN'T RESPONDED TO MUCH OF ANYTHING that had been said lately. He vaguely remembered stopping for a time at a traveler's lodge to stock up, eat, and have their wounds cleaned, though his father's leg had only grown worse from the spider bites. Erevan tried to recall whether their stop at the lodge had been today, yesterday, or the day before, though he wasn't sure as his mind was focused on something else. But now as they trudged through the stinking fungus-filled bog west of Bogudos for which the city got its name, he knew exactly where they were. And despite the croaking toads and chirping crickets; with every muddy step, one word rang in his mind, *princess*.

"Why didn't you tell me?" he asked. Both Nya and Sir Lee stopped in the swampy trail ahead of him, where the bottom of the sun neared the horizon and turned back.

"Would you look at that, he speaks," Sir Lee said sarcastically. *How long has it been since my last words?*

"Finally alive again, are you?" Nya joked, looking at him with an amused grin.

Erevan didn't return the smile. "Why didn't you tell me?" he asked again. *The king and princess laughed about treating kids like criminals. Kids like my friends. Kids like me.* The thought haunted Erevan endlessly. *Nya was the one laughing.* Whether she had changed since then or not, he didn't know, but it made his blood boil either way.

"Tell you what?" Nya asked, her lip curled up as though she was genuinely lost.

"That you were a princess," he said through gritted teeth. "What else could I be talking about?"

"I don't know, Erevan, you haven't said anything in a week. Honestly, I was starting to think we were being followed by a ghost."

A week?

"There's no way it's been a—whatever. Just answer me."

"If you had known, what would it have changed?" Nya asked. "My mission remains the same. I have to get the mirror back to Nyumbafro."

"Why though? What does Nyumbafro want that mirror for anyway? And why are we giving it up? Couldn't New Lanasall use the mirror?"

"For what?" Nya asked, laughing condescendingly. Or maybe it *seemed* condescending because he knew she was a princess now.

"The same thing you're using it for."

"We're not going to use it for anything," she said. Erevan sneered. Her face looked honest. But she'd also looked honest when she'd lied about being a courier.

"I find that hard to believe."

"Why? What's really bothering you, Erevan?"

"I don't like you people. Never have, never will."

"You people?" she asked. "What's so wrong with being royal?"

"You *all* lie. And you take what isn't yours. And you use people like me to get what you want. Like you're doing right now."

"You know me, and you know I'm not like that."

"Do I? How well do I really know you, Nya... excuse me, Princess Niysidialana," he said, giving an exaggerated bow. She stared long and hard at him, her expression unreadable.

"Ask me anything, Erevan, I'll tell you whatever you want to hear."

"Exactly. You say what people want to hear, not the truth."

"You're being ridiculous," she said, pointing a finger his way. He folded his arms. There were too many strange holes in her story. Why was she being chased by a spectre? Why was the Magistrate of New Lanasall giving away a powerful magical artifact? Why would Nyumbafro send a princess instead of an actual courier? He wished it all made more sense than it did. He hadn't questioned these things before like he should have, because deep down...

I really like her. No. Erevan shook his head. *She's just another wealthy liar, I can't trust her.*

Finding the answers to the questions, though, could prove difficult. He could ask her, but she'd surely lie. *No, she wouldn't. I know Nya.* Did he? *Ask her, she's not a liar.*

"I have a question."

"Let's hear it. I promise I'll tell you the truth."

"Why is it you're the one carrying this mirror back to Nyumbafro? Why did they send a princess?"

"They didn't."

"Then why are you the one delivering it?"

"I... can't tell you."

Erevan gave a hysterical chuckle. "Of course not. There's always another secret with you, isn't there?"

"I told you he'd act like this," Sir Lee said to Nya. *Hold on.* Erevan turned to him.

"You knew?" Rage burned Erevan's veins. *Was everyone a liar?*

"Longer than you? Yes. The princess told me because she was concerned about what you might think of her if you knew," his father said so casually that it made Erevan more furious.

"You're both nothing but liars!" Erevan spat, then he marched off. He ignored their calls of his name and slogged past the slugs and insects on the outskirts of Bogudos. He knew there was one person in town who'd tell the truth about the things he needed to know, and he knew just where to find that person. So, he walked until a battered building puffing out sour smoke from its chimney appeared. *The Lazy Lizard*, Bogudos's seediest tavern. Its wooden sign housed a smirking lizard resting against a tree with a pint of ale in hand.

Despite its reputation, Erevan found it a good place to find work when he'd been desperate for coin in the past. Bogudos had a hefty demand for crooked deeds to be done. Dark memories came back as he strode onto its rickety porch, populated with the same types of rogues, rascals, and ruffians as always.

The townguards, of course, liked to pretend the tavern didn't exist and refused to come anywhere near it. Not that the rest of the city was much better. Most people in Bogudos didn't even bother to lock their doors at night. What was the point when you knew your weekly robber on a first name basis?

Erevan walked into a scene he knew all too well. The scent of cheap, watered-down ale filled the air while his eyes scanned the room. Spacious enough that one wouldn't bump into anyone accidentally while walking around but cramped enough to make one wary of who was eavesdropping on their conversations.

In one corner, several hooded figures whispered amongst themselves at a table, preparing for some illegal act Erevan knew better than to get himself involved with. In another corner, a couple of cloaked men sharpened knives. A third corner was the focus of an intense Wizards, Witches, and Warlocks game.

His gaze shifted to the far wall of the tavern, where his eyes rested on the centerpiece of it all, the bar. High stools sat around the low curved, faintly polished countertop. The bartender, a brawny dwarf. Bumgrim Mountaincoat. His coarse black hair was tied back into a ponytail that no patron had the guts to call delicate. He grinned the moment he saw Erevan and gave a bar-shaking laugh, literally.

"Oi! What I tells ya, the kid's back, now cough up," Bumgrim demanded of a bald man sitting at the bar, who craned back and frowned at Erevan. He grumbled something, took a swig of ale, then reluctantly dug in his pocket and tossed a few coins onto the bar counter. "Come 'ere boy, lemme see ya," the bartender said, slipping the coins into his pocket.

Erevan took a breath, then made his way to the bar. Every eye in the tavern watched as he did so. The bartender motioned to the bald man as Erevan approached, and the man got up from his chair and walked off, taking his cup of ale with him.

"Take a seat, boy."

"I'd rather not."

"I won't ask twice."

Erevan stood for as long as his mind told him was safe to silently rebel, then he begrudgingly sat where the bald man had been. Bumgrim pulled a dirty rag from his pocket and began wiping the countertop. "So, let's 'ear it, why'd ya come back?" the dwarf asked.

"It's my home," Erevan said, resting a swamp-stained sleeve on the freshly wiped counter. The bartender growled in annoyance and Erevan removed his arm in an instant.

"Ya rode down the Raging River all the way to New Longaiya and ya happy comin' back to this rat-infested city?" he asked, cleaning the counter again.

"I'm not afraid of a few rodents."

"I watn't talkin' 'bout that kind of rat," Bumgrim said, nodding to the liars and cheats that filled the room. "Lee don't like ya mixin' in wit' this crowd."

"Do you see him here?"

Bumgrim frowned deeply, scratching his beard. "No, I don't. And that's exactly why I says it. One day ya'll be glad to know ya had someone lookin' out for ya all this time. Not all the kids 'round 'ere do."

"Yeah, sure," Erevan grumbled. "Anyway, I didn't come here to talk about him. I need to know everything you can tell me about spectres." If Erevan didn't know Bumgrim better, he could've sworn the dwarf flinched.

"Spectres are immortal, what else ya need to know?" Bumgrim said, busying himself with cleaning a glass.

"Where are they from?"

"Torva. Or so my people says. It's a land far north of the western world, forever 'idden in storm clouds no ship can pass through."

"Sounds like a sailor's tale," Erevan said. "I thought the dwarven homeland was north of here."

"It is… or was. Before they invaded. They take over everything they see."

Erevan crossed his arms. "So, if I sailed north, I'd find a country of spectres in underground dwarven passages?"

"If ya sailed north now, ya would be headed into pirate territory and never make it fifty miles off coast. The seas have changed since we left."

"Why would pirates still risk sailing that way if the Torvans are as dangerous as you say? Shouldn't they have run into each other by now?"

"Why don't ya ask The Sunken Six?" Bumgrim grumbled sarcastically.

"Who?"

"The pirate captains controlling those waters. Listen, all I knows is those Torvans invaded our homeland. We had two choices, fight and die, or flee. Most of us fought. There were calls to every corner under and overground that dwarves lived. Many raised their axes together to push the Torvans back."

"Did you fight?"

"I brew beer, sonny," Bumgrim said. "I left my foolish kin to get themselves killed if they wished while I sailed south. That's how I came 'pon these lands. And kept my life."

"You don't regret abandoning them?"

Bumgrim scowled. "I didn't abandon them," he spat. "I live for them. If we had all been too prideful to walk away, we dwarves would be no more," Bumgrim continued. "When an army marches to an enemy city in war, do all the peoples in that city stay and die at their hands? Course not, they send scouts out to warns neighboring cities and outposts, and they sneak their lords away to avoid capture. If an enemy has an advantage, hold ya time until ya can strike back."

Erevan frowned thoughtfully. The whole idea sounded cowardly. But it also sounded like something his father would say, and sometimes cowardice and wisdom were easy to mix up.

My father. Nya told him who she really was and not me. Erevan exhaled; he didn't come here to think about that.

"Eh, why am I tellin' ya any of this, ya too young to understand," Bumgrim said, shaking his head at Erevan's sigh.

"I get it. Sometimes the best way to fight, is to not fight at all," Erevan said and Bumgrim stared hard at him as though the words couldn't have come from Erevan. Though understanding an idea and liking it were two different things.

Suddenly, a familiar hand touched his back. "Erevan?" A girl's voice. He turned but knew who the voice belonged to before he did. Selea, his old... friend. She was as pretty as ever, and her eyes were still cat-quick, tracking every subtle movement he made. She used to joke she had a furry tail to go along with her sharp-toothed smile, which always reminded him of a kitten. And that was the exact smile she gave him now.

"I didn't recognize you when you first walked in. Your hair is longer," she said, reaching up and curling a dreaded lock over her finger.

"I was thinking about cutting it."

"You shouldn't, it's cute."

His cheeks went warm. Bumgrim grumbled, walking back to the kitchen, "So that's why ya came back."

"For me?" she asked, her slender eyes lighting up.

"I—uh…" Erevan stammered, scratching his head.

"You're staying then?"

"Maybe," Erevan said. What did he mean, *maybe?* He wasn't still planning on following *that other girl*, was he?

"You're always welcome to join me," Selea said.

"Picking the pockets of merchants?"

"It's a life," she said with a scandalous grin. The fine, blue yarn scarf around her neck contradicted the worn tunic she wore. Surely, the prize of some noble theft. "Besides, I have an interesting job lined up." Two men from the corner rose, brandishing their knives. Erevan grabbed the hilt of his sword, but found relief in seeing them threaten each other, cursing back and forth. "You're jumpy."

"Not as jumpy as Tinny the time he sat on that barrel of muskweasels," Erevan said, chuckling. "Remember when we were all out in the bog and heard a roar?"

Selea gave a wistful giggle. "And he peed his pants, even though it was only your stomach?"

"I hadn't eaten in two days," Erevan said, still laughing.

"It's really quite sad, I can't believe we can look back and laugh at things like this," she said, failing to stop her own laughter.

"We've got to remind Tinny about that when we see him. Does he still live in that old yellow house near the market?"

Selea shook her head. "Tinny's dead," she said, and all the happiness and laughing was gone in an instant.

"What? When?!"

"Not long after you left. Typical mugging if the story's to be believed. I saw him lying in the middle of the road the next day. People stepped over him on their way to the market without so much as an acknowledgment. I had to carry his body home so we could bury him."

"Who killed him?"

She shrugged. "Like I said, official story is a mugging. But someone said they saw him beat one of the townguards in a game of Wizards, Witches, and Warlocks. Won a couple gold pieces from it. I heard the guard was furious."

Erevan's mind flashed back to the day Isaiah was caught and how Tinny had shouted at him and Selea. Angry not because the plan hadn't worked, but because they'd put themselves in danger without Tinny being there to have their backs. *Three little thieves,* he had said. *Erevan, you two saved Selea, but at what cost?*

Isaiah sacrificing himself; that was the cost. Erevan pushed the thought away. "You think the townguard killed him?" he asked, forcing his mind away from mistakes he hoped to soon amend.

"Wouldn't be the first time, would it?" Selea let out a long sigh. Then she leaned in close enough for Erevan to feel heat warming up his cheeks again. "I'm getting out of here," she whispered.

"The tavern?"

"The city. Bogudos is nothing but quicksand waiting to sink us all."

"Where are you going?" Erevan asked.

"I've been thinking of traveling back to the home country. Touring Lanasall, seeing the capital, the people, the schools, it sounds nice. You should come with me."

"Lanasall isn't close. You'd be journeying for weeks, and it's dangerous out there in the wild."

"I'll take the well-known roads, and sleep at the traveler's lodges," Selea said.

"Those lodges are expensive, and you'll need to buy a mount."

"I'll have all the money I need."

"From what?"

She leaned in tighter and whispered, "Tonight. I've scored the perfect job with some Heritourians from Rifton. We make our move at sundown. It's quick and pays well... *really* well."

"Rifton? Why are they on this side of the river?"

"They're townguards chasing some outlaw."

"You're working with townguards now?" he asked, and Selea frowned.

"We both know I don't have the luxury of turning jobs down."

Erevan folded his arms. "What's the job?"

"All I have to do is steal from some lady coming to town. She's got a couple mercenaries, but we'll have a bigger squad, it should be easy."

"What're you supposed to steal?"

"Some kind of weapon. It's disguised as a mirror."

Air left Erevan's lungs so fast he feared it would never return. Selea wasn't talking about just another lady. She was talking about Nya.

"Heritourians gave you this job?" he asked, again.

Selea nodded. "I told you, they're townguards from Rifton. I heard of the job weeks ago. I was starting to think it wouldn't happen. Seems like that lady took forever getting to town."

"She was delayed."

Selea's face curled in confused surprise. "How do you know?"

"I'm the one protecting her," he said. This was bad. Someone had sent word of them. Pirates from the Coral Coast, perhaps? No. Whoever it was knew about the mirror. *The spectre?*

"You?!" Selea exclaimed. Several of the shady fellows nearby looked their way. She went back to whispering, "Since when are you a full-on mercenary?"

"I—it doesn't matter, just don't do the job."

"Erevan, it's a lot of coin."

"Enough to kill me?"

"I told you, I'm only after the mirror."

"But I doubt that's all *they're* after. They probably plan to kill her too."

"Who cares? This job could change my life. She's just some rich lady."

"She's so much more."

Selea snapped her head back, eyes wide, looking surprised, offended or both. *Why am I defending Nya?* Erevan asked himself.

"I see," Selea said, taking a step back. "I hope I don't see you there tonight," she said, turning to leave, then she stopped for a moment to speak. "One last thing. Your little brother Scoti has been hanging out at The Thieves' Den lately. He's trying to get in on the job tonight too," she said, then she walked out the tavern, not even giving him a chance to respond.

He wanted to chase after Selea. There was so much more to say and to ask. But he also needed to warn Nya and his father. Then there was his little brother. If the Heritourians found out who Scoti's family really was, there's no telling what they'd do to him.

They were surely already planning to kill Erevan and Sir Lee. There wasn't much sunlight left and Erevan didn't have time to do all three things. He had a choice to make.

Chapter 26

Friendship & Family

ZALE KEPT CHOOSING TO AVOID AIREYAL. The frown etched across her face had been stuck there for over a week. He was late to every history lecture where he would choose to sit as far away as possible from her, then he'd rush out the room as soon as they were dismissed. *What did I do wrong?*

She had asked herself that question so many times and that loathsome inner voice, which had all but disappeared for a while, came back with so many answers. Her least favorite of which was, *he just doesn't like you.* But that was the answer that kept creeping back into her head. *He does though, doesn't he?* He said he wanted to kiss me. *But he didn't.* Why not? *Because he doesn't like you.*

Then there was her other problem. The scaly one. Not to mention her mother. Aireyal had skipped every magic lecture since their argument. They didn't argue often. Disagree, sure. But the other night was different. Fractured.

Regardless, Aireyal stood before her mother's study, ready to apologize. Once she found the courage to knock on the door, that is. *You've been standing here for half an hour. Just knock.* Aireyal raised her hand, then dropped it. *What do I even say?*

Suddenly, the door opened on its own. Her mother took a step out in a hurry, a cup of tea in hand, then paused, seeing Aireyal.

"…" Aireyal tried to say *sorry*, but it came out as nothing. She wrung her hands together as her mother studied her face.

"I'm sorry too," her mother said, wrapping her in a hug.

"How'd you kno—"

"Because you're my daughter, and moms know everything. Come inside," she said, directing Aireyal into her study, which was chaotic as always; one stack of books even towered a couple of inches from the ceiling.

"Weren't you headed somewhere?"

"It can wait."

…

"How are we? The two of us, I mean. Are we…"

"We're fine," her mother said, hugging her tighter. Aireyal gave her a half-hearted hug back. She wasn't sure she'd be able to move on so quickly from the things her mother said the other night. As a little girl, she'd looked at her mother as a hero. An impossible beacon to live up to. Now she wondered if she'd ever feel that way again. Her mother must've sensed some of the doubt in Aireyal's spirit because she gave one of her forced smiles. "We can wait on a decision with the dragon. You don't have to rush."

Aireyal cringed and sat down on a sturdy stack of tomes near the door as her mother walked deeper inside and leaned comfortably against her desk. Of all the secrets her mother held from her, the secret power of dragonslaying was one she wished she had never learned. The thought of killing a baby turned her stomach to a gurgling fountain of sickness.

"Won't you get in trouble if someone finds out you're hiding a dragon here?" Aireyal whispered, though there was no one else around.

"I won't tell if you won't," her mother said with a jovial smile.

Aireyal tried to return it, but her face turned to a frown instead. Choosing the fate of a life wasn't something to be taken lightly. *What's worth more, life or choice?* Docent Tolk's question from the first day of school pricked the edge of her mind.

Scarlet couldn't make choices on her own; she was only a baby. That meant Aireyal had to decide for her, right? But being the last living dragon in a country full of people that wanted her dead didn't sound like a good life to live. It would likely be one of pain and suffering. Perhaps a quick death now was the merciful thing to do. *You're only thinking that because of what you'll get out of it,* the inner voice told her.

Aireyal shivered. Was the temptation of no longer being magicless affecting her judgment? *We have laws and rules for a reason.* That's what she'd said about Nodero. And she believed it then. Did she still? *Probably... maybe.* Zale pointed out in the Crypt of Infamy that she wasn't following the rules herself. Zale. She could use his help right now.

"What's wrong?" her mother asked, bringing Aireyal out of her thoughts. Aireyal couldn't say that she'd spent the better part of the past week in her room. Her hideout spot since the *non-kiss*. In her room only one person could see her cry. And she'd been doing a lot of that lately. Her sleeves were soaked. Not just today. Every day. Since the *non-kiss*.

"Aireyal? Did you hear me?" her mother asked. She craned her neck Aireyal's way, her mouth pressed thin with worry, though she hid it by sipping a cup of tea. A cup Aireyal recognized. She had painted little flowers on it herself years ago as a gift for her mother. Though her mother's expression now was far from the delight Aireyal had seen that day, and she felt herself mirroring the worry. "No matter what you're going through, it will pass in time."

That was a hopeful thought. Aireyal's spirit lifted an inch from the muck it was in. "Did father ever do anything that upset you?" she asked. Her mother spit out her tea. They didn't speak about Aireyal's father. *Ever.*

"What makes you say that?" her mother asked, looking as though she'd been punched.

"Never mind. Forget I asked, sorry."

A long silence echoed around the room. Her mother took another sip of tea, her hand trembling as she did so. Then she looked at Aireyal long and hard.

"Your father did a lot of things that upset me," she said, pushing herself from the desk and taking another sip of tea. Though this time, a small smile snuck its way onto her lips as she walked to Aireyal.

"Then why'd you marry him?"

"Because he also did a lot of things that made me happy." Then she gave a little pinch to Aireyal's cheek. "Best of all, he gave me you."

A little ray of sunshine came back to Aireyal's heart. *That was nice to hear... even if it did come from my mother.* "So then, it was worth all the other times? Even when you didn't understand why he was doing what he did?" she asked cautiously. Her mother studied her face.

"Aireyal, what are you really trying to ask me?"

Aireyal squirmed around on her seat of books. *Should I tell her about my... what was Zale to her?* She tried not to think of an answer. "I uh... um," she said, then started wringing her hands together. Her mouth refused to open to say more. Red flushed her cheeks just from thinking about it.

"Oh, that's what this is about."

"I didn't even say anything. How do you kn—"

"I'm a mother, we know everything," she said, sipping her tea. "Casilda and I have had a few conversations about you and that boy."

That boy.

"Then I suppose you know we haven't been talking lately," Aireyal mumbled.

"Hmm, I didn't know that." *So much for moms knowing everything.* "But I do know there's a big dance going on tonight. So, I'm guessing this has to do with that?" *Tonight? The dance is tonight?!*

Aireyal forcibly closed the jaw she hadn't realized she'd dropped. "That complicates things." *He's not going to go with me.*

Who cares? There are more important things going on, the inner voice noted.

So? That doesn't keep it from hurting.

"I can only help if you let me know what's bothering you. I was a young girl once too, you know," her mother said, taking another sip. Aireyal looked at her mother, trying to imagine her in her youth. *Maybe my mother hasn't always been old.* Aireyal didn't have much experience on the *boys* topic herself. Actually, she had *no* experience.

"A boy likes you if he says he wants to kiss you, right?" Aireyal asked. Her mother spit out her tea, *again*, and her eyes nearly bulged out of her skull.

"I didn't realize you were already that… involved," she said, taking an extraordinarily long time to say the word, *involved*. Then she squinted at Aireyal. "How old are you again?"

"I'm sixteen, Mother."

"Right," her mother said, clearing her throat. "To answer your question, yes. That would indeed mean what you think." Aireyal noted her mother's choice of not using a specific word. "But I don't think you and that boy sh—"

A shrill yawn cut through the room. Aireyal turned to see Scarlet waking up on a soft chair. Her mother gave her a knowing look.

"I'll sit down and figure out what to do with her tonight," Aireyal said.

"What about the dance?"

"I don't think I'm going," Aireyal said, shrinking in her seat. Her mother frowned.

"You should. It's a fun time. All the other kids will be there."

Aireyal groaned. *That's exactly why I don't want to go. They're already making fun of me everywhere I walk.* She didn't want to get made fun of at a dance too. Especially not when all the other kids were going with someone.

"If it makes you feel any better, I'll be there directing errand runners for the ceremony. I think it'll do you some good to get out of your room with your head buried in books all day. You can go to the dance with your friends."

Having a night to dance and eat and laugh and not care about anything did sound good. It might be exactly what she needed, but there was one big problem with that plan. "I don't have any friends," Aireyal murmured. Her mother's lips wrinkled with worry again. She started to say something but didn't. Then again, what was there to say? Nobody was socially senseless enough to risk the shame of being a magicless girl's friend. Aireyal was going to be alone for the rest of the year.

They sat there awkwardly for a few more minutes before Aireyal gave a half-hearted goodbye and slinked back to her room.

Re-reading *The Adventures of Allia* for the thirty-seventh time was the best way to spend her evening, she decided. But just as she was nearing the chapter where Allia faced off against the archers of Elvangard, the door swung open. Morgana glided in with her usual strut, then froze and stared at Aireyal.

"You're not getting ready?" Morgana asked, heading to her wardrobe.

"I'm not going to that stupid dance."

"Why not?" Morgana asked, stopping.

"Because I don't want to," Aireyal said. It wasn't necessarily a lie. Besides, Morgana didn't need to know that—

"What about Zale? He'll be waiting for you."

"Who told you that?" Aireyal asked, tossing her book down.

"That is what one of the boys was saying. You are not going to make him go alone, are you?"

Aireyal was too stunned to speak. Her eyes flicked over to her desk. The bracelet he made for her was sitting atop it, as it had been for quite a few days. *I should go.* His last words to her echoed like a bell. She at least wanted to ask him what happened that day. Was he too nervous to kiss her?

"Aireyal, the dance is in half an hour, you have to get ready now," Morgana said. *Half an hour?* Aireyal looked out the window; there wasn't much sun left.

"What do I even…" Aireyal wasn't sure what to say. The only formal events she'd ever gone to were for her mother's accomplishments, and her mother got her dressed and ready for those. But she'd have to do it herself this time. Aireyal scanned her bookshelf. *Aha.* She pulled out a worn book.

"You cannot be serious," Morgana said, her hand to her mouth holding back a snicker. Aireyal's cheeks warmed.

"It's called *Modern Looks for Balls and Festivities*," Aireyal said stubbornly.

"Modern for grandmothers maybe."

Aireyal looked at the painting of the lady on the book's cover. She could imagine her mother sporting a similar bun in her youth, complete with a sundress and a cup of tea. *Perhaps Morgana had a point.*

"Leave this to me," Morgana said, scurrying over to collect combs, perfumes, and more, then motioning for Aireyal to sit at the beauty desk in front of her giant mirror. Aireyal did so cautiously.

"Do I really need to look fancy for everyone?" Aireyal asked.

"It is not about everyone else. It is about making yourself look the way you want," Morgana said. "Think of yourself as a delicious cake."

Aireyal couldn't help but laugh. "What is that even supposed to mean?"

"You are perfectly tasty just the way you are. But if you want to be extra elegant," Morgana said, running a comb through Aireyal's hair.

"You can add frosting, filling, and fruits." She continued combing with one hand and pulled out a brush with the other. "Wouldn't you like your cake to be extravagant too? You could be vanilla, chocolate, banana…" she kept going on listing so many cakes that Aireyal wondered if Morgana was hungry and compensating for it.

Swish, swish. Keeping track of what Morgana's hands were doing was impossible. They buzzed around Aireyal's face in a swarm. A fluff of powder here, a brush of the hair there. When Morgana reached for a dark bottle of perfume, Aireyal closed her eyes. It smelled like sweet cherries and chocolate, which made her start thinking about cakes too.

"Chocolate cake does sound tasty."

"Don't be absurd, Aireyal. You cannot have your cake and eat it too."

"Why not? It's my cake."

"No, you *are* the cake. Haven't you been listening?" Morgana said, her face completely befuddled.

Aireyal giggled. "I have no idea what you're talking about."

"All you need to know is that you look scrumptious. Have a glimpse," Morgana said.

Aireyal slowly opened her eyes. She was herself but, different. Her hair was curled and pinned up in elaborate braids that should have taken way longer to do than they did. Her face's normal blemishes were gone, replaced by an even peachy color. It made her dull eyes stand out for once. She… liked it.

"Thank you," Aireyal said, beaming at herself for the first time in her life. Then she noticed the scar that the girl with the brooch gave her was still there. She reached up instinctively to touch it, then stopped herself, not wanting to ruin Morgana's work.

"Don't worry about it. Whoever gave you that scar has great taste, it gives you character," Morgana assured with a smirk. Aireyal's stomach flipped like a playing card at the comment. *Did she say that because she's the one that gave it to me? No. Of course not. If she were trying to kill you, why would she be helping you get ready now?* "Let's get you a gown and some jewels," Morgana said, rushing to her wardrobe and flipping through choices of every color. There was just one problem.

"Morgana, I don't think any of those will work."

"Why not?" Morgana turned back, her eyes watching Aireyal anxiously.

"We're not exactly the same." When Morgana didn't get her point, Aireyal waved her hands in the shape of a slender hourglass and pointed at Morgana. Then cupped them into an unwanted potato and pointed at herself.

"Nonsense," Morgana said, then returned to her fumbling in the wardrobe. Morgana clearly didn't get it. They weren't even *close* to the same height, let alon— "Here we go," Morgana said, pulling out a deep, vermillion red gown. It was gorgeous. Sleek all over with thin straps and flowery ruffles along the chest line. It was far too ravishing for Aireyal to wear. "Come on, get up," Morgana said, pulling Aireyal out of her chair. She measured the dress against Aireyal's figure.

It will fit.

"How—"

"I bought this for *you*, Airy," Morgana said. *Airy.* She was starting to like that. "I figured if you wanted to go to the dance, you would need something to wear," she said, nodding happily when she saw the measurements were correct. This was the nicest thing Morgana had ever done for her. The nicest thing *any* girl had ever done for her.

Aireyal squeezed Morgana in a big hug. "Thank you so much."

"You're welcome," Morgana said, pushing away, her face squished red.

"Sorry."

"It's fine," Morgana said, taking in a breath. "Now, don't let all this hard work go to waste," she said, fluttering a hand over Aireyal's face. "Get dressed and tell me how it went when you get back."

"You're not coming?" Aireyal asked. Morgana shook her head 'no'. "I hope you change your mind. I could use someone there who's on my side."

~ *Chapter 27* ~
Scoti's Scorn

EREVAN NEEDED TO GET TO SCOTI'S SIDE, *NOW.* Rain puddles resonated with purpose as his footsteps splashed through them in haste. He made his way to the Thieves' Den. If he was going to find Scoti, it would be here.

Red light flared in the window as he waded through the weed-filled yard, but it dimmed as he got closer. By the time Erevan walked up the porch and knocked on the splintered door, the light was gone.

And there was no answer at the door. Instead, the soft shuffling of feet and near silent whispers among voices inside was the response. The shuffles moved closer to the door, as did metal and wood in the air before a scruffy voice spoke, "Knocking on this door is a bold choice, uninvited."

"I'm not looking for trouble," Erevan said, holding his hands up. It was pitch black inside, but he had a feeling they were watching him.

"Then what are you looking for?" the voice asked.

"A young boy, Scoti."

The door swung open to reveal five men, two on the left and three on the right side of the door, all armed with swords and twisted frowns. They wore silver and blue leather armor with a boar's head embroidered into it. Townguards from Heritour.

In the center, the shortest of the group stood with a dagger pointed at Erevan's chest. A boy. Scoti. His orange hair shimmered under the fading sunlight that spilled in from the door. "Erevan?" Scoti realized, eyes wide. "I heard you were dead."

"No, I'm quite alive for the time being. Unless you plan to stab me," Erevan said, nodding toward the dagger in his brother's hand.

"Ah, sorry about that, we were expecting someone else. Come on in," he offered, lowering his weapon. A couple of the men at the door let out disapproving grunts.

"I'm here to take you home," Erevan said, watching the townguards.

"Can't. We have a job tonight," Scoti said, his adolescent voice cracking here and there.

"I've heard." Erevan crossed his arms.

"You know? How long have you been back?"

"Not long enough, apparently. Let's go."

"I can make my own decisions," Scoti said.

"Bad ones, obviously. I'm trying to do what's best for you," Erevan said, taking a step forward.

"Careful there, don't put ideas in the boy's head," said one of the men, moving between Erevan and Scoti.

"I think it's time you leave," said another of the Heritourians to Erevan.

"I'm not going anywhere without Scoti," Erevan said, then he turned to his little brother. "Why are you here anyway, what could they possibly offer you?"

"They pay me for something I'm good at," Scoti said. Erevan glared at him. "What? It's not like I killed someone."

"Do you even know who you're working with?"

"Does it matter? The coin I get helps put food on the table, and that's what a man must do."

"You're not a man, you're a boy. And there are other ways to make money."

"That pay a lot less," Scoti said, rolling his eyes. "I'm doing something that helps people, and you're mad?"

"Helps? Do you even know what you're about to go do?"

"Get something back that a rich lady stole," Scoti said. "And the coin goes to us, people with nothing. Isn't that what you always used to talk about? Besides, you've done far worse for money."

"I didn't have a choice," Erevan said, taking another step forward. Two of the Heritourians moved toward him.

"I'm gonna ask you one last time to head out," said the one that answered the door. He was the tallest of the men. He had a beard, and like the other men, had blond hair. In fact, their faces all looked similar. Relatives perhaps? Regardless, it didn't matter.

"I'm not leaving without him," Erevan said, reaching past one of the Heritourians towards Scoti, but the burliest of the townguards pushed him away.

"Back off," the man said, brandishing a blade. Erevan drew his own sword.

"Don't hurt him!" Scoti shouted, pushing the man. The man stumbled for a second, then snatched Scoti.

"Put your hands on me again and you're gonna get your throat slit," he said, putting his sword at Scoti's neck. Erevan rushed forward and slammed the man's face against the wall as hard as he could, pinning him there with his sword. There was a *crack*, then a *clack* as something hit the floor.

"Threaten him again and I will end every last one of you," Erevan snapped. The man smiled and Erevan realized what the sound had been. As did the other men, who cackled. One reached down to pick up what had fell. The stout man's tooth.

"You were already uglier than Adamin, now it's worse," said the man who'd picked up the tooth.

The stout townguard gritted the rest of his teeth at Erevan. "I'll kill you," he growled.

"Leave the kid alone, he's just trying to protect his friend," one of the other Heritourians said, pulling the stout man away from Erevan. "We're already running out of time. We need to get ready."

"We're men of Heritour, we don't run from battle," said the stout man.

"This isn't war, let the orphan go. The cut's bigger without him anyway," said another of the men.

"Scoti, let's go," Erevan said, staring down the stout Heritourian until Scoti walked out of the house. Then Erevan followed, keeping his eye trained on the townguards.

"Better hope we don't meet again, *drow*," the stout man said as the door closed. *Don't worry, we will.* If they were after the Frostfire

Mirror, he'd see them again. But Bogudos wasn't the place to fight. Not near his mother and little siblings. Speaking of which...

"What were you thinking?" Erevan said, fuming at Scoti. The boy sneered, walking off in the rain, which had briefly calmed to a light drizzle. Erevan followed. "I'm talking to you."

"Mother needed help. She hurt her back working at the mill, not that you care. And there are two more kids at the orphanage now."

"Don't say I don't care."

"You and father left ages ago. You were only supposed to be away for a few weeks, Uncle Aeric is already gone."

"It's *only been* a few weeks," Erevan protested.

"It's been a month and a half."

"No, it hasn—" Erevan started, then stopped, counting in his head. *Had it really been that long?*

"You abandoned us."

"I was training to become a mercenary so I could help make honest coin."

"You left an old lady and a bunch of kids to fend for ourselves. I was the oldest, and I'm twelve.

"That doesn't mean you should be taking jobs with thieves."

"They're townguards. Besides, taxes went up again this month, and we couldn't afford it with two more mouths to feed," Scoti said.

"You can't let every kid in the city into the orphanage."

"Tell that to my mother."

"*Our* mother."

"You don't get to say that after leaving us to go play father's favorite soldier."

"So that's what this is about. Whatever your problems are with father, they're childish," Erevan said, though the words were hypocritical. He needed to apologize to his father himself when he saw him again. Erevan sighed. "This isn't the time to lecture you. I have to know about that job you were trying to do."

"I don't need you babying me."

"Could you stop being a brat for two seconds? I'm asking because the people they're after are me and Father."

"You're the escorts for the important lady?" Scoti asked, squishing his face in a look mixed with disbelief and suspicion. Erevan checked several times over his shoulder, making sure there were no eavesdroppers before nodding.

"Which makes me wonder why you were hired for the job in the first place."

"Because I look *unassuming*. That's what I've been told. I've stolen things from all kinds of people lately," he said, raising his chin high. Erevan gave him a soft bop on the head.

"That's not something to be proud of. It's going to get you mixed in with the wrong crowd. The type of people you were with today."

"I told you already, those guys were townguards. They're the law, they police Rifton."

"Doesn't mean they're good guys!" Erevan snapped. "Townguards just killed my friend Tin—" he caught himself and took a deep breath, lowering his voice. "Those men are after the girl we're protecting, which is why I need to know what their plan is."

"They want to get a magical weapon from that lady. Supposedly, if we don't wrap it up, it'll freeze our hands to ice."

"It's not even a weapon."

"The Krilows seemed convinced," Scoti said, shrugging.

"Krilows?"

"That's the name of the Heritourians I was on the job with. They're all brothers, I think."

"Who were you supposed to give the mirror to?"

Scoti shrugged. "We were going to sail overnight to Rifton to hand it in. But they didn't say to who."

The spectre? Erevan had seen his father stab the spectre through the heart, but that wasn't proof their assailant was dead. He could be waiting for them in Rifton. Erevan's mind lingered on the memory of slicing the elf's chest open only for him to stand back up, uninjured. *Spectres are immortal.* Bumgrim's words settled like a chill, haunting Erevan for the rest of their walk home.

When they arrived at the orphanage, its windows were cracked, like he remembered. All three stairs to the porch creaked, squeaked, and squawked, like he remembered. And the little house's ruined red paint was peeling off all over, though he remembered a time when it had been a beautiful, bright red.

As they walked inside, their mother fussed at one of the little kids for getting their clothes dirty. "And that's why you can't go rolling around in the grass," Mrs. Eston scolded, standing by the single table in the kitchen, dining, and everything else room, except bedroom. There was one small room around the corner for that.

"But I don't like skirts," a little girl whined back.

"Then—" Mrs. Eston stopped and turned when she heard Erevan's footsteps on the old, groaning wood of the floor. "Erevan! Thank Evlynna, you've made it back safe," she said, placing aside a ragged broom on the wall that had the least amount of mold infesting it and scurried over, one hand rubbing her back.

"What about me?" Scoti asked. Mrs. Eston glowered at him.

"You need to stop running off," she said before turning back to study Erevan's face. "You look thin. Has your father been feeding you?"

"I'm fine, Mother," Erevan said. "I do need to talk to him though." And by talk, he meant apologize. His father was many things, but a *liar* was not one of them. They also needed to get away from the orphanage before sundown, and it was only half an hour away at best. Just being here was a bad idea.

"Your father went out to the apothecary to get his leg checked. He said he was feeling numb after a bug bite he got on the road. And I see he lost the hat I made him. That man couldn't keep track of his own hand if I wasn't there to show it to him," she fussed, though she did so with a smile on her face. Erevan wondered if she'd seen his father's missing finger yet. Either way, she rambled on, "Oh, and I told him to grab some bread from the baker's for me on the way back. I used the last of it to make some beeberry bread. Would you boys like some?" she asked, pointing to the table where the bread was surrounded by several chipped plates. They both instantly shook their heads. She frowned. "Well, Miss Nya seems to like it."

Erevan went through a series of emotions so fast he wasn't sure what he'd even felt. Surprise, probably. Nervousness, maybe? Shame, surely. "She's here?"

"Yes, she is," said a familiar rebellious voice. Nya came strolling around the corner. Her usual swagger had been replaced with a look of uncertainty as she stared at Erevan.

"Nya's been a joy," Mrs. Eston said, beaming at her. "I hope you don't live far. I'd love to have you come back."

"I'm not sure I'd call it close," Nya said in a neutral, unreadable tone.

"That's a shame, Erevan's getting to the age w—"

"Thanks, mother," Erevan said, stopping her. He wasn't sure what she was going to say next, but he refused to find out. A long, awkward, silent, tension filled the room. No one moved and no sound was made, other than the rain picking up outside.

"More bread?" Mrs. Eston asked, rushing to the tiny table in the center of the room. She cut the partially charred bread on it in half, then placed it on two plates, making sure to give Nya the uncharred piece. Erevan's slice wasn't so lucky.

"Why don't I get a piece?" Scoti asked.

"You can share with your brother," Mrs. Eston said, shooting him a quick warning stare. Scoti leaned over, looking at Erevan's blackened bread, which could've been mistaken for a scorched potato.

"Never mind," the boy said, stepping back.

"Let us pray," Mrs. Eston said, motioning aggressively for Erevan and Scoti to close their eyes. She continued when they did, "O blessed Evlynna of the stars above, bless us with grace when we are curt, bless us with mercy when we are crude, bless us with health when we are hurt, and bless what we eat, purify our food. Afide."

More little faces peered around when Erevan opened his eyes.

"Who's that?" one asked, looking at Erevan.

"She's pretty, right, big brother?" asked another at the same time, pointing at Nya.

"Back to your room, all of you," Mrs. Eston said, grabbing her broom to shoo the children away.

Nya smiled. "You have a delightful home, Mrs. Eston, it's quite cozy. And the bread is delicious," she said, taking a bite. Loud crunching followed, but Nya ate it happily.

"I'm glad you like it," Mrs. Eston said, shuffling around the corner, sweeping. Erevan looked down at his own bread. He risked taking a bite too. Delicious, it was not. He'd had good beeberry bread before, its sweet honey taste melting in the mouth, but never from his mother's kitchen. He dropped the rest of it back down on his plate, and Scoti snorted. Erevan turned to glare his way, then looked back to see Nya still watching him intently. They needed to talk. But privacy was impossible inside the house.

"Nya," he started, not sure what to say next. Her eyes widened... then narrowed when he didn't continue.

A crash outside caused them all to turn. Before Erevan could move, several children ran from the other room and headed outside.

"What was that?" one asked.

"I'm gonna find out!" yelled another.

Oh no.

"Stop!" Erevan shouted to the kids, but they ran on, ignoring him. He sprinted after them outside. Lying there, unmoving on the cold ground was Sir Lee, blood running in droves from his open mouth.

~ *Chapter 28* ~
Elegance & Escorts

T HE GROUND OUTSIDE WAS COLD, BUT THE autumn air was cooler. Aireyal waited, shivering outside the decorated doors of The Banquet Hall, which had been repurposed for the dance. Zale hadn't made it yet, and she kept peering at the charm bracelet around her wrist as if it had the power to make him appear.

Messengers ran in and out the doors and couples passed her to go inside every so often. She had learned to look away when they did; the eyes of pity she received from the first few were like spikes to her soul. The rest laughed at the lonely, magicless girl.

She must have looked ridiculous, dressed up in the radiant red ball gown Morgana had given her with fancy curled up hair and a shiny necklace, all so she could stand by herself. Surely more so with the fire-colored leaves of the hedges around her cut in the shape of wisping flames. And the ribbons swirling in intricate loops through them, tying high above the open doors of the hall which housed a feast of laughter and singing within.

Aireyal sighed as yet *another* couple passed by her, headed inside. *What could be taking Zale so long?* The festivities started almost half an hour ago, and most people had arrived even earlier. Perhaps Zale knew showing up fashionably late was what the most impressive guests did. But Aireyal had the awful feeling he wasn't here for another reason.

He isn't coming.

No. Don't think like that.

A laugh, no, a snicker, brought her out of her thoughts. Priscilla Hornbuckle, Aireyal's official freckle insulter. She walked up to Aireyal, arm in arm with Winston Ellisburg from her history lectures. Both of them dressed classily in all white. They'd have something snippy to say for sure.

"You look pretty for once today," Priscilla said to Aireyal. *Wait, what?* Was that a compliment? Aireyal fumbled, unsure how to react. She eventually gave a courteous smile in return.

"Thank y—"

"With all that red, I almost mistook you for a big rose. Then again, they are pretty every day, so they couldn't be you." And there it was. Aireyal's smile faded, and Priscilla's grew in its place as an overly dramatic expression crossed Priscilla's face. "Where is your escort?" she asked Aireyal, peeking sarcastically under one of the hedges. "Did they get lost?" Priscilla paused and looked to Winston. "She looks rather lonely, don't you think?"

"Perhaps her escort is invisible," Winston said, squinting his eyes and scanning the area snobbishly.

"They're waiting for me inside," Aireyal lied, hoping her burning cheeks didn't give away the truth.

"I hope so, I would certainly hate to see you wait out here all night," Priscilla snickered, then she and Winston headed inside, arm in arm.

Where was Zale? Did he even plan to come? What if he was sitting in his room laughing at her too? No. Good thoughts. *He likes me.*

Does he?

I think so. Maybe he's in trouble or hurt.

You're at a school, there's nothing dangerous here.

Except killer tigers. What if it—

No. Don't think like that.

Ignoring her inner panic worked… for a while. But after the couples stopped walking past her, everything was becoming clear. *He's not coming.* Her mind started wandering into questions again when a familiar voice spoke…

"I'm sorry I didn't get here earlier." But it wasn't Zale. It was her mother. Aireyal tried to respond, then she realized her voice was croaky and awful. How long had she been crying? "I saw you standing out here all alone, but I had to finish a few ceremony affairs. Why aren't you inside?"

Aireyal felt the newest tears as they tumbled down her cheeks. Her mother's arms wrapped around her in an instant, and a cloth wiped under Aireyal's eyes. For this moment, at least, she wasn't going to complain about being treated like a baby. Instead, she leaned further into her mother's arms and sobbed until her eyes were red and stuffy. She was a fool. A stupid, *lonely*, fool.

"I'm sorry your night isn't going as planned."

Aireyal stared solemnly into the ball where the other kids danced, laughed, ate, and sang; cheerful faces everywhere.

"I only wanted one single night. One night that I didn't have to worry about dragons or mirrors or magic or anything. One night to not care and to—" her mind thought of Zale and their *almost-kiss*. "Never mind, it doesn't matter."

"Aireyal, I love you more than anything in the world and I've tried to give you everything I could to help you, but—"

"It's not your fault I can't do magic, mother. You tried to teach me, and you bought all the best books for me to study an—"

"That's not what I was getting at." Her mother gave a sad smile. "The one thing I don't know how to give you is belief in yourself. You are the smartest, hardest-working, most caring, and knowledgeable girl I have ever taught. And I'm not just saying that because you're my daughter. I genuinely believe you can do anything that you put in the time to study," her mother said, then she sighed. "Even if it's not me, I hope someone will help you find a piece of yourself to believe in." Morgana had tried, but even that hadn't seemed to help her. Though perhaps false confidence wasn't enough. Maybe Aireyal had to be the one to believe in herself. Her mother let out a wistful sigh. "You know, I didn't go to my first school dance."

"Why not?" Aireyal asked, perking her head up, her voice still soggy and horrid.

"I got asked to the dance by two boys at the same time in front of everybody. Your father and a boy named, *Claro*," she said, frowning at, Claro. "I didn't know which one to choose. And so, instead of choosing, I pretended to be sick, and faked my sickness for weeks until after the dance was over. All because I didn't want to hurt someone's feelings for choosing another suitor," she continued. Choosing between multiple admirers? That was a vastly different problem than the one Aireyal had. "The reason I'm telling you this story is to let you know, I wish I would've gone to that dance."

"With whom?"

"I was sixteen, Aireyal. It didn't matter who I went with, even alone would have been fine. The point is, I should've enjoyed myself instead of worrying about those boys." She gave Aireyal a squeeze. "And I want you to go in there and have your one night to not care and have fun like you wanted to, even if that means you have to do so alone."

"She doesn't have to be alone," a voice said. Aireyal looked up. Morgana. She was beaming in a black dress. Or lavender. No, it was both. Shifting colors under the light. "I thought you promised not to let all my hard work go to waste," Morgana fussed, taking the cloth her mother had and dabbing under Aireyal's eyes.

"Sorry."

Morgana smiled. "What am I going to do with you?"

"I didn't think you were going to come," Aireyal said. Morgana gave a half shrug.

"I wasn't, but then I got word you were out here all alone."

"Word from whom?" Aireyal asked. Morgana peered over at her mother, and the two of them exchanged a look that suggested they had talked. "You told Morgana?"

"As Grandmage, I'm required to sit through all the opening speeches here, but that doesn't mean I can't send someone else out to deliver a message for me should the need arise."

More tears came to Aireyal's eyes, but this time she didn't care. She grabbed both Morgana and her mother and gave them the biggest hug she could. It might have been a silly notion, but she hoped they felt how much she appreciated them by how tightly she held on. Both their faces were red by the time Aireyal let go.

"I have some errands to run for the festivities," her mother said, sighing. "You two, have fun." She gave Aireyal and Morgana a final smile, then headed off and away from the ball.

"Shall we?" Morgana asked Aireyal, extending her arm. Aireyal took it, unable to resist smiling.

"We shall," Aireyal said, and they strolled into the bright lights of the ball.

Chapter 29

Three Little Thieves

THE BRIGHT LIGHT OF THE SUN FADED, AS DID Sir Lee before it. "Father?" one of the little girls asked, staring at his broken body, but Sir Lee didn't move. It would've bothered Erevan less if she had screamed out; the silent horror in her voice was much worse. Her expression was blank, waiting for her mind to process what her eyes witnessed. She should've never seen her father like this.

"Go back into the house, all of you!" Erevan ordered. None of the kids moved, their gaze fixed on their father. Erevan's eyes drifted too, trying to see if the man still drew breath, and for now, at least, it appeared he did. But they weren't good breaths. His father wheezed quietly, lying flat and disturbingly still on the muddy ground before the porch. His head sat in a small pool of his own blood, which ran off in the rain into a bag of bread at his side.

Erevan looked up. Six sinister figures stood in hooded cloaks under the rain. He couldn't see their faces, but he knew who they were. He recognized the boar's head armor of the five Krilows. And he recognized the other. Selea. He'd know her body anywhere. But regardless of their past together, she was in the group responsible for attacking his father. Erevan was going to make them pay for that, *all* of them.

"You're supposed to be the good guys!" Scoti shouted at the Krilows, ripping his dagger out. Erevan yanked Scoti before the boy could run forward, and pulled him close.

"No," Erevan warned in a low voice. "I need you to get all our brothers and sisters inside. Lock the front door, then all of you sneak out the back with Mother and run."

"I'm staying to figh—"

"For once in your life, stop arguing and do what you're told!" Erevan shouted at him. Scoti fired a frustrated look back, but he *did* listen, shuffling their little siblings into the house and slamming the door behind them.

"I'm with you, Erevan," Nya said, her eyes narrowed in fury. Erevan nodded to her. They needed to talk, but they could do that later. For now, they had to save his father as he'd done for them. But how? Nya still didn't have any dust for sorcery. He'd lost her belt and pouches to the wolves.

"So, you're her," Selea said to Nya. "I can't lie, I expected more."

"I told you not to take the job," Erevan said, glaring at Selea. "Your issues are with me. Leave everyone else out of this."

"Seems you have issues with everybody," said a voice Erevan recognized as the stout Krilow brother he'd pinned against a wall earlier. The same man that threatened to slit Scoti's throat. "Thank Evlynna I get to see you again. And so soon too."

"It's two of you left and six of us. Let's not make this harder than it needs to be," the tallest Krilow said. *Two of you left.* Erevan dared another glance at his father. He was bleeding out fast. If he wasn't bandaged up soon, he'd die from blood loss. Erevan drew his sword.

"Nya. Get my father out of here, he needs help."

"I can't leave you out here alone. They'll kill you."

"Yes, we will," the stout Krilow said. The tall one nodded and two hooded figures sprinted at Erevan. One was the stout Krilow. Erevan gripped his sword. *Come die.*

Erevan swung with murderous intent. Straight for the Krilow's head. Ducked. The man charged into Erevan, grabbing him with both hands. He pushed Erevan back and against the house's wall. *Thud.*

Erevan prepared another swing, then a fist came into view. Slugged. Then again. Nya screamed somewhere as he was punched a third time across the jaw. Then the stout Krilow slipped around to Erevan's back and grappled him into a headlock for another cloaked Krilow standing before him. Blood washed off the second Krilow's fist in the rain. Erevan's blood.

"Scum," he said, then hit Erevan in the face a fourth time. Rain blurred Erevan's vision. Or maybe that was the dizziness of being punched so many times. He still managed to see Nya being snatched and a blade pushed to her neck as Selea ripped through Nya's traveling pack. Hatred boiled through Erevan's veins. Selea wasn't some common thug like the rest of them. She'd been his friend since he was five years old. This was *betrayal*.

"I want my turn too," said the stout Krilow holding Erevan.

"Fine."

A quick knee to the gut. Then another blow to the head sent Erevan's face to the muddy ground. But he was picked right back up. He wasn't sure who was where anymore. Two or three, maybe four people stood hovering over him. It was hard to tell if he had double vision or if two Krilows had walked over. What he did know was that two people were holding him back now.

Slam! Another strike to the gut. This one forcing him to throw up. "You're gonna die nice and slow kid," said the stout Krilow, tapping Erevan on the cheek, preparing his next beating.

"My finger!" Selea's voice cried out in agony. *Good. She deserves to be in pain.* "That mirror is colder than ice."

"Didn't you hear what we told you? Hold it with some cloth," the tallest Krilow's voice said. Erevan looked over to him standing over his father. "Sir Lee, Knight of Grier. You're quite famous where I come from," he said, and kicked Sir Lee in the stomach. Sir Lee didn't move.

Erevan did. He wrestled against the two men holding him. But the stout Krilow blasted Erevan in the chest.

"Sit still, boy."

Cold rain pouring did nothing to douse the fury burning within Erevan.

"On second thought, infamous is a better word for you, Lee. You abandoned Heritour. And now you pay for that dishonor with your life," the tall Krilow said, pulling out a sword.

The front door to the house burst open and Scoti ran out with a knife.

"Scoti, no!" Erevan shouted, coughing up blood, but Scoti had already jumped at the man standing over their father.

"Get away from him!" Scoti cried. "I won't let you Krilows get away with this!"

The man smashed his pommel into Scoti's face. *Crack.* Bones broke and Scoti hurdled into the mud, but he hopped back up. Then the tall man put a blade to Scoti's neck.

"Drop the knife, kid," he ordered, but Scoti refused, flailing helplessly at the man.

"Leave my brother and father alone!" Erevan yelled at the top of his lungs. Tinny's life had been taken by townguards. He couldn't let his family die at their hands too. He fought to no avail against the men holding him and the rage inside him grew.

"Evlynna's breath, they're all a little orphanage family," said the voice of the stout Krilow in realization. "Isn't that sweet? A tooth for a life, seems like a good trade, don't you think?" he asked Erevan with a chuckle. "Your father first, then you."

The tall Krilow held Scoti off with one hand and raised his blade over Sir Lee with the other.

"No!" Erevan swung his head back and headbutted one of the men holding him. But he was struck again and had his head grabbed and pointed toward his father.

"Watch, boy."

The sword cut through Sir Lee's back and into his heart. He didn't cry out in pain, but life drifted from his father's eyes.

Erevan was sure he screamed. But he didn't hear it. He didn't hear anything except the blade piercing into his father ringing in his ears over and over. His vision blurred red. And every feeling of warmth, happiness, and peace left him. The pain in his body was gone, but his heart felt like it had been stabbed along with his father. He fixed his eyes on the hooded figures before him. *I'll kill every last Krilow.*

"You're next," the stout Krilow said to Erevan, placing a sword at his neck.

"Stop! Don't hurt him!" It wasn't a plea. It was a demand. "Or I'll break this." Selea's voice. In one hand, she held the mirror up in a cloth; in the other, she held a dagger pointed at the mirror.

"You wouldn't dare," one of the Krilows said.

"Try me," Selea snapped back.

"If you do that, we'll kill you too."

"I don't care. You aren't going to lay another finger on Erevan. Let him go."

The Krilows looked at each other and exchanged several expressions. After a few seconds, a decision must've been reached silently because the sword at Erevan's neck pulled away.

"Little Scoti too, he's just a kid," Selea said, and the tall man wrenched the knife from Scoti then released his grip on the boy. Scoti fell to Sir Lee's side, grabbing hold of his father and wailing out tears.

"Now, give us the mirror," one of the Krilows said to Selea.

"After you let Erevan go," she said, nodding to the two men still holding him. The moment they did, he was going straight after the tall man that killed his father. "Erevan, don't." Selea was looking right at him. Her expression hard and full of warning. She knew exactly what he was thinking.

Every eye was on her. Erevan's, the three Krilows around him, the tall one standing next to his father, and the one further off still holding a blade to Nya's neck.

Nya. She looked petrified trying not to provoke the man to violence. Erevan couldn't let her die here too. He had to get her out somehow. The hands holding Erevan grudgingly let go, then the men around him started inching towards Selea. She slowly stepped away.

"Erevan," Selea said, and his eyes snapped up to meet hers. "Three little thieves. I'm Isaiah. She's me," Selea said, nodding to Nya. *What's that supposed to mean?* Selea smiled at him, then took off running with the mirror.

"You stupid girl," snarled the closest Krilow. He let go of Nya and chased after Selea. Erevan understood her plan now. He ran, grabbed Nya's hand and sprinted the other way as fast as he could. Footsteps hounded in their trail, but he didn't turn.

"Forget those two. Everyone after the girl with the mirror!" the voice of the tallest Krilow ordered. The footsteps behind them changed course but Erevan kept running with tears in his eyes, pulling Nya alongside him, hoping he could save the life of at least one person he cared about tonight.

Chapter 30

Ballad & Ball

ONIGHT WAS PERFECT. LAUGHTER, SINGING, AND the smell of delectable food filled the air. A crowd of gowns fluttered frivolously past Aireyal and Morgana who sat at one of the elegant round tables, sipping on iced red tea. They spent their time watching other people at the dance, but it was more fun than Aireyal could've imagined.

"Look at him," Morgana said, nodding to a skinny boy who slipped by a few dancing couples to get to the dessert table. He hovered over one of the little cream-drizzled muffins that Aireyal had just finished stuffing her own mouth with. "What kind do you think he will go for?" Morgana asked. The boy struggled to decide between a vanilla, chocolate, or britaberry muffin.

"Vanilla probably… maybe," Aireyal said.

"Why do you think that?"

"Because he's wearing white, I guess," Aireyal said with a shrug. Morgana giggled.

"I don't think that's how it works," she said, and Aireyal laughed with her.

"It's a one in four chance, right?" Aireyal said, shrugging again.

"There are only three flavors of muffins," Morgana said, double-checking the table of sweets.

"He could also choose nothing," Aireyal noted. Morgana rolled her eyes.

"You're too smart for your own good," Morgana said. "I think he wants chocolate. Look at his eyes, they keep darting back to the chocolate muffin."

"I suppose you're right," Aireyal said, realizing Morgana's statement was true. After a few more seconds of deliberating, the boy finally reached down to grab one of the muffins. He picked up a britaberry one, took a satisfied bite, then walked off. The two girls looked at each other, then burst out laughing.

"I guess we were both wrong," Morgana said between giggles. Aireyal laughed until her sides hurt, and she snorted. She wasn't sure why it was so funny, maybe it was because it was such a silly thing to laugh at in the first place. Or maybe it was because Morgana kept laughing along with her, not even stopping to say a word about Aireyal's snort. *Is this what having a friend is like?* "That's him!" Morgana blurted out suddenly. Aireyal's heart did the annoying flutter thing before she even looked up. Morgana pointed to a tall boy with black hair, and Aireyal's heart continued its flipping, sinking back down like an overused anchor. "He's the one who told me Zale would be here," Morgana said, getting up. Aireyal's feet followed before she could even think.

"Have you seen Zale?" Aireyal found herself asking the moment the boy noticed them. He looked to Morgana first, then noticed Aireyal.

"Recently? No," the boy said.

"You said he would be here, Tyus," Morgana said.

"No. I said he'd try," Tyus corrected. "At least, that's what he told me. Zale looked a little busy last I saw him, said he had important things to do." *More important than being here with me?* Aireyal's fingers caressed the bracelet Zale gave her. "Excuse me, I have to get back to my escortee… unless you wanted to trade places with her, Morgana."

"I would rather wake up with a Kahamian knife at my neck in the middle of a winter night." The comment was so specific Aireyal couldn't help but wonder if the headmistress had threatened Morgana with it before. Either way, Tyus hurried off and out of sight. Aireyal groaned, wishing she had Morgana's unflappable attitude. Pretending not to be hurt from the news was—

Twang! Loud lute strumming. A line of musicians filed into the room across from the chorus of singers already present. They all stood on a short, elevated platform in the middle of the hall. The two groups glared back and forth, competing for volume. The lute had the upper hand for a while, until a high-pitched voice rang over them.

There is one place where elves roam free
Beneath the waves of the Sunlit Sea
In the realm of wood that's filled by tree

This is the place you should live and be
Lanasall, beautiful land for all
Where joy rains like a waterfall
Before your country we stand tall
Lanasall, beautiful land for all

Apprentices from around The Banquet Hall coupled up and started dancing to the song. Before long, Morgana stood up humming the tune too. She nudged Aireyal several times to get her to join in, but Aireyal shook her head. She never liked their country's anthem, and she disliked dancing more. People who danced stood out. Not to mention her mood had soured after what Tyus told them. "Don't be so bottled up, it'll be fun," Morgana said, taking a hand to tug at Aireyal's arm.

"I don't dance," Aireyal said, planting her shoes on the floor to keep from moving.

"Neither do I," Morgana said with a chuckle, using her other hand to pull Aireyal too. "We can embarrass ourselves together," she said, hoisting Aireyal up next to her.

"People will see—"

"Aireyal, look around, everyone here is focused on themselves."

Morgana was right. All the other kids' eyes were on their partners. "Come on, just have fun for once," Morgana said, offering Aireyal her hand. Aireyal took it and followed Morgana's movements, swaying to the music. Aireyal tried to give her a smile, but her heart was still too sore. "I am sorry about Zale."

"It's not your fault," Aireyal said.

"You wouldn't be here if I didn't tell y—"

"Morgana, it's fine."

"You don't sound fine."

Aireyal dropped Morgana's hand and stood still. "Because I'm not," Aireyal said, holding back tears welling in her eyes. "I want to be fine, but it still hurts." Morgana's eyebrows turned in pity and Aireyal dropped her head. "I hate how I let myself feel. He hasn't talked to me since..." *The non-kiss.* "A really long time," Aireyal said, drooping her shoulders. "Why do I even care so much? I wish I were like you. You don't let anything bother you. That must make life easy."

"Aireyal, look at me," Morgana said, taking her hand again. She didn't speak until Aireyal lifted her head up. "A lollidrop is hard on the outside, but inside it's softer than any other candy." The words were sweet, but there was a solemness to Morgana's tone. Aireyal thought of all the things Morgana must've been through growing up under Headmistress Markado's prowling watch.

"I'm sorry, I didn't mean t—"

"It's fine," Morgana said, but the smile she gave was even less convincing than Aircyal's.

"If you ever want to talk about it, I'm here," Aireyal said, and Morgana's mouth turned into a real smile.

"I have never met anyone like you," Morgana said, chuckling. "I'm supposed to be cheering you up, not the other way around." Morgana swayed in time with the music again, bringing Aireyal with her. "Tell me something, why did you choose to come here to Darr-Kamo, knowing you were magicless?"

Aireyal followed Morgana in the dance for several long moments before she responded. "There were a lot of reasons," she said at last. "Part of me believed that if I came here, I'd be able to learn magic."

"Magic is not something you learn as much as feel, just like dancing."

"But if you don't know the right steps—"

"Then you can make them up on your own," Morgana said, shuffling her feet randomly.

"I don't think that's how it works," Aireyal said, keeping in time with the music.

"That is the problem. You *think* too much. Let your instincts take over," Morgana said, still shuffling against the rhythm, but somehow making it look natural. "So, why do you care about learning magic this much? Is it the pressure of being the Grandmage's daughter?"

"No, it's far more foolish than that. Thinking about it now makes me realize how crazy of a plan it was."

"What plan?" Morgana asked as the song ended in the background.

"I came here to start the first steps of becoming a Senate-Mage so I could help create changes here for people who need it the most. Not us, but you know, for people like the one's begging outside The Home of Parliament every day," Aireyal said. Morgana stared at her for a moment as though trying to judge if Aireyal was being serious, then she laughed.

"That is the most Aireyal thing I have ever heard," she said, and Aireyal blushed.

"I told you it was foolish, I don't know what I was thinking," Aireyal mumbled. "I've been nothing but terrified since I stepped foot on these grounds."

"You were thinking like you always do. About other people. Honestly, the world would be a much better place if more of us were like you," Morgana said, and Aireyal scoffed.

"A world full of magicless cowards doesn't sound so great," she said, and Morgana squeezed her hands gently.

"Cowardice is refusing to face the things you know you must. Bravery is trying to succeed even when you know you might fail."

Aireyal couldn't help but smile. *Maybe she's right. Just maybe.*

"You're awfully cherry," said a snooty voice. Priscilla Hornbuckle stalked over to them with Winston Ellisburg, a tart expression wrinkling her face. She even brought followers this time that stood behind her, nodding along self-importantly. Of course the guardians of good times would show up now. Aireyal took a step from Morgana and turned to them.

"Hello," Aireyal said in as cold a tone as she could manage, though it still came out slightly polite. She needed to work on her *rude* voice. Priscilla didn't respond, instead she craned her neck to Morgana.

"Why are you with little Miss Magicless? You should come with us instead," she said. Priscilla glowered at Aireyal, then turned her nose up and looked back at Morgana. Aireyal stepped back to her table and took a sip of tea, hoping it would excuse her from the conversation.

"And should I stand to the left or right of your little minions' formation behind you?" Morgana asked the girl sarcastically. Aireyal spit her tea out on the floor, snorting. The minions shot her evil looks, while Priscilla's face went redder than Aireyal's dress.

"You don't get to laugh, Ando, you don't even have an escort!"

"Yes, she does, I am right here," Morgana said. Priscilla's mouth fell open as her eyes flipped back and forth between Aireyal and Morgana.

"I—But I thought…" Priscilla said, fumbling, then she composed herself. "Nice scar, Ando, it almost distracts me from how ugly you are," she said, stomping off, tailed by her horde.

"You are too nice. Next time, put her in her place," Morgana said to Aireyal. "I'm going to get another muffin. Do you want one?"

"Sure, I'll take a britaberry one, thanks."

Morgana eyed her. "The scar really does look good on you. Make sure to thank the girl who gave it to you when you see her again," she said with a knowing wink, walking off.

Aireyal ran her finger over her scar, then a chill of realization crept down her spine. *I never told Morgana who gave me the scar. She knows because it is her. I'm such a fool. The signs have always been there, I've just been pretending I didn't see them.* The dark hair. Access to the headmistress's office to steal the mirror. The scar comments. *But why?* Clearly, she wanted to save the dragon, but then why was she in the library the first night of school? Zale hadn't even remembered her. Unless. *Had he lied about that?* Zale and Morgana had been in the apothecary together. *He wouldn't lie to me.* Or would he? *He isn't here now a—*

A hand touched Aireyal and she jumped. "Calm down, I'm just bringing you a muffin," Morgana said in a muffled voice, her own face stuffed with a tiny chocolate muffin. She held a vanilla one out to Aireyal. "They were out of britaberry. I blame that boy from earlier," she said, smiling. Aireyal accepted the muffin and tried to fake a smile, but the slightest narrowing of Morgana's eyes indicated she saw right through it. "Sorry, I didn't know it was that important to you. I can ask to see if they're making more brita—"

"Vanilla is fine," Aireyal said, forcing herself to take a bite. It was good, not *britaberry* good, but good. She tried to fake another smile, but her face fell into a frown.

"I'll go get you a different muffin," Morgana said, returning the frown.

"Morgana, there's nothing wrong with the muffin."

"Then what is it?"

"I don't know how to say this..." Could she really accuse Morgana? *I have to.* She couldn't. *I HAVE TO.*

"What?"

"You're her, aren't you?" Aireyal asked, closing her eyes. She waited several moments for... she didn't know what. A maniacal laugh? A series of deadly spells heaved her way? Thunder suddenly crashing outside?

When Aireyal peeked out, Morgana's mouth was curled in confusion.

"I'm who?"

"The girl with the brooch," Aireyal let out in a whisper.

"Who?" Morgana repeated, twisting her brows as though she were utterly lost. Maybe Morgana wasn't faking. *Stop being naïve, of course she is.*

"You're the one who gave me this scar, right?" Aireyal asked, feeling less certain with every word as Morgana's face squished more and more in bafflement. Maybe it wasn't her. *But it has to be.*

"Aireyal, what are you talking about?" Morgana's voice was calm, but she frowned deeply. Was she faking? *Of course she is.* "Why would I be here if I wanted to hurt you?"

"I..." Aireyal didn't have a good answer to that. Morgana shook her head.

"I cannot believe you," Morgana said, stomping off into the crowd.

"Wait." Aireyal followed, squeezing through the sea of people, trying to keep an eye on Morgana's ever-changing dress. But person after person shoved Aireyal every which way, making the task impossible.

It was only made worse by the fact she was too short to see over anyone. When she reached the other side of the crowd, Morgana was nowhere to be found. Instead, Aireyal's eyes found Headmistress Markado staring directly at her. An icy shudder went down Aireyal's back. *How long has she been watching me?*

Thud. A troop of Lanasall townguards stormed into The Banquet Hall, each adorned in armor. The one in front carried a small, terrified-looking creature in his hands with big red eyes and scaly black skin. Scarlet.

"May I have your attention, please," the headmistress said, trying to conceal a triumphant smile on her face. "I would like to announce that *I* have uncovered an attempt to hide a dragon here on these grounds. An attempt by Grandmage June Ando, whose crimes will be punished as quickly as possible."

~ *Chapter 31* ~
Falling Feelings

MOVE AS QUICKLY AS POSSIBLE. RUNNING MEANT he didn't have to think. Didn't have to feel. And Erevan didn't want to feel anything ever again. It would be easier that way. Selea had screamed in the distance as the Krilows caught her, and Erevan had heard them turn to chase after him and Nya afterwards. And now, even after they'd run so far that the Krilows surely had no idea where they were, Erevan kept running.

"Slow down, please." Nya touched his shoulder and he collapsed face-first into the muddy ground of the street. It wasn't that she'd pushed him; he was just ready to fall.

The water on his face might've been the rain that hadn't stopped pouring or it might've been tears. He didn't care either way. He just didn't want to think abou—

"I'm so sorry he's gone," Nya said, kneeling beside him.

"Don't talk about it," Erevan said, his voice hoarse. His chest was sore like it had been heaving up and down for some time. Maybe he *had* been crying, or it could've been from the lingering bruises left by the Krilows. *They deserve death.* Erevan punched the squishy ground. Rage. That was an emotion he didn't mind feeling. He welcomed it. *The only one I should be mad at is myself. I let this happen. I chose to find Scoti. I chose to let him die.*

Soft, caring hands pulled Erevan's face out the mud, sitting him upright. Nya's hazel-brown eyes stared into his. It seemed like they'd lost some of their brightness… or maybe the brightness was gone from him.

"Erevan…" Nya started, looking like she wanted to say something else. Instead, she wrapped her arms around him in a warm hug. At least, he thought that's what warmth felt like, he couldn't quite remember. "I'm so sorry," she said again, her voice breaking. *Is she crying too?* The sobs that followed answered him as she shuddered.

Shame. That was another emotion he felt. Not that he wanted to, but he deserved it. *I watched him die and did nothing.* No, not nothing. *I ran like a coward.* "I should've fought them. I should've killed them all," he seethed out. *He needed me and I didn't help. I wasn't even here for Tinny. And Selea, now she's…* Erevan clenched his fists until they hurt, then he clenched harder.

"There was nothing you could've done. It wasn't your fault," Nya said tearfully. "We did the only thing we could."

"He's my father. I should've avenged him," Erevan said, slamming his fist deeper into the ground. Then something sparked in him. Something he never thought he'd feel again. Something he wasn't sure he deserved to feel. *Hope.* "I know where they're headed." He could still avenge his father.

Nya looked at Erevan, a fire burning in her eyes. "Where?"

"Rifton."

She hopped back on her feet in an instant and offered him her hand. "They stole my mirror and killed a good man. We're not going to let them get away."

Erevan took her hand. "No, we aren't." It might've been in his mind, but he thought he felt another sliver of warmth as she helped him to his feet.

They were near the western border of town from the looks of it, heading back in the direction of the farms and towards Garolek. Erevan turned around. East. That's where they needed to go. To the docks on the other side of town to get a boat and sail for Rifton. If they hurried, they could get to the river city tomorrow morning. Erevan started forward, but his legs were sore. *How long have I been running?* Regardless, he pushed himself, moving eastward.

"What's the plan?" Nya asked, following him.

Plan? He didn't have one of those. But he knew what he wanted to do. "I'm going to kill every last Krilow."

"Erevan, we need to think. Be smart about this. There's five of them. We can't take them on alon—"

"Watch me," he said. Fury consumed him as he saw his father murdered in his mind on an endless repeat. Erevan knew he *should* come up with a plan, but he couldn't, not right now.

"That's stupid, you're going to get yourself killed," Nya scowled, walking in front of him and planting down her feet.

He pushed past her. "I don't care, it's what I deserve."

"No, it's not." She grabbed his shoulder. That feeling of warmth again. It felt good and he hated her for it. *I don't deserve to feel good right now.* Erevan tried to shrug her hand away, but she held fast. "I'm not going to watch you throw your life away."

He moved to walk off again. "Why not? It shouldn't matter to you what I d—"

"It *does* matter to me," she said, stepping in front of him a second time. Her eyes were full of grief and regret, like she was staring at a corpse. And maybe she was. He might've already been dead. "Seeing you like this hurts. Please don't do this to yourself."

"You don't need me."

"But I want to," she said. Then Nya's eyes widened like the words surprised her. She took his hand in hers, frowning at him. "Erevan, you're the most frustrating person I've ever met. You don't admit when you're wrong, you never think before you do anything, and you're terrible at Wizards, Witches, and Warlocks."

"If this is supposed to make me feel better, you're doing a terrible job," he said, and a grin snuck its way onto the edge of her lips as her nose wrinkled. Another tiny bead of warmth came to him from her smile. Almost enough to want to go on, even if just for a little bit.

"You're also honest, you try to do the right thing, and you look out for those that can't help themselves. And that's why, despite how much you infuriate me every day, I always want you by my side."

Heat was flowing through him now. The rage was still there, but it had calmed, replaced by... *comfort?* Nya gave him another hug and for the first time in what seemed like a lifetime, he wasn't angry at himself. He wasn't sure if he deserved it, but he hugged her back anyway. "Thank you," he said, holding her in his arms.

Erevan had no idea how much time passed, but he didn't want to let her go. Nya was the most daring person he'd ever met, the greatest sorcerer he'd ever seen, and the one person who could make him feel better now, even when he didn't want to. "I'll stay by your side until the end," he said. "I'm here whenever you need me." She shifted and he stared into her big, beautiful, brown eyes. Their usual brightness was back and livelier than ever. "I'm sorry for all those things I said before." He hadn't forgotten his words to her on the outskirts of town. The anger he'd had at all the secrets she'd kept from him.

"I know," she said, then she glanced down at her boots. "I should've told you earlier. There are so many things I should've told you. So many things I still have to tell you." Nya looked back up at him and tensed like there was some great burden she carried. Erevan gave her a gentle squeeze.

"We've got a long walk ahead of us, I'll listen to whatever you want to say. And if there are things you don't want to say, you don't have to," he said, forcing himself to let go of the embrace he wanted to stay in forever, and head east.

Nya followed, uncertainty in her tone when she spoke, "Are you sure?" she asked, and he nodded. "Then I should start by telling you the truth about my journey. I'm not supposed to be here," she said, then leaned in to whisper as they walked. "The Magistrate of New Lanasall delivered a message to the King of Nyumbafro about a strange mirror."

"Why would she send a message to him?"

"Because she knows we collect all the magical items we can. And because she wanted to sell it. New Lanasall is starving for coin and from our travels it's clear the citizens aren't happy with their leadership. The Magistrate is not a queen, she could be removed." Erevan thought of the rising taxes. Nya was right. "We knew it was one of the Frostfire Mirrors of Torva from her description."

"Torva? That's where the dwarves say the spectres are from."

"They're right. And that's why I knew we had to keep the Torvans from obtaining the mirror, but the price she asked for was far too high, so my father turned her offer down."

"But you came anyway," he said, and she nodded.

"I'm the only person who both dared to defy the king and could get enough gold to do so. We all knew what the mirror showing up here meant. The Torvan Empire is on their way to the western world. That crusader was the first of an entire army, I'm sure."

A chill traveled through Erevan's bones. "What do they want?"

"To conquer. Everything and everyone. You either become a part of their *divine* empire or you perish," she said.

"How do you know all this?"

"I hear many things in the palace."

"You live in a palace?"

"I wouldn't be much of a princess if I didn't, would I?" she whispered, giving him her signature smirk, then it faded. "But it seems Heritour has found out about my travels."

"And it's against the Treaty of Rifton for anyone from Nyumbafro to set foot inside of Rifton," he whispered back, and she nodded grimly.

"Let alone a princess. If they see me, a conflict that extends across nations will follow. We have to find the mirror and get out undetected."

"I'm not leaving until the Krilows feel the same pain they caused my father," Erevan said, anger flowing through him again. Mostly at the Krilow brothers, but some at himself too. *You're nothing but a liar.* His last words to his father. He would never get the chance to apologize for them, but he could avenge him. Nya was right though; he needed a plan. His father wouldn't want him to go on without one. *A man must think before he acts.* He'd never hear his father speak those words again, but he could still follow the man's guidance. *He's gone forever.* The cold hand of despair wrapped its way around Erevan once more and his whole body slumped. Nya frowned.

"Erevan, I'm so sorry."

"You don't have to keep saying that."

"Yes, I do. I can't help but feel responsible. If you hadn't met me, Sir Lee would stil—" she paused, her voice breaking. "I didn't know him as long as you, but I know he was a good man. He saved me from that crusader, and now I'm alive while he's..." Tears formed in Nya's eyes and her hands shook. "And now he's dead because of me. It's the curse of the throne. That's what my father says. To go on every day knowing that when you make a mistake, good people die. It's why I hope I'm never queen. I don't think I could..." she trailed off again, staring at her hands as though they were stained with blood. Erevan put an arm around her as they walked toward the docks.

"You don't have to be queen today," he reminded her, and she leaned into him, letting her breaths move in time with his heartbeat.

"Thank you," she said, her voice soft and low.

"I'm here whenever you need me."

"I know."

Chapter 32

Reunion of Revelations

T HE HEADMISTRESS MIGHT NOT HAVE KNOWN IT,
but she was probably Aireyal's least favorite person ever. The
lady droned on and on merrily while everyone at the dance, even
the townguards that had arrived carrying Scarlet stood intrigued
by her words. Well, everyone except for Aireyal. Instead, she
stood, arms folded, as the headmistress explained Lanasall law
and why hiding a dragon must be punished and how they'd all
hear about even more tomorrow.

Aireyal had anticipated the headmistress doing something
horrible to her before the year ended, but sending her mother to
jail wasn't on the list of expectations. Then again, Aireyal's inner
voice kept telling her something else. *Your mother will be going to*

jail because of you. If Aireyal had made a decision about Scarlet earlier, none of this would've happened.

"This news hurts no one more than myself. Grandmage Ando was a dear friend of mine," the headmistress said. *Liar.* "But don't worry about that *criminal*, she is already been retained for your safety and will not be causing any more trouble."

Aireyal stomped out the hall. All the eyes in the giant room followed her, but for once, she didn't care. Not even the sympathetic looks from the burly, dragon-carrying townguard gave her pause. She had to talk to her mother, but she needed to do something else first. She needed to find out the truth about Morgana.

Her footsteps carried her across the school grounds toward their room. Everything made sense if Morgana had been playing Aireyal like a fool from the start. But it hadn't seemed that way from how she had reacted to Aireyal's accusations. *She had to be lying, right?*

Then again, if Morgana was trying to save Scarlet, was she a bad person? But what could she have to gain from freeing a dragon? Some blood magic sacrifice ritual, perhaps? Maybe that's why she'd been in the library that night. *If* that was her. Whatever the reason, Aireyal was going to go through every note, scroll, and tome Morgana had until she found an answer. If Morgana hadn't gotten there first, that is. Aireyal had no clue where the girl had gone after disappearing from the dance.

Creak. The doors to the girl's dormitorium opened wide and Aireyal hurried inside its marble halls, picking up her pace. Maybe her mother could make sense of everything. She might have some piece of the puzzle Aireyal was missing. But when would she get another chance to talk to her? *She's going to jail because of you.* Aireyal tried to shake the thought away, but it stuck fast like eyes on a compelling book. *I can't keep waiting and hoping. I have to start acting.*

And she had the chance to do that now. Aireyal slipped down the empty hall, into her room and shut the door. *No sign of Morgana.* Aireyal headed straight for Morgana's wardrobe, remembering the dust the girl had hidden there when she tricked Aireyal into telling Zale she was magicless. *Did she really trick me, or was I going to tell him anyway?* It didn't matter. This wasn't the time to think about that.

Aireyal noticed a handwritten note sat atop Morgana's desk. She crept over to read it.

Sincerest star
And brightest ray
You surely are
My deepest grey
They thank you for, the warmth of day
And curse me for, ending your stay
Beacon you are, providing hope
For all like me, you're our last rope
My glow shall fade
In milky bloom
But you're my shade
Against all doom

What?

Morgana writes poetry? Aireyal squinted at the letters; it was Morgana's handwriting for sure. *Who cares? You need to find something on the dragon, or the brooch.* Aireyal placed the letter back on the desk, then scampered over and opened Morgana's wardrobe. *So many dresses. And shoes. And pouches of dust.* But no... what is it she was looking for anyway? The brooch itself? The jagged knife? Another note? One where Morgana confessed everything?

Would that even do any good? Aireyal's mother wasn't in the trouble she was in because of Morgana, at least, not directly. Aireyal sighed and picked up one of the pouches of dust. *None of this would've happened if I could do magic.* She opened the pouch and poured some dust into her hand. Blue dust. *I have to learn soon. I can't keep waiting.* She sighed again, then moved to put the pouch b—

Aireyal paused. Behind where the pouch had been was a small chest. *Could this be what I'm looking for?* An ominous glass raven decorated the top of the box. *What are you hiding, Morgana?* Aireyal reached to pick it up.

Szchla! A ghoulish shriek and a dark mist spewed from the chest.

"Countru!" Aireyal shouted in what was either instinct or fear, tossing her dust forward and closing her eyes. A brilliant flash blinked and Aireyal squeezed her eyes open. The mist was gone. Aireyal peered around and didn't see any dust. *Did I just do magic? Or...*

A faint glow faded from the bracelet on her arm. *Did I do that?*

"Hello? Is someone in there?" an all-too-familiar voice asked from somewhere in the hall. Aireyal's blood froze. She sprinted for the door, swinging it open to get out befor—

Crash! Aireyal smashed into someone.

"Ow," she said as her elbow slammed into the ground.

"What are you doing here?" The tone of someone obviously not happy to see her. She looked over to see Zale picking himself up off the floor. He wasn't wearing the formal clothes of someone going to a dance. He had on adventuring clothes and a bag over his shoulder. Aireyal's mouth opened but nothing came out. He offered a hand to help her up, but she ignored it, standing on her own.

"I think the question is, what are *you* doing here?" she asked. His face dropped, proof he could hear the irritation in her voice.

"I don't have time to explain, but you need to leave. *Now*."

Her frustration grew in a storm. "You've been avoiding me for two weeks, and that's all you have to say?"

"I don't have time for you right now." Aireyal blinked in shock. She shrunk smaller than a pebble; one that had been crushed under Zale's boot. "That's not what I meant."

"It's what you said."

"I—please just go, I'll talk to you later," he said. Aireyal ripped the bracelet he had given her off and shoved it into his chest.

"Don't bother."

Footsteps clattered in the hall behind her. Aireyal spun to see the girl with the brooch walking her way.

"A lovely surprise to see you," she said, looking at Aireyal. Her hood covered her face in shadow, but it didn't matter anymore.

"You don't have to keep faking your voice, I know who you are," Aireyal spat. *The evil chest of darkness was obvious enough evidence.*

"You told her about me?" the girl asked Zale. *Told her? So, they're together.* Aireyal turned back to Zale. His face was stiffer than a dead tree.

"I didn't say anything," he said through thin, barely moving lips.

The girl turned back to Aireyal. "Impressive, maybe you're as smart as he says you are. I wish that could change things," she said, then she pulled out her jagged knife.

"Don't," Zale said, jumping between the girl and Aireyal. "Let me." Then he turned to Aireyal. "Dormia." A blaze of green light flashed, then everything faded away.

RIFTON'S MARKETPLACE BUZZED UNDER THE BLAZE of early morning sun's light along the city's watery shore. Merchants and customers shouted everything from food prices to town gossip and everything in between. The fishermen were the loudest of the bunch.

One of them, a fisherman named Fisu, was ferrying Erevan and Nya across the Raging River. He didn't speak much or ask many questions. But upon seeing Nya would pay him twenty-five gold coins to get them to Rifton, he had happily obliged, even agreeing not to mention seeing them.

Nya kept her hood and gloves on from before the time they reached the docks of Bogudos and all the way here as Rifton's shores came upon them. She was completely concealed like she'd been the day Erevan met her. He followed her lead, wearing his own hood. They both agreed that being here long wasn't a good idea. They needed to find the mirror, *fast*. And that meant finding the Krilows.

"Swamptrout from the rivers, my food always delivers!" a fisherman called out from his stand in the marketplace, surrounded by hungry faces.

"Scales already sheared, this way for fish that's seared!" another shouted from somewhere in the marketplace. Every fisherman in town seemed to have their own distinct phrase. Probably a necessity because competition looked high. At least two dozen fishermen yelled over one another as people flocked into lines for food.

"Get it here and not there! Fisu fish is always Fisu fresh!" Fisu called, jumping from the boat and hurling a net full of fish toward his own stand, which housed detailed paintings of blue fish chasing each other on expensive fabric. "Sure I can't convince you two to stay until these are cooked?" he asked Erevan and Nya, nodding to his fish.

Growl. Erevan's stomach reminded him how long it'd been since his last meal. Though he knew eating what Fisu was offering would only make him think of the man that was supposed to teach him how to fish. His father. And how he'd *failed* him. A freezing gust of shame swirled inside him. "No, we can't afford to stick around," he said, helping Nya out the boat after he got out.

"Then maybe you could *afford* to help my memory falter again," Fisu said, setting a cooking fire with a log at his stand.

"But you've already been paid," Nya said. Fisu shrugged.

Erevan's eyes narrowed, though Fisu probably couldn't see it under the hood. "Maybe we should see if you can *afford* for your entire stand to burn down," Erevan said, moving over to the fire.

"No need for that. I've forgotten everything," Fisu said quickly, but Erevan stared him down anyway, until Nya touched his shoulder.

"Come on, Erevan," she said, pulling him away. "There's no need for that."

"Sorry, I'm not in the best of moods," he said, following her into the market.

Erevan's hand slid instinctively to the hilt of his sword every time someone raised a suspicious eye their way, which was more than once. "Just keep moving," Nya whispered each time, her hood still pulled over her head.

"I used to complain to my father because he never let me come here to the *great* city of Rifton," Erevan whispered back, "But now I see he only wanted to protect me," he continued, watching as they passed several craftsmen selling paintings to a clamoring crowd of people. One man gave them another crooked eye, whether that was because he saw their skin or because they were wearing hoods in broad daylight was impossible to tell. "My father didn't want the townguards mistaking me for a Nyumbafroan."

"I can see why he was afraid they'd arrest you," Nya said. Another eye, and they sped up their pace through the marketplace.

"He was afraid they'd kill me," Erevan corrected. "Looking the part is enough for death around here."

"Things shouldn't be this way. Someone needs to take the first step by putting aside their differences."

"Who?" Erevan asked, looking at the crowd around them. Nya had no answer, she just kept walking, staring ahead as though lost in thought. "It's not like these people care that the ones protecting them are murderers. They're too busy wasting their coin on useless things," Erevan said, shaking his head at a lady who bought a portrait.

"Paintings aren't useless, they're art. It's culture."

"You can't eat culture."

Nya chuckled softly. "Maybe not, but it is the spirit of its people," she said, still whispering, then nodded to one of the paintings. It was of a man who cheered proudly in a fine tunic as one pig raced ahead of other hog competitors on a muddy trail. "Heritour enjoys much success of late and their art reflects it."

"What's art from Nyumbafro like?" Erevan asked, and Nya bounced with excitement.

"It's a blend of creativity and sorcery. Hopefully, one day I can show you. I think you'll like it."

"I'm not sure I'll ever have time. I should go back to help my mother, especially since…"

The sun was bright and hot, but a chill came over Erevan all the same. One that froze his heart to ice. *His father was dead.* Nothing could change that now. Nya placed an arm around his side and the warmth from her made it better, but he was still cold.

"We're going to find them Erevan, they're in this city somewhere," she said, her voice held back an anger as though it had moved from him to her. He looked through the crowd, searching for anyone with the build of one of the Krilow brothers. It wasn't the most effective plan, but it was an easy enough task. Too easy, in fact. There were at least twenty men in sight who could've been one of them. He scanned faces for the yellow beard of the tallest Krilow, but locating him in the sea of people shoving their way through and shouting in the marketplace was impossible.

"I don't think we're gonna find him like this," Erevan said. Nya nodded, her head moving back and forth between the masses as well.

"There is one place we can look, or rather ask," she said. "The church of Evlynna."

"Why there?"

"The Krilows spoke her name a couple of times. I'd bet the people at the church know their faces, maybe even where they live." *The irony.* Men of the church, *murderers.*

The church of Evlynna wasn't nearly as hard to find as the Krilows themselves. The silver bell atop its giant tower had been ringing through the morning at the top of every hour. It was also the tallest building in the city, making it impossible to miss. Erevan and Nya made their way to where it stood as the centerpiece in the middle of the city.

The church gleamed so perfectly that it came off as smug. The buildings around it were flawless too, clean of all the filth and broken windows Erevan was used to in New Lanasall. And everything around led to the church. The paved roads converged like rays of the sun to its glass doors. And painted glass adorned the windows depicting a lady of golden hair with a basket of food, handing it off to the joyous faces around her. Evlynna. Erevan had seen her face many times, having been shuffled off to the church as a child by his mother constantly.

"There are more people than I expected here," Nya said as they entered the light-filled glass doors. More than a hundred churchgoers mingled about, some praying, others talking, and others still sharing food at tables. Their faces were all happy; some genuine, others less so.

"Do you see them?" Erevan asked, searching the crowd for the Krilows, but they were nowhere to be seen. Nya had no better luck.

"Would you like some bread, dearie?" an old lady asked, pausing before them with a basket full of fresh rolls. She bore one of the many genuine smiles in the room. *Growl.* The smell of honey wafting through the air was enough to convince Erevan's hungry stomach to get a roll. "Evlynna, bless you," the lady said with a smile. Evlynna *blessed* the roll from the taste of it. Warm, flaky, and delicious. "You look in need of a few more meals," she said, surveying Erevan's thin frame. If she noticed his skin, she didn't care. "Fresh food's served every morn an' eve here. No child goes hungry in the city if we can help it," she said, smiling.

"Thanks... but we're just visiting," Erevan said in between bites. "We're looking for someone. Do you know anyone by the name Krilow?"

The lady's smile faded. "You aren't here to cause trouble, I hope."

"I assure you, we aren't," Nya said. "They're dear friends of ours. We were hoping we could get a word with them," she lied. Erevan clenched his fist at hearing the Krilows called *friends,* even for the sake of getting information.

The old lady placed a hand on her hip. "You'd do well to speak to their other friends," she said, waving a hand towards several of the priests donned in red robes moving about, then headed on her way, offering bread to all she could. Erevan and Nya exchanged looks of concern before heading over to the nearest priest.

The man frowned at Nya, then perked up to force a smile. "It is disrespectful to wear a hood in the house of Evlynna," he said, his eyes fixed on Nya. Erevan could only hope its shadows hid her face from the man's prying gaze.

"I have a horrid burn on my face. I don't want anyone to see it," Nya lied.

"Evlynna judges us not for our appearance, but rather the valor of our hearts," the priest said tightly, then he reached to pull at Nya's hood.

She sprang several steps back before his grasp landed. "Don't t—" she stopped herself from whatever she was going to say, and Erevan took a step in between them.

"We're looking for the Krilow brothers, we were told you could help us," Erevan said, blocking the priest's inquisitive eye on Nya, and for whatever reason, the man made no comment on Erevan's hood.

"Gryson Krilow was here earlier this morn. He spoke with Rorulo, one of your kind. Gryson had a few questions before the Krilows' trip into Nyumbafro." *Nyumbafro? Why would they go there?* "Rorulo is up in the bell tower now."

"Thank you," Erevan said, ignoring whatever the, *your kind,* comment was supposed to mean. He tugged on Nya, pulling her away and up the stairs to the bell tower. Waiting around for the priest to start asking questions didn't seem like a good idea. They'd somehow been able to get around the city so far undetected by Rifton's authorities and he liked it that way.

And so, they moved. But the bell tower's winding ascension seemed to go on forever. They traveled up until they could see the top of every building in the city through the windows, then they went up some more. A commotion of some sort occurred below them at the base of the church. Shouting, and plenty of it. Clattering too. Nya sped up her climb.

"Slow down," Erevan called.

"Something's not right," she said. "That man spoke of Rorulo like he was from Nyumbafro. But if he is then..." she trailed off, picking up her pace again.

She was right, it didn't make any sense. Erevan scrambled in a rush behind her.

Up.

And up.

And up even more.

Nya finally reached the top and let out a horrified gasp. Erevan hopped up behind her. The body of a Nyumbafroan man hung from the bell, littered with arrows. One of them had a note attached. Nya grabbed it and Erevan read over her shoulder.

Dear Princess,

If you are reading this, you have broken the Treaty of Rifton with your presence here and will be considered an instigator of war. At this very moment, you are surrounded. Come quietly and we will consider taking you as a prisoner of war instead of a more forceful action.

−Sir James of Hamildale, Captain of Heritour's 3rd company

"They've been waiting for me. It was a trap," Nya said, turning to Erevan. Then her ears perked up along with his, and they stared out into the city. "Oh no."

Marching. A company of at least a hundred soldiers flew the blue flags of Heritour with silver boars embroidered on them. The soldiers closed in from the market, headed straight for the church.

~ Chapter 34 ~
Divine Duty

SPLASH, AIREYAL SAT UP AND STRAIGHTENED her head. The bright morning sun blared at her, and tall grass tickled her skin. She squinted ahead as a rock fell into a lake. The same lake the shadow tiger attacked her in. Her heart skipped a beat, and she snapped her head around, searching for the creature. But it was nowhere to be found… or rather, *seen*. Instead, by the bank stood a lone figure. The girl with the crescent brooch.

Morgana. Her hood still covered her face, and her back was turned, staring away from Aireyal at the lake, but Aireyal felt an anger building at her all the same. Vague memories of seeing her with Zale in the school hall came back.

"Why are we here, Morgana?" Aireyal asked. The girl turned and pulled her hood down.

"Maybe you aren't as smart as Zale thinks," she said. It wasn't Morgana. The elven girl before Aireyal had dark hair like Morgana's, maybe even a shade darker if that was possible, but there were no defiant purple streaks. The roots of this girl's hair were white as snow as though she'd dyed it this dark color long ago and it was starting to fade. Her face was paler than Morgana's too and when she spoke, her voice was only a little higher than Morgana's, though it fluttered a hair more. "Bugs will fly into your mouth if you leave it open like that."

Aireyal promptly shut the jaw she wasn't aware had dropped. "Who are you?"

"A servant of the divine as all righteous beings are," she said, raising her chin as though reciting a memorized oath.

"Why are you here?"

"To complete my mission of service to my home. The Torvan Empire," she said. Torva. It wasn't a dwarven tale. It was *real*. And if she was Torvan, that could mean Zale was too. Not from the Felaseran Forest, like he'd led Aireyal to believe.

"If your mission is saving the dragon, we're on the same side."

"That is certainly what Zale believes," the girl said, reaching into the grass. When she pulled her hand up, it held the Frostfire Mirror. It showed a lively city of people meandering about selling everything from fish and fabric, to pots and paintings. There was a shining bell tower in the not-so-far distance. Wait. The girl was holding the mirror in her bare hands, like Zale had.

"It's not burning you."

"Because I am not impure." *Impure*. What did that even mean? "Does ignorance infect all who live upon this unsettled rock?" the girl asked. She had the mystique of a much older lady, but from her face she couldn't have been more than a couple of years older than Aireyal.

"Rock?" Aireyal repeated.

"This tiny place you call a home."

"The school?"

"The western world."

The western world was *not* tiny. There were four fully-fledged countries here, not to mention the Kahamian League, the goblins, and other creatures that lived on the land. This was the largest region in the world, wasn't it? "How big is Torva?"

"Twice the size of this rock." Aireyal's eyes widened to the size of the sun. "You're so ignorant." The girl pulled out her curved dagger and twirled it. Seeing it again made every hair on Aireyal's neck stand up and she resisted the urge to touch her scar. But the Torvan girl didn't make a move to attack. She tossed another stone into the lake, instead, tapping her foot impatiently. "Where is he?" Her eyes looked to the cabin nearby. *Zale*. She had to be talking about him. The fires within Aireyal heated up. She stood from the bank and when the Torvan girl didn't move to stop her, Aireyal marched to the cabin.

She burst through the door then slammed it shut as hard as she could, which was a rather unimpressive creak. Inside, bags of animal food were torn and spilled, rope was flung everywhere, and there was an awful stench, like rotted meat.

"You're awake," Zale said, his face going paler than it already was. He was standing over two bodies. Two *dead* bodies. One was an apprentice she'd seen walking the school grounds before, a short boy who was always feeding the birds. The other body belonged to a docent. A lady with blonde hair.

"Did you…" Aireyal couldn't even fix her mouth to utter the rest of the words.

"No. You know I wouldn—"

"I don't know you at all," she snapped. Zale looked away, his hands clenching on the adventuring bag over his shoulder. His eyes passed over the dead bodies and cringed.

"This is Vale's work."

"The girl outside?" Aireyal asked. Zale nodded, then turned to the dead boy and shook his head.

"He was bringing a message to Docent Irwi. They wanted her to check on the dragon's health. It seems the dragon will live, for now. If only to be used as a political token. Perhaps a swift death like the docent here would've been more merciful," he said, looking at the body. "You should leave before Vale comes. She never stops searching for prey, and she strikes when they least expect it." He peered nervously at the closed door.

"Why are you speaking about her like an animal?"

"She's a purifier, it's what she does."

"Purifier?"

Zale groaned. "You don't want to know," he said, and Aireyal stomped her foot.

"I can decide for myself what I want to know, thank you," she said. "Like…" she opened her mouth several times, unsure what she wanted to ask first. *Who are you? Why did you bring me here? You lied about everything, didn't you?*

"What is going on?" was what she finally settled on.

He sighed. "I'm sorry. I never should've gotten you involved in this."

"Involved in what?"

His shoulders drooped. "This mission, and the crusade that will follow it."

"I don't know what that means."

"I know," Zale said, beginning to fumble through the room, searching for something and refusing to look her way. He combed over shelves and under sacks of animal food.

"Aren't you going to tell me more?" Aireyal asked when it became clear Zale wasn't saying anything else.

"I'd rather not."

"Why?"

"Because I'm afraid you'll hate the answer... and me."

Aireyal narrowed her eyes. "Keeping me in the dark with your masquerades isn't making me fonder of you. Vale already told me she's from Torva. Are you?" she asked, and Zale paused, distraughtly tight-lipped. *But maybe that was acting too.* "If Torva is some great warring empire like I've heard, why didn't they send an army?"

"I never said they didn't."

Is he serious? "So, what are you, some kind of scout?" she asked, and the disturbed look that crossed his face told her no. *Unless he's lying.* Probably. *Maybe.*

"Bringing the mirror back is the only way I can return home." He sounded like he was telling the truth. *He's lying.* "It doesn't belong here anyway. It'll only bring trouble... bloody, peaceful trouble." He looked like he was telling the truth. *He's lying.* Zale turned for a moment to face her. His beautiful blue eyes full of a deep, supplicating sorrow. *Don't look at his eyes. They lie too.*

"You only talked to me because you knew my mother had the mirror. You never cared about me at all." That was why he said he didn't have time for her. That was why he didn't bother showing up for the dance. That was why he didn't kiss her. *You're such a fool.*

"I do care," Zale said, sounding sincere. *But he's been pretending the whole time.*

"Liar," Aireyal seethed.

"You have to listen to me." He moved over to place a hand on her shoulder. His touch was cold and foreign, and she smacked his arm down.

"Don't touch me," she warned, and he took a step back.

"Pleas—"

"Don't even talk to me," Aireyal said in a voice lower and more dangerous than she'd ever spoken in before, then she headed for the door. Aireyal didn't know where she was going, but it was somewhere away from him. Her hand snatched the door open only to see Vale blocking the way, quickly examining Aireyal's distressed expression, then Zale's.

"Igra ogriu assilia riyno," Vale said to Zale in Sylvan, her tone flat as stone. *I'll kill the ogre.* At least, that's what Aireyal thought she said. But that didn't make any sense, she must've misheard her. Vale flipped her dagger, watching Aireyal with predatorial eyes.

"If you hurt her, I will—"

"Aoi igra haltiadoriyno?" Vale asked in a haunting laugh, cutting off Zale. *You'll stop me?* Aireyal was sure that was close to what she had said this time. "Aoi assilianisi unolo." *You're not a killer.*

"Aoloino iseegro uliada," Zale erupted, his voice was so threatening Aireyal turned back to check if it was him at all. *Don't make me become one.* She must've misheard him; Zale wouldn't say something like that. Then again, who was Zale? "Aireyal, take this. It will protect you," he said, walking between her and Vale. His hand held out the bracelet he'd given her before. "If you hate me, I understand. But please put it on."

"Magi gro igra arro," Vale said. Aireyal didn't know the meaning, but her voice was hurt. "Lizer—" Vale started, but he cut her off.

"I'm destined to be a traitor this day no matter what I choose to do!" Zale shouted in common, then he shook the bracelet in front of Aireyal. "Please, take it." Aireyal clutched it reluctantly.

A long, silent staredown between Vale and Zale ensued, as though they were testing to see if the other would move. Then at once, both of their ears perked, and their heads spun to the surrounding trees.

Zale turned back, looking at Vale. "Ioa nanalo trast ule riyna," he said. *We shouldn't still be here.* Or something close to it. Or perhaps, he had said, *we shouldn't have come here.* The phrases sounded somewhat similar.

"Ubiqu gladi draco pilgaba. Krisi isi trastule alio alio." That time, Aireyal hardly understood anything at all. Something about a dragon and armed guards. She looked out to the trees. What were they afraid was in there?

Aireyal found out, several seconds later.

"Docent Irwi, are you out here? They need your assistance in checking the dragon's health." Morgana's voice. She emerged moments later. Her face mirrored Aireyal's feelings of dread as she laid eyes on Vale, who turned back to Aireyal, twirling her dagger.

"This is lovely, you two can leave this world together."

Chapter 35

Stifling Standoff

TOGETHER, EREVAN AND NYA MOVED IN perfect step. Running was Nya's best plan. And Erevan ran alongside her back down the steps of the bell tower which were infinitely longer now that they were being pursued. Chatter grew below them in the church's main room and when they made their way down in a frantic rush, every eye was on them. The people didn't move but continued to stare as Erevan fled the building with Nya behind him, searching for somewhere to hide.

"Where are we going?" Nya asked. Erevan turned back to look at her.

"I don't know," he said as they ducked between buildings and into alleyways while thunderous marching came from every direction. The Heritourian army was close. *Too close.*

"You're in front, how do you not know?"

"Running was your idea."

"Then let's head back to the docks. We have to get out of this city," Nya said.

"What about—"

"The mirror? I have to let it go for now," she said.

"For now? They're going to hand that mirror off. After everything that's happened, you're giving up?" Erevan asked, stopping in an alley untouched by the sun.

"You don't understand. I don't have a choice, Erevan. If I'm caught, it'll be war, or worse." She walked up to him, her eyes twinkling with guilt.

"Then I'll get it. And I'll go through every Krilow in my way."

"Alone? There are platoons of Heritourian soldiers out there," she said, looking back. "If they know you were with me then—"

"I'm not going to let my father die for nothing."

"Erevan, you'll never—"

"Nya, I'm doing this. I couldn't live with myself if I didn't." He felt that cold pain cutting through his blood again. It wasn't a good idea; he knew that. But he couldn't run away. Not again. Not after all they'd been through. *All they'd lost.* He just needed to think of a way to do it without killing himself. *A plan.*

"If you're going, then I'm going with you," Nya said.

Erevan shook his head. "You don't have to do that."

"Yes, I do," she said, inching closer to him. "Whatever happens, we do it together."

"Are you sure?"

"Whether you like it or not, you're stuck with me," Nya said, her mischievous smirk forming.

"I'd like that a lot," he said, smiling back. Then she leaned forward and *kissed* him, immediately jerking her head back as quickly as she'd moved in. Erevan's face went fire hot.

"Sorry," she said, her eyes wide open. Erevan opened his mouth to respon—

Ring! Ring! Ring! The church bell was going off, but that same thunderous echo overtook it. Erevan dared to look up. Sunlight glistened off the silver armor of Heritourian soldiers. Their footsteps clanked on the paved cobblestone of the road. Civilians scuttled out the way of the army, not in fear, but rather in pride. Some chose to salute the blue flags waving high in the sky.

The army shouted orders to evacuate the area, and so the people did. "Why are they clearing everyone out?" Erevan asked.

"So they can murder us in cold blood," Nya said. On the front line of the host before them was a young soldier, carrying the very thing they needed.

"He has the mirror," Erevan said. They were too late. The Krilows had already delivered it. And to the Heritourian army of all places. The man before them carried the mirror, wrapped in cloth around its edges and tied to his quiver's chest strap along with a scroll of parchment in his gloved hand. *There's no time to plan, we've already lost.*

"I think that's him," Nya said.

"Him who?"

"The one who wrote the letter," she said. *The captain.* "I have an idea... a stupid one."

"How stupid?"

"Just follow my lead," she said as the Heritourian army closed in. She walked out of the alley onto the cobblestone street in plain view of the soldiers. Erevan followed, hating the plan already. The army marched until they were only a few yards before Nya, then stopped at once on their captain's command. "Are you, Sir James?" Nya asked the young man holding the mirror. He had markings on his armor in blue that suggested some sort of rank.

"I am. And you trespass on Heritourian land, princess," he said, standing up straight.

"You're a bit uptight," Nya said. A chorus of aggravated grunts came from the army around Sir James, though he stayed silent.

"It's probably not smart to annoy an entire army," Erevan whispered to Nya.

"Princess, you are under arrest in accordance with the Treaty of Rifton. Come peacefully and we shall not harm you," Sir James said, and his men moved to surround them.

"So I can be used like a bartering piece in a game? I'd rather not," she said and another chorus of grumbles from the army followed. One of them being a man muttering, *just kill her*. But Nya smirked. Was her plan to make them angry? If so, it was working. And although they were already surrounded by an unmoving wall of troops, more footsteps marched and shouted in the distance. *How many soldiers do they need?* "Sir James, I hope you'll hear me out—"

"No, princess. You shall hear *me* out," Sir James said, a hint of irritation budding in his tone. "A violent man, I am not. And that is the way I'd prefer it to stay."

"Is that why you brought all these soldiers to arrest one girl?" she asked. Sir James didn't look amused.

"Bind them," he said and half a dozen armed men around him walked forward as did another group from behind them. Resisting would be pointless, and possibly deadly, so Erevan let his hands be tied with rough, skin-scraping rope, as did Nya. "Perhaps now you will be more agreeable," Sir James said with a smile as his men stood guard around his new captives. Then he pointed at the mirror. "How does this weapon work?"

"It's not a weapon, it's a mirror," Nya said.

"That is not how it was described to me."

"The men you received it from stole it from me. I'm sure they were only trying to increase the sale price. The word of a thief can hardly be trusted after all," Nya said. Sir James grinned wider.

"Oh, but my information is not from those men," he said. "It is from the Magistrate of New Lanasall herself. And her words have all rang true so far." *The Magistrate?* But she was the one that wrote the note that started Erevan on this journey with Nya in the first place. Why would she tell Heritour of it too? She could start a war if she wasn't careful. "You seem surprised, princess. Shall I read one of her letters out to you?" Sir James asked. Nya's eyes widened as Sir James unrolled the scroll in his hand. "To the Captain of Rifton, I bring grave news. It has come to my attention that none other than the Princess of Nyumbafro is traveling to Bogudos carrying a magical weapon of great destructive power disguised as a simple mirror. I fear this is part of a larger plot by Nyumbafro to begin another war. With concern, but always hoping for a brighter tomorrow, Magistrate Luxa." Sir James put the letter away and looked at Nya. "Now, I ask again. How does this weapon work?"

"It's not a weapon."

"I tire of your lies, princess."

"She's not lying," Erevan said. *She might be.* But the Heritourians didn't need to know that.

Sir James looked at him. "And who are you?" he asked.

"I'm Erevan."

"I hope you understand, *Erevan*, that assisting the princess is a crime under Heritourian law."

"Leave him out of this," Nya warned.

"You don't make the rules in my country, princess," Sir James said, then motioned to one of the men standing next to Erevan. The man grabbed Erevan and pulled out a sword, bringing it to Erevan's neck. He struggled for a moment helplessly with his hands bound. "You may not be expendable, princess, but Erevan here is. Last chance, how does the weapon work?" Nya's face twisted, but she didn't speak. "I've all but lost my patience." Silence followed, except for the constant marching and shouting behind them in the city that grew ever closer to the street they were on. "Five." *He's counting the seconds until I die.* "Four."

"It's not a weapon," Nya said again. Sir James groaned.

"Two."

"Please listen to me," she pleaded.

"One," Sir James said, and the blade at Erevan's throat squeezed tight.

"You need both!" Nya shouted. Sir James motioned again, and the man released the sword at Erevan's neck right away.

"Need both what?" Sir James asked.

"There are two mirrors. They only form a weapon when together," Nya said. Erevan glanced over at her, but she refused to look back at him. Her eyes stared straight ahead at the captain. *Is she lying to him?*

"Where's the other mirror?" Sir James demanded.

"Far from here, it's in Lanasall," Nya said.

"Lanasall? You plan to obtain that one too?"

"No, I don't want the other mirror."

"How then will you make the weapon?"

"I don't want the weapon. I'm trying to keep it from falling into the hands of those who would destroy our very way of life."

"Whose hands do you speak of?" Sir James asked.

"You wouldn't believe me if I told you."

"I insist."

"Torva, home of the spectres you've heard of in tales from dwarves," she said. A round of laughs came from the men around Sir James.

"Your jest falls on the wrong ears," Sir James growled.

"Out of my way! I will speak to your captain!" shouted someone behind them. Erevan turned, but seeing through the rows of soldiers was impossible. The soldiers, though, had turned too, watching whoever was forcing their way through. Which, from the sounds of the growing marching and shouting, was another army.

Soon enough, elves, most of them with skin deeper brown than Erevan's own, made their way past the Heritourian ranks. The elves were donned in black and red, many carrying spears and shields embroidered with the faces of lions. An army of Nyumbafroans. There were at least as many of them as there were Heritourian soldiers, but each Nyumbafroan was strapped along the waist with pouches of dust. *Are they all sorcerers?*

"Your presence is not welcome here," Sir James said as a Nyumbafroan soldier pushed his way forward to where Erevan and Nya stood tied up.

"I would say the same to you, who stole our lands like a fox in the night," the soldier said, and a roar of approval came from the other Nyumbafroan soldiers who were pushing through as well behind their leader.

"By standing in this city, you dishonor the Treaty of Rifton," Sir James announced.

"You speak of dishonor while you threaten royalty as a commoner," the Nyumbafroan leader said, then he turned to Nya. "Princess," he said, kneeling to one knee. His soldiers did the same. Many of them stared at Erevan angrily until he followed along a moment later.

"Stop that, Erevan, get up," Nya said. "You too, Quan," she said to the Nyumbafroan leader. "And the rest of you," she said, and they all rose.

"Forgive me if I don't bow to criminals too," Sir James sneered to a chorus of approval from his own soldiers. The Nyumbafroans shouted several things back his way that must've been elvish curses, and Quan's eyes ignited with wrath.

"How dare you, Heritourian pig—"

"Quan, please," Nya glared, her hands still bound. "I'm trying to avoid violence, not start it."

"Forgive me, princess," Quan said, bowing and taking a step back. She turned her attention to Sir James.

"I'm sure neither of us want to see today end in bloodshed. Why don't we resolve this peacefully?" Nya asked.

"You are the one who called a foreign army into my city," Sir James said.

"I did no such thing, I assure you," Nya said, but Sir James sneered again. Then she turned to Quan. "Why are you here?"

"We were warned of Heritour's plan to imprison you, princess," Quan said.

"Warned from who?" she asked.

"The Magistrate of New Lanasall," Quan said. *The Magistrate?* Was there anything she wasn't involved in?

"Why'd she have to drag our country in the middle of this?" Erevan groaned. The last thing New Lanasall needed was to become part of Nyumbafro and Heritour's rivalry.

"It appears you've dragged *yourself* in the middle," Quan said to Erevan sharply.

"Quan, stop. Erevan has saved me more than once, I trust him with my life," Nya said, then she turned to address Sir James as well. "It seems we have a common foe, the Magistrate seeks to manipulate us all," Nya said, looking back and forth between Sir James and Quan.

"What proof have you of the claims you've made?" Sir James demanded of Quan.

"My word," Quan said.

"That means nothing to me," Sir James spat.

"I don't care what you believe. Release the princess or we will do it for you."

"Quan, you aren't helping," Nya snapped.

"You are all trespassing on Heritourian soil and as such are in violation of the Treaty of Rifton. You shall be tried in Heritourian court for your offenses before King Thomas," Sir James said.

"This is not your land, and we don't answer to your king," Quan said.

"You shall," Sir James warned, then he turned to his soldiers. "Arrest the princess's army. Any who won't come willingly can stay here as a corpse." The Heritourian soldiers drew their weapons.

"You can try," Quan said, bracing his spear against his shield. The other Nyumbafroan soldiers did the same.

"We don't have to do this," Nya pleaded.

"I am done trying to negotiate. Boars of Heritour, charge forth!"

Chapter 36

The Pious Purifier

VALE LOOKED POISED TO CHARGE AT ANY MOMENT, whirling her dagger. Breathing felt dangerous, so Aireyal decided not to. "This is the girl that cut you, isn't it?" Morgana said from the top step in front of the cabin's door, which was still blocked by Vale. Aireyal nodded but cringed. She'd wrongly accused Morgana at the dance, but now wasn't the time to apologize, that could come later. Vale didn't acknowledge either of them, instead focusing on Zale, now clutching her dagger tight in her palm. A shiver of fear trickled through Aireyal. Zale had infuriated her with his lies, but she still ached at the thought of him getting hurt.

"Please don't," Zale pleaded to Vale, but she closed her eyes, then cut across her own palm until it bled. Zale reached into his bag.

"Igra elkario alvia moi," Vale whispered in what sounded like a prayer. *Even on distant land must I purify,* is what Aireyal was nearly certain the words meant. Then without warning, she spun in a blur at Morgana. Her blade would've connected if not for Morgana tripping off the steps trying to step backward and falling into the tall grass.

"Ventu!" A gust of wind knocked Vale from the door and down into the grass below too. The spell had come from Zale's outstretched hand. He offered the other to Morgana, helping her up as Vale rose too. "You'll need this," he said, extending a pouch of dust to Morgana from his bag.

"Solio, amata kilola," Vale said to Zale with such venom that poison could've dripped from her lips. Aireyal didn't know what was said, but the emotion was enough to guess the meaning of her words. And Vale's eyes were burning, *literally.* A thin, smoky, white trail floated up from them, fading in the air just above her head.

"I'm doing what's right," Zale spat back at Vale.

Vale pulled a handful of dust from her bag and threw it up in the air. "Luxa!" Vale shouted and a light as bright as the sun burned Aireyal's eyes, the pain remaining even after she closed them. "Terru!" Vale said. Aireyal squinted, but her eyes were still dizzy and half blind. Her ears, however, worked fine. Feet shuffling, grunts of pain from Zale, a dagger swinging through the air. *She's going to stab him!*

"Please stop, I'll give you whatever you want!" Aireyal screamed as loud as she could. When her eyes came to, Vale had a dagger placed at Zale's stomach by the bank of the lake. Morgana stood several feet away with a handful of dust. "You want the mirror, right? It's yours, take it. But please, leave him alone. His life is worth more than that mirror."

"No, it isn't." Aireyal had expected the words to come from Vale. But instead, it was Zale who spoke them.

"Aoloino morta talami," Vale said back to him in warning. *Don't choose death*, that's what her words meant.

"Igro morta talami riyno, tuani gara felir," Zale said, dropping his head but not before Aireyal caught a face full of regret and sorrow. *I'd rather die by choice than live without freedom*, is what he said.

"Lizer morta bugoka," Vale said, narrowing her smoking eyes at Zale like a predator preparing to strike, her dagger unyielding below his chest. *Death to betrayers*. Or something similar to that, Aireyal was certain.

"He's not what you're here for. You wanted the mirror and now you've got it," Aireyal said. "Just leave. Please. I am begging you. You don't have to hurt anyone."

Unmoved, Vale responded, "Don't speak." Then she stabbed Zale in the stomach and kicked his body into the lake. He cried out, sinking into its waters, a trail of blood circling behind him.

"Zale!" Aireyal screamed, running after him. Vale was already throwing dust Aireyal's way though, and Aireyal closed her eyes, as though doing so would in some way save her from the girl's spell. *I'm going to die.*

"Aquo!"

An intense gurgle spurted from the lake and Aireyal braced for impact as she ran, but nothing hit her. Someone else slammed to the ground. Aireyal opened her eyes; Vale was on the ground in a puddle. Morgana had cast the spell. But before Aireyal could think any more, she fell forward, face-first into the lake.

Splash! The same colorful fish swam around, but somehow, they appeared grimmer this time. Aireyal scanned the waters; a stringy trail of red floated down. Zale's body drifted below it.

It was only now that she remembered she couldn't swim. Her heart picked up its pace and her hands started trembling.

You can't save him. You're too weak, the inner voice told her.

No, I'm not.

You're a coward.

I don't have to listen to you.

…

The voice didn't respond this time.

But this wasn't a moment to celebrate. Her hands were still trembling. She had to fight her nerves. She and Zale would both die if she didn't. *Focus. This will pass.*

Aireyal closed her eyes. One. *This will pass.* Then two. *This will pass.* Three. *This will pass.* Four. *This will pass.* Five. Her eyes popped open. Focused. Alert. Her heart still beat fast, but she was *finally* in control.

I can do this.

With a push, she kicked her feet forward. *Don't think, just act.* She dove down to where Zale's body had sunk at the bottom of the lake but as she grabbed him with two hands, blood red eyes slit open before her.

Aireyal didn't wait for her fears to be confirmed. She pulled Zale straight for the surface. A roar bellowed below, and she kicked her short legs as fast as they could go. A muffled scream came from someone, but Aireyal was too focused on reaching land to know if it had been her or Zale.

Another roar shook the waters as they made it above water and Aireyal pulled Zale to shore, then several feet further until they were hidden in the tall grass. She rubbed her blurred, stinging eyes, then Vale's shrill voice rang with indifference in her ears, "Why save the dead?"

Was he dead already? Aireyal placed one of her hands over his chest, checking for a heartbeat.

ROAR! Aireyal's head whipped around at once, but there was nothing there except the sun's rays shining down upon them. Vale, who stood on the bank, turned too. "Terru!" Vale shouted, firing dust toward the ground in the roar's direction. The earth shifted around invisible feet, encasing them. But not for long. With a quick series of stomps, the tiger broke free. Then a scramble of paws pounded toward Vale. "Ven—"

She didn't get to finish this time. Vale was sliced across her face and fell to the ground, where several more slashes carved her. The shadow tiger was going to maul her to death.

"Let her go!" Aireyal shouted, trembling within the tall grass.

A low growl hummed through the air, and the assault on Vale stopped. Then clawed footprints stalked towards Aireyal's voice. But after several steps, they stopped. A faint light sent Aireyal's eyes down. The bracelet Zale gave her glowed.

"Noxa!"

Aireyal looked back up. Every shadow pulled together, converging in darkness around Vale. A bewildered roar came from the tiger, and it slashed the shadows. But when the darkness passed, Vale was nowhere to be seen. The tiger scraped for several more seconds at the ground where she'd been before skulking its way back into the water. Aireyal looked again at the bracelet, but its glow was gone. *What was that?*

She waited several *excruciatingly* long moments, watching the lake for any more movement, before turning back to Zale. He wasn't moving and his eyes were shut. She placed her hand over his heart again.

Pump, pump.

He was alive. She leaned down and held him as tight as she could. Water trickled from her face, either from the lake or tears, or both. She didn't care; Zale was breathing. *Barely*, but breathing, and that's all that mattered. She needed to get him back to the school where someone could help him. Aireyal tossed one of his arms over her shoulders and stood awkwardly, trying her best to handle the added weight.

One clumsy step forward. Then two. Thre—

"Aireyal."

The voice was soft as a feather and half-dead. She turned to Zale, staring at his unconscious face before discerning it wasn't him who'd spoken. "Aireyal," the voice said again. Her eyes combed the grass around her. A sliver of purple hair stuck out. Morgana. She was bleeding on the ground. It was only now Aireyal realized the scream she'd heard in the water hadn't been from Zale or herself. It was Morgana.

Aireyal moved over and reached down clumsily helping Morgana over her shoulder, while still holding up Zale. Step by step, foot by foot, she lumbered toward the school's main grounds with both of their tall, bleeding frames slumped over her. Carrying one person was hard enough, but two took every muscle in Aireyal's body. *Don't think about the weight, just keep going.*

Left foot. Right foot. Left. Righ—

"Thank y-you, Airy," Morgana croaked, barely opening her violet eyes.

"I should be the one thanking *you*," Aireyal said back. "For everything." Morgana smiled and closed her eyes again. Aireyal still hadn't apologized for all the things she'd said at the dance, but she knew Morgana needed her rest, so she stayed quiet.

Left. Right. The minutes seemed to turn to hours as Aireyal went from strainfully walking to painfully dragging her feet. She'd hoped she'd meet someone along the way who could help her carry one of them, but no one was in sight. The sun melted her from above, and yet she didn't pass a soul near Sybill Observatory, the stone maze, or the bell tower as she went by. Her limbs had all but given out when she reached the bottom of the hill that led up to the apothecary hut. She'd never make it to the top. *I have to. They'll bleed out and die if I don't.* Aireyal forced her legs up the steep incline.

Left. Right. Lef—

She went tumbling down, crashing, and dropping Morgana and Zale in the process. One, or both of them groaned out in pain.

"I'm so sorry," Aireyal said, brushing grass and dirt from their faces. "I'm not strong enough." She looked back up the hill. *We're so close.* But she couldn't do it. She might be able to drag one of them up the hill, but if she somehow managed to do that, she wouldn't be able to make it up a second time. "Someone, please help!" Aireyal shouted. But the gentle breeze was her only answer. "If anyone's out there, please come help, I'm begging you!" she yelled out again. But there was no help to be had. *Where is everyone?*

Another pained groan came from either Morgana or Zale and Aireyal turned to them. Their faces were always a little pale, but they were more colorless than usual. Tears welled in Aireyal's eyes. *No.* It wasn't the time for that. *I refuse to let them die.*

Aireyal took a deep breath, then a second, and a third. She stood up and marched up the hill alone. *If I can't bring them to help, I'll bring the help to them.*

Getting up the hill took more than she thought, however. Aireyal's legs wobbled and she nearly fell back down, but she managed to lean her weight and fall forward instead. Then, steadily and surely, she crawled the rest of the way up the hill. Forcing herself on her feet one last time, she barreled into the apothecary hut. No Casilda, *as usual.* No matter, Aireyal scoured the walls, grabbing book after book and scanning them for remedies. Then she grabbed a basket and shoved the most useful books and a host of ingredients, herbs, and cloth into it. She snatched a pitcher of water with her other hand, then hurried out the hut.

Aireyal's legs shook just from the sight of the tall hill. She wasn't going to make it back down before they gave out. *Forget it, I don't need to walk.* She sat down, placed the basket in her lap, and slid her way down the hill like a child. But there was nothing carefree or fun about this. Her hand held the pitcher of water as carefully as she could, making sure not to spill it over.

The moment Aireyal reached the bottom of the hill, her hands were fumbling through the basket. *Accidents, Bruises & Cuts* was the first book she pulled out. Then *Bleeds & Bandages.* Aireyal's eyes skimmed back over the pages she needed. *Hopefully, I've studied enough to do this right,* she thought to herself, then she went to work.

Her hands trembled, but she ignored them. She didn't *really* know what she was doing, but the instructions in the book were clear enough. At least, on the basic things. She scrubbed her hands with water and soap, then tapped at their wounds with cloth to stop the bleeding. There wasn't enough cloth though, so she settled for *slowing* the bleeding instead. Then Aireyal washed their wounds with soap and water before wrapping them in kael leaves, which according to the books were the best natural choice for preventing infections. Finally, she held the leaves over the wounds in place with the little clean cloth left. *That'll have to do for now.*

"Aireyal?" She jumped at the sound of her name. But this time, it wasn't Morgana. "It is you, little chicata." Casilda. The lady strode Aireyal's way. "I didn't expect to see you here, wh—" she stopped, noticing the two bandaged bodies before Aireyal. "Qi morta! What happened to them?"

Aireyal opened her mouth, but she struggled to find the right words to say. "There was a girl with a knife," she started.

"She didn't happen to be wearing a brooch, did she?" Casilda asked. Aireyal's eyes popped open.

"You know about her?!"

"I didn't think she was real," Casilda said. "The morning of the second day of school, I found Zale half-conscious, right up there." She pointed to the front door of the apothecary. "He was talking in his sleep and mentioned her several times. I figured he was dreaming nonsense when he said she was from T—"

"Torva," Aireyal finished for her and Casilda nodded. "I'm afraid that girl is very real and very dangerous." Another groan of pain. Aireyal glanced down at Zale and Morgana. Then she looked back to Casilda. "Please save them, I did all I could."

"You've done admirably." Casilda peered at the bandages before patting Aireyal on the shoulder, then the lady turned to Zale. "Up you go." She pulled him gently to his feet. "I'll be back for her in a moment," Casilda said, then she headed up the hill with Zale.

"Thank you," Aireyal said, then she fell back flat on the grassy ground and let her limbs rest. The breeze and Morgana's soft groans of pain were the only sounds in the area. A few minutes later, Casilda returned. "Where is everyone?" Aireyal asked her.

"Headmistress Markado called a school-wide assembly. I'm still supposed to be there too, but I'm a busy lady… and sometimes I get tired of hearing our headmistress talk," Casilda said with a wink. Aireyal knew the feeling. "When I didn't see you there, I figured you'd decided not to come after what transpired last night, and that Zale here might've been consoling you. But it seems I was quite wrong," the lady said, hauling Morgana up.

"Thank you," Aireyal said again.

"Of course. Helping people is my job," Casilda said with a smile. "And if today's any indication, it might be yours someday too."

Aireyal smiled. "Maybe," she said, and closed her eyes.

"You aren't coming up with us?" Casilda asked.

"Go on ahead, I'll be up in a few minutes," Aireyal said, but she knew she wasn't moving anytime soon. She took a deep breath and let her body sink into the grass.

When Aireyal opened her eyes, she was in the apothecary hut, its sweet smells surrounding her. Ointments, gels, and bandages were lathered and wrapped around Morgana and Zale's resting bodies. Casilda scurried back and forth, picking up an assortment of herbs from different bowls on the shelves.

"Good to see you're up," Casilda said to Aireyal. "I figured I'd carry you here instead of letting you sleep on the ground."

"Thank you," Aireyal said, then she turned back to Morgana and Zale. "Will they recover?" she asked.

"I hope they will. For now, they both need lots of rest."

"Thank you for everything."

"You don't have to keep thanking me, dear," Casilda said with a smile.

"Oh, sorry."

"You don't have to apologize either. If you hadn't slowed the bleeding, these two would be in much worse shape. Though I must admit, I've never treated cuts like the ones they have before."

Aireyal thought back to the night she'd escaped Vale and the maze. "The knife that cut them is the same one that gave me the scar across my cheek. I think it has some kind of magic imbued in it."

"Then it is a twisted and vile magic," Casilda said, frowning, and Aireyal looked out the window in thought. *Was saving Vale the right thing to do?* Aireyal rubbed her hands together nervously then felt the bracelet Zale gave her still on her wrist. She examined it closely. *Some kind of magic is in this too.* Magic she didn't yet understand. Magic she wasn't sure had anything to do with her. *What makes it work?*

"Aireyal." The familiar voice sent her body cold. She looked up to see Zale's eyes the saddest blue she'd ever seen.

"I'm so sorry," he said. Hearing his voice again made her happy he was alive, but angry he'd lied to her. She was hurt with betrayal, and giddy he'd been loyal in the end. She wanted to run over and kiss him, and she was disgusted and never wanted to see him again. Above all, she was ready to crumble like a home burned from the inside out. Breathing was impossible.

"I can't do this right now," she managed to wheeze out, before turning and rushing out the door. It was a little easier to breathe outside, but as Aireyal stared up into the cloudy sky, she wondered how long it would be before she was ready to face him.

Chapter 37

Sword & Sorcery

THE FACE OF A DEAD SOLDIER FELL BEFORE EREVAN, detached from its body. Spears stabbed. Blades cut. Armor and shields clanked and crashed, while arrows and spells rained down. Bloodied bodies from both armies fell all over.

Erevan lost track of everyone who'd been at the front of the battle. When the first soldier had charged, Quan grabbed Nya and retreated into the army of Nyumbafro. Sir James had stepped back behind the first line of his soldiers and drew his bow. And the young Heritourian captain wasn't missing, ending the life of every Nyumbafroan soldier he shot at.

"Aargh!" groaned a man near Erevan, who was hit with an arrow in the chest. There was no time to worry about him, a sword came at Erevan's neck. A Heritourian soldier. Erevan ducked just in time to see a spear stab the man through the heart. Before he could check to see if the man was dead, another arrow flew past his head. Then a shout of pain came from behind him.

This wasn't a street fight in Bogudos. This was the first battlefield Erevan had been on and he hoped it was his last. "Come with me." There was no time to say no.

A hand grabbed Erevan and pulled him back into the Nyumbafroan ranks. Quan. He cut the ropes binding Erevan's hands and tossed him a pouch of red dust.

"You look more out of place than a furless camel in snow. I can tell you're a stranger to war. You should go home, boy," Quan said over the violent shouts around them. "Ventu!" He threw an air-powered spear at a Heritourian charging their way, dropping the man in a single blow.

Quan was tall and well-built, but his beard suggested he was more seasoned than he probably was. He looked ten years older than Erevan at most.

"I have to make sure Nya's safe," Erevan said, glancing around but wherever she'd gone in the sea of soldiers was impossible to know.

"That's Princess Niysidialana to you," Quan warned. "Harm shall not come her way, she's in the hands of our fastest riders."

"But can they fight?"

"There's no need, they're leaving the battle."

"I still want to make sure she isn't hurt," Erevan said.

"Run that way, if you wish to follow her," Quan said, pointing behind them. "She's likely gone by now. Headed on horseback to a boat waiting on the river to take her back home."

Erevan didn't waste another second, he ran back in the direction Quan showed him, pushing past the army. From the looks of things, the soldiers of Nyumbafro would be fine. They were winning so far, if barely.

The shouts of battle thrashed in Erevan's ears with each step, and so too did the clamoring of hooves. But they were getting further away by the second, even as he sprinted.

When he burst out from the final line of soldiers, he saw Nya. She was at least fifty yards away, galloping past buildings on a black horse, saddled behind a Nyumbafroan soldier. Two other soldiers galloped behind them, and Erevan could see Nya's arms waving about as she argued with them fiercely.

"Izea totua, Hua hua olialat!" she yelled in what sounded like elvish, but the soldier whipped the horse's reins forward toward the river, ignoring her completely. They were already a third of the way there. Erevan couldn't catch a galloping horse, but he forced his legs after them anyway.

This might be the last time I see her.

Erevan told himself his legs weren't getting tired, but it was more of a lie with every step. The distance between him and the horses grew until Nya and the soldiers with her reached the docks where a small boat waited for them. The soldiers disembarked, and Nya shouted angrily at them some more, but she walked to the boat, nonetheless.

Erevan had hardly made it halfway to them when another horse, a fast white steed, appeared in front of a building far ahead of him. It galloped straight for the boat, and as Erevan's eyes locked onto its rider, his blood chilled. A white helmet with horns protruding from it and smoke flowing from its eyeholes. The spectre, adorned in his white armor. The spectre's sword was already drawn as he closed in, headed for Nya.

A second wind of energy hit Erevan and he dashed forward. One of the Nyumbafroan soldiers raised a spear, only to be cut down by the spectre as he dismounted with leaping crisscrossed strikes. A second soldier reached for her pouch of dust, but her hand was cut off in a violent stroke. Then the spectre thrust his sword through her heart and placed two quick crisscrosses there as well. He turned to the last remaining soldier, who stood defiantly between the spectre and Nya.

Erevan was close now, only several dozen yards away. But not yet close enough for sword fighting.

There's still one thing I can do.

He reached down and pulled out as much red dust as he could hold from his pouch. *Be free. Let go of everything. Mother. Scoti. Tinny. Selea. Isaiah. Nya. Father.*

"Ventu!" A swirl of wind blasted forth at the spectre.

"Countru!" the spectre shouted, spinning and tossing blue dust at Erevan's gust. The air scattered in blue shimmers. But Erevan's efforts weren't a complete failure. The soldier guarding Nya slashed the spectre while he was distracted, cutting him across the elbow.

Blood spilled and the spectre dropped his sword, but didn't even acknowledge the pain. *Was he undead? Some already deceased warrior?*

"Aquo!" Nya shouted. A small wave washed onto the docks, knocking the spectre's sword into the river. *She must've gotten more dust from the Nyumbafroans too.* And her spell came with perfect timing. Erevan had just arrived, and he swung at the spectre.

Missed. The spectre spun and tossed out dust from his good hand in a circle. "Ventu!" A ring of wind knocked both Erevan and the Nyumbafroan soldier off their feet. Erevan's head crashed down onto the cobbled stone of the docks.

Crack.

He knew exactly what the warm, stinging sensation at the back of his skull was. But he refused to pay it any mind. Instead, Erevan stood back up to face his foe once again.

As he did, the last remaining Nyumbafroan soldier was sliced twice across the heart with his own sword, now held by the spectre.

"Darren!" Nya screamed. A tear slid its way down her cheek, then she scowled, her eyes trained solely on the spectre.

"Trastule mala prudi, divelk wyana nolozo," the spectre said coldly to Nya. Suddenly, the milk-white mist formed again from thin air.

Erevan dashed forward into it, swinging. But his strike was parried and a well-placed kick from the spectre sent him right back to the ground. The spectre's sword was already cutting through the air, down at him.

"Aquo!" Nya shouted from right next to Erevan. The spectre dodged a wave of forceful water slamming against the docks, stopping his attack. "Don't rush, Erevan. We do this together," Nya said, and he nodded, scrambling to his feet. *Patience. Think. Plan.*

The mist was thick, but the spectre was down one good arm thanks to the Nyumbafroan soldier's blow, he'd have to choose between sword and sorcery, he couldn't do both effectively. They could beat him. *Use your advantage.* Erevan waited as Nya drew two handfuls of dust, then he went in for a strike. Deflected. But it didn't matter.

"Ventu!" Nya shouted.

A gust of wind ripped partially through the mist, knocking the spectre off his feet and giving Erevan better vision. He stabbed down. But not quick enough. The spectre rolled out the way, hopping up in a hurry.

Erevan swung again. *Dodged.* And again. *Parried.* It didn't matter.

"Ventu!"

A sweeping gust from Nya. This time, the spectre jumped to dodge it, leaving his chest exposed. The opening Erevan needed. He thrusted forward, stabbing the spectre straight through the heart. The mist dissolved and the spectre stumbled back, dropping his sword. Erevan picked that sword up too and with a fell stroke, sliced the spectre's ghastly helmet off, leaving him headless. Then Erevan kicked him off the docks into the Raging River.

"Come back from that."

The spectre's body and helmet floated away along the waves, leaving a trail of blood behind them. Nya exhaled. Erevan turned, she looked as weary as he expected, and he imagined he appeared the same. Once the rush of battle left him, he'd be sore and aching.

"Poor Darren." Nya dropped to her knees, wiping her eyes of budding tears with one hand, and closing the man's eyes with the other. He was an older man, with grey freckling through his black beard. "I know you've never met him, but Darren was like an uncle to me. He's been a member of the court my entire life." She pulled the man's lifeless body in for a hug. "He even taught me how to ride a horse when my father was too busy."

"I'm sorry," Erevan said, reaching out to her.

She smiled weakly when he placed his hand on her shoulder. Then she shook her head and laid Darren down softly. "I wish this senseless violence didn't have to happen. So many people are going to lose their lives today."

"It's not your fault. There's nothing you can do about it."

Nya stared at the bloody ground beneath Darren for a long moment. Her face twisted and turned as though trying to come to a decision. "Alioyatta! I am the Princess of Nyumbafro, of course I can do something about it. Come on," she said, getting up and hopping back on the horse she'd arrived on.

The moment Erevan jumped on behind her, they were off, headed right back for the battle in the city. From afar, it looked like there were more soldiers from Nyumbafro still standing than Heritourians. "I think your people are winning," Erevan said.

"Nobody wins in war. The only thing worth celebrating is everyone not being dead."

"Well, everyone isn't dead yet. What's your plan? Why are we going back?"

"To keep the rest of them alive," she said, whipping the reins faster. Though with every yard they pushed forward, another body fell. Some on either side, though as the numbers dwindled, Nyumbafro continued to pull ahead. When they were finally in earshot, Nya started shouting.

"Soldiers of Heritour, there's no need for you or any more of your countrymen to die here today," she said, as they rode through what was now only several dozen soldiers on the two sides combined. "Please, lay down your arms and be spared," she said, but her words fell on deaf ears. The fighting continued as did the death. Nya's face dropped.

"The only voice they'll listen to is their captain's," Erevan said, pointing ahead in the battle where Sir James was still letting arrows fly.

"Captain, a word please!" Nya shouted at the top of her lungs. The city-torn battlefield was quieter than before, but the screams of death were far from silent. And the stink of death was far worse, like piles of sour meat left under a cooking sun. "I request an end to this bloodshed!" This time, her words were heard loud and clear.

"Hold!" Sir James commanded, and in an instant, his men stopped their assault, assuming defensive positions. The Nyumbafroan soldiers paused as well, watching their counterparts with as much distrust as they were being eyed with. Each waited for the other to throw another blow. But none came.

"What's the meaning of this? Why are you back?" Quan demanded as Nya rode to the center of the battlefield. "Where's Dar—"

"Dead. Like the rest of you will be if you don't stop this madness," she said, anger bubbling in her voice as she dismounted.

"If your sister were her—" Quan started, but Nya cut him off.

"Silence. She'd agree with every word I said. And she wouldn't want to see so many of us dead either. None of our families would." Then she turned to Sir James, who had lowered his bow, and walked to him. "I'm sure you and your men have families too. Look around. Is dying here worth never seeing them again?" All the anger in her voice before, had turned as calm and soothing as the melody of a harp.

Why are you being so nice to the enemy?

"Heritourians do not retreat," Sir James said bluntly. "Least of all from those who would murder us in our own city."

Nya frowned. "Who's that?" she asked, pointing to a dead Heritourian soldier at the captain's feet near one of their blue, boar-bearing flags.

"His name was Lucas."

"Did Lucas have a family?"

Why are you asking? Erevan wondered, and from the looks of everyone around, they were thinking the same thing.

The captain nodded. "A wife and two children."

"I'm sure he was a good man," she said, looking out to the other Heritourians, ignoring the grumbles of disapproval from her own people. "I see several dozen more men like Lucas, one strike away from their children being fatherless. You call us murderers, but you are the same if you would willingly send your men to unnecessary deaths. Is that what you want on your conscience?"

The captain paused. "You would let us go? Why?" he asked.

"Because I'm a good person. And so are you, which is why you're going to help me end this," Nya said, smiling wide. "Your people can go back home, and so can mine. But..." she said, raising a finger. "Not before you give me back the mirror you stole."

And there it is, Nya's goal. Groans of contempt came from the Heritourians. Sir James gazed at the mirror still wrapped in cloth on his quiver's strap.

"So, your speech was merely an attempt to get your hands on this weapon?" the captain asked, shaking his head.

"No," Nya said. "You're outnumbered and if we continue this fight, you'll all end up dead. But I'd rather not pluck the mirror from your corpse. I'm trying to give you a chance to live, please take it."

"What guarantee have I that you will not attack if I hand the mirror over?"

"I give you my word. Hopefully, that is enough," Nya said, extending her hand for a shake.

James stared at it for a long while. "You ask for no small amount of trust."

"If there's ever going to be peace, we have to start trusting each other," she said. Then she looked down to the faces of those who had not survived. "Soldiers of Nyumbafro, drop your weapons."

Quan opposed her immediately, "We can't do that, the Heritourians are still armed, they could attack us—"

"I am well aware," Nya snapped back at him. "That is the entire point," she said, eyeing the Nyumbafroan soldiers that remained, all of them still clinging to their weapons. Many of the soldiers turned to Quan, their eyes pleading for his assistance. "Don't look at him. He's not royalty. Isn't that right, Quan?" Nya asked, watching him intently.

"Yes, princess," Quan said, but not before a moment of hesitation. He dropped his spear and shield, then bowed to one knee before her.

"Now, I believe I've made myself clear to the rest of you. Drop. Your. Weapons." It took another half moment before the soldiers followed her orders and a chorus of clanks rattled the ground. All the eyes, both from the now defenseless soldiers of Nyumbafro and the armed ones of Heritour, turned to Sir James.

"Orders, sir?" one of his men asked.

"Lay down your arms," Sir James said, pulling the mirror from his person and handing it to Nya. At first, only the closest soldiers stopped and followed his command. Then Sir James yelled it again louder and the message became clear to all. And so, the battle of Rifton was over.

~ Chapter 38 ~
Frostfire

AIREYAL WALKED OVER TO HER MOTHER'S STUDY for what might've been the last time. She raised her hand and gave a soft knock.

"Come in," said the familiar voice from inside before Aireyal could even knock a second time. She pushed the door open to see the headmistress lounging in her mother's study chair, plundering through a neat stack of notes and papers on her desk. The place looked... *uncluttered*. The desk, the books, the floor; everything was in order. Aireyal's eye twitched as she strode to the center of the room. "I heard you have had quite a busy day," the headmistress said cheerily. Her tone suggested they were friends. Aireyal frowned.

"You could say that," she said, unamused.

"You are a bit gloomier than I would expect for someone who has recently avoided death," the headmistress said, remaining pleasant. Aireyal didn't respond. "Let us cut to the necessaries, shall we? I called you here for a few reasons." She paused, like she expected Aireyal to ask her why. When that didn't happen, the lady continued. "First, I would like to know what exactly happened this morning, the reports of your account do not exactly sound plausible."

"I'm assuming those reports included what I said about the girl from Torva?" Aireyal asked, and the headmistress's eyebrows arched for the shortest of moments before coming back down.

"So, that part is true," the lady said, more to herself than acknowledging Aireyal. "As is the news that she took the Frostfire Mirror?"

"Maybe. It was a little hard to focus with an invisible tiger stalking around us," Aireyal snipped. The headmistress smiled.

"*Us*. Yes, I heard that young Mr. Varron was there as well… *if* that is his true name." The headmistress said, pausing. "I also heard he was with the girl, is that true?" Aireyal hesitated, she couldn't bring herself to confirm the statement. Her eyes flicked away. "I understand you two were close, Miss Ando, but I need to know if the boy was involved," the headmistress pressed further. Aireyal looked everywhere in the room except at her. "From that non-response, I shall assume he was."

Aireyal snapped her head up to object, but despite her mouth opening, she couldn't bring herself to lie. "He's not a bad person," was what came out instead.

"That remains to be seen."

A long silence ensued. Silence enough that the innocent chatter of kids in the distance outside the window was louder than anything inside the room.

"If you don't mind, I'd like to go back to the apothecary and check on—" Aireyal started, only to be cut off.

"I *do* mind. There are still several things I want to ask you," the headmistress said, plundering through more of Aireyal's mother's papers. Aireyal's eye twitched again, but she forced her face to remain neutral. "How would you like to come live with me this summer?"

Surely, I heard her wrong. "What did you say?"

"Don't be so alarmed, Miss Ando, it was your mother's idea."

"I'm going to ask her if that's tru—"

"Unfortunately, you cannot. She was taken away last night."

"To where?"

"Somewhere secure," the headmistress non-answered. "She will have to speak before the Senate in the coming days, perhaps more than once. I hope all goes well for her."

"No, you don't. And why would my mother ask for me to stay with you?" Aireyal nearly shouted, though she already knew the answer.

"She might be locked up for quite a while."

"Because of you." Aireyal narrowed her eyes.

"I did my civic duty as any law-abiding citizen should."

"You betrayed her."

"She betrayed Lanasall. Your mother admitted that. Luckily, the dragon she tried to hide will finally be—"

"Killed?" Aireyal finished for her. "She's just a baby."

"I can tell you are rather... passionate about this, but I am not here to argue with you," the headmistress said, opening a handwritten note on the desk.

"Then what are you here to do? Other than snoop through my mother's things?!"

The headmistress tossed her hands up. "Do you believe everything I do has ill-intention? Has it never occurred to you that I am *not a bad person*?"

"No, it hasn't."

"Then perhaps I should inform you that what I am seeking is research your mother found about the Frostfire Mirror," she said, turning away to examine several papers side-by-side. "Since its whereabouts are now unknown, it is even more imperative I find all I can."

"How did you ever get that mirror in the first place?" Aireyal asked. The headmistress looked up at her and smiled.

"Well, well, there you go. Now you are asking the essential questions," she said before dropping her head back to the papers, flipping through page after page.

"Aren't you going to answer me?"

"The people who need to know the answer to that question already do. You, are not among them," she said, not even bothering to look up.

Aireyal scoffed. "Then can I go now?"

"There is one more thing I need to say. It seems fortune has smiled upon you."

Aireyal didn't try to soften the deep frown on her face. "How so?"

"All school activities are postponed due to your incident. So, congratulations, if things stay this way forever, you will get to avoid the inevitable and stay enrolled at this school."

Aireyal turned to leave, wishing she'd never come here to participate in the headmistress's games. But she stopped for a moment upon reaching the door, turning back one last time to the headmistress still sitting there, plundering. "I have something to say to you too."

"Hmm?"

"Do you remember what I said when you asked me why I came to this school?"

The headmistress raised an eyebrow. "No. I tend to forget things that aren't important," she said. Aireyal took the comment, unflinching.

"I told you it was so I could protect people from those that would abuse their power," Aireyal said, and the headmistress gave an indifferent grin.

"Lovely—"

"And I meant it," Aireyal said. "You've asked me question after question, and yet not one of them was about your daughter. Morgana almost died today. Do you even care?" Aireyal hissed, stomping her foot.

The headmistress's grin faded. "I have given Morgana everything she needs not only to survive, but to thrive. If she fails to do either, it is her own fault."

"No. *You* failed Morgana," Aireyal said. "You don't deserve to call her your daughter. You haven't earned the right."

With that, Aireyal left. She wasn't sure what the rest of the year might hold for her, but at the moment, she didn't care. If the systems in place could put someone like Mirvana Markado in the chair of power, then perhaps they needed a bigger change than Aireyal had once thought.

After a long sigh, Aireyal moved forward. She couldn't be bothered to think about the Frostfire Mirrors, Torvan purifiers, or even school. Her mind dedicated itself to wishing those closest to her would make it through whatever was to come.

Over the course of days that turned to weeks, the deaths of both an apprentice and a docent at the lake cabin didn't sit well with anyone. Constant rumors and fear of more attacks had temporarily at first, then permanently closed Darr-Kamo for the rest of the year. The headmistress's job was in jeopardy, and all apprentices had been ordered to return home.

Aireyal sat alone in her room, clothes packed up and books stacked away. She read the last pages of *The Adventures of Allia* with a bittersweet smile on her face. Hearing about her favorite adventure again gave her some form of solace, but her mind kept racing back to all that had happened. And all that would.

Her mother still hadn't been cleared of wrongdoing. And that meant Aireyal needed somewhere to stay. But she also wanted to make her way to the city of Rifton in Heritour. Something big was going to happen there. Something people were referring to only as *The Summit*.

Apparently, some kind of battle broke out in Rifton involving a princess the same day as Vale's attack at Darr-Kamo. Solid details were scarce, and rumors were abundant. Everything from both sides joining hands to sing songs of peace, to the princess single-handedly stopping the battle was said. The one thing that was clear was that leaders from all the countries in the western world were going to assemble to discuss findings, assess blame probably, and ultimately decide on what to do with the problematic city of Rifton and its surrounding lands.

News swirled Aireyal's head with questions, like word that this princess carried a magical mirror. But most concerning was that Aireyal's mother was expected to speak at this summit, giving her account of all the events at Darr-Kamo this past year relating to the mirror, the dragon, and the Torvans. And her testimony would determine if her name was cleared.

However, she wouldn't be alone. Zale was also expected to speak at this summit in all the same fashions, except Aireyal had the feeling that the odds were stacked out of his favor.

Aireyal hoped that if she went to Rifton, the summit might hear her account of the events as well, and that she'd be able to spare more than one life if she did things right. That wasn't the only reason she wanted to go though. If every country was going to be there, she might be able to meet this Princess of Nyumbafro for herself. Maybe she'd be able to help Aireyal learn the secrets of the mirrors and why Torva seemed ready to stop at nothing to retrieve them.

Knock. Knock. Knock. Aireyal jumped out of her thoughts at the sound of her door. She looked up to see Morgana, *mostly* healthy again, holding a letter.

They still hadn't truly talked about their argument at the dance yet. Aireyal wasn't sure how to word all the things she wanted to say. She'd never had a friend she needed to apologize to before because she never had any friends. She also hadn't mentioned seeing the malevolent looking chest in Morgana's wardrobe or the wicked mist that spilled from it.

"What are you thinking about?" Morgana asked.

"Oh, nothing too important," Aireyal said, forcing a smile. "Is that for me?" she asked, pointing to the letter. Morgana nodded.

"It's from your father."

~ Chapter 39 ~
Ventras

EREVAN STOOD AT THE BACK DOOR OF THE orphanage before the freshly made grave for his father. Behind him, his mother and siblings wept, and he clutched the shovel in his hand to avoid doing the same. But it was no use.

Erevan dropped to his knees at the grave as the empty dreariness of a cold heart conquered him again. "I'm so sorry," he cried, tears falling on his father's sword below. "I was too weak to save you."

"Erevan, don't talk like that. It wasn't your fault," Nya said, wrapping her arms around his shoulders. The sweet smell of the flower she carried and the feeling of warmth overtook him as she laid a hand over his. "We'll make sure we didn't lose him in vain."

He looked up at her with tear-stained eyes and nodded. The faces of the Krilows flashed in his mind. If they were headed to Nyumbafro, so was he.

"O blessed Evlynna of the stars above," his mother's voice sobbed behind him. "I pray you'll guide Lee in his journey now. He may not have believed in you, but he was a good man. A wise man. And a caring one. I pray you'll keep him safe until the day I join him and we're together again. Afide," she said, then broke down into another surge of weeping. Erevan turned back and gave her a hug along with all his little siblings. All except Scoti. He'd decided to stay in the house. The boy blamed himself for their father's death and no one could tell him otherwise.

"What are we going to do without Father?" one of the little girls asked.

It took a long time before Mrs. Eston answered her between sobs. "We'll find a way somehow."

"What about the tax man? He'll be back next month," another kid asked nervously.

"Don't worry about that." Nya's voice. "Sir Lee helped me against all his inhibitions. If it weren't for him, I don't know where I'd be right now. I'll make sure that all of you are taken care of for as long as you live," she continued. "And Mrs. Eston, I know it doesn't make up for what's happened, but I'll get you as much coin as you need to build the school you've always dreamed of," Nya said, her voice beginning to falter, like the rest of them. Then she walked back to Sir Lee's grave. "Thank you for everything. I'll never forget the last words you said to me." She placed her flowers on his grave. "You were a great man. Almiata, mo nala. Rest in paradise."

She cares. Nya's a princess and she cares. More tears flooded Erevan's eyes. She was unlike anyone he'd ever met. There were a lot of people with power and fortune, but maybe… just maybe… *she might not be the only one that cares.*

Nya departed not long after to speak with Quan about a host of things, including one special request from Erevan. But Erevan and his family stayed at his father's grave for hours, first in mourning, then in melancholy retellings of the many things they remembered him for. His calm demeanor through their hard times together. His patience for all the kids when they made mistakes. And above all, his undying love for children that were outcast, shunned, and rejected by their own kin.

"You're leaving, aren't you?" Mrs. Eston asked Erevan as they remained outside together after all the kids had gone back in the house.

"How'd you know?" he asked.

"A mother knows her children," the lady said, giving him a saddened smile. Then she pointed at his father's sword. "You should take that with you. He always wanted you to have it one day."

"I can't tak—"

His mother waved him off. "It's well made and worth more than you know. It'll do nothing but attract thieves in this town," she said, looking back at the house. "There's one more thing I want you to have. Your father's journal of his time in Heritour. I know he's never told you why he left, but in those pages you'll find understanding of more things than one."

"What kinds of things?" he asked, but she shook her head.

"It's his story, I'll let him tell it to you in his own words. He planned to share that journal with you when Isaiah got out. But now, I'm not sure if that will ever happen."

"It will. Nya's sending word to her people to deliver coin and negotiate his release."

"Scoti told me she was an important girl, but I didn't realize she had that much authority."

"She's the Princess of Nyumbafro," Erevan said, and his mother's jaw dropped.

"And she's doing all this for us?" her mother pondered as a thankful tear slipped down her cheek. "That girl really cares about you, Erevan. Remember that when things are bleak. That's what always got your father and I through the toughest times."

"I will," Erevan said, staring at his father's grave once more. "And I'm going to find the men that did this to him."

"I don't like hearing you talk that way. Violence only brings more violence," she warned. "Being away from home changes a man. Don't forget who you are on the road."

"I won't, I promise."

Many days later, Erevan stood tall, leaning over the starboard side of the massive Nyumbafroan galleon ship he rode upon with Nya. Sea shanties filled the deck behind them between orders of the ship's captain as the sea's waves pulled them ever closer to Nyumbafro's shores.

Erevan clutched his father's tattered journal in his hand. "You have that look again," Nya said, frowning.

"I have to avenge him," Erevan said.

"Are you sure that's what he'd want?"

"You're saying I should just let the Krilows go?"

"I won't tell you what to do, Erevan," she said, then paused for a moment, choosing her words carefully before speaking again. "Nyumbafro is a big country. It might not be easy to find them."

"I'm patient," Erevan said.

Nya laughed. "You've come a long way."

"And yet we have so far to go."

She squinted at him. "We?"

"We're in this together, right?" he asked.

"Until the end," Nya said, before pausing again. "If that's what you want."

"Why wouldn't I?"

Nya pulled the mirror out and ran a finger along its edges. "Because I have a feeling this mirror we're bringing back to Nyumbafro will cause more trouble than it will solve."

"It'll be fine, I'm sure. You have a master sorcerer at your side now."

Nya laughed. "Is that what you're calling yourself? You haven't even got a handle on the basics yet," she said, smirking. "And there's *so* much more to learn."

Erevan smiled back and peered into the mirror, which showed nothing but the sea, as it had for many days. "What are you planning to do with that thing?" he asked.

Nya looked at him and frowned. "I'm hoping the king can answer that."

"And if he can't?"

"Then someone at this summit will," Nya said. *The Summit.* Erevan had read the note from the messenger bird that announced a grand meeting of all the western world's countries. But if he knew anything about wealthy and powerful people, lots of lies and backstabbing were coming next.

"You're going to the summit?"

"I'm a princess, Erevan, I doubt I'll have a choice," Nya said, chuckling. "You should come too."

Suddenly, a note floated out from the mirror and almost flew out into the breeze, but they each grabbed a side of it with an outstretched hand. Then they pulled it back and read the sole line on the note.

Winne pilli ule, garabaozo yild riyno, lolo, trasta ventras tatiamito

Elvish.

"What does it say?" Erevan asked.

"The first part is from the ancient text of *The Anima*," she said, studying the words. "What is lost, will grow when found."

"And the rest?"

"But the ground floats by the... windstone."

~ *Chapter 40* ~
# Epilogue

WIND WHISTLED THROUGH THE CRAGGY, eroded stone banks of the Lagoona Jungle. Rowen Mountaincoat wiped his brow of sweat and dipped an empty bucket into the waters of the Raging River. Though it hardly *raged* this far down. He looked along its path, thinking of his cousin in Bogudos. Bumgrim was finally fixing his shabby tavern up, even if only for the sake of attracting new customers.

Rowen had received word of a major gathering soon to come in Rifton. It would be too many people to fit in one city, and once Bumgrim followed his advice and cleaned up The Lazy Lizard, travelers might make it their tavern of choice. A good business plan, if Bumgrim listened to it; his cousin wasn't like the apprentices in his lectures. *Docent Mountaincoat, are there any books you recommend I read to supplement today's lecture?* Rowen chuckled, recalling the words of Aireyal Ando on her first day. If only Bumgrim had her determination to learn. Rowen sighed.

That poor girl, he thought to himself. She might never see her mother again. A shame too, Grandmage Ando was always one of his favorite people, happy to share a cup of tea with any who asked.

Rowen pulled his bucket back up and looked into its pristine water. Or, mostly pristine water. A milk-white helmet floated inside with horns protruding from either side. Rowen dropped the bucket at once and turned, rushing away from the bank. *I've escaped them once, and now the nightmare lives again,* he thought to himself. *No.* He stopped, then turned back to the water.

Running wouldn't solve his problems. If the world was to be rid of this evil once and for all, they would have to fight. And they would have to do so together.

Special Thanks

Stories are not made by one person alone, and while there are far too many people to thank, (like the fabulous librarians, educators and book-lovers sharing this book) this story would not have been the same without the following; first off, you, dear reader, who continues to inspire me to write when I am weary and restless! To Lamont Kristian Turner, who helped make sense out of the western world, thank you for all the times you told me how stupid some of my ideas were. And thank you for being my friend before I knew how to be a good person. This story would not exist without you and I pray you find peace in your next journey. Thank you Sarah, my sweet love, not only for the amazing cover art, but for being unbelievably supportive and caring the entire way. I love you.

To my awesome critique partner Doug Hilson, thank you so much for trudging through a messy draft and giving me invaluable advice on fixing that one character in particular. Thank you Vernon E. Williams for providing developmental editing this story needed. Thank you Dr. Tyra Seldon for providing line and copyediting that cleaned this manuscript up so much and thank you for all your insight and advice on the world of writing as well. Thank you Belle Manuel and Nicole S. Arnold for lending your excellent proofreading skills, you both caught things the rest of us missed after many *many* reads. Thank you JonahPaul Butterfield for the marvellous map, it truly brought the western world to life. Thank you Danielė Buivydaitė for the incredible chapter art, it's been a dream of mine since I was a child to have those in the book, and every drawing is wonderful. Thank you to all the amazing beta readers, Carla Buzz, Maddy D., Kenzie Farrington, Lashandra G., Shalin Gray, Daniel Hamilton, Yuliya Liberman, Matthew Patterson, Jessica Seevers, and H.L. Storm; your feedback helped refine the rough edges of this story and gave me the motivation to keep writing. Thank you Biblaridion for teaching me how to make conlangs, I would have been lost without you.

Thank you Dr. Ann Wagner-Hill for teaching me the importance of multiple perspectives. Thank you Fawn Harris for teaching me that our stories matter too. Thank you Jason Thornton for placing me in a community of us. Thank you John L. Hank for treating me like a genius. Thank you Michelle Brown and Dr. Gene Harris for giving me a chance. Thank you Maura Heaphy for introducing me to Octavia E. Butler. Thank you Corrine McConnaughy for sharing some of your political expertise.

Thank you Chris for being my friend through many years and for constantly holding me accountable by asking when the book was coming out, lol. Thank you Ken for great memes, nerd-talk and convos about real-life. Thank you Kc for checking up on me and making sure I'm ok. Thank you Samantha for always keeping it real. Thank you Anthony for always being honest with me. Thank you Jelani for introducing me to Sarah and for sending me memes to brighten my day. Thank you Gabi for giving me way too many ideas in D&D. Thank you Crissy for running it down with me. Thank you Ak for all the random animes you recommended to me and for asking me questions about things I never would've thought about. Thank you Cola, Emma, Michael, Moe, Rose and Sal for giving me a reason to actually act like an adult and pretend I knew what I was talking about.

Thank you Gregg Stefan Lee for being my best friend and never giving up on the fact that we can do better. Thank you Cedric Brentley for making sure I actually got this book done. Thank you Ebony Kimble for encouraging me to keep grinding. Thank you Moe Quteifan for pushing me to keep writing. Thank you Devin Pompey for making me a much better person, I'm sure your Hogwarts letter will arrive soon. Thank you Eric Kiefer for all the nights of Halo and pizza. Thank you Grant Johnson III for being a real one.

Thank you Vernita Williams for being my big sis and always doing the best you can with what you're given. I'm so proud of you. Thank you Jordyn Moore for taking care of the people around you and thank you Jamyah Moore for loving the people around you. Thank you Anita Williams for being my fellow artist. And thank you Vernon Williams for introducing me to so many of the influences of this story.

Ok, time to write the next book, I'll see you all soon…

CPSIA information can be obtained
at www.ICGtesting.com
Printed in the USA
LVHW101544070722
722976LV00020B/528/J